Embers and Ashes
by
Katelynn R. Butler

Copyright © 2024 by Katelynn R. Butler
Published by Aisling Books, an imprint of Winged Publications

Editor: Cynthia Hickey
Book Design by Winged Publications

All rights reserved. No part of this publication may be reproduced, stored in a retrieval system, or transmitted in any form or by any means—electronic, mechanical, photocopying, recording, or otherwise—without the prior written permission of the publisher. The only exception is brief quotations in printed reviews. Piracy is illegal. Thank you for respecting the hard work of this author.

This book is a work of fiction. Names, characters, Places, incidents, and dialogues are either products of the author's imagination or used fictitiously.
Any resemblance to actual persons, living or dead, or events is coincidental.

Fiction and Literature: Fantasy

ISBN: 978-1-965352-18-2

DEDICATION

To all the angry girls with fire in your hearts.
Let it burn.

Chapter One

It had been two weeks since Valentin had been shipped off to the Coalition territories in search of my father, and four weeks since I had been in this cell. Twenty-eight days. Six-hundred and seventy-two hours. Forty-thousand-three-hundred and twenty minutes. Two-million, four-hundred and nineteen-thousand, two-hundred seconds. Give or take. Trying to count while interrogators probing one's deepest memories is rather difficult.

As soon as Valentin's boots left the ground – some aircraft or another whisking him away on his mission to right my mistake – the goodwill from my jailers ended. The blinding white of my cell became my new normal. It was blank and bare, like the room I had been kept in for my previous interrogation. White, metal furniture bolted to the floor. White sheets and a white blanket on the cot in the corner. White four walls, white ceiling, white lights, white flooring, white door, no shadows. I was even dressed in a white, fitted, long-sleeved shirt and pants. No shoes. No socks. My earrings were gone—nothing I could use to attack someone else or hurt myself.

Except for the sheets, which – when I had snapped after a long interrogation session – I had wrapped around the woman's neck so tightly that her face turned purple. I then learned they kept cameras somewhere in my cell because guards with sedatives and blockers burst in, restraining me to the cot.

I should have known they had cameras.

Purple and red. Blotchy. The colors I painted on the interrogator's face were the only colors I had seen in weeks, and I was already forgetting what they looked like. The white erased everything. Everything except the memories.

Félix. The black and orange of his armor ripped off, splayed open over the red and black of his brown, burned skin. The smell of his singed hair and flesh. The shiny, bloody, metallic smell. His shrill screams of pain, then his silence, my sobs, and my screaming that left my throat raw even now.

The memories of the pain in my skull, on my scalp, my neck where glass and debris embedded themselves and they shaved away my long blonde hair to clean and stitch the torn skin back to some semblance of what it used to be.

Scars now pebbled those places, and the soft fuzz growing on my head was not long enough to see the dark gold color I *thought* it should be but I couldn't remember. I could not even remember what I looked like.

Amalie once said I was pretty. So did Jax, and Himawari – her name meant sunflower and sunflowers were yellow, I still remembered what yellow looked like – and Félix. And Valentin… In so many words. But I could not see my face physically or in my mind's eye. I saw *their* faces in such vivid detail, but mine was a blur with colorless hair, a formless body, and dark, soulless eyes.

Even in my interrogations, I was a smudge on the landscape reliving every memory. Especially the ones I could not recall voluntarily. A small ghost of a girl hiding under her desk in her bedroom while her parents shrieked at each other, having learned long ago what happened when she screamed at them to stop. When she tried to protect Mother from Father's big scary voice and hands. Black, purple, blue, green, and yellow stained her skin long after. Not where anyone could see, of course.

Mother had not thanked her for it.

Tiny, blurred hands as the ghost girl gripped baby Amalie tightly to her chest the first time she ever got to hold her. Amalie's bright, baby blue eyes stared calmly up into the colorless mass of the girl's face, unflinching at her dark eyes.

A small, slip of a thing as she sat at her parents' table while they entertained people she recognized. People who worked with Father. Neo-traditionalists. Coalition sympathizers. People of all shapes, appearances, and sizes — all saying the same thing. Magic was bad, magic was dangerous, magic was evil, and they must go back to the old ways so the Gods would forgive them and return. Back to the way everything was before the Civil War changed everything. They spoke unknowingly that the daughter of the man they dined with possessed such an atrocity. She, herself unwilling to divulge.

A vaguely blossoming shape of a pre-teen girl as she sat under her desk, crying from a formless mouth and tears pouring from black hole eyes. At the same time, her parents stalled the representative from Heliorious Academy who had come to pick her up because it was past admissions and she had been accepted.

The representative was nice, with warm, tan skin and raven black hair with shiny eyes like a starlit sky, a scar marring the skin over one of those eyes. She had sat under the desk with the ghost girl and wiped her eyes with a handkerchief that smelled of clove and cinnamon. Helped her pack her clothes and most important belongings into her suitcases, and hurried her away from the falseness her parents spewed.

"I am shocked," she had said as they entered the awaiting car. "They kept you from your rights, but they congratulated you in front of me."

"Why did you come?" the girl had asked instead of responding in kind.

"Because your parents wouldn't want to deal with the scandal of withholding you from your chosen educational establishment. Especially when you had been readily accepted," the woman explained, handing her a recyclable bottle of water.

"They will be angry with me."

"And me."

They were silent for a moment but for very different reasons.

"Are you scared?" the girl asked, gripping the water bottle in her small, blurry hands.

"No," the woman replied with a grin that showed teeth that were a little too sharp. "And neither should you be. They are only as scary as you let them be."

And the girl smiled wryly back, with her mouth without a shape, knowing that her parents did not need her help being scary. The woman I would later learn was the headmaster of Heliorious Academy herself – Rajani Kader.

But I couldn't *truly* see any of it. Not the way I remembered Félix lying on the ground in Portnith, dying.

And I lay there, on my cot. In my colorless cell, with my sheared, scarred head. Tears, leaked once again from my unseeable face as my stomach growled for the umpteenth time in the vague shape of my body because the white, bland food they gave me had been drugged and I would not eat it.

Because when I slept, I *could* see it. Black and red flesh, shiny and raw and bloody. It did not matter; I saw it when I was awake too. Not even the white could erase that.

They came every day. Took away my picked at tray of food and replaced it with a new one that I would barely touch. I would only eat enough to keep me alive and to prevent the drugs mixed in from knocking or dulling my senses too much.

They would hook me up, climb into my memories, and turn my insides out searching for answers. Searching, searching. *S e a r c h i n g.*

Until the thrashing started and the needles came and pierced my skin, injecting me with the substance that took away the very thing that made me, me.

My vision would blur, my hearing would dull, and my words would become slow and thick in my mouth. My veins would burn with ice, and the spark inside me would nearly burn out, and I could barely reach it to keep it aflame. Then came the strange burning in my chest, pushing back at the ice.

It gave me the courage to fight. I would fight, because that was all I knew how to do – one would think they would learn but they never did – and I would end up restrained to my cot, shrieking and crying as they delved further into my mind where I did not want them to go, where *I* did not want to go. I did not want to see those memories.

But I saw.

Valentin's arms were around my vague form as I cried from a featureless face. As he stroked my nonexistent hair. I saw the warmth in his face. I heard the words he spoke to me as I poured my heart out to him.

I saw his hands on my waist as we danced at the gala, the garish red blush that was flushed on my white, colorless face.

Saw us fighting in the rain and mud.

Watched as he might have kissed me.

As I almost wished he would have.

As he said those four words.

"…I believe in you."

Chapter Two

He believes in me. Kate believes in me. He believes in me. He believes in me. He believes in me. He believes in me. He believes in me. He believes in me. He believes in me. He believes in me. He believes in me. He believes in me. He believes in me. He believes in me. He believes in me. He believes in me. He believes in me. He believes in me. He believes in

*me. He believes in me. He believes in me. He believes in
me. He believes in me. He believes in me.* **But I do not.**

Chapter Three

The screams. They were building in my throat, under my skin, in my head, under my tongue, under my chewed-up fingernails, in my lungs, and every hidden part of me.

They were mine and not mine.

Félix's – favorite color is pink. Jax's – a small scar on his left thigh. Himawari's – her name meant sunflower and sunflowers were yellow, but now I could not remember what yellow looked like anymore. Valentin's – he believes in me, he believes in me, *he believes in me*.

The burning started again, and the oily, black thing in my chest slinked around my neck to stifle the screams but they kept coming. And coming and coming until it was just gargling that came out of my throat, and they once again took away my blankets and sheets, and my cot was left bare, and it was cold and white and nothingness.

It had been three weeks since Valentin left. That would mean five weeks of this torture. Thirty-five days. Eight-hundred and forty hours. Fifty-thousand, four-hundred minutes. Three-million, twenty-four-thousand seconds.

Or, I thought it had. I could not tell anymore. Could not count. I did not even know if it was Victorisday or Warsday.

But the screams – the red, black, blood – the cries, the oily black hole in my chest, the dulling spark were all still there.

I could feel it and see it all, even if my eyes could not focus anymore.

"Do you think she has poor eyesight?" someone asked.

"What?" another replied.

"She keeps saying she can't see," the first one said, talking as though I was not in the room with them, strapped to my cot. "Her ability is called foresight – a sight and sense sharpening skill. Maybe with her magic being blocked it stopped it from helping her normal eyesight, which may have been poor without the magic."

"Huh… It's a possibility. I'll ask Dev and we will look into it."

Now they would break into my mind. They had spent too much time talking already. This time, I barely even fought it when they did.

Chapter Four

Félix – favorite color is pink. Jax – a small scar on his left thigh. Himawari – her name meant sunflower and sunflowers were yellow. Valentin – he believes in me. Félix – favorite color is pink. Jax – a small scar on his left thigh. Himawari – her name meant sunflower and sunflowers were yellow. Valentin – he believes in me. Félix – favorite color is pink. Jax – a small scar on his left thigh. Himawari – her name meant sunflower and sunflowers were yellow. Valentin – he believes in me. Félix – favorite color is pink. Jax – a small scar on his left thigh. Himawari – her name meant sunflower and sunflowers were yellow. Valentin – he believes in me. Félix – favorite color is pink. Jax – a small scar on his left thigh. Himawari – her name meant sunflower and sunflowers were yellow. Valentin – he believes in me. Félix – favorite color is pink. Jax – a small scar on his left thigh. Himawari – her name meant sunflower and sunflowers were yellow. Valentin – he believes in me. Félix – favorite color is pink. Jax – a small scar on his left thigh. Himawari – her name meant sunflower and sunflowers were yellow. Valentin – he believes in me. Félix – favorite color is pink. Jax – a small scar on his left thigh. Himawari – her name meant sunflower and sunflowers were yellow. Valentin – he believes in me. Félix – favorite color is pink. Jax – a small scar on his left thigh. Himawari – her name meant sunflower and sunflowers were yellow. Valentin – he believes in me. Félix – favorite color is pink. Jax – a small scar on his left thigh. Himawari – her name meant sunflower and sunflowers were yellow. Valentin – **he believes in me.**

Chapter Five

Red. Bloody, scarlet, and hot. All of the white was dyed red. Who had done it while I slept? Had they done it while I was drugged…? I had eaten too much of their bland white food and now they painted the white room red. But my head was attached, or at least I thought it was. When one is beheaded, one is still alive for at least four minutes. That is two-hundred and forty seconds one attempts to breathe as blood and oxygen leech from one's brain, creating hallucinations as the life fades from the body.

I lifted my hands as far as possible, reaching for my face. I had to crane my neck a little to touch it, but it was there. My head was still attached to my body.

So, I wasn't hallucinating because a wrathful queen had beheaded me. But everything was so red. Red. Red. Red. *Red.* **Red. *RED. RED. RED. RED. RED.***

I screwed my eyes shut, but the red was still there behind my eyelids.

My heart was beating. Fast. Too fast. I was dying. I could not breathe. I was dying. Dying, *dying,* **dying**. Then there were needles in my arms, in my legs, and my face was wet, and I tried to brush it away – even as they pulled at my weak arms – but my hands came away bloody, and the screaming returned, but this time the blood was not Félix's. It was my own.

When I awoke everything was white. Back to the way it was. There was no red. There was no one looming over me, waiting to lop off my head. But white was worse than red, and I wished I was dead.

My head was pounding.

My heart was throbbing.

My teeth were aching.

The black burning hole in my chest threatened to burst wide open and swallow me whole, devour me with glistening needle-sharp fangs, and drag me into the nothingness that was its domain.

But that dull, barely there spark of flame refused to let it grow. Its sputtering light ate at the edges of the hole, pushing it back, warding off the fangs. Just barely.

I wondered how much more of this I could take before it extinguished entirely.

When I awoke next, they were back—waiting, watching, their holonavs at the ready, prepared to take down the most minute neurological signal I transmitted.

Exhaustion and malnutrition weighed down my limbs. I would not have been able to move even if I was not restrained to the bed.

Drip, drip, drip went the IV attached to the once toned arm that was attached to my once healthy torso. It appeared that they refused to let me die of malnutrition, even after violating my mind over and over to the point where the memories and images were tormenting background noises.

After forcing me to eat drugged food. After breaking me into tiny, jagged pieces.

It was white, so perhaps this was real. This specific white color did not appear during those times. It was not in my memories.

No, I felt clarity for the first time in a long time. They probably had something other than nutrients in that IV drip.

The sound of it was so loud in my ears. The buzzing in my head drowned out the voices of the interrogators. Why had they not hooked me up to the machine yet? Why were they just standing there? I almost wished they would begin another session so they would stop their staring.

My eyes shot to the right at the blip of a deactivating holonav, the glow of its holographic screen disappearing. One of the three interrogators had shut it off and left the room. Then another, until it was only me and one final interrogator.

My vision was so blurry now I could barely make out that it was a male figure. It was easy enough to make out the dark color of his skin, but I could not see his features or his hair—if he had any.

"Daux," he said in a deep, rich voice that I recognized, but could not place. Would not place. I would have to travel through those memories without them forcing me to and I was too tired. So tired.

"Daux," he repeated with more authority.

I answered with a noncommittal hum.

He sighed and moved closer to the bed; I was too weak to flinch.

"We have gone through your memories enough times to know you have given us a full account without omitting anything, or having your mind altered."

I scoffed mentally. My mind was altered all right. Had I more strength, I would have been flinching at any sudden movement or noise. My mind's eye was nearly constantly plagued with things I did not want to see.

The red, black, bloodied skin. The acrid smell of burning hair and flesh. The choking feeling of smoke-filled air. Félix's prone, broken body. Valentin bleeding out in front of me. The *thwack* of the rifle butt slamming into Jax's back. The feeling of blood running down my face and the back of my neck, the sharp, stabbing pain. The fear of being unable to locate Himawari.

The crazed laugh of my father.

My own, shameful failure.

They were all hurt because of me. My father escaped because of me.

But I had not facilitated it.

There was no conspiracy—at least not one that involved me. Spec Ops and the NAF had gained valuable information because of that mission, and we had taken out a vital Coalition base. We had gained traction in protecting New Palogenia and the many refugees who wished to escape into our borders—magical and non-magical alike. I would not have been able to pull that off had I been aiding and abetting my father. He would not have allowed it.

"I never would have helped him…" I said, my voice raspy from disuse. Or from screaming. I had not been allowed to speak during these long, long weeks, but I could hardly tell if the words were even coming from my throat or my head.

"We know that now," the interrogator said, remorsefully.

Ha, *remorse*.

Where was that when I was trying to claw out my own eyes? When they drugged my food so they could slip into my mind uninterrupted? When they dragged up my childhood, or the small happiness I had found, and when that all came crashing down around me. Over and over and over and over and *over* until my mind broke and I could barely think for myself until they pumped me full of whatever was in this IV drip.

"For what it's worth," the interrogator said, moving to

stand next to my cot. "I am sorry for this."

I did cringe away that time, causing a roiling bout of nausea in my empty stomach. Anger – so intense that the tiny ember inside me blazed for a moment – arose within me.

Weakly, I strained my neck to look up at him. Now that he was closer, I could make out more of his features. Dev, the man who gave us our first Spec Ops tour, had shaken my hand and given Félix a fist bump. One of the other interrogators had mentioned him, I remembered.

I wanted to reach up my emaciated hands and wrap them around his throat, squeezing until the life left his body. To rip his skin to ribbons with my jagged nails. To flay him alive with my dulled magic.

But I settled for retching on his shoes.

There was nothing to empty from my stomach but bile, however, the satisfaction I got from his disgusted cry – his jump backward a fraction too late – made up for it. Even if the vomit did only get on the slip-covers he wore to muffle the sounds of his footsteps. All part of the rouse to break me.

I grinned up at Dev with bile-slick lips, falling back against the cot with a weak thump. At least I knew what he did for Spec Ops now, not that I was surprised.

"We are releasing you."

What?

My head snapped to the side, so hard that my teeth clacked against each other. Though I could not see Dev clearly, he could see me. My expression, whatever was there, splayed across my face. I was sure there was rage, hurt, anger… but I felt more. I was being let go, just like that?

"That's right," he continued all business, scrolling through his holonav. "You will be free to go as long as you attend mandatory psychotherapy appointments at pre-scheduled times and take temporary blockers while you are not undergoing missions."

So… they were going to starve me, torture me, *destroy me*, then just let me go? Set up appointments with doctors to make themselves feel better about the torment they inflicted on me? And then they expect me to work with them – *for them* – again?

As if he read my mind, Dev continued. "Of course, you will need some time to build up your strength again before taking on any sort of mission. But we need you, Daux if we're going to take on this threat. We gleaned valuable information from your memories and you are instrumental in our plan to capture your father."

"*Screw* that," I rasped, the spark flaring up and then dulling into a flickering ember. Greasy, oil-slick black attempted to envelop it, attempted to *devour* it.

"If you wish to retire as a civilian, we can't stop you," he said with a few taps to his holonav. The manacles on my hands and feet snapped open with a click. "But I will inform you that the government will take control of your sister's care as she is part of the investigation as well, and you will not be allowed access to her."

No.

No, no, no!

They could *not* have her. Who knows what they would do to her? She was *my* sister. *Mine.*

"Well played," I rasped, tugging my wrists from their resting place. "Always have a bargaining chip in your possession. They taught us that at the Academy."

It was very clever. And just as cruel. To his credit, though, Dev had a sickly shade of puce tinging his skin and I suspected it was not due to the vomit marinading on the ground between us.

Was his squeamishness because he knew me? Liked me even? Perhaps. Dev was a kind person despite his profession, that much was evident in his prior treatment of me. Of my teammates.

"So, you will be accepting your reassignment?" he asked.

I pulled my feet from the open restraints, marveling at

the blurriness of my vision. My toes were fuzzy blobs and my depth perception was off. But I could still see the significant amount of weight I lost, the muscle mass that had shrunken in my attempt to gain some semblance of control. I wondered just how much I had lost, and how long it would be before I could feel normal again. *If* I could ever feel normal again.

Would I be "accepting" my *reassignment*? What a joke. They were going to take *my* sister away if I did not. I had no choice. If they wanted, I would fling myself off the roof of Spec Ops HQ just to keep her safe.

I fixed Dev with a long, bleary stare.

"I accept."

Chapter Six

The round metal frames felt cool and uncomfortable on my face. I had been tested apparently while I was in custody, and foresight not only heightened my five senses while I used it, but it also enhanced my naturally poor eyesight involuntarily. The Spec Ops requisition office had taken it upon themselves to procure me a pair of corrective glasses. Remedial surgery was off the table for the moment, I was told. I needed to gain back all the weight I had lost during my incarceration, and I needed to help bring my father back first. They could not wait for me to recover from surgery on top of the weight loss and muscle atrophy.

I pushed the frames back up my nose for the umpteenth time as I sat in the hard, uncomfortable wheelchair, waiting. After hours of nutrition drips and pacs – laced with blockers, of course – I was wheeled from the interrogation chambers and into a therapist's office where I was assessed and made to talk about my experience.

Dr. Castillo, a gentle-looking woman in her mid-forties with black hair and onyx eyes, listened intently with nods of compassion and murmurs of encouragement or sympathy. But I knew she did not care. She was only doing this because she was contracted to. When I had given her what she wanted, I was handed a prescription card and another with an appointment time on it—along with her personal phone number so I could "call whenever I needed her".

Bullshit.

Now, though, I waited in a hospital corridor that smelled strongly of disinfectant and sadness after yet another check on my vital signs. White and beige colored the walls and floor, which was not so bad because I was now wearing black from head to toe, and all the healers wore a myriad of colors on their scrubs.

Now I remembered what yellow looked like. There were so many shades and hues.

And also orange, and brown, and red, and black but I only felt numb, not excited. Nor was I scared—just vacant numbness.

Until the large double doors opened and through them stepped Félix.

From what I could see, there was no sign of any scarring he could have had. Where the burn marks on his face were, only healthy brown skin remained. No shiny pink puckering or black edges.

He even *looked* happy. I could barely bring myself to stand and meet him. The chair creaked as I shifted, and he rushed toward me. A smile broke out across his face, dimpling his cheeks. He had lost some of his baby fat during my imprisonment. Otherwise, he looked... as though nothing happened.

And I, shorn hair, glasses, with noticeable weight loss... Scars rippling over the back of my head and neck. I looked very different. But he was *smiling* at me.

I could *feel* the remaining pieces of my heart splintering. I watched as they tumbled out of the inky black hole in my chest, and fell to the pristine hospital floor, staining it a bloody, messy red.

"Daux!" Félix shouted, snatching my attention back to the present as he attempted to lift me out of the wheelchair in a bear hug.

There were no bloody pieces of my heart on the floor... My chest was whole and unblemished beneath my black shirt.

His arms wrapped around me tightly, whether to hug me or reassure himself that I was there, I didn't know. But it was the first time I had been held since Valentin came to tell me goodbye. That little ember flickered in recognition, driving back the darkness temporarily.

I held Félix tighter for a few more seconds before the healer hovering by his station helped to deposit me back in the chair. A smile threatened to tug at the corners of my lips as I looked up into Félix's beaming face. Whatever he went through did not appear to have affected him as it did me, and I was glad for it.

"The others are waiting in the lobby," Félix said, taking the handles at the back of my chair to roll me forward. Even with all the nutrition drips and pacs I still felt so fragile – so angry – that Félix noticed.

The whole elevator ride down to the hospital lobby Félix kept his hand in mine, squeezing it every so often. Each time he did so, it was like a jerk back into the present, forcing me from the fearful numbness of my mind. I both welcomed and resented the action at the same time and hated myself for that.

Two familiar, hesitant smiles greeted us from the sitting area when the doors opened. Jax and Himawari hurried over. The former dressed in a riot of colors as usual, and the latter head to toe in deep violet and charcoal.

Himawari was the first to point out my hair since Valentin left.

"It looks good on you," she said, a wobble in her voice. She had known exactly how much I loved my hair, and how much it meant to me.

I knew that she was placating me, trying to make me feel better. But I did not feel better. I felt worse. It was a roiling, swirling, noxious feeling that started low in my stomach, and I felt bile rise in the back of my throat.

The slick, hot, burning feeling at the back of my neck returned. I resisted the urge to rub the scarring and reassure myself that I was no longer bleeding. That I was safe. I could do that when I was alone when no one was watching, waiting to report on my well-being.

Félix squeezed my hand again.

"Thank you," I rasped, my throat aching and raw merely from answering the therapist's questions. I wanted to go home.

"We will," Jax assured me, because I had apparently spoken aloud, reaching forward as if to touch me, but pulled back as though he had been burned.

My eyes flashed down to see if there had been an accidental flare of magic, but nothing was on fire. I was pumped too full of blockers to do anything, even if I wanted to. The heavy, ice-cold feeling dampened anything I could have conjured forth. No, it was my emaciated muscles that caused him such a visceral reaction. Another crack formed in my already shattered heart.

"Not here," I hissed at the clear question in his eyes.

Whatever had been done to them during their interrogations and imprisonment had been milder than what I had endured. I was grateful for that. I would not have wished the torture I underwent on many people, especially not my best friends.

Best friends…

Ah, how the righteous have fallen. I, the jaded, friendless protégé gladly suffered some of the worst possible torment for her newfound *friends*. It was like a cartoon holovid or one of those heroic novels I had devoured during my time at the Academy. *Pathetic.*

I was pathetic, just like my father always told me. Not for having friends, not really. But for caring. For allowing so much feeling to cloud my mind. For caring, loving, and wanting *more*. So. Damn. *Pathetic.*

The ride back to our dormitory was punctuated by meaningless, vapid small talk. My teammates bore tired, slightly haggard appearances which offset their cheerful conversation uncomfortably. Of course, it was for my benefit, but I did not participate. I merely sat there, staring out the shuttle window as the pristine city of Heliorious shone brightly in the fat radiant sunshine.

"Daux," Himawari began hesitantly as she unlocked the door to our rooms with her holonav passkey. "There is something we need to talk about."

"You're telling me," I muttered. There was much to discuss once we got inside. To plan.

But that was not what everyone else had in mind, because once the door swung open a small shriek came from inside and a small body flung itself into my arms, sending my chair rolling back a few feet.

Sobs wracked the tiny frame I clutched to my chest, soaking quickly through my shirt to my skin with tears. Amalie. It was my sister. They had not taken her from me, but they had also not treated her well. Her pretty blonde hair was matted and dull, and her body was tense.

"What the—" I started, but she only sobbed louder, muttering incoherently.

Jax took hold of my chair and pushed us inside before the noise attracted an audience, Félix taking up the rear and shutting the door behind us. Amalie's thin frame would leave bruises the next day, but I still held her as tightly as I could, smoothing her tangled hair back from her forehead and murmuring soothing nothings as I glared up at my friends.

"*What* is going on?"

Chapter Seven

My mother had been taken into custody, shrieking and cursing. It would have been amusing had Amalie not been witness to the whole thing. Had they not bundled her into the same vehicle as our mother. Had they not kept her in an overcrowded foster home while Mother was processed and I was in custody. A home filled with strangers. They waited until today, the day I was *released*, to bring Amalie to my flat. My friends had tried to convince them to release her into their custody multiple times, but the care system refused. Eventually, a Spec Ops agent had to "personally convince" them to stay away.

I would have laughed had I been there to witness my mother's humiliation and shame. I would have jeered as she screamed the same obscenities that she always said were unfit for a girl's pretty lips. I would have celebrated as she felt the same indignity I had been forced to endure because of her husband, my father.

As it was, I could find no pleasure in her suffering because Amalie had borne the shame as well. It was not fair that our parents did this to us. It was not fair that I was shunned because I had magic, nor that Amalie had to stay home and bear their expectations and emotional brutality. Or that they left us to fend for ourselves because of their crimes.

Though we were now on the couch in the living area—safe, comfortable. Amalie still sat in my lap, despite Jax's insistence that I was not well enough to hold her. The challenge in my eyes defeated his half-hearted attempts before he could even try to take her from me. She was *mine*. No one was going to take her from me now. *Ever.*

My trembling hands combed through her long, blonde hair, gently pulling through the tangles as she hiccoughed against my chest, tears long spent. It had taken her several minutes to calm down, or at least quieten enough for Himawari to explain what in *Eturnus* was happening. Since I was the next of kin, the same Spec Ops operative that had warned my friends to stay away from Amalie had dumped her on them to wait for my eminent release. I had been too afraid to seek out my grandparents for fear of angering my father while I was at the Academy, and too afraid of what I would find after I graduated to search on my own.

When I asked why Amalie had not been given over into their care, I had to find out from Himawari that they had admitted themselves into a care facility a few years before my Placement. The Spec Ops agent who brought Amalie to the flat had told her, explaining that since they were in the care of the province, they were unable to look after a child.

After being dropped off, Amalie refused to leave my room, barely eating, only sneaking out to use the bathroom when she could be sure no one was around to grab her. Because of my and my parents' arrests, she was also being monitored and unable to attend school in person. For the most part, my teammates had left her alone, only checking on her to make sure she ate *something*. They did not want to traumatize her further.

They had also been interrogated; though, for less time than me. Félix's interrogation was even shorter than Jax and Himawari's due to his injuries, which were now – thankfully – healed. That did nothing to dispel my anger, my *rage*, at the mere fact they had been met with suspicion at all.

My stance on the matter when Spec Ops interrogated me the first time, was naïve. They could care less about what truly happened. They could care less about the *truth*. A scapegoat is what they needed. Someone to blame, to torture, so it looked like they had the situation under control. And they brought my friends into it, all because they were guilty by association, just as I was guilty of being my father's daughter.

Talia had gone through a similar interrogation process as me, emerging from her cell like a husk of her former self. Félix had gone to visit a few days after her release last week, only to see the light gone from her eyes and the door slammed in his face by Gwyn. Talia's team lead never did trust me, and probably wouldn't ever now. Not that I cared.

I only worried for Talia.

Gods, this was such bullshit. Where was the 'utopia' in this mess we were in? How could Spec Ops and the government claim to serve and protect the citizens of Heliorious, much less the rest of the NAF when they did this to my friends and my baby sister?

I listened in horror as my teammates – my *friends* – told tales of being followed home by angry Spec Ops operatives who threatened them just for knowing me. Thankfully, these agents never made it into the flat and would have been taken down easily had they tried. Of how they too were being forced to take blockers until we were all deemed fit for duty. The rage boiled inside me, burning hotter with each word. With each sniffle from the girl in my lap.

It had not slackened by the time we all sat down for dinner. Clear broth and plain bread for me and roast meats with mashed parsnips, spicy glazed carrots, and the same bread I was given for everyone else. Félix and Jax had done the cooking tonight and had outdone themselves, even on my food. While my food was bland, it tasted rich and heavenly compared to what I had been fed while incarcerated.

Though I was angry – no, furious – dinner seemed to be going well, and no one noticed because they were content to let me remain silent. It was enough to listen to their idle chatter and hear the scrape of utensils against dishes. It was enough until Amalie slammed her fork down onto the table, causing everyone to jump.

"Would you *stop* doing that?" she demanded, glaring at Félix who blinked back at her owlishly.

"What is he doing?" I asked, turning toward her in shock.

She had never acted this way before, at least not in front of me.

"Playing with his food!" she flung her slim hand out accusatorily, pointing to his plate.

Félix had arranged each item on his plate in perfect rows and was taking precise bites of each in the order that suited him. My brow furrowed as I looked back at the fury on Amalie's face and the confused expressions of my friends. He had always done this, as long as I had known him unless the meal was soup or something he liked to mix. It had never bothered anyone else, so I never really paid that much attention to it.

"Félix just does that," Jax told her gently, side-eyeing me.

"It is rude and dumb," she insisted, crossing her tiny arms over her chest.

"Amalie," I snapped, shooting her a fierce glare.

Félix, who looked utterly confused and embarrassed, made to push away from the table before I placed my hand over his to stop him. He did not meet my eyes, instead keeping them trained on his perfectly arranged plate.

"Amalie," I repeated, softer this time, waiting for her to look at me. "Félix is autistic. He likes to eat his food in certain ways and is *allowed* to eat *however* he wants to. This is his home and we are not going to tell him how to act here. It is a safe place for all of us, do you understand?"

"No," she hissed, her nose scrunching in displeasure. I used to think that was cute, but now it reminded me horrifically of my mother. "He is just dumb and needs to eat like the rest of us."

That reminded me of my father.

"Are you finished with your meal?" I asked, fury simmering beneath the softness of my voice.

"Yes, why?" she asked, tossing her hair. I wanted to gag at the action. How many times had I done that as well, in subconscious imitation of our mother?

"Go to my room," I commanded softly, putting the full force of my authority as a Spec Ops team leader into my tone. "And do not come out until you are ready to apologize to my friend for insulting him."

"Daux, it's okay, really—" Félix tried, gripping my fingers tightly.

"It is absolutely *not* okay. Amalie, my room. Now."

With a rage in her eyes that matched my own, Amalie glared at me and then stormed off to my room, slamming the door behind her so hard that the walls shook and the picture frames rattled against them.

I let my head fall into my hands, meal all but forgotten.

The next few days had not been much better. Amalie grudgingly apologized to Félix, though we could all tell she did not mean it. Jax said it was because she was scared and angry, just acting out. But I knew better. My parents had begun to poison her, and now it was coming out like venom oozing from an open wound.

The worst part was, that I had no idea how to fix this. How could I reach her, guide her, when I could barely help myself? I was a floundering, weak mess who condemned her friends to unimaginable torment simply because of their association with me. I could barely get out of bed to use the bathroom by myself, so frail was I.

I did have one idea, however. Once Jax awoke to help me into my wheelchair – with regular meals and physical therapy I should be back on my feet in "no time", the healers had said – I rolled myself to my writing desk and began penning a letter. Amalie was at a counseling appointment I had scheduled the night before, indicating a crisis. She had been neglected by my parents, and the state, for too long and though I did not trust Dr. Castillo to help me – as she was in Spec Ops employ – I knew Amalie needed someone to talk to who was not me.

Plus, she would not be around to bother me while I wrote to our maternal grandparents. I had no idea if our parents had poisoned her against them, but I needed to be careful. My letter was about her after all.

Once it was finished – at least three drafts later – Himawari came to fetch me for my first physical therapy session. I went, grudgingly, with her to the front room where a man in a white coat waited, holonav activated. He was plain, unassuming with unlined light brown skin and dark hair and eyes, framed by thick soda bottle glasses.

"Ah," he said, looking up from his holonav at me, moving across the room to shake my hand. "Ms. Deveraux, a pleasure to finally meet you. I am Dr. Jai Ahmed and I will be your physical therapist for the duration of your recovery. Sometimes I will have assistants joining us for observation, but for the most part, it will only be you and me—and a friend, of course, should you wish it. I would like to start in your flat, just in the beginning, so there are no distractions."

He smiled amiably at Himawari and she returned it. I, however, resisted the urge to roll my eyes. If Spec Ops needed my recovery to move along so quickly, they should not have tortured me to begin with. They should not have tortured my friends or left my little sister to fend for herself. What they should have done was let me prepare better and go after my father with a team of operatives.

But no. This was what they chose. And I would make them regret it.

"Himawari," I said, handing her my completed letter. "Will you post this and ask Jax to join me and the Doctor?"

"Sure," she said with a soft smile. "Do you expect a reply

during your session?"

"No, it's to my grandparents." I wheeled myself fully into the living area.

Himawari promised to check the mail for a response later in the day and left to get Jax, who followed her out to the living area, before leaving to post the letter.

"Jax Aldridge," he said, holding his large hand out to shake Dr. Ahmed's. Jax was not a hulking man by any means, but he seemed to tower over Dr. Ahmed in every way, from the top of his braided crown to the leather sandals he wore on his feet.

It had the desired effect.

Dr. Ahmed swallowed hard, eyes flickering between my innocent expression and Jax's friendly one, and stuck out his hand. "Dr. Ahmed," he stammered.

"Pleased to meet you, Doc. Should we get started?" Jax asked, moving to lift me from my chair with minimal effort. His arms were warm and comforting, they felt like coming home. Were we alone, I would have wept.

Instead, I willed back the tears, letting them build into the blindingly hot pit of anger that burned constantly in my chest. I had wanted Jax with me to intimidate the doctor – I didn't like the way he smiled at Himawari – but now I was grateful for his physical presence for my own sake.

"Ye—es," Dr. Ahmed said, pulling up the diagrams on his holonav. "Let's try setting her on her feet, shall we? I think you would be the best companion to join us from now on."

Jax agreed and did just that, holding me upright by my waist when I began to shake.

"You got this, Daux," he whispered in my ear.

And we began.

The session was excruciating. The goal was to build up my muscle mass as quickly as I possibly could, and I also had to almost relearn how to walk. Being strapped to a bed for weeks will cause one to lose basic fine motor skills. Who knew?

By the end of it, I was a sweaty, cursing mess. Jax and Dr. Ahmed fared no better. My glasses had fallen off twice and I had made to grab them instinctively, launching myself from the contraptions I had been strapped into, knocking my body against the furniture as I was held aloft.

To say I was frustrated would be an understatement.

To say I was *upset* would be an understatement.

No, I was enraged. I felt betrayed by my own body, something I had learned to count on more than anything else in this world. If I could not rely on myself, then who could I rely on? The easy, clichéd answer would be "my friends". Yes, that was probably true, but it wasn't so simple. Especially when the last time I relied on them, it got them all arrested.

"Let's wrap this up for today's session," Dr. Ahmed said, pushing his glasses up his nose. "You have made an excellent start, Daux. Most excellent. You will improve very quickly if you keep up this level of intensity during our sessions."

"How many weeks?" I snapped as Jax helped me back into my wheelchair. I wanted a shower, food, and a nap in that order. But more importantly, I wanted to be able to use my own body again.

"We—ell…" Dr. Ahmed said, drawing out the word. "It is hard to say. It could be as little as two weeks to see improvement or as long as several months."

"Months?" I gasped in shock, fingers digging into my thighs.

"Well, yes, in the worst cases. But with the medication and advanced therapies, you will be receiving it should not take that long," he assured me with a timid smile. I could tell he was glad for my blocked magic because I would have thrown him through a wall were I able.

"Thank you, Doctor," Jax said with his smooth easy smile, interrupting before I could say something everyone else would regret.

He nudged my shoulder and gave me a pointed look. I rolled my eyes, crossing my arms over my chest.

"Thank you, Dr. Ahmed," I said insincerely.

The doctor did not seem the least bit offended, probably used to similar behavior from other patients. He smiled pleasantly at us before gathering up his things and then leaving. The relief I felt at his departure was palpable. All I wanted to do was collapse somewhere and cry.

But as fate would have it, Jax turned to me and gave me a long, searching look.

"What?" I snapped at him, attempting to wheel my way toward my room.

"Your eyes…" he hedged; expression tight.

"What about them?"

"They're—"

My hand flew to my eyes, nearly smacking the glasses from my face. Jax blinked a few times, grabbing my hand away so he could look deeply into my eyes. What was he searching for?

"Nothing," he said finally with furrowed brows. "They looked almost black for a moment. But they're green now."

"Must be the glasses." I shrugged and pulled away, hoping to escape to my room.

I had noticed the same thing a few times, looking into the mirror at the dressing table in my bedroom. A flash of darkness across my irises, so quick that I was not sure I had even seen it. And when I would remove my glasses to investigate, all I could see was the green-gold of the ocean staring back at me the only black being the pin-pricks of my pupils.

I wanted to return to my room, to yank my sweaty clothes off my body and fling myself into the bed to sleep my problems away. But not before I investigated the strange black shadow that flashed over my eyes.

But that was not to be my fate, as it happened that

Himawari returned from running errands. She insisted on helping me shower with the special soap she *just* purchased to help me feel better. Jax insisted I do so, against my protestations, stating that I smelled. Bad. So, begrudgingly, I allowed Himawari to wheel me into our shared bathroom where she pressed the button on the shower for hot water.

I was silent as she set about gathering loofahs, nail brushes, a wide-toothed comb, nail trimmers, and the brand-new lavender-scented soap she purchased. She set everything on the edge of the shower and pressed the button that activated the retractable sitting ledge, then turned to me.

"Let's get you out of those clothes." She placed my glasses on the counter, helped me pull my sweat-drenched long-sleeved t-shirt over my head, and then helped me shimmy out of the sweatpants I stole from Félix's clean laundry basket when we returned home. He did not mind.

Once I was completely undressed, she reached for me, placing her hands under my underarms and *pulling*. My sore, weakened muscles protested with a shrieking pain, but I grit my teeth and tightened my core as much as I could to help her. It did not amount to much, but even without using her magic Himawari was strong.

With little struggle, I was sitting on the cold ledge while Himawari fiddled with the buttons on the shower, attempting to raise the water to a temperature that was comfortable for both of us.

Soon enough, *hot* water was streaming from the faucets and Himawari was throwing her clothes onto the bathroom floor before closing the shower door. She had a purple two-piece swimsuit underneath her clothes, which was something I thought was rather amusing as warmth flooded over my aching body. While the water showered down over me, Himawari sprinkled healing salts and steam-dissolvable muscle-relaxing solvents onto the floor.

The scent of roses, peonies, and lavender assailed my nostrils and I was floating. My eyes slid shut against the blurry bathroom. I hated the indistinct unfocused way I saw the world now, but my glasses fogging up in the steamy shower would have been incredibly annoying.

When the water finally drenched my shorn hair and body, Himawari carefully sat down next to me on the ledge. The warmth of the water contrasted starkly with the coolness of her hands, but it wasn't unpleasant. Her hands were always cool and soft. I thought she could have been a healer with those hands, had she not been born into a shadowmancing family.

The spark in my chest responded with a warming flicker but quickly dulled. The blockers were doing their work well, dulling my senses and my magic. Fueling only my ire.

Himawari hummed softly as she worked a floral-scented oil into my short, wet hair, massaging my scalp with such precision I would have fallen asleep right there in the shower had I not been tasked with washing my body—as much as I could by myself. It was nice. This was nice. Friends were supposed to take care of each other in this way. To bond together over the rituals of cleanliness and beauty.

A sudden, vivid memory of Talia sitting on the counter painting her toenails while I showered in the communal dorm bathroom surfaced, hitting me like a ton of bricks. We were laughing, she had made an excruciatingly bad joke and I had thrown something at her from the shower. I could not remember what it was, but she looked at me with such an offended expression that I burst into laughter, almost slipping on the shower stall's wet soapy floor and falling.

And now she was likely in the same state as me, weak and barely able to care for herself. Because of my incompetence and failure. Because I was incapable of arresting my father. And she only had Gwyn and the twins to help take care of her. Would they help bathe her? Would Talia even want that?

Warm water pouring over my head pulled me from my thoughts. Himawari's long-nailed fingers worked into my scalp, shampooing it gently.

"I know it's hard," she commented softly over the sound of the water and bubbles. "But let's try and remain present in this moment, okay? I think it would be good for you."

Anger bubbled in my stomach, and I wanted to direct it at her, but I could not. Not while I was unable to fend for myself, not when she was being so kind to me. That would not be right. Besides, she had a point. If I let myself dwell on how miserable I was, then I couldn't do anything about it. No, I had to focus my rage.

"Okay," I agreed, allowing her to guide me through my breathing exercises while she rinsed my hair out, and then conditioned it.

One breath in, hold it. One breath out. One breath in, hold it. Just like I had taught her once.

One breath out. One breath in. Hold it. One breath out. One breath in. Hold. One breath out. In. Hold. Out. In. Hold. Out. In. Hold. Out.

A soft knock roused me from the deep slumber I had fallen into after Himawari helped me to bed, a pair of soft, fleece pajamas covering my body in their velvety warmth. It was dark and warm and safe. I had not felt so safe in a long time.

The knock sounded again, jerking me *back* awake.

"Come in," I called groggily, face pressed into the pillow.

The door opened, light spilling into the room for half a second before someone stepped inside and closed it, making their way over to my bed. It dipped under their weight as they climbed in. A large, warm hand smoothed over my hair and I knew who it was immediately. The spark in my chest burned away some of the black, oily darkness at his touch. Burned back some of the ice in my veins.

"Fé," I mumbled into the pillow. "Do you need something?"

"Himawari told me to wake you up for dinner," he explained, his fingers running through the tangles in my growing hair. "And Valentin yelled at me when I walked in on you two cuddling last time, so I figured I better knock."

Had the lights been on, I would have given him a glare that would have sent him running from the room; however, I was far from angry. While that moment was mortifying, to say the least, it had become a fond memory, something that helped to ground me.

It had nothing to do with the fact that I had fallen asleep in Valentin's room, nor the fact that I had fallen asleep in his safe, warm arms, my face pressed into his toned chest. It certainly had nothing to do with the fact that I replayed that very memory each night to help me sleep.

Of course, it didn't. That would be ridiculous.

"Thank you," I mumbled, attempting to push myself off the pillow.

"You also have a letter waiting for you," Félix informed me, hopping off the bed to help me into my chair, turning on my bedside lamp as he went.

"Oh," I said in surprise. I had not been expecting a reply so soon, and I said as much to Himawari when Félix and I entered the dining room.

She, Jax, and Amalie were all seated around the table already. A steaming pan of stir-fried meat and vegetables sat in the middle of the table, rice seasoned with broth and spices, plain broth, and dumplings surrounded the dish. My stomach growled.

"I checked while Jax and Félix were finishing up dinner," she said passing me a bowl of broth and two small dumplings with a small bowl of rice. "I know you were looking forward to the reply."

"I appreciate it," I said, breathing in the heady scent of the foods I was allowed to eat.

Amalie looked as though she wanted to say something, a few things maybe, but looked at me and then looked away, keeping her lips tightly closed. Despite her dark mood, the rest of us had a nice dinner. We talked and laughed like old times – though Valentin was not with us – and ate until our stomachs were full.

Amalie did not make a single comment on Félix's eating habits. She didn't even look at him, which wasn't good either, but at least she was avoiding an argument. Perhaps Jax was right, and she was just taking out her anger on what she supposed was an easy target. It was a distinct possibility.

But I just knew that the poison our parents tried to shove down my throat – and almost succeeded in doing so – was bubbling beneath the surface of her cherubic face. In her stomach the way my anger constantly roiled. In her palms, the way they balled into small fists. Yes, she may be angry and looking for a fight, but my parents had given her one and I intended to dismantle it from the inside.

I would not have them ruining her. I wouldn't.

Chapter Eight

By the next morning, I had still not drafted a reply to the message I received from my grandparents' carer. The missive the care facility sent said they were unwell and unable to write back, but encouraged me to visit them at my earliest convenience. If they were unable to dictate a reply, what state would they be in should I work up the courage – and the strength – to go visit them?

I thought about messaging Talia – Félix had said she was in the same shape as me – but I chose not to. I did not want my first message to her after my release to drag her down. No, I would wait until I had something happy to share. Soon, I hoped.

Hope. I scoffed internally.

What did I have to *hope* for?

I lay facing the ceiling on my bed, unable to move my sore muscles. What muscles I had left anyway. For the first time since I had left the hawkish scrutiny of my mother's gaze, I hated my body. I hated how it looked, how it felt.

I hated that even if I had chosen to starve myself, it atrophied to this weak, pathetic excuse of something that was supposed to keep me alive. Even if my mother wished me to starve myself as she had, she would be critiquing me now.

You are too thin. No one will want you looking like that. Her voice floated through my mind as I lay there, unable to escape.

And your hair! It was so beautiful and long. It is all your fault you look like this, and that nasty bunch of "friends" you have surrounded yourself with.

"Shut up," I snapped, voice raspy with sleep.

"I didn't say anything," Amalie said petulantly from the other side of me, the sound of Mother's cruel laughter fading quickly from my mind.

Grumbling an apology that she did not accept; I slid from the bed and dragged the wheelchair closer so I could pull myself into it. I heard her rustling on the other side of the bed as I struggled to lift myself into the chair, my muscles screaming with every movement. Then Amalie's dainty arms were wrapped around my chest, pulling my body upwards so I could slide into the chair with the ease I would not have had on my own.

Tears welled in my eyes but I did not let them fall, instead grabbing my glasses off the bedside table, and sliding them onto my nose. Amalie was angry with me and yet she still helped me. If my parents' poison had truly dug its way into her, would she have done so?

I did not have time to say more than a quick thanks before Himawari came to fetch me for my therapy appointment that day. Before I left, I caught a glimpse of Amalie's frozen expression over my shoulder. The ember in my chest faltered at the sight and I quickly turned away.

Coward. My mind whispered in a combination of Mother's voice and my own. *Coward. Coward. Coward.*

With each foul whisper, the inky black hole in my chest dimmed the ember of my magic slightly. With each flash of Amalie's green eyes set deeply into the cold mask of her face. How could I push back at the darkness when I knew the condemnation was deserved? How could I fight when I knew the whispers were true?

Therapy was just another round of senselessness. Dr.

Castillo sat across from me and whispered murmurs of concern at what I endured. She even seemed emotional herself – to my wicked satisfaction – when I explained the way the interrogators tore the memories of my father using blockers on me from the recesses of my mind.

But when I brought up my anger at the way I was treated, at the agents who tortured me, and even the Overseer and the NAF for allowing such inhumane practices, she cut the session short. She stated that because I was still showing signs of defiance against what was essentially a rehabilitation program, she needed to rethink our working relationship as I was making her feel unsafe.

I just blinked momentarily, nodded, and wheeled myself through the lobby and outside to wait for Félix to come to fetch me on the next shuttle to the office. Her? *Unsafe?*

I tried not to laugh as the hot end-of-Melodie sun shone down on me. The idea was as ludicrous as they came. I, barely mobile, on blockers, and weaker than the day I was born made a *therapist* feel unsafe with non-threatening words. Just general expressions of anger and malcontent. So upset that she felt as though she needed to threaten our "relationship", as she called it, with termination.

Again, I had to force back a laugh. Then my mirth at her cowardice dulled somewhat when I realized that her threat of termination could reflect badly on me. Even if I went back in there and groveled for her forgiveness, Dr. Castillo was more than likely going to flag what I said in her notes for whoever was going to be reviewing them at Spec Ops HQ. That was bad for me.

I could feel the anxiety fluttering around in my chest like a nest of angry hornets trying to bust their way through, and my normally paper-dry hands became slick with sweat in the hot summer sunshine. Gods above, below, and wherever else—I was going to go back to prison. I was royally screwed.

Because when they reviewed those notes – under the

guise of national security – I would be marked as deviant, as dangerous. Again. And they may decide I was not worth their trouble, and just imprison me again, leaving Amalie all alone. She would be left all alone to fester with the filth our parents poisoned her with.

No. That angry voice that sounded like Mother in the back of my head hissed.

My sweat-slick hands dug into the armrests of my wheelchair to steady the rage that burned within me, igniting the ember once again. I could almost taste the fire in my veins at the way it burned in my chest. The euphoria I felt at its burning would have terrified me had I been in a position to do anything about it.

There was nothing scarier than a woman backed into a corner with nothing to lose, except a woman with everything to lose.

I had everything taken from me once, and I was not about to let that happen again. Even if I had to rip out my father's heart with my bare hands and toss it onto the Overseer's desk myself. I was not about to let them take away everything my parents never let me have. I would burn Heliorious to the ground first.

"You look like you want to murder that stop sign," Félix commented from beside me.

I jumped in my chair, looking up at him in shock. When had he gotten there?

"Let's just go home," I grumbled, wheeling myself toward the shuttle I had not noticed drive up. "I have a PT appointment later."

"Nah, we're going to get frozen mangonadas," he said brightly, grabbing the handles on my chair and wheeling me onto the shuttle. "You've got plenty of time before PT. Why'd you get out so early anyway?" he asked as he settled us in the disabled seating.

"Don't want to talk about it," I ground out through my clenched jaw.

I did not want to go get frozen mangonadas with their chilled, fruity, and salty spiciness. I wanted to sulk in my bedroom and plot what I was going to say to Dr. Castillo in our next session. To plan exactly how I was going to make Spec Ops regret releasing me. To figure out how in the lost names of the Gods I was going to make my father pay for what he had done.

Félix got his way, though – I was unable to put up much of a fight – and we were sitting outside the mangonada place on a shaded patio covered in colorful greenery from hibiscus to zinnias. Félix looked healthier than ever in the warm glow of the sun. His hair had grown longer, curling well past his ears and down his neck. A light dusting of stubble shadowed his jaw and upper lip like he was allowing it to grow. His eyes were covered by dark sunglasses, but I knew behind the frames they would be sparkling with mirth despite my dour mood.

My heart squeezed at the sight of him slurping down the cool drink. In the white room, I had only pictured him riddled with bullet holes, dying slowly as he bled out on the ground. Now here he was, larger than life and completely healthy.

I began to hate myself even more than I already did for allowing myself to be manipulated into thinking he was going to die—that he *was* dead. For starving myself and fighting back instead of allowing them into my mind unimpeded. If I had let them have what they wanted, had I not fought against the injustices they were doling out upon me, I might be as healthy and happy as Félix was right now.

Finally, a harsh laugh escaped me.

"What," Félix asked, excited.

I had interrupted him, but he seemed happy I was engaging.

I felt bad for misleading him and took a large gulp of my drink, savoring the cool, but spicy sensation as it made its way down my throat. I probably wasn't cleared to have this by the nutritionist, but I was breaking rules now—not abiding by them. I wasn't going to be that girl anymore. I was not the girl who blindly followed authority.

"Nothing," I answered mysteriously, injecting as much mischief into my voice as I could. "I'm just happy you're here with me."

At least that was honest. I was incredibly happy he was there with me. Not dead and riddled with bullet holes.

"Oh," he said, at once looking bashful and out of place. "Thank you."

Then he launched himself back into his tale of how he and Himawari nearly burned down the house the other night, nary a Valentin to put out the fire with his ice magic. He watched me carefully when he said that, glee upon his lips. But I did not give him the satisfaction of knowing just how my heart lurched when he spoke Valentin's name. No, I was going to let the little meddler stew as I finished my mangonada, then made him pay for another.

By the time we returned – full of spicy, fruity drinks and snacks – Dr. Ahmed was ready and waiting in the living room, polishing his soda bottle glasses. Félix chuckled to himself and went to fetch Jax, my team-appointed assistant for PT, leaving me alone with the doctor.

"Good afternoon," I said brightly, throwing the young doctor for a loop.

Up until now, I had been at best standoffish and at worst, embarrassingly rude to my physical therapist. The sunshiny smile I was giving Dr. Ahmed now was incredibly contrary to my previous behavior. It was satisfying to watch the confusion cloud his eyes behind his thick glasses. The voice I had dubbed as my mother's echoed in the back of my mind, cackling at my manipulation.

Since the fiasco of my appointment with Dr. Callisto that

morning, I decided I was going to play them at their own game. Defiance was going to get me nowhere. It hadn't while I was incarcerated and tortured. Let them think I was improving. Let them think I was playing along. And just when they thought they had me wrapped around their fingers, I would show them my fangs. Mother liked that idea.

"Good afternoon," Dr. Ahmed stammered, brows closely knit across his forehead. "How are you feeling today?"

"Oh, just great," I enthused, perhaps too cheerily because a deep frown crinkled Dr. Ahmed's relatively smooth face.

He quickly brought up the screen of his holonav and began typing something I could not see. I would have to fix this quickly, or my plan would be ruined before it even started. That was the problem with me. I was too black and white. I had to find the grey.

"I mean, I had a great afternoon with my teammate," I interrupted as he typed furiously on his holonav's interactive screen. "He picked me up after my therapy appointment and we went out for a snack. He noticed I had been feeling down and thought a pick-me-up would be good before you came over."

That stopped Dr. Ahmed in his tracks, and he blinked a few times. Then he deleted whatever he had written down and sat on the couch facing me as Jax entered the room. He eyed me suspiciously, noting my cheerful disposition. Félix had no doubt told him about my dark mood earlier, and that I had gotten out of my appointment early.

"How has your strength been?" the doctor asked clinically. "And your soreness?"

"Strength-wise," I began slowly making eye contact with Jax from across the room. "I would say I have noticed some improvement. I can sit for longer periods without fatigue and use my arms more. Walking is harder, but my teammates have been helping me every day. Isn't that right, Jax?"

At Jax's name, Dr. Ahmed turned and smiled. After that first day when I had used Jax to scare the doctor away from

Himawari, the two had grown rather friendly, much to my annoyance. But I couldn't control who Jax was welcoming to.

"That *is* right," he agreed sunnily, sauntering into the room. "And her soreness hasn't improved much, but we are keeping up with her mobility and stretching."

"I am trying to work on those relaxation techniques you recommended," I supplied, though my trying was more at the insistence of my teammates rather than personal initiative. Dr. Ahmed did not have to know that, though.

Quickly, he resumed typing on his holonav and stood. Jax moved to help me from my chair, holding me upright on my unsteady legs. I wasn't so unsteady that I couldn't stand on my own anymore, the doctor had not lied about rapid improvement, but it felt nice and secure for Jax to help me. With him there, I knew I would not fall. Dr. Ahmed suggested upping my protein intake – something my nutritionist recommended I do as soon as my stomach could handle it – and we began.

Once again, like all the other appointments, it ended with me sweaty and exhausted. However, this time, I allowed a polite goodbye and a smile to Dr. Ahmed. Jax and the doctor both were flabbergasted, but the latter said his goodbyes and left without much incident.

"Daux," Jax called, stopping me on my way to the bathroom.

"Yeah?" I asked, looking back at him.

"I don't know what has gotten into you today, but I am so proud of you for trying to change your attitude," he said with such sincerity that my stomach lurched.

Guilt crashed into me like a tidal wave and I was almost washed away by the sensation. The realization that I had not only lied to Dr. Ahmed, but to my friend made me feel physically ill. Mother's laughter cut sharply in the back of my mind, the sensation of her long nails ghosting over my scarred scalp.

"Thank you," I choked out, wheeling as fast as I could into the bathroom, and slammed the door behind me.

Mother did not deign to follow, thankfully leaving me alone with my misery and self-loathing. I moved mechanically, pulling myself from the chair and into the shower, leaving the glasses on the countertop and ignoring the black shadow that crossed over my eyes in my reflection. I allowed my breath to move through me slowly, hoping to calm my racing heart, but it did nothing to soothe the feeling. It did nothing to relieve the aching in my chest.

Relief still had not found me when I was finished with my shower and wrapped in my bathrobe. I slid on my glasses and opened one of my drawers at the sink, hearing the clattering and rolling of syringes and vials. A lump of fear began forming in my throat and I attempted to swallow around it. My eyes began to burn and my vision blurred with unshed tears of rage.

I had not allowed my friends to help me administer my blockers. I could not bear to let them see me in that state. It felt shameful, like something to hide. Félix would have been the only one to understand, as Berserkers were required to take temporary blockers off assignment due to their unstable magics, but I did not want his help.

It is the punishment for the sins you have committed and are committing. I thought as I filled the syringe with clear blocker fluid and lined it up with my thigh.

I shoved the memory of Valentin kneeling before me as he injected me with a blocker earlier this year.

I had no use for such images.

No use for the fluttering in my chest the image of Valentin's hand on my bare thigh conjured.

With a sharp cry, I stabbed the needle into my thigh and pressed the plunger on the syringe. A burning flooded through me like a fever, burning my insides out. Boiling me alive. I fell back against my wheelchair with a gasp as the heat seized me, stiffening my muscles and snapping my bones taut in my joints. The syringe was still stuck in my leg and I watched as it trembled, my body shaking uncontrollably.

For a moment, I had made the mistake of looking into the long mirror at my reflection. My face was twisted into a furious sneer instead of contorted in pain, black tears leaking from my shadowy eyes.

Weak. Mother's voice jeered at me. *Pathetic.* It spat.

And as the burning heat seized me once again, my vision was ripped away from my reflection toward the ceiling. I wanted to scream, but I could not. My jaw was locked tight and the muscles of my neck closed around my throat. I could barely even breathe.

Panic began to settle in my chest, and my seizing hands grabbed at the syringe, yanking it from my flesh. It clattered to the ground but I barely heard it over the raucous laughter in my ears, over the cries of pain, and bellows of fury.

And then, as though it had never happened to begin with, the sensation was gone and I was left with the same familiar icy feeling I always had when taking a blocker.

Panting, I rubbed the tears from my eyes, surprised to find they were not black when I pulled away. My gaze flashed to my reflection and I saw nothing out of the ordinary, except my face was as red as if I had just completed a forty-two-kilometer run without stopping and my forehead was slick with sweat.

Snatching the empty blocker vial off the counter, I turned it over and over expecting to find something wrong with it. Perhaps it had expired? But it was still well within the safe-to-use date. Such reactions to blockers were not uncommon… However, I never recalled experiencing one. Except maybe while I was incarcerated. I hallucinated far more than was necessary on the chemicals the interrogators pumped me full of.

Was the reaction caused by my incarceration? The stress on my mind and body certainly could have changed how the blocker felt and reacted inside me. But this was the first time since my release that this had happened. Could it be a fluke?

A knock sounded on the bathroom door, causing me to jump and lurch for the dropped syringe.

"Duax?" Jax called from the other side of the door. "You okay? You've been in there a while."

"I'm okay," I croaked out, throwing the empty syringe into the biohazard receptacle. "Just taking a blocker."

"Okay…" Jax paused. "If you need help, just holler."

"Will do." I turned on the sink to drown out anything else he could have said, splashing cold water onto my cheeks – uncaring if water got onto my glasses.

The idea that I would not only have to lie about my feelings and moods – but about my physical condition as well – to my friends did not sit right with me.

I have no other choice. I thought angrily.

If they knew what I was thinking, then they could be endangered, and I could not have that. If they knew what had just happened with the blocker – the hallucination – I would be locked up in a mental care facility. So, if I had to lie to everyone to protect them, and myself, I would.

Chapter Nine

My progress over the next few weeks continued to shock and awe my therapist. Well, faked progress. She *did* help me work through the lingering fear and anxiety surrounding the torture I underwent, but I never made Spec Ops or the NAF government out to be the "bad guys" in her presence again. Those feelings of anger, of bitterness, did not go away. I held onto them with a grip like a vise, biding my time until I could unleash them on the world.

And I would too.

I would make them pay for their continued torment when they knew I was innocent. I just didn't know how. I was not about to give up those feelings, my plan for revenge until I knew where to strike and strike them hard. But how to do that without causing a major societal or governmental collapse?

I had not quite figured that out, so I would continue to wait patiently until I could act.

Amalie still refused to talk to any of us, and I could not bring myself to head down to my grandparents' assisted living facility to talk to them about her. And at that time, I was so angry with Amalie anyway that I hardly felt the need to bother. Not to mention that I felt betrayed by my grandparents as well. Mostly for them getting old and not protecting me and Amalie from our parents.

I knew the blame I placed on them was unfounded, but I

couldn't help but feel they were partially responsible.

After a few weeks, physical therapy and strength training quickly began to restore me to how I was at the beginning of my time as a Spec Ops prisoner. They finally cleared me for some bodily restorations with healers, which would allow me a moment's reprise from blockers, and I could not wait for that moment.

The burning sensation and hallucinations did not return, which I was grateful for. Just the ice-cold numbness I regularly felt with blockers that made my chest ache.

The first healing session was taking place today, and I had been able to forego my nightly blocker to prepare. The ember of my magic flickered brightly, the thrum of flame warming my blood and flushing my pale skin. It burned back at the hole in my chest, cauterizing the edges slightly. It did not stop the weeping black sludge I saw in my mind's eye. I often had to rub my sternum to remind myself that there was not a real wound there.

But magic was healing, even if it wasn't healing magic itself.

A ping from my holonav dragged my attention away from my breakfast of banana protein pancakes that Félix insisted on drowning in syrup and butter because: "It's good for you!"

Not that I disagreed. Sugar, fats, and carbs were exactly what I needed along with the protein. It was just… rich. So much so that it nearly turned my stomach.

I forced myself to finish nonetheless. I did not want to disappoint Félix or bring any unnecessary attention to myself. I was sick of people watching me – sick of people poking and prodding at my mind and body – and wanted to be left alone as much as possible. Which was not much, if at all. Especially with Amalie living in my room with me.

Félix finished his breakfast much faster than I had and had already cleaned up most of the dishes when I had finished eating. He smiled at me when I slowly made my way over to the sink, plate in one hand, crutches held tightly between my arms and sides. Thankfully, he did not try to help me as I struggled my way over. It would have been infinitely more frustrating. I finally fully understood why some disabled individuals preferred not to be helped or babied by those around them. I knew what I could do, even if it was slow going.

Himawari and Jax were out on a menial task that did not require a full team, so I, Félix, and Amalie were alone at the flat this morning. My sister decided on cereal in front of a vid in the common room, which I was grateful for because she had continued her pointed silence at every meal.

I dreaded having to take her with me to the healer's office this afternoon, but there was no way I could leave her all alone. And I needed Félix with me in case I fell on my crutches.

"Ready to go?" Félix asked as I placed my plate in the sink.

I held back a sigh. "Let me get Amalie."

"'Kay." He waved me off, scrubbing the sticky syrup from my plate with steaming water.

By the time I made it out of the kitchen, Amalie was already on her way to bring her bowl to the sink, a determined look on her face. I was loath to think about what that could mean.

"Are you about ready to go?" I asked her softly, dreading her response.

She looked up at me, her green eyes hard and her mouth pursed. Her small hands were gripped tightly around her ceramic bowl as though she was afraid to drop it.

"Yes," she said finally. "I need to brush my teeth first though."

"Okay, I still need to get my boots on and that will take a minute."

"I'll hurry."

I blinked at her as she brushed past me. I had told her

there was no need to rush… but the way she held the bowl was tight and determined.

On my way to my room to grab my tactical boots – the easiest pair to maneuver in – I heard Amalie's soft voice coming from the kitchen.

Where Félix was.

By themselves.

I nearly turned around, then I registered what she was saying.

"I can do it," she said, sounding frustrated.

"I know, but I'm offering if you don't want to," Félix replied, louder than her.

"I… I need to learn."

The kitchen was silent momentarily and I was scared to move lest Amalie realize I was eavesdropping.

"Do you want me to teach you?" Félix asked.

I realized his voice had deepened while I was away. My heart squeezed at the realization—at how mature he sounded.

"I suppose," Amalie answered him primly.

"Cool," Félix replied.

The water started again and I hurried toward my room as fast as I could on my crutches.

Sitting in the hard plastic chair in the healer's office was a relief. Félix sat to my left, Amalie to my right, as we waited for my call back into the office. It was a bland room, as most waiting rooms were, with generic art prints and photographs lining the beige walls. The chairs we sat in were the same color as the grey tile floor.

A shiver ran up my spine at the seemingly perpetual cold of healer's offices, and I tugged the sleeves of my long-sleeved black shirt down to my wrists. I wished for my long hair, wished that it could settle around my neck and ears to warm me. The cool air prickled gooseflesh at my neck and I felt a scowl twist my neutral expression.

My booted toes tapped against the tile, folding my arms over my chest to ward off the chill. Félix slid his arm around my shoulders, pulling me closer to his side despite the armrest dividing us. He was squeezing one of his stress balls, one of his earbuds in his opposite ear—no doubt playing music of some sort. His other hand tapped out a beat I recognized on my arm.

I would have smiled had Amalie not looked over at us from her lesson on her holonav, a sour expression on her face. She said nothing, only observed us with obvious displeasure before returning to her work. I supposed that whatever goodwill Félix had gained this morning no longer applied. I shook my head at her and leaned my head back against Félix's arm as I waited for my name.

I only had to wait a few minutes before the healer's assistant stuck her head through the door and searched the room. She was small, with a round freckled face, red curly hair, green eyes, and round glasses that looked like my own. She wore lilac scrubs with little white cats printed on them.

Her voice was soft, lilting. A Highlands accent from Eidolon.

"Daux?" She called.

I struggled to my feet, pulling my crutches under my arms, grimacing at the way my body still strained. But I was here to help my recovery. And I was pleased, if not thankful, that whoever my handlers were had allowed healing sessions in my rehabilitation program. That would make all this easier, and faster.

The healer's assistant smiled and opened the door wide for me but I stumbled a bit on my way over. A gasp escaped me, but I regained my footing, pausing momentarily to catch my breath.

"Aren't you going to help her?" Amalie hissed from behind me.

"Nah," Félix said. "The PT said we're supposed to let her do it herself or she won't get stronger."

"But she's—" Amalie began to protest.

"I'm okay!" I called through gritted teeth. "I'm *fine*."

She fell silent and I turned to look over my shoulder at her and Félix.

Amalie's mouth was drawn in a thin line and her color was high, her bright green eyes shimmering as though she was about to cry. Félix was looking between me and her, a nervous sweat breaking out in a sheen over his bronzed skin. He knew how to comfort *me*. He knew that holding my hand a squeezing it with his breath triggered my response. He knew that I would want to be touched, to be held in some way and that it grounded me.

Amalie was a whole different beast.

And Félix was beginning to panic.

"I'm okay," I said again. "Just catching my breath, promise."

Amalie eyed me suspiciously, pale brows furrowing.

I gave her a wan smile, hoping that it came off genuine. Then she looked over at Félix one more time, her mouth working as though she wanted to say something to him. He looked at me, then back at her unsure of what to do.

"I'm headed back," I said, turning toward the healer's assistant. "Take a breath and play nice. I'll be out in a bit."

I did not wait to see how they responded to my command. I wanted to get this healing session over with. I knew it was going to be uncomfortable at best and I was ready for it to be over.

The assistant took my vitals, comparing them to previous charts on her holonav as she worked. Her tongue clicked against the roof of her mouth as she looked over my previous weight, and then looked at the weight I was now. But she said nothing, which I appreciated.

"The healer will be with you shortly," she said with a sweet smile and led me to the examination room.

"Thanks," I mumbled.

Moving to stand in the center of the bland room as the assistant shut the door, I wondered where I should sit. The exam table would be difficult with my crutches, but the chairs along the back wall would be annoying to get out of as well. Especially when the healer was to heal me.

A knock sounded on the door, and the healer poked her head in with a bright smile. She was a small woman. Young, round, and pleasant-looking with golden brown skin that seemed to glow. Brown eyes framed by thick lashes and a round face. Her dark brown hair was tied into a knot at the nape of her neck, and her scrubs were a light blue, printed with clouds.

"Daux Deveraux?" She asked, entering the room.

I nodded my response.

"I'm Healer Martín," she said with a smile, closing the large grey door behind her. "I'll be working with you today, and for the rest of your sessions."

I nodded again, staring at her intently.

"May I help you onto the exam table or would you prefer to do it yourself?" Healer Martín asked after a moment of awkward silence.

I appreciated the question but resented it all the same. I did not *want* help. I wanted to be well again.

You won't be well until she heals you, stupid girl. The voice that sounded like Mother's said.

"Help," I said through gritted teeth, then softened my voice when I saw the startled expression on her face. "Please. I'm having trouble getting up and down."

Her soft smile returned and she guided me to the exam table, placing her hands under my arms to help me up onto it. She was surprisingly strong, but one would have to be if one was a healer. I recognized her, but could not place her in my memory.

"Daux," she mused, looking over my chart on her holonav.

She tapped at her bottom lip a bit, her eyes narrowing as she read each section carefully. Horror dawned on her face for a moment at whatever she read there before schooling her features into a mask of pleasant calmness. Then she took my crutches from me and leaned them up against the door.

I felt naked without them but did not protest.

"You've been through a lot recently, haven't you?" Healer Martín asked.

I could hear the sympathy in her voice though she tried to disguise it. Anger flared in my gut, but I grit my teeth against it.

I will not lash out at the healer. I thought to myself sternly. *I will* not *lash out at the healer; she is here to help me.*

"Yes," I said through my clenched teeth.

She looked me over, noting the haphazardly growing hair, my still abnormally thin frame, and the exhaustion bruising under my eyes. "Lie back, please."

Slowly, I lowered myself onto my elbows, cursing myself for shaking with the effort. A breath in, a breath out. Expanding my stomach, then deflating it. She helped me arrange myself comfortably on the exam table, then pressed her hand to my heart, listening.

I never understood how healers could hear a person's heartbeat without the aid of traditional medical equipment. Their abilities were far beyond my comprehension, but I still watched her with rapt fascination. She ran her cool hands over my face next, then down my neck, shoulders, torso, pelvis, and legs. Slowly, and carefully, scanning the front of my body and internal organs for anything out of the ordinary.

Besides the obvious, of course.

"Let's get you flipped onto your stomach now, okay?" Healer Martín suggested, taking my glasses and placing them on the small wash station next to the exam table.

I used as much of my strength as I could to help her, which was more than I thought I had. It was easier to move lying down. My muscles did not protest as much.

Face down on the exam table, I began to feel small. Vulnerable. I could not see what the healer was doing in this position. Where her hands wandered was beyond my observation, and that meant beyond my control. I flinched when her cold hands pressed at the base of my skull where my scars decorated my flesh.

Those scars were likely noted in my medical chart, as the wounds would have been noted on my arrest intake evaluation, but it felt like an invasion of privacy for her to touch them. I wanted to snarl at her to keep her hands to herself. I wanted to set this boring, sterile room on fire. The hole in my chest began to expand, the inky blackness pressing outward toward my other organs.

Instead, I took a deep breath, igniting the ember in my chest to push back the sludge leaking from my metaphorical wound. Then I let it go.

"Am I making you uncomfortable, Daux?" Healer Martín asked, probing my sore muscles gently.

I did not know how to answer. She *was* making me uncomfortable. I hated the feeling of her hands on me, reminding me of everything that was broken about my body, but if she did not touch me then she could not do her job and heal me. Then I would not be whole again, physically.

"If I am, we can take a break," she said softly, pausing her hands just above my backside. "There is no need to rush through this. Trauma can often make physical touch difficult, especially during medical procedures."

"I'm fine," I snapped, pressing my face into the sterile paper on the table. "Just get on with it, please."

Wordlessly, she continued her exam. I did not need to be reminded of my *trauma*. It was with me every second of every day. I could not be rid of it, as much as I would like to. I would endure, as I had always done, as I would continue to do.

Moments later, the healer had completed her exam and

turned me over onto my back once again, then placed my glasses onto my face.

"There, that part is complete. Now, let's take a moment to go over what I've found before we get started on healing," she said, taking a seat on one of the chairs lining the wall.

Watching her carefully, I motioned for her to continue. I wanted this over. I did not care what she found.

"You have severe muscle atrophy from lack of activity and malnutrition," Healer Martín started, observing me with unabashed sympathy now. "It is a miracle your body did not shut down on itself. Some of your internal organs do show damage, but nothing that I cannot handle. The scarring on the back of your head is fresh enough that I may be able to reduce it entirely during our healing sessions if you would like. As for your eyes…"

"I know," I said, interrupting her. "It would either be surgery or a more intensive healing procedure that would take precious recovery time."

"Which I have been given instructions not to do, at present," she continued.

"I can wait."

Her lips pursed, but she did not continue. Instead, she stood and moved to the sink and began to wash her hands, then she turned toward me with a deep sadness in her eyes and I realized where I had seen her before.

She was the first girl who received her Placement at my Placement ceremony. Katalina Martín, with her shining eyes and excited smile. I hoped to any God that was still listening that she did not remember me.

But I could tell from the look in her eyes that she did.

"I will need to undress you so I can work on your muscles from a cellular level," she informed me, her hands hovering over the hem of my shirt. "The fabric will interfere with the regeneration process. If you are uncomfortable, we can undress you on one half and redress you before moving on."

I shrugged and helped her pull my shirt over my head, then struggled into a seated position to help her undo my boots and remove my pants. Nakedness did not bother me. It was inevitable with dorm life. Talia on the other hand hated people looking at her body. I knew, with a pang in my heart, that she would be undergoing similar procedures to me. That she might even be seeing the same healer and would have to suffer the indignity of undressing in front of a stranger. All because of me.

"I'm going to begin," Healer Martín started, the light green glow of her healing magic turning my pale skin a sickly shade of puce. "This may hurt, and your muscles will be very sore for a few days after the procedure."

I clenched my jaw and nodded. I was already in pain. I did not care if I was sore for a few more weeks strengthening my body – healing it – if I was going to be able to move on my own again. If I was going to be healthy again. I would *endure*.

I always did.

And when her cold hands descended on my body and the excruciating burn of her magic began to flow through me, I welcomed it. I would take this punishment for my failure, for dragging Talia through this, for allowing Félix to be hurt, for Amalie's rage that mirrored my own. I would accept it for Valentin's exile, however temporary.

I. Would. Endure.

Chapter Ten

I made it ten steps out of the healer's office before I nearly collapsed. Félix rushed to catch me before I landed on the sidewalk, leaving Amalie to grab my crutches. Pain lanced up my arms and legs, burning up through my torso and into my jaw. My head lolled as though my neck had broken, but I could not lift it.

Healer Martín had said weakness and pain would be significant side effects of the healing process. The effects of the restoration procedure should wear off by morning and I would feel significantly stronger. However, I now felt as weak as a newborn as Félix maneuvered me from his arms to his back.

Amalie fluttered about like a butterfly, grabbing my crutches, and adjusting my clothes all while I lay against Félix's back unable to move my screaming muscles.

"Y'okay?" Félix murmured, standing to his feet.

"Mmm," I mumbled back, not trusting my voice to be anything less than a scream.

"Let's get her home," Amalie demanded, gesturing for Félix to follow her to the shuttle terminal.

He followed dutifully, promising to go back out and get me a pitcher of mangonadas if I could make it home without passing out.

I could have wept.

I think, from the wet spot on the back of his blue t-shirt, that I did.

Back home, Amalie and Félix propped me up in bed and I helped them activate my holonav's screen to stream some sort of trash show. Félix left shortly after, promising to return with snacks. Amalie stayed in my room with me, leaving only to grab ice packs and towels when the pain grew too much.

She placed them behind my neck, on my legs, and my abdomen all without a word. So, she had not forgiven me. I did not blame her. Our parents had filled her with their bigoted nonsense, their judgmental attitudes, and I had called her out and embarrassed her in front of strangers. Right after our mother was arrested, our father abandoned her, and me nowhere to be found. She was just as unmoored as I was. I had no right, nor the energy, to match her anger.

Amalie had earned it, as misplaced as it was.

She sat on the chaise lounge, her earbuds while she worked on her homework. Effectively ignoring me, except to look up every fifteen or so minutes to see if I was still breathing.

Soon, Félix was back bearing the promised snacks, and mangonadas so I no longer had to worry about Amalie. At least, I did not have to worry about her alone. Félix eyed her warily, setting down a to-go cup filled with sweet and spicy slush next to her along with a bag of gummy candies shaped like worms.

Blinking up at him, Amalie flushed a bright pink and took both of his offerings with a confused expression on her face.

"Thank you," she whispered, seemingly unsure of her own voice.

Félix just smiled at her and headed over to the opposite side of my bed, setting the drinks on the side table and the snacks next to me.

"How long have you had those on?" he asked, gesturing to the ice packs covering my body.

I was about to shrug but thought better of it.

"Amalie got them for me maybe twenty minutes ago," I said.

My jaw ached.

Nodding, Félix moved around to my side of the bed and pulled all the ice packs off. He tossed one to the other side of the bed but took the rest to the kitchen to refreeze. When he returned, he placed the ice pack on his torso and settled onto the stacked-up pillows next to me. Then he held up a to-go cup to my lips, offering to help me drink.

I gave him a look.

"What?" he said. "D'you not want one? I thought you liked these."

"The ice pack," I croaked out.

He looked down at his abdomen. The pack was in the exact spot where he had been shot. Exactly where my father had shot him and I had failed to stop him.

"Oh," he murmured. "The healers said it could ache sometimes, especially after strenuous activity. It will go away with time, apparently."

I made a non-committal hum and gestured weakly for my drink. He passed it to me without another word, shutting down my holonav and pulling up a different show on his device. I sipped at my drink, watching whatever Félix had turned on for us to watch without registering anything other than pain.

Félix still felt the bullet wounds in his abdomen. He still remembered lying on the ground, skin burned and bloody. As long as he remembered this pain, I could accept my own. I would not complain. I would take it. I would endure.

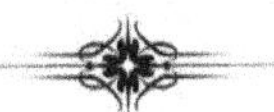

Both the healing and physical therapy would continue for

a little while longer but with decreasing frequency of visits, and more effort on my part. My legs were finally beginning to hold strong as they stood underneath me—barely a tremble for several minutes. I hardly had to use the chair anymore as crutches were now my main mode of support.

I could not bring myself to feel pride in my accomplishments, merely a fierce determination. A sense of relief as a goal was checked off my list.

My hair had even begun to grow rapidly due to the healing. It was now below my chin and I could pull it back into a stubby ponytail and clip back the sides. It was not as long, or as strong, as it used to be, but I was happy to have something to brush through. And not that it was very important, but I was beginning to feel pretty again.

My face was no longer sunken in and sallow, despite my eyes still having a hard glint to them beneath the round glasses I had to wear while on blockers. What is more, my body was still too thin... but I was beginning to fill out rapidly and my musculature was returning.

For the first time in a while, I would allow myself to imagine what Valentin would say when he returned. *If* he returned.

Nothing graphic or inappropriate. I couldn't bring myself to even think such thoughts about him, though I still had the memory of him on his knees before me to keep me too embarrassed to fall asleep some nights lest it followed me into my dreams.

No, I would merely imagine his eyes lighting up his travel and mission-weary face when he saw my hair growing in again. When he saw that I had survived what the interrogators had done to me and come out with my head held high. When he saw the hard work I had put into coming back from my near-dead state – one I was sure he knew I would be in when I left that awful white room.

I prayed to any of the faceless, nameless Gods that were still listening that I would be strong enough to face him when he returned to me. I prayed he would not be as changed as I had become. I prayed for things I could not name or form into words. I prayed that one day, I would be able to do so, that I would be brave enough to face my demons and my feelings for Valentin. Because I knew that right now, I could barely face getting out of bed in the morning.

My prayers were cut short by the sound of screeching and thuds coming from the hallway and living room.

Grumbling, I dragged myself out of bed, grabbing my crutches to pull myself onto my feet. Surprisingly, I did not feel like I needed them too much at that moment, but used them anyway. Poking my head out of my bedroom door, I saw Félix in my wheelchair rolling at top speed down the hallway, stopping short of my bedroom door. The tires squeaked against the wood flooring, as did his shoes. His face was a mottled pink when he met my eyes with the barest hint of shame.

"This thing is fun, Daux," he crowed, rolling back and forth lightly. "I don't know why you didn't like it."

I rolled my eyes. "Maybe because I'm not strong enough yet to roll around in it like that."

"Oh, right," he said in a small voice.

Before he could even begin to apologize, Amalie ran into the mouth of the hallway, stopping abruptly when she saw me.

"Fé," she called, voice unsure. "Hima said it was my turn now."

"I'll be right there," Félix said, turning back to grin at her. "I'm being made to share."

I rolled my eyes again, but this time with more affection – and a little bit of shock. Amalie was *playing* with Félix? And interacting with Himawari? Giving them *nicknames*?

It felt as though I had awoken in a parallel universe and I did not know whether I should go back to bed and try waking up again or roll with it. Ultimately, as I watched Félix roll himself back down the hallway to Amalie and then push her around the flat at full speed, I decided to stay awake and dress for the day.

Since moving around was easier, I did not need help from Amalie or Himawari to dress. Jax had offered but I could tell he did not feel comfortable with that, and nor did I. Still, I dressed in a loose red t-shirt and clean, grey pajama bottoms, as Félix had stolen his sweatpants back from me.

When I exited my bedroom finally after dressing, Himawari was seated in my wheelchair, Amalie and Félix pushing her at full speed around the flat. I blinked at them and shook my head, grateful that the flat was soundproofed. And that paint would not be too expensive if they just so happened to ruin the walls.

By the time I reached the kitchen, I realized that my soreness from my last session with Martín had finally abated. It was taking less time for the feeling to fade each time, and with each session the stronger I felt. The crutches I used now, as I moved about the kitchen, were nearly unnecessary.

The thought filled me with pride, and the ember in my chest flared with excitement. Then dimmed slightly when I remembered I would need to take a blocker this evening. I had to take them after the effects of the healing regeneration wore off; orders from the Overseer herself, and the replacement governor who took my father's place. Edda Faris, an elderly woman who held the title before him.

Interim Governor Faris had immediately branded my father a traitor after his defection and had taken to monitoring my actions as well, through reports from the Overseer.

They both believed temporary blockers were the best course of action in case I was to defect and join my father; as if they had not threatened Amalie's safety if I did not cooperate with them.

I shook my head to clear it and set out to make my tea. I had lost my appetite.

My sister's laughter rang out in the flat around me,

echoed by Himawari and Félix's while I sat, alone, in the dining room. I stared into the cup, watching while the dark leaves leeched into the water. The hole in my chest responded in kind, bleeding into the flame in my chest, swallowing my heart.

"Daux, you are doing fabulously!" Dr. Ahmed exclaimed at my progress.

I was crossing the room in the downstairs training facility, unaided by Jax or my crutches. My balance was off, and my body was shaking with the effort but I had made it to the turning point without mishap. Turning to face them and make my way back, I caught sight of myself in the mirror.

My once-tanned skin was several shades paler under the fluorescent lights, my short hair – pinned back with Himawari's sunflower hair clips – was dull and slick with sweat, and my eyes…

I could have sworn they were as black as an antimatter hole in space for a moment, but they flashed a poisonous green behind my glasses. It was like my irritation had chased away whatever had been hiding there.

I shook my head, observing my form. My face was filling out and I looked less malnourished and more… weak. My muscles quickly filled out thanks to the physical therapy and regeneration procedures. I was beginning to look a bit more like myself again.

Reaching up behind my head, I felt for the place my scars used to pebble my skin, but they were nothing more than smooth patches where my hair refused to grow. Healer Martín had said they were new enough that she could reverse them entirely since they had healed so well this far, and I was looking forward to the day I would no longer feel their presence at all.

"Okay, Daux?" Jax called, a look of worry flashing across his handsome face in the mirror's reflection.

And... a black flash across *his* irises.

"Yep," I called back, tearing my eyes away from my reflection to look at him full-on. "Just taking a breather. I'm ready to make my way back."

And I did so without incident. No matter how much my muscles had been regenerated, if I could not relearn how to coordinate them after so much disuse and damage, I would experience muscle pain and tension – at least, that was how Dr. Ahmed had explained it.

"You are doing remarkably well!" He said, eyes glittering behind his glasses. "It's extraordinary! I never expected you to come so far so quickly. It usually takes months to see this much improvement, and it's only been a few weeks."

There was a time I would have blushed under his praise – anyone's praise – but I merely smiled. It was a fake smile, but a smile nonetheless. "It is all thanks to you and my healer."

"I could do nothing to help you without your hard work and cooperation," Dr. Ahmed insisted.

I ducked my head, hoping to appear sheepish instead of annoyed by his praise. We quickly moved on to my bodyweight exercises, weight training, and balance exercises with Jax spotting every step of the way – always ready to step in and catch me or a weight if I was about to harm myself. If I was sweating at the beginning of the session, then I was completely soaked to the bone by the end of it.

I gasped breath into my lungs, finally allowing myself to collapse to the black foam mats covering the floor. Despite all the progress Dr. Ahmed proclaimed I was making, I felt as weak as a child after all the strength training I had just gone through, and all that I had been doing. I knew I was going to be sore later. All I wanted was an ice-cold shower to combat that as much as I possibly could.

"That is enough for today," Dr. Ahmed said, typing up his end-of-session notes. "Let's get you back up to your flat so you can relax for the rest of the evening."

Evening?

I looked toward the large windows and saw that while the sun was still hanging in the sky, it was quickly lowering, painting the sky with oranges, reds, and pinks. Had I really been working this long? No wonder I was exhausted.

"Help," I demanded, lifting my hand weakly so Jax could grasp it.

He hauled me to my feet with a laugh, clapping me on the shoulder with his large hand, nearly sending me sprawling toward the mats again. He caught me quickly, his hands barely slipping from how sweaty I was.

"Sorry," he said, though from the hint of laughter in his voice he did not sound *too* sorry.

I turned my head to face him, my brow raising slightly. Then he did laugh, and I smiled for real this time.

"Let's get you to the showers," he said once he had quieted down. "You're gonna start smelling soon."

"Wow," I snarked, grabbing my crutches. "Thanks so much."

"You're welcome!"

I flipped him off, smiling, and took off ahead of him and Dr. Ahmed toward the corridor. I did not bother to listen to their conversation as we walked. I just wanted to clean up and eat something before I had to inject myself with another blocker tonight. I could almost feel the freezing pain lancing through my veins, or… or that horrible burning sludge-like sensation that happened previously.

I wanted to be sick, remembering that feeling.

When Dr. Ahmed left the flat after doing an after-session survey, I made a beeline for my bathroom. Soon, my sweat-soaked clothes were in the laundry hamper, Himawari's clips were back in her drawer, and ice-cold water was spraying from the shower heads.

A light rap of someone's knuckles on the bathroom door made me pause with one foot in the shower. I huffed an exhale and grabbed my bathrobe, tying it securely around my waist before answering the door to see Jax standing there, a look of concern and bewilderment on his face.

"Yes?" I asked, a little annoyed.

"I just…" he paused, looking deeply into my eyes.

I wanted to flinch away; he was looking too closely at me, looming over me like the God of Judgement when it still had a face and name. I did not like it. The way he was staring seemed like he was trying to see deep inside of me as Dev and his interrogation team had. My jaw tightened and I crossed my arms over my chest. The last time he thought he had seen something he said it was a fluke. So, why was I so nervous?

"What?" I snapped.

"Nothing," Jax said finally pulling back. "I thought I had seen something when we were downstairs."

"What did you see?"

"I…"

"What did you *see*, Jax?"

He stared down at me, dark brown eyes swirling with confusion and some other indiscernible emotion. His hand reached up to push the hair away from my eyes. There was a flash of something dark across his eyes again but I blinked and it was gone. Then he dropped his hand.

"When we were downstairs, I thought I saw your eyes go black again, like the other day," he whispered as though he did not want to be overheard. "But it must have been a trick of the light. It had to be."

"I just… I saw…" I started but Jax pulled away, shaking his head.

Jax's eyes had just swam with shadows. They had done it downstairs too. Were we both seeing things? My heart began to pound thunderously in my ears. What was happening to us? To me?

"Forget it, Daux," he said lightly, smiling at me and ruffling my hair. "Enjoy your shower."

Then he was gone and I was alone. Silently, I closed the bathroom door and pressed my back against it, trying to regain control over my heartbeat. Shaking my head, I tore off my robe and ignored my reflection in the mirror. I did not want to see if that same shadow I saw in Jax's eyes reflected in mine. I did not want to see if my pupils swallowed my irises whole.

The ice-cold water of the shower engulfed me with lung-aching intensity. Lowering myself to the floor, I lay down and let it wash over me the way the rain washed over Valentin all those months ago. I wished he was here. He would know what to say about all this. Whether to tell me I was crazy or something *was* wrong.

I took a breath. And then another, letting the water wash everything away.

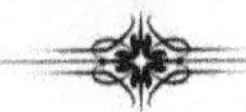

After a dinner of chorizo tacos and pork steamed buns – Félix and Himawari unable to decide which they wanted for dinner tonight, had decided to make both – I found myself alone again. Jax and Amalie were cleaning up the kitchen and after he would take her to pick out ice cream to take back home, Himawari had gone out to see Rhiannan for a moment, and Félix was gaming in his room.

I could not put it off any longer.

Sighing, I closed the bathroom door behind me again, leaning my crutches up against the counter, and began rummaging around for a vial and sterile syringe. I found them, then rolled one leg of my oversized sweatpants to mid-thigh.

Valentin's icy gaze flashed before me.

Do you want me to do this for you? The ghost of his

words whispered over my skin and I shivered.

Yes. I wanted to say. *Yes, please help me.*

Coward. That ugly voice in the back of my head snarled.

Rage flashed through me and I filled the syringe, flicking it to rid it of any bubbles. With shaking hands, I plunged it into my leg, a gritted cry of pain slipping through my teeth as fire burned through my body. My reflection's eyes seared black into mine, and I wanted to call for Jax but all that would come out of my mouth was a breathy sob.

Gods, it hurt.

Sweat poured from my forehead onto my face and down my neck. My whole body seized up, and without the support of my wheelchair, I stumbled back into the wall, cracking my head sharply against the drywall. My ears rang, the sound of that voice cackling riotously in my mind. Bile and brimstone rose in the back of my throat as I fell to the ground, another cry of pain slipping past my lips.

I barely registered the knocking on the door, or its opening until Félix appeared above me, pulling me upright and checking me over for damage.

"Daux, are you okay?" he was saying over and over.

I could not answer him. My jaw felt like it was wired shut with the pain.

"Hey, hey," he crooned pushing my hair back from my face. "Breathe, breathe with me."

Gripping my hand tightly, Félix squeezed it and took a breath, squeezing again to release it. I tried to breathe with him, despite the burning in my veins finally reaching my heart. He was holding my gaze, or trying to. I could not keep from trembling, nor could I help but to flinch when I saw a flash of shadow cross his eyes.

He released all his breath in a muffled yelp when my hand clamped down on his. I could hear the popping of his bones as he wrenched it free, shaking it and clenching it to see if anything was broken. It was not, because he placed it on my shoulder this time and resumed his breathing.

I followed along as best I could, the flame reaching my throat now. It tasted like smoke and blood. I wanted to be sick, but Félix held my gaze, breathing with me until the burning finally settled into a dull ache in the center of my chest.

"Daux," he whispered. "Are you okay?"

I nodded, fisting my hand in his t-shirt.

"You don't look okay," he said, brushing a tear away from my cheek. I had not realized I had been crying. "You don't need to lie to me."

I inhaled a huge gulp of air.

"'M not," I breathed.

"Well, that's not a typical reaction to a blocker…" he said, reaching for the vial on the counter. "You've been taking them for years. You shouldn't feel so much pain, if any. And if you do, it wouldn't make you react like that."

"It's… just… an intolerance!" I hissed through gritted teeth, my breath heaving in my chest.

"Daux, it's not normal for you to develop a blocker intolerance this late in your life," Félix protested, staring at me incredulously. "And if you had an intolerance this bad, then you'd need medication to counteract it or have yourself blocked permanently. At most, blockers cause a cold discomfort and a minor amount of pain, not… whatever this was."

"I'm. Fine." I ground out through my teeth.

"Sorry, but you're not."

"Get out."

"No."

His fingers fluttered at his sides, the blocker vial forgotten, eyes scanning me with his too-observant gaze. I felt stripped bare, skin flayed, before him. He knew how it felt to have to take blockers all the time, to have his flame extinguished. Félix may enjoy not exploding with magic every negative emotion, but he knew how the icy burn in his veins felt. It took your breath away.

Félix even knew enough people who took blockers regularly to have expertise when it came to blocker intolerance. It did not just randomly develop. It was like an allergy. One was born with it.

And it did not cause your eyes to turn black.

It did not cause you to see shadows where there were none.

Félix was hard for people to read, but not me. I could see the gears in his head turning, trying to figure out what I was thinking, attempting to discern what was going on with me.

"I'm fine," I repeated softer this time.

"I don't think I believe you," he retorted.

I would have smiled if the burning heat in my veins had not continued to smolder. Félix's tenacity was always endearing.

"I'm gonna finish playing my game," he said, pushing himself to his feet. "You're coming with me."

Without giving me much of a choice, he pulled me to my feet and grabbed my crutches, helping me situate them under each arm. Then he opened the bathroom door for me, letting me pass him before guiding me toward his room.

He pulled a second chair up to his gaming table – Jax's for when they played multiplayer games. Reactivating the main console, the holo-screens flared to life showing a dramatic opening scene. Then Félix grabbed a stress ball and a handful of small objects from his shelf, gesturing for me to sit next to him as he plopped down in his chair.

I sat and he tossed his things down on the table.

"We're having calm time," he explained, turning on a soothing synth-pop band and muting the game. "You can play with some of those and we're gonna chill out."

"And if I don't want to?" I hedged; voice low – dangerous.

"Then you can go sulk in your room and I'll make Amalie have a sleepover with Hima," Félix snapped back, his fingers tapping riotously on the surface of the gaming table.

I was upsetting him. There was no need to be difficult, much less on purpose, but I was *angry*. Why was this happening to me? And who was he to tell me what to do? *I* was the team leader, not him.

With a frustrated sigh, Félix tossed a fidget toy and his favorite pink stress ball into my lap and picked up his controller.

"Calm time," he repeated and pressed play.

So, I sat there, angrily squeezing Félix's favorite stress ball and listening to the melodic sound of the woman's voice filtering through the speakers. The characters on the screen acting out their individual melodramas distracted me enough, that I eventually crossed my legs up in the seat, playing with the toys Félix had gathered for me until the wee hours of the morning. Listening, feeling, breathing. Breathing. In and out. In and out. In and out. In. And out. In. And out. In. Out. In. Out. In. Out.

Chapter Eleven

After my next physical therapy session, Dr. Ahmed exited the flat practically floating with elation. I had made it through yet another session without instilling the fear of our long-gone Gods in him and, according to him, I was making such excellent progress I might be cleared for small-scale missions soon. This *was* good news. I was not pleased about being forced into working for Spec Ops against my will, but it was going to be nice to get back to something familiar. Something besides sitting in this flat with Amalie glaring daggers at me. And the haunting shadows in my teammates' eyes.

Or having someone wheel me around because my arms would give out.

Even though I would be under the thumb of the Overseer and my colleagues, I would have some semblance of independence. Something I so desperately craved.

Another thing that improved my mood was that Félix had not pressed me on the matter of the blocker incident. Other than a few searching glances, he had left me alone about it. I still had not understood what was happening myself, and I didn't need his scrutiny to figure it out. I could deal with it alone. I *would* deal with it alone.

As soon as Dr. Ahmed was out the door, Jax scooped me up in his arms with a shout of joy.

"I am *so* proud of you!" he exclaimed; his face

practically radiant.

"I'm just glad this is almost over with," I said honestly, a pleased grin splitting my cheeks nearly in half.

He was just about to spin me around again, a snarky retort on his lips when the front door crept back open. We both craned our heads to see if Dr. Ahmed had returned, maybe having left something behind in his delighted stupor. But the man we saw in the doorway was not Dr. Ahmed – it could not have been him; he didn't have a key code to the flat.

It was someone tall and pale – blond. Someone with ice-blue eyes I recognized almost immediately despite the hair change.

Valentin.

The rush of emotion that filled my chest at the sight of him would have knocked me to the ground had Jax not been holding me in his arms. And from the way Valentin was looking at us, it appeared that he didn't much like what he was seeing.

Jax set me down immediately, an elated grin breaking over his face which belied the uneasiness in his eyes. Valentin… My heart lurched at the sight of him. I wanted to run to him, throw my arms around him, and never let him go, but my feet were rooted to the spot. He merely stood there, observing us with the cool expression I had become so familiar with.

"Val, you didn't tell us you were coming back," Jax said, striding toward him, hand outstretched.

As though it were never there to begin with, Valentin's cold demeanor dropped, a warm, animated smile crossing his lips. "Wasn't allowed, confidential."

The two shook hands, and then Jax – unafraid of male affection – pulled him into a bone-crushing hug. When Jax released Valentin, he looked between us, eyes widening and flashing mischievously.

"I'll, uh… I'll leave you two alone," he said slowly,

before leaving the room.

Only when the sound of his door clicking shut reached our ears did my tears spill over, and at once, Valentin rushed across the room, sweeping me into his arms. Oh… It felt like all my problems fell away in his arms. I wanted to stay there forever, and if the way he was holding me was any indication, he felt the same.

"Valentin…" I breathed, clutching my hands in his thick, black jacket.

"Daux," he murmured, lips in my hair.

Would he kiss me now? I was hopeful but apprehensive at the same time. Did I want him to kiss me? I did once, but that was before my mind was turned against me. I didn't know or understand my feelings now. But if he did, and I wanted him to, what would that change?

Everything.

If Valentin kissed me, it would change everything, and I didn't know if it would be for the better. But before I could make up my mind, he pulled back, his face awash with relief. He lifted his hand to my cheek, stroking it reverently with his thumb.

"I prayed they wouldn't break you," he whispered, eyes wet and shiny.

"They almost did…" I whispered back, a lump forming in my throat.

They *almost* did. But they did not, and I would *break* them for trying. I would find whatever little cracks they had in their armor and worm my way into them to destroy them from the inside out like they had tried to do to me. And I would enjoy every second of it.

"I missed you," he said, eyes searching my face.

I did not know how to respond to that. I should have felt elated, overjoyed even, but I only felt a tiny flutter in the hollow, void-like cavity in my chest. I was not the same girl he had left behind. I was not even sure who I was anymore, much less that optimistic, naïve person.

"I missed you so much," I said around the lump in my throat.

It wasn't a lie.

Thinking of him, the rest of the team… It kept me from breaking apart entirely. All I wanted was him next to me, holding my hand, rescuing me. Perhaps the thought of him did keep me somewhat sane. He did say he believed in me after all. That was enough to pull me from that place or keep me from breaking entirely until I could get out on my own.

"I thought of you every single day…" My words came out in a shuddering gasp as I pulled him close again.

I didn't ever want to let him go.

"I did too…" he admitted, stroking my back.

I could not help but think that if my hair were there – as long as it used to be – he would be running his fingers through it. He admitted before he left that he liked my hair; I felt ugly without it. Many people could pull off the buzzcut I once sported, or a well-shaped version of the length I had now – which was not much. Would he think the same? That I was… less attractive? Was he even attracted to me? Did he even like me in that way?

I could not believe I had never asked. It never really mattered until my heart began… to do whatever it was doing right now – fluttering like a hummingbird's wing, making me feel sick and elated at the same time. He had been in love with his team leader before me… but maybe she was a one-time thing? Or maybe he wasn't even attracted to me at all?

Maybe he loved me, but in a friendly way, like Félix who sat on my bed with me when I could not be bothered to leave it. Or Himawari who helped me dress, kissed my cheek, and comforted me through this point of weakness. Or Jax, who danced with me in the living room just to make me smile. Or even Talia, who used to sit in the bathroom with me because I was too anxious to shower alone.

It would rend my heart in two for him to reject me, so I did as I always had. I kept those feelings bottled up inside me, hiding them just out of sight.

Valentin held me until my tears dried, in that quiet way of his. He did not need to fill up the silence with words. He said what he wanted to say, and that was that. There were no frilly words of comfort, no pleading for me to dry my tears. I did not need that. I did not *want* that.

And he knew it.

I pulled away first, my legs still shaky from retraining them, but I held my own. I could for a while now, and I was proud of that. I was proud of myself. I was proud that I had funneled my anger into recovering my strength instead of destroying myself like I had wanted to do.

Had I done that, I would not have been able to see Valentin again. I would not have been able to see anyone I cared about again.

"Are you hungry?" I asked abruptly, grabbing my cane, and started toward the kitchen.

"Yes," he answered, following me, confusion cracking through his carefully placid expression.

I began grabbing leftovers from the fridge without really thinking about what he might want, placing them all on the counter for him to choose. I knew he liked spicy food though, and Félix had made something the other night…

Valentin was looking at me, his eyes bored holes into my back where I felt his stare. My stomach fluttered – whether in nervousness or excitement, I was unsure. I did not turn around to return his gaze.

"I will heat you something up if you want," I began, my hand tightening on the countertop. "So, you can have some time to yourself, put away your things… shower maybe?"

"Do I smell that bad?" His voice was right behind me, warm and soft.

"Oh…" I breathed, feeling that spark inside me respond to his tone. "No, you don't. Sorry."

"I was teasing you, Daux." I could *hear* his smile when he spoke behind me.

"Oh…"

The spark, the lingering ember of magic – of my very *identity* – leaped and flickered brightly, threatening to burn the blockers out of my system and engulf me. My limbs began to shake, but it was not from the strain of standing or using my significantly less weak muscles. No, it was for a much different reason than that.

"I don't want to be alone right now," Valentin admitted, placing his hand on my shoulder to turn me around.

I could understand that. I could understand just as well as wanting to be completely left alone. I wanted both simultaneously sometimes. But if he kept his hands on me, as platonic as the gesture was, I was going to explode.

"I thought you were reassigned," I said, swallowing thickly as I allowed myself to face him.

"I was," he replied, keeping his hand where it was, burning a hole through my sleeve. "But I was mostly alone for my missions."

"I'm—I'm so sorry."

"Don't be, Daux. None of this was your fault."

That is where he was wrong though. All of this was my fault. It pained me that he could not see it.

"It is not *your* fault," he insisted, bringing his palm up to cradle my cheek.

My heart was beating a mile a minute in, threatening to burst through my chest. I wanted to hold him again but I could not make my body move, could not make it respond out of fear of what would happen if I allowed myself that amount of self-indulgence.

"When I told you that I believed in you, I meant that," he told me, his other hand was now resting on my waist, and I was going to die. "I do not say those things lightly."

"I know," I rasped with a smile, trying to keep the tears from my eyes. The warmth radiating from his hands was going to melt me. "You made that very clear when we first met."

"I was a total ass," he laughed.

Gods, he had such a beautiful laugh.

"Yeah, you were."

"I bet you hated me."

"I did. But I don't anymore."

Something in him froze at my words and flickered in his eyes. Then all at once, his expression changed, blazing a smoldering heat that threatened to burn me alive. His hand tightened on my waist, and the one that cupped my cheek trembled, inching into my hair.

"Is that a promise?" he whispered, reverence on his breath.

Reverence for me? Me?

I blinked. My brain could hardly form a coherent thought. I could scarcely breathe. And, embarrassingly, said the first thing that came to mind.

"It's a threat."

As soon as I spoke, mortification crashed into me. I could feel the blood drain from my face, making me feel even weaker and more lightheaded than before.

Idiot! I thought savagely.

However, Valentin smiled. Then his smile turned into a laugh, one that was deep and genuine. It reminded me of the first time I had heard him genuinely laugh while we were touring the Spec Ops living facility. This one was different, but it held the same happy quality. It made my already shaking knees weak.

And just as quickly as it came, his laughter trailed off and the blazing look returned to his eyes. My stomach clenched as he leaned closer, and closer, and closer until his lips were a hair's breadth from mine. Then the sound of a bag thumping on the floor made the both of us jump and look toward the sound.

Amalie stood at the entrance of the kitchen, arms crossed, a glare forming on her pretty face. She was back early from her counseling appointment. Then she spoke to

me directly for the first time in forever.
"Who is this?"

Chapter Twelve

My eyes flickered between Valentin and Amalie, my heart beating a mile a minute. He and I had moved apart, but the suspicious look had not left Amalie's face. Nor had she uncrossed her arms, or moved from her spot in the doorway. It was almost as though she was blocking us in.

"Who is he?" Amalie repeated, tapping her foot against the tile floor.

The rhythmic pattern beating in tandem with my heart, and the pounding in my head. I wanted to take Valentin by the hand and lead him away from the flat, from anywhere Amalie – or anyone else who would bother us – would be. But I really couldn't do that, not when she was talking to me again, no matter that it was nearly an accusation.

"This is Valentin Angelov," I explained, introducing him to her. "He is a member of my team. You would remember him from the Placement Ceremony."

Her already bitter expression soured and she shook her head. "This guy is blond. Angelov had black hair with other colors in it."

"I had to dye my hair," he clarified evenly, attempting to smother his mirth at the situation.

Was I the only one embarrassed? Probably.

"Can't you guys use glamours?" Amalie sniffed, shifting her weight.

Valentin's neck strained against a laugh that threatened

to escape. "Yes, but in case my magical energy was too low or I was caught, I needed some sort of physical disguise."

Amalie blinked at his explanation, then nodded and turned to me.

"Do you hug all your teammates like *that*?"

A choking sound emanated from my throat and I held onto the countertop for support, nearly knocking the containers of leftovers to the floor. Valentin quickly moved to steady me, placing his hand on the small of my back, and before I knew what I was doing, one of my hands was fisted into the black fabric of his shirt.

In horror, I looked back toward Amalie who quirked her brow at us.

"Mhm," she hummed and picked up her bag. "I've seen what I needed to."

Seen what? I could feel the heat rising in my cheeks. *What* did she need to see?

"Amalie, wait," I begged in embarrassment, attempting to go after her.

"Please let me know when it is time for dinner," she asked in a small voice, more polite than I had heard in a long while. "I have homework from my counselor and my online classes to do."

I blinked for a second before nodding. "Sure. I'll come get you."

With that, she turned on her heel and left. Neither Valentin nor I were very much inclined to resume our embrace after our first interruption, and Valentin found that he was not as hungry as he initially thought. I was getting rather exhausted from standing so we put away the leftovers and made our way into the common area where I sank into the couch with relief. My body was *much* stronger than it had been, but I still tired easily.

Valentin seemed to understand.

"I have seen a lot of operatives come out like this after intense interrogations," he explained softly when I asked him about it. "It's something I hoped wouldn't happen to you. I expected you to fight, and you look like you fought hard."

"Why didn't you tell me what they would do?" I asked, unable to help feeling a little bit betrayed.

Shame colored his expression, his voice. "I only had a limited amount of time to speak with you, I wish I would have told you what could happen... but the Overseer explicitly told me not to, that my investigation would help you, and..." his voice faltered, a pretty flush forming high on his cheekbones. "I had other things I needed to say to you."

The thundering sensation had returned to my heart, making my throat close up. The way he was looking at me... Valentin's eyes were no longer frozen over but blazed with blue fire. Burning, burning, burning, attempting to consume me. If I could be burned alive by that look alone, I would have died happily. Instead, I spoke.

"That you believed in me," I said shakily around the blockage in my throat.

"Yes," he whispered hoarsely, as though even that one syllable was too difficult for him. "Yes, I did then and I do now."

Flame engulfed me and I had no idea what would quench it. I was ablaze with happiness, elation, rage, and so many undiscernible emotions. I wanted that flame to burn me to ash. It likely would have had Félix not rushed into the flat at that exact moment and screamed with excitement upon seeing Valentin and me together on the couch.

This brought Jax running, no doubt worried that Valentin and I had murdered each other – or at least left a bloody mess on the floor for him to clean up. Himawari, who had also been out with Félix but left behind in his rush to get home and probably continue his game, rushed through the door, eyes alight with panic. Even Amalie peeked out from my room, curiosity shining in her otherwise dull expression.

Félix tackled Valentin onto the couch with a whoop, sending the piece of furniture back a foot or so with me still on it. I blinked in surprise, remembering that Valentin had cultivated relationships with everyone before our final mission, not just me. Then a pleased smile broke out across my face and I joined the hug from the outside, earning a delighted squeak from Félix and a long bout of grateful eye contact from Valentin.

When we pulled away, Félix was scrubbing his eyes furiously, attempting to hold back tears of joy. "We were worried we would never see you again," he admitted.

"As was I," Valentin said gravely.

"So, you are back for good?" Himawari asked hopefully after a beat.

Valentin looked at me, then each of our teammates in turn. His lack of answer sent my heart thundering in my chest, this time out of pure panic rather than its earlier melding with anticipation.

Was he truly back for good? Or was this only a small visit? I almost hoped he would not answer; I was not sure my heart could take it if he said he was unable to stay with us. Unable to stay with *me*.

Then he smiled and my heart nearly shattered in two. It was so beautiful it could have lit the sun aflame like the Gods had designed it that way. It certainly caused the ember inside my chest to burn with even more intensity than before.

"I am *staying*; I'm not going anywhere," he promised, but when he spoke, he spoke directly to me. The message was intended for everyone, but the way his eyes held mine – the timbre of his voice – Valentin was speaking directly to me.

I could have wept.

Tears blurred my vision, but I blinked them away. There was no reason to get emotional in front of everyone, though they likely would have understood. Félix was still very misty-eyed himself.

We all stayed like that for a while, sitting and talking – sometimes laughing – until Jax and Himawari disappeared into the kitchen to prepare dinner. The rest of us followed, and I even noted Amalie joining us on the fringes, taking her "homework" to the dining room table to listen to our conversation. A strange sensation came over me just then. An almost… peaceful feeling. It lasted well into the night, leaving me confused.

Long after, I lay in bed next to Amalie, my skin still burning in all the places he touched me. Still tingling as though his eyes were still on me. It hardly felt like two walls and two doors were separating us. I so desperately wanted to go to him, to tell him how I was feeling, but the cowardice in me rose, staunching the flame a bit. He would not want me. Not at all. Not with all this hot, ugly rage inside of me.

No. I was damaged.

Broken beyond repair. I had been wrong, and so had Valentin; the Spec Ops interrogators *had* broken me. They had beaten and crushed my will, and I came back out of that white room broken and wrong. Angry. Vengeful. Something I hardly recognized, even though I still wore the same familiar face I was born with.

I wasn't going to saddle Valentin with that, even if he did want me. Even if he did like me – love me. Or whatever it was we felt for each other. It was not possible. I was going to crash and burn one day, and I could not allow him to stand too close when it happened.

Chapter Thirteen

The door loomed before me, like a horrid gaping mouth belonging to the corpse of a long-dead god. Flat two-hundred and ten. Talia's flat. The place I could not bear to wheel myself down to when I had been released from that white hell of a prison.

Talia and I had messaged each other on numerous occasions, but I could never bring myself to try and see her. I felt much too guilty. At first, my friends were annoyed, criticizing Talia for not coming to see me either. I could not bring myself to feel that way; it wasn't her fault. Gwyn, her team leader, hated me. Hated our whole team for what happened the day my father escaped. Hated us for what happened to Talia.

He would not allow her to see me, and she was too weak to bring herself. At least until she began improving her health and her strength as I had. Last night I found a note slipped under my front door. It was from Talia.

It read:

"Daux,

As you can see, because I left you this note all by myself, I am regaining my strength. We have talked about it, but I wanted to show you because I know you would not believe me unless you had proof. So, I snuck out and left you this.

Anyway, Gwyn and the twins will be gone all day tomorrow, and maybe even into the next day and I think you should come see me. We can be alone, like old times with no one to bother us. It's been too long, and I hate having to hide our holochats and messages. I'll be telling Gwyn to get his head out of his ass presently.

I will await your visit.

Your loyal Huntress,

Talia"

Could she have messaged me? Yes. Was she dramatic? Also, yes.

That was Talia, and it was what I loved about her.

Now I stood outside her door, my palms slick with sweat, staring at the maw of a doorway like a dead god that wanted to swallow me whole. I could not bring myself to knock. What if Talia was as altered as I had been? Holochats never did a person justice; the camera was never as accurate as in real life. And I was scared of what I would see when she opened that door and let me in.

Then the god would swallow me whole.

Before I could raise my balled fist, I heard the lock click from the inside and the door swung inwards revealing my best friend.

I let out the breath I absolutely knew I was holding.

Talia looked haggard, but other than that, she looked her normal self. Her lounge clothes hung loosely on her willowy frame, thinned by the torture she endured. Her impish smile was still there, stretching across her freckled face, giving her amber eyes a mischievous twinkle. She still had her hair. She still had her spark.

Talia was okay.

And I was not.

I did not know how to feel about that, but I did not have time to dwell on it because Talia pulled me inside her flat and slammed the door. Then she wrapped her thin arms around my thin body and held me as though she thought I might disappear. A wetness spread through the black sweater I hastily threw on before I left and I knew Talia was crying.

As a good friend, I would not acknowledge it. She didn't

like people staring at her when she cried. It made her feel silly.

I did not want her to feel that way.

When she pulled away, Talia's face was dry, though her eyes were rimmed with red and her smile was a little wobbly.

"I missed you," she whispered, aware she was on the verge of tears.

"I missed you too," I said around the lump in my throat.

We embraced each other simultaneously, allowing the tears to flow, both refusing to acknowledge the other's torrential emotions with anything other than reassuring squeezes. We stayed like that for what seemed like hours, just holding each other until the sobs turned into hiccoughs, and the hiccoughs into sniffles, and the sniffles into silence.

After a moment, Talia practically dragged me to the couch in the common area of their flat. It was decorated similarly to mine with two couches, an armchair, and bookshelves, with a place to watch vids and play games. The only difference was the coloring, which was dark and earthy to reflect both Gwyn and Talia's tastes while also accommodating the twins' preference for brightness with pops of color around the room. It was cozy and I could see Talia was very comfortable in this space.

"How have you been?" I choked out around the lump that my throat refused to swallow.

"Horrendous," she laughed, but there was a hard edge to it. "As I'm sure you also have been. Why is everyone so Gods damned perky all the time?"

"Or treating you like you're about to fall apart?" I supplied with a knowing smile.

"Exactly!"

"I would rip out my hair if I had enough of it."

Talia gasped at that, her honey-brown eyes growing wide and horrified as she brought a hand to my shorn locks. Her teeth found purchase on her bottom lip as her fingers slid through my still very short hair. Then, she began to laugh.

Softly at first, almost sounding like sobs again before it changed to the sound that I loved oh so much.

It emanated from deep in her belly, and some might have found it obnoxious, but to me, it was one of the most comforting – one of the happiest – sounds in this Gods' forsaken world. I was so glad to hear it in person once again. So glad to be with *her* once again.

Talia… she understood.

She understood the pain and the anger inside me, not only because she knew me better than anyone else, but because she too underwent an unjust interrogation. She too understood having her insides flipped out for perfect strangers to see, and judge her innocence or guilt. She understood the weakness of her body deteriorating because she would also have refused to eat that drugged food. She would know the feeling of her mind breaking at the seams, desperately clawing at the edges, hoping her body would break before her mind did.

"I'm sorry about your hair," she said ruefully, her expression full of sorrow. "I know how much you loved it."

"It will grow back," I said dismissively, waving my hand.

Talia pursed her lips and looked as though she were about to argue, but before she could, I grabbed her wrist, drew her arm around my shoulder, and curled into her side. My distraction had worked, for now. Talia held me, jaw tense, but did not speak the thoughts I knew had to be running through her head.

I had been too dismissive. I had not shown enough grief. Talia had known just how important my hair was to me, and I had brushed it off. Of course, she would be suspicious. However, she also knew exactly what I had been through, and that, too, kept her from prodding me where I did not want her to.

Instead, she switched on a vid, something mindlessly entertaining, and I sat in the shelter of her too-thin side as we watched the characters on the screen flit by in inane scenarios that were mind-numbingly comforting. We chatted intermittently about the vid, the actors, and many other things avoiding the topic I knew Talia was so desperate to discuss.

Me.

I would not talk about that. It did not need discussion. I was *fine*. I would *be fine*. And I would continue to be *fine*. I would make sure of it.

Once the vid was over, I began to stand, but I realized Talia's arm was still wrapped tightly around my waist. A quick peek at her face told me that she had fallen asleep. Nothing would wake her short of an auto wreck happening right next to her, so I settled myself back into her side and closed my eyes, letting the exhaustion wash over me like I used to back at the Academy when Talia would spend the night with me.

The couch was not the most comfortable place to sleep, especially considering the worry that one of Talia's teammates would return. Gwyn namely, the twins were still cordial with me but I did not want them to report my visit back to him accidentally. I had enough problems; I didn't need threats from Gwyn on top of them.

Before I knew it, though, Talia was shaking me awake and speaking in that groggy rasp that was oh-so-familiar to me.

"Hey, hey," she was saying. "It is *so* late. Wake up, wake up."

I glowered up at her, pushing her face away from mine and settling back down on the couch. She laughed but did not relent, and I allowed myself to be pulled into the kitchen for a dinner of junk food and ice cream. Talia did not bring me, or my feelings up again for which I was grateful. But when it was time for me to go, when I pulled back from her embrace, I noticed a brightness in her eyes that she tried to blink away.

Instead of acknowledging it, I kissed her cheek and held her close once more. The pain in my chest was a dull, heavy thing. Lying to Talia was not something I enjoyed. She deserved so much better than that, so much better than a best friend who would put herself above her, so much better than my lies.

When I pulled away finally, the shine was still there, but it was trailing through the freckles on her cheeks and dripping onto her sweater. Instead of wiping it away, she grabbed my hand and kissed it, waving me on. After the door closed behind me, the pain in my chest exploded and I allowed myself to feel every stinging wave.

Chapter Fourteen

Himawari and I stood side by side in the bathroom, cleaning up after an impromptu workout session. Jax and Valentin had taken it upon themselves to order takeaway, leaving everyone a restful evening after all the stress we had been dealt. I hardly needed help walking anymore, my cane leaning against the long countertop as I applied a moisturizing cream to my face, and Himawari had wanted to get some training in together. Something we had not done by ourselves in a long time.

After we had taken turns showering, Himawari pinned my hair back with little black moth pins this time, clipping the sunflowers into her hair. Both of us wore fluffy bathrobes in our favorite colors, red and purple. Beside me, she massaged her face with a jade roller, her skin glowing with moisturizer and serum.

It was often the case that we gave each other private time in the bathroom, but it was nice to share it with her, especially lately when I had to be monitored for fall hazards. Himawari liked her privacy and I respected that, but I missed Talia clinging to me like I would fall apart without her. I suppose I had…

I sighed, glancing down toward the drawer where I stored my blockers and syringes in. I would need to administer one tonight, and I might as well do it while I was thinking about it. Forcing my hand to open the drawer, I pulled out a small vial and syringe, grimacing at the clear liquid that extinguished my flame.

I felt Himawari's gaze on me like a dead weight and I turned to her, brow raised.

"Do you want some help?" she asked hesitantly, setting her jade roller down on the counter. "Fé said you had a fall last time."

No. I wanted to say.

Of course, I did not need help. I did not *want* help.

Which was a lie.

"Please," I whispered, shoving the vial and syringe toward her.

After carefully washing her hands, Himawari took them without a word, unwrapping the syringe and filling it with the dreaded clear liquid inside the vial. I shuddered and lowered myself to the ground, pressing my back to the cupboard doors.

Himawari knelt next to me, pushing my bathrobe up my legs to access the injection site.

"Are you okay?" she asked.

"No," I exhaled in a shuddering breath.

Tears burned my eyes and my breaths were coming in erratic gasps. Panic was beginning to overtake me, canceling out all rational thought. I was *terrified* of the burning sensation I had experienced with the last few blockers I had taken. I was terrified of the shadows I was seeing in my friend's eyes. Of the blackened irises in my own.

Of the voices in my head that were mine, but not.

"Can you breathe with me?" Himawari asked, placing a hand on my chest.

"I-I can try," I answered honestly.

She smiled, then pulled an exaggerated inhale through her nose. I mimicked her, and then we exhaled. We repeated this over and over, all the while she lined up the syringe with my thigh, plunging it in unexpectedly with my next exhale.

I forced a startled yelp back down my throat and continued to breathe steadily as Himawari injected the blocker into me. Instead of the horrid flames licking through my veins, the initial burning cold shocked through my thigh. Then the ice flooded my veins, making me shiver. Tears slipped down my cheeks and I choked on a hard lump that had formed in my throat without realizing it.

Himawari removed the syringe and tossed it in the biohazard receptacle before settling down next to me. She slipped her arm around my shoulder and massaged the injection site with her free hand, warming the ice-cold sensation the blocker always left behind.

Her body was warm next to mine as I trembled on the cold marble and her lips pressed a kiss into my short hair. I did not turn, fearing the shadows I might see in her eyes. Or, for the fear of the blackness she might see in mine.

"I hate this!" I seethed through my teeth. "I *hate* this."

"I know, Daux," Himawari whispered tearfully. "I hate it too."

I'm going to make them pay. I promised mentally. *They will burn for this.*

We sat there until the tears stopped burning my eyes – until I could breathe evenly again. And when I gathered the courage to look at Himawari, I saw that she had been crying too.

"Hima… I…" I started, my throat closing in on itself again.

"I know," she interrupted, pressing her forehead to mine. "I know, Daux. I hate them too. It feels like they dull the sunshine in my soul and all that's left is the shadows."

My heart squeezed painfully in my chest at her words. Knowing that Himawari was experiencing the same feelings I was—the same as the rest of the team—should have brought me comfort, but it did not. Despite the chill running through my veins, anger burned hotly in my gut, and my jaw tightened to the point of pain.

"Can," she started to ask, then took a deep breath. "Can you help me with mine?"

With my forehead still pressed against hers, I nodded, bringing my hand up to cup her cheek. Our eyes met, and I saw a flash of shadow crossing behind her irises. The muscles in my jaw fluttered and instead of yanking away like I wanted to, I pulled her close so I could no longer meet her gaze.

After a beat, I released her, and she stood to grab her blockers from her cupboard.

Repeating the process for Himawari was not any less daunting, but this time both our eyes were dry. I noted the way her body seized, the way her jaw clenched, and the weak cry of pain that left her lips.

Was there something in these blockers?

Were they somehow stronger than the label on the vials said they were?

I held her until her trembling stopped, massaging the injection. It was cold, as it should have been, but when Himawari pulled away to go dress, I noticed that her eyes seemed devoid of light. Like mine had been.

But then she blinked and it was gone.

By the time the takeaway arrived, we were dressed and smiling as though nothing had ever happened. But I had seen the shadows in her eyes. I had felt the tremors that had wracked her body. I knew we were not okay. I did not know what to do about it.

Though all of us, excluding Valentin, were on blockers, I decided it might be a good idea to do some training using the outdoor facility. We needed to be able to use our weapons in the instance that our magic failed us for whatever reason, and this was a perfect time to prepare for such a scenario.

It was odd, being out here again together. Other teams stared at us openly as we made our way to an empty space but I paid them no mind. I could tell Félix was uncomfortable, his posture rigid and fingers tapping against his legs. And Himawari appeared unsteady on her feet. Jax even appeared tense.

The only one of us who seemed to be unperturbed by the attention we were getting was Valentin. Which, was unsurprising. He always had a cool head, and he was known by reputation even to Academy students.

He was used to stares.

If there was anything the onlookers wanted to say, they could say it to my face. And from the way they all turned away when they met my returning stare, they would not be doing that any time soon.

"Ready to get started?" I asked, turning to my teammates.

They all made eye contact, not wanting to be the first one to answer.

"More or less," Valentin shrugged after a beat.

"Then let's go," I said and set up a basic simulation on the console.

It was one of the easier ones programmed for combat, not magic. Respawning sets of coalition enemies that grew more difficult the longer we stayed in the sim. Good for me, because my movements with my rapier were still clumsy and uncoordinated. The others seemed to be in better shape than I was, thankfully, but we had been out of practice fighting as a team for a good while now.

By the third wave of them, my sword arm was aching and I could barely see because of the sweat in my eyes. It was exhilarating. In my weakened state, I had thought of nothing but returning to my previous strength and ability but I had forgotten how I loved the rush of battle.

I had not particularly enjoyed killing – as much as it was necessary for my profession, I hardly thought about the act with pleasure – but crossing swords with an opponent, using my armor against another's bullets, outwitting an opponent?

It was something I relished in.

I was back-to-back with Valentin, a ring of simulated soldiers surrounding us. Strangely, I felt my magic flicker within me, waiting to be let out, directing me to burn the soldiers where they stood. But I had taken a blocker the night before? Ignoring the feeling, I nudged Valentin in the back, wordlessly indicating our next move.

As soon as the soldiers charged, we spun, my rapier stabbing deeply into the soldier closest to me and Valentin's sword slashing through two others. They dissolved immediately, and the holograms returned to the simulation. Knocking the rifle of an advancing soldier away, I pressed forward, the tip of my blade lancing his throat.

Before I could make the kill, a sharp pain lanced up my side and I turned to see a tall man with long black hair and black eyes looming over me. A wide, feral grin split his handsome face in two, showing all of his teeth. I gasped, stepping back as a warm wetness spilled over my side. Looking down, I saw that there was a large slash down my side, ripping right through my tactical armor and into my flesh.

Pink muscle gave way to white bone and red blood. I would have vomited if not for the white-hot fury boiling inside me. Raising my sword at the simulation soldier, I felt the flame in my chest bloom, churning against the blackness that resided there.

But a simulated soldier could not harm me, not at this setting at least. And not to this extent. It would be impossible.

The man took a swipe at me with clawed hands and I stumbled back, pulling at the flame in my chest, begging it to fight back against the blockers and save me from whatever this *creature* was. I tasted smoke in the back of my throat and gasped, a spark dancing over the fingers on my left hand, my sword arm trembling with the shock.

"Daux!" Himawari called from across the training

ground.

I slowly edged to the side, keeping the man in my sights so I could at least catch a glimpse of Himawari. When I saw her in my periphery, I couldn't believe what I was seeing. Despite having taken blockers the night before, Himawari was wreathed in shadow.

Chancing a glance down, I noted that my shadow was missing. It had been called to Hima's aid… but how? How had she been able to manipulate it in the first place when her magic should have been blocked?

Before I could even form the words in my mouth, I was launched backward, my glasses flying from my face as I flew. My brain immediately conjured images of Portnith, Félix on the ground bleeding, Valentin attempting to hold his shredded side together, the square flying below me as I was blown feet over head into a storefront.

Just as I was sure I was about to hit the ground and potentially break my neck, strong arms encircled me, halting my descent. The smell of ozone and sunshine assailed me. Jax.

I looked up and saw the cold expression on his face, his braids flowing behind him with the magical energy he was exerting. His nostrils flared and a shadow passed over his eyes.

"Who are you?" Himawari demanded, pointing her staff at the man, her shadows whirling around her like an icon of the God of shadow incarnate.

He stood stock still, head cocked to the side as he observed us. "I am known as Fear – or Despair," he spoke at last, and his voice was terrible, like boulders crashing against each other. Like the wind during a hurricane. "I came to see how you were progressing. I am *most* pleased."

"Let me go, Jax," I hissed, and he released me.

From behind the man, *Fear*, I saw Félix dancing on the balls of his feet. His hands were clenched around his conductors, which had gone white-hot with his magic.

But that couldn't be!

We were all on blockers.

My hand flew to my face, and I realized that my glasses had been knocked off. So how could I see? How could I see any of this? I remembered that I had smelled Jax's magic. I could not smell magic – at least not well – while I was on blockers. And I had clearly smelled ozone and sunshine. And where were the simulation soldiers?

"Rage," Fear said, his voice like a purr.

It instilled such dread in me, that I froze.

A stirring fluttered in my chest at the word

"All will be revealed," he said, then his mouth opened in a terrible howl that curdled my blood and pierced my brain.

Félix's hand protruded from Fear's chest, a black substance oozing from his body and fanning out in front of him from the impact of Fé's magic. Fear's heart landed with a wet squelch in front of me. It was still attempting to beat, black sludge spewing out of it as it shuddered, attempting to keep the body behind it alive. I moved with morbid curiosity to pick it up, but one of Himawari's shadows ensnared my wrist, preventing me from touching the organ.

Félix's fist retracted from Fear's body, and it slumped forward onto the ground with a surprisingly heavy thud. It shook the ground around us as though he weighed an impossible amount for his elongated frame.

Then, before our eyes, the body crumbled into dust along with his blackened heart. Something was chanting in the back of my head, which I shook to try and clear, but the noise only grew louder and more insistent.

"Daux!" I heard over and over.

I shook my head again, this time opening my eyes to Valentin's ice-blue gaze.

"You all right?" he asked, concern lacing his tone. "You froze. I had to halt the simulation."

I looked around to see the holograms frozen in place and realized that Valentin had not been wherever I just was either.

"I…" I paused, pressing a hand to my face and knocking my glasses askew.

Hadn't they fallen off?

Félix, Jax, and Himawari were all approaching, a glazed-over look in their shadowy eyes. I opened my mouth to ask them if they remembered Fear and if they remembered that Félix had punched a literal hole in his chest, but the shadows had cleared by the time they reached us. My mouth closed, lips pursing.

"I'm fine," I whispered, looking at each one of them in turn.

Then, I spun on my heel and marched away, ignoring Valentin's call for me to return and Jax's telling him to leave it. I had seen the tendril of a shadow swirling around Himawari's shoulders, the flicker of lightning around Jax's knives, and the smoke curling around Félix's fingertips.

As I walked, my fist clenched and I ignored the way the sparks danced around my knuckles and the ember blazed in my chest. What I had seen was not a simulation. It was… I did not know what it was, but it had been real. Whether I hallucinated it or not, it had been real. My friends were on blockers, but their magic was active, just like mine. That was impossible. Just as impossible as this Fear creature appearing out of nowhere. I did not know what to make of it but I was sure it had something to do with the shadows I was seeing in my friends' eyes and the black holes I was seeing in mine.

Chapter Fifteen

It was not long after Fear appeared to me that the team and I were called into the Overseer's office. Jax, Félix, and Himawari had not said anything to me about the vision, hallucination – whatever it was – and I had not gathered the courage to bring it up to them. Valentin had not been a part of it, so I could not go to him, and I would not have even if he had been because he would have bombarded me about it immediately. So, I left it.

What could I say anyway? That I was seeing things? I could not lead this team if I was hallucinating, and they knew that. They would be compelled to report the incident, and I would lose everything. My chance at apprehending my father, Amalie, my life. I would not jeopardize that. I would die first.

Nervousness coursed through me as we made our way to the Overseer's office. She wanted to interview me personally before we went on a low-stakes mission back to the Cassacania coast. Back to the place where my father escaped from my clutches. We needed to look over the trail left behind, the cause of the fire, and the safe house my father had brought us to when we were captured.

At least, that was what she claimed. I was fearful one of my teammates had told her about the incident on the training grounds and that I was being relieved of my position. But I did not have to worry long. The Overseer made no mention of the training ground incident during the meeting, and the mission she was assigning us sounded easy enough. A lot of walking and using foresight perhaps which would be taxing on me at first since I would be coming off blockers for the investigation. It was to be a several day's long mission to allow time for me to adjust and rest as needed. They were, of course, bringing in other trackers to help, and using the intel Valentin had gathered while he was away – intel he was not allowed to share with me. But I was the only one who knew Charles Deveraux better than anyone else. Well, better than anyone else who was willing to help that is.

The thought of going into the Overseer's office again though… filled me with an immeasurable amount of dread. And rage.

Gods, this anger made me so tired. It sapped the energy right out of my bones. The blockers probably were not helping with that either.

But here we were. It was too late to turn back now.

"Come in, Team Deveraux," the Overseer called.

When we entered the room, each of us dressed in our armor, her eyes were guarded and wary. She still did not trust me. Well good, she was right not to this time. Not after she ordered my second interrogation.

"You look well," she commented as we stood before her desk. "All of you look healthy."

I nearly scoffed but held in my resentment. I did not need to anger the Overseer further. I needed her to know that she may have broken me, but I came back. And I came back more dangerous than she ever thought I would.

The Overseer wanted to interview each of my teammates to see if I truly was improving. If I was being "retrained properly". Himawari scoffed when we were sent from the room.

"Like this is some sort of Coalition territory that requires retraining programs," she continued incredulously.

It was not uncommon for "retraining" to happen when a person defected to the Coalition. It was either that or imprisonment. The tactic was looked at rather unfavorably by instructors at the Academy – especially the ex-Spec Ops agents. I now knew why, having to go through it myself. We had no idea it would ever be used in a situation like this.

Do not question, do not fight. The Government is *always* right; Spec Ops is always watching to protect you. It is for your safety.

Yeah right.

The interviews went on without incident, each of my teammates returning to me in the waiting area with varying degrees of annoyance they did not dare show the Overseer. Valentin appeared particularly stormy when he returned, reminiscent of his early days with our team.

I wondered if he had discussed his secret mission during his interview. I made a mental note to ask him about it when we had time, hoping he would not just tell me it was classified. That would be particularly annoying since we had been brought in here to be evaluated for a mission that pertained directly to what he had been doing overseas. Searching for my father.

"Well," the Overseer began, steepling her fingers when we all returned to the interior of her office. "It appears that your teammates believe you fit enough to return to duties despite some initial misgivings from your psychiatrist."

I resisted the urge to roll my eyes. Of course, Dr. Castillo would have flagged my comments about feeling betrayed. It was why I fed her what she wanted to hear until she agreed to clear me and reduce our sessions.

"I am pleased with your progress, Daux," the Overseer continued, watching me carefully.

"Thank you, ma'am. I am glad to be getting back to work," I lied through my teeth with a saccharine smile.

With a nod and another long look at me, then the rest of my team, the Overseer waved us away. We all breathed a collective sigh of relief when we exited the exterior of her office, anxious that she would still somehow hear us inside.

We were to leave Mournsday. That gave me two days to figure out childcare for Amalie. I couldn't just leave her in the flat, that would be neglectful. None of my teammates could stay behind with her either. The Overseer's instructions were very clear. She wanted all of us present on this mission. Likely to make sure we were all following protocol to the letter, and perhaps to have more eyes on me.

Just in case the interrogations had not been enough to detect any foul play on my part. Which was absurd. They searched every facet of my memories. But dwelling on that did not resolve anything. It certainly did not solve the problem that I had no one for Amalie to stay with.

I was still pondering the issue on Godsday afternoon, lounging on the couch in the living area. Had Talia not been in the same weakened condition as me, I would have asked her. She was one of the only ones who knew what Amalie and I had gone through with our parents. Talia would have been able to handle her. I could not ask her though. According to her messages to me since our last visit, she was improving as quickly as I was, but there was still Gwyn to deal with.

Whenever I passed him in the corridor, I would receive the iciest glare I had ever gotten in my life. And I was on a team with Valentin Angelov: the master of ice magic and cold rage. I had no idea his affection for my best friend ran that deeply, but it must have been from the way he treated me. I could not trust Talia with Amalie, not with him around. Talia might not be strong enough to stop him if he were to lash out at my sister because of me.

Of course, I would never blame Talia for such a thing. That wouldn't have been her fault, but Amalie was making minute progress. I could not risk any sort of occurrence to make her distrust me, my team, or magic users any more than she already did.

Hatred for my parents flared up in me once again, making me feel sick to my stomach as I lay on the couch in the common area trying to decide what to do. I had other friends, but could I trust them? Whom did I know that would be good with a… well, frankly bigoted child with lots of terrible ideas to unlearn?

Talia was the only person I could think of. The twins too. But Gwyn threw a wrench into those plans.

"What are you thinking about?" a cool voice asked from above me.

I sighed and grabbed my glasses from the end table on the side of the couch where my head lay, sliding them carefully onto my face. They gave me headaches as I was still getting used to having them sit on my face, and I wanted to lie down without them for a bit.

I did not need to see to know who was standing above me, though.

I would recognize that voice from the depths of the underworld.

Valentin stood above me, an amused expression on his handsome face. His now blond hair was slicked back away from his face. He had no business looking so pretty. It just was *not* fair.

"I am trying to decide who would be a good fit to watch Amalie while we go on our mission," I said, sitting up. "Talia is the only person I can think of besides our teammates, and neither of those options is going to work."

Who knew taking care of an eleven-year-old would be so difficult?

Still, I wasn't my parents. I was *not* just going to dump her on someone. Not when she barely trusted anyone anymore. I could not do that to her, I would not.

"What about Rhiannan?" Valentin asked, sitting down next to me.

Rhiannan… I hadn't thought of her. She had younger siblings and was even friendlier than Talia. She would be perfect… except.

"Meera and Willow hate my guts," I sighed, my head

falling into my hands.

My glasses were surely smeared now and Valentin plucked them from my face, cleaning them carefully with his black t-shirt. I averted my gaze from the pale sliver of his abdomen that peaked out from beneath his hem. He did *not* need me ogling him.

"I have it on good authority that those two are off on a small mission while Rhiannan and Hawthorn are at home transcribing the intel," he told me, holding my glasses up to the light for inspection.

"I can't ask them to watch her while they work," I protested.

Then, Valentin's cool fingers hooked around my chin and tilted my face toward him. My brain nearly short-circuited and I swallowed. Hard. Before I could say anything else, or embarrass myself with the gibberish that was sure to spill from my mouth, Valentin slid my glasses back onto my face and released me.

"Rhiannan has a photographic memory," he reminded me, standing to his feet and stretching his arms up into the air. "She will be able to remember and transcribe everything in no time, especially with Hawthorn there."

I once again averted my gaze. "I suppose you are right…"

"Of course, I am. Now you should ask her before it gets any later."

As it turned out, Rhiannan was more than willing to keep an eye on Amalie for me. We had messaged each other off and on since my release, and she told me how Meera and Willow resented me for getting everyone arrested despite her telling them that I was innocent and Spec Ops was just looking for a scapegoat. She felt responsible for her teammates' negative feelings toward me and wanted a way to make up for it even though I told her over and over that Meera and Willow were grown and could form their own opinions of people. And that Amalie had been slightly indoctrinated by my parents' bigotry.

Rhiannan would not budge on the issue and insisted that Amalie was welcome in her flat whenever for however long and that she could get along with her despite some bad parenting. *That* I believed. If anyone could make friends with a person of Amalie's current disposition, it would be Rhiannan.

She was a force to be reckoned with, and if she decided you were going to be her friend… then you had no chance. Just as I hadn't stood a chance. I did not regret it though. Not one bit. Especially now.

"Thank you," I said in earnest, standing in front of Rhiannan's flat with Amalie at my side. "You really should let me pay you for this, you know."

"I will not hear of it!" Rhiannan dismissed me, kneeling to Amalie's height with her signature sunny smile. "Your sister told me you like mint chocolate ice cream?" she asked, waiting for Amalie's nod of affirmation. "Good, that's what we're having for dinner!"

I was about to open my mouth to protest, but the shocked and excited look that came over Amalie's face was so similar to how I had known her before our parents' arrests that I nearly wept. Was it the healthiest choice for a growing child? No. But neither was holding onto an explosive rage and half-baked revenge plot. Amalie could have ice cream for dinner now and again if it made her happy.

Specifically, if it were a situation where I had to leave her alone while I went on a mission, like this one. I felt so guilty, but there was nothing to be done about it, and Rhiannan had already agreed. We were already *here*.

"I have to go now, Amalie," I said, passing Rhiannan Amalie's go-bag with all her toiletries, coloring books, stuffies, and clothes. Everything else she needed would be on her holonav.

"I don't want you to," she protested, her brow furrowing and she hooked a finger into the space between my breastplate and hip armor.

It was the first amount of affection she had shown me since the night I forbade her from bullying Félix. I blinked down at her, my heart swelling three sizes, but she kept her gaze on the floor. Bashful or petulant, I could not tell, but from Rhiannan's wry smile, I thought it was the former.

"I know," I soothed, brushing my still-thin fingers through her silky blonde hair, surprised that she let me. "But I will not be gone long."

"What if they arrest you again?" she snapped, her fingers tightening on my armor. "Where will I go? I don't want to go to foster care."

Rhiannan looked at me, concerned, before placing Amalie's bag in the entryway and taking her free hand. I was grateful for what she said next because I was much too angry to speak.

"Your sister has lots of friends, that includes me, sweetheart. We are not going to let anyone take you away from her, and we won't let you become a ward of the state."

The blinding rage I felt at the NAF and Spec Ops for what they had done to me paled in comparison to what they had inadvertently done to Amalie. Her only living grandparents were in an adult care facility, her parents had abandoned her and were sent to prison respectively, and I had also been arrested. It wasn't fair.

It. Was. Not. Fair.

"Daux," Himawari called from the end of the hall. "We've got to go."

I shook my head to clear it and knelt to hug Amalie, who was still squeezing Rhiannan's hand tightly. She released my armor to hug me back, fat crocodile's tears drenching my neck before I could pull away.

"Promise you'll come back!" Amalie demanded, holding

her pinky up.

I swallowed and wrapped my finger around hers. "I will always come back to you, Amalie. I promise."

She nodded, her chin wobbling, and turned to follow Rhiannan into her flat. I waited until the door was shut before turning on my heel and marching toward my teammates at the lift, watching with varying degrees of emotion.

Félix was openly teary even though Amalie had been rude to him; Himawari looked as though she wanted to hug me; Jax *did* hug me, his braids brushing against my cheeks with a wave of coconut scent; and Valentin… Valentin looked murderous.

It was not because we were leaving Amalie behind, or because he disapproved in any sort of way. No, he was angry because she and I had been put in this situation to begin with. I wondered for the first time if this had been a regular sight for him. The injustice of it all.

A sister, with no other options, was forced to leave her younger sibling alone with strangers so she could provide for her. So, she could bend to the will of masters who would take that child away for minor disobedience.

I wondered if he had gone through what I had when his team had been murdered. There would be no record of it if it was an involuntary interrogation. Spec Ops did not like records of them torturing their own to get around if the subject did not agree to it. Like I had the first time I was interrogated.

I wondered if that was what had made him so angry.

If that was why he was so terrible in the beginning when our team was first formed.

If he was so wrathful that there was hardly anything left in his heart but that hot, painful feeling of rage. If it was so consuming that he could barely sleep, eat, or think of anything but righting that wrong.

Even if he had not undergone an interrogation, I felt as though I understood his anger better now.

But I didn't understand what had changed anymore.

My eyes hardly left him as we descended to the ground floor. I watched every movement – even down to his blinks. His posture was tired but relaxed. His smiles were easy, with no sign of the old tightness I had been accustomed to before he tried to be a better teammate. Where had that anger gone? Would that happen to me one day?

Did I even want it to?

Chapter Sixteen

Portnith was exactly as I remembered, sans all the fire and rapidly crumbling buildings. The smell of burning still lingered in the air though, the same way it lingered in my nostrils. A flicker of Félix's body bloodied on the ground sent a wave of nausea through me so sharp I almost vomited on one of the guard's boots.

I would not have cared to do so, other than the fact that *I* would have been embarrassed. So, I swallowed back the bile and stepped out of the auto into the hot sun. Humidity instantly clung to any exposed skin on my body and wormed its way into my armor, making the bodysuit underneath cling to me uncomfortably. When I looked around at my teammates, they appeared to be in similar shape to me.

Himawari held a hand to her nose and mouth almost as though she were trying to breathe through non-existent smoke. I pressed a hand in between her shoulder blades, my fingers tangling into the dark purple fabric of her cloak. She looked up at me with tears in her eyes. I had been right. I was not the only one who still remembered.

The screams of the dying and injured did not just haunt me. They haunted all of us, and here we were. Forced to come back before any of us could even be deemed remotely ready, all because Spec Ops believed it necessary that *we* be the ones to find my father and bring him back.

A punishment for letting him escape, of that, I was entirely certain. They all but told me as such.

Coming here and being tasked with finding him was the smallest punishment they could inflict upon me. They already did so much worse.

"Okay," Jax said, coming up to stand behind us and placing his hand on Himawari's shoulder. "Where do we begin?"

"Well," I started, looking around at all the people assigned to keep an eye on us. "We should probably start with the building my father brought us to in the first place. The people who came after will have searched it, but we know his movements and thoughts better than anyone else who would have gone over the place."

I ignored the scoff from an officer behind me. Ignored the flare of anger that threatened to shoot from my fingertips in a blast of flame. It felt good to have my magic back, but I could not lose it here. I was finally starting to feel whole again.

Valentin had no problem confronting him though. He strode straight up to the man and looked him up and down. The officer was of average height and build, tan, brown eyes, and brown hair. Nondescript as they come. Valentin towered over him, but to his credit, the officer held his ground. It probably helped that he held an automatic rifle between the two of them. Not that Valentin's magic could not silence him permanently in the amount of time he could get a shot off.

A wicked part of me wanted to see that.

But I did not get the chance.

"Is there a problem here?" Valentin asked.

Perhaps that would have been the wrong reaction had this man been a higher-ranking officer or general, but he was not. Therefore, we outranked him. And he knew it.

"No sir," the officer ground out, clutching his gun to his chest.

"What is your name, Officer?"

"Adams."

Valentin looked him over once again, frowning. Then his

frown turned into a glower. Then he looked positively murderous.

"Listen to me, Adams, and listen to me well. We are here to aid this investigation because we have knowledge that you do not. Do not piss us off, because we *will* leave and I *will* make sure it is known that it was your fault. Do I make myself clear?"

Adams swallowed and nodded as though he bought Valentin's bluff. We could not leave even if we wanted to. Not everyone here knew that.

I smiled. "Valentin, I am ready to get started."

"Okay," he agreed, not taking his eyes off Adams. Not even when he made his way back to me and the rest of the team.

It was an endearing gesture, but unnecessary. Nonetheless, I was pleased.

It was clear some of the people here did not appreciate Spec Ops agents being here in any capacity. My father's escape and the subsequent destruction had led to more than a little mistrust in the capabilities of Spec Ops agents and magic users. Adams' reaction to us was potentially a combination of both sentiments, which only made the feeling in my stomach about this investigation worsen.

"Which direction?" Jax asked, wrangling Félix away from a debris pile. "C'mon man, we need to wait for the go-ahead!"

"Fi—ine," Félix whined, allowing Jax to haul him back.

It was nice seeing them goofing around, but we were here for an investigation. An investigation I was already feeling apprehensive about. I wanted to be back to Amalie as soon as I possibly could. I was concerned about her, even if Rhiannan was sending me hourly updates on the shenanigans they were getting up to – even knowing I could not respond. Rhiannan and Willow had somehow convinced Amalie to let them give her a makeover – something Himawari could not even persuade her to do – and set up a whole photo shoot for me to look over when I had some downtime.

I was anxious to get back to her… but a nagging feeling in my stomach made me think that her fun would be ruined the moment I set foot back in the city. I almost thought that she would be better off without me, then remembered the fierceness in her eyes when she made me promise to come back to her.

Steeling my spine, I looked each of my teammates in the eye. Then, for the first time in weeks, I activated my foresight. The thrill that ran up my spine nearly knocked me to my knees as color exploded before my eyes, as the sounds of the faraway ocean and nearer rebuilding efforts erupted in my ears, and the smell of brine and mildew assailed my nostrils.

I felt whole again.

For the first time in months, I felt whole again.

The hot trickle of tears trickling down my cheeks nearly burned as I wiped them from my flesh. Now was not the time to go getting all emotional. I had a father to track.

My father, to my knowledge, did not have magic; if he did, he most likely took blockers regularly to render it obsolete. He always made it seem that I got my magic from my mother's family anyway, but he might have drowned away his ability with injections.

This would make tracking him difficult as I didn't have a magical signature to follow, but if I focused hard enough, I might be able to find something. Since he was my father, I may be able to combine my signature with his to track his movements. It wouldn't be as strong as if he had a magical signature of his own, but it was better than nothing and would allow me to track his movements if it was successful.

However, any sort of signature might no longer be there since it had been so long since my father or I had been in Portnith.

But, as I watched with increasing relief, a silver band

began to form. It was small and wavering, but it was there.

"This way," I said, signaling the others to follow me. "I suppose we could have just asked where that hideaway was, but I wanted to exercise my magic."

"You don't need to explain that to us, Daux," Félix said trotting along beside me.

His face was taut beneath his smile, and my heart nearly stopped in my chest. The smell of blood and gun smoke filled my senses, and I had to shake my head to clear it, making the tracking band waver until it almost disappeared.

"I'm sorry we had to come back here," I whispered so my voice wouldn't break around the lump rapidly forming in my throat.

"Don't be." He waved me off, but I could tell he was still tense.

My jaw tightened. Okay, we were here and we had a job to do. We needed to finish it and finish it fast. That was easier said than done, though. Much easier. I would honestly rather be pulling out my teeth right now than reliving that horrible day again. Rather than watching my teammates relive it.

Eventually, we came upon the building my father had spirited us away to. It had been picked over by guards after the attack on the city, but they did not have the intel I did. They did not have the intel Valentin had.

"What are we looking for?" I asked him once we entered the building.

"Well…" he mused, looking around the space.

It was a regular, small-scale coastal storage facility. Grey walls, grey concrete floors, and minimal natural lighting from the small windows that were high above our heads. I knew for a fact that further into the building, there had been modifications to block out any natural light at all. The Coalition and its supporters seemed to have an affinity for this type of architecture. Probably due to their lack of creativity and joy.

"There is something I need you all to know, and you

cannot tell anyone. This is highly classified," Valentin said finally, face grim.

We all looked at him expectantly, waiting for him to speak once more.

He took a deep breath. "Charles Deveraux was already planning on defecting the day we attacked their base… And somehow, without us knowing, he chose this location. A location we were set to attack a major Coalition base in."

We were all silent. This information was nothing new to any of us as it was something we had surmised during our escape. But Valentin rarely did or said anything without reason, so, we waited patiently for him to continue.

"We suspected he may have had inside information on Spec Ops intentions in this area," he said, his eyes refusing to meet mine.

This was also something I had suspected. But the leak could not have come from me. We shouldn't have trusted others to help us on that mission… But there was no other way. We had to ask for help, or we would not have been able to pull it off – the surveillance and the destruction of the base.

Valentin knew that, and I could tell he was ashamed of this knowledge. Ashamed that people he had traveled with thought I was a traitor like my parents. I wanted to take him in my arms and tell him it would be all right – that I knew he did not think that way about me – but that wouldn't be appropriate just now.

"What did you find on your mission?" I asked, clearing my throat.

"From the task force members, we left back at HQ we discovered that there was strong evidence of a leak," he said, still not meeting my gaze. "Not from any of us, and it is likely the leak was not even intended to be a leak. It was potentially 'office gossip'."

"So how did it get to Charles Deveraux," Himawari asked, horrified.

"Since their focus was mainly on Daux and our combined teams for an extended period of time, the task force is still looking into it." Valentin shook his head.

This was so stupid. They were all so focused on me while he was out searching for my father that they likely wasted an opportunity to find the real leak. To find the real reason my father essentially had me framed. The anger boiled inside me and I had to fight to tamp it back down.

"It doesn't matter now," I said finally. "Valentin, you didn't come here with your task force, why not?"

Now he looked at me and I could see the shame and rage in his gaze. It was suffocating. Intoxicating. It was like looking in a mirror. He eventually broke our gaze long enough to explain.

Valentin's placement on that task force had been more of a punishment than anything. It would have been more effective to interrogate him, but they wanted him separated from the rest of his team. The team he had finally accepted after so many years of team hopping and being alone. No, an interrogation would not break him. Not this time.

Knowing that each one of us was locked away in those soundless white rooms, our thoughts and memories being harvested like grains were enough to make him compliant. Enough to punish him.

They refused to let him come to Portnith to investigate because they feared he would try to escape back to the capital and attempt to free me and the others. So, he was forced overseas to try and find my father, even though they were never sure where they should be looking.

I felt sick at his admission. He *knew* we were going to be tormented and he could not tell us. He *knew* if he did try to tell us or stop the torture in any way, they would make it all worse. And he would never see us again. He would be without a team once more.

That was his torture.

Once again, I understood his previous anger. I

understood his shame, his rage, and his grief. So much had been taken from him, and whether he had been interrogated for the deaths of his former teammates or not, he was assuredly blamed for it. I too had been acting on orders from on high when everything fell apart. But it was not those who gave the orders who had taken the blame.

I felt like I understood him better than ever; though, I still was able to reunite with the friends I had lost. Valentin had not been so lucky the first time. For a moment, I was struck with the fact that it could have been much worse for me. I could have never recovered from my ordeal – physically in any case. Mentally, I was still very up and down. My friends could have been taken from me forever, or treated exactly as I had been.

"Thank you," I whispered, not trusting my voice, and waited for a beat before continuing. "Let's search for anything here. Valentin, you take Himawari and Félix. Jax and I will go in the opposite direction. We will communicate if we find anything."

My teammates agreed and off we went in separate directions, no one taking note of the lingering look I gave Valentin's retreating form. Or so I thought. Behind me, Jax's smile was wider than it had been in weeks, but I did not notice. I had a lot to think about.

Chapter Seventeen

Jax and I only found evidence of the helicopter my father escaped in in our part of the warehouse. It had been stored there for a long time it seemed, how long, I was unsure. My father's signature was the strongest there, though. And there was obvious evidence of a large, airborne vehicle even if the scene had been trampled by military and Spec Ops agents since the defection.

"Why would your dad use a helicopter?" Jax asked as we stood there, observing the large open space. "It's clunky and old-fashioned."

"That is exactly why he used it," I answered, looking at the high ceilings and hangar-like doors at the front of the building.

"You mean he wanted to be caught?" Jax sounded incredulous.

"No, since we did *not* catch him. If he used a jet like we do, it would have been harder to conceal," I explained. "My father likes old-fashioned things, if that is at all a surprise. Hardly anyone would question why he would want such a machine, much less fly it if it were discovered here. It would be easy to explain away, and by the time he was ready to defect, none would be the wiser or able to rally their jets in time to bring him back."

Jax sighed, running a hand over his face. He was tired, like me. Like all of us. The constant surveillance we had been enduring had not allowed anyone to rest, or the opportunity to see their families. I hoped we would be able to rest for a little while after this mission. Maybe Jax would get to see his father and brothers. Maybe Himawari would get to see her mom and grandmother. And Félix his entire immediate family.

That would leave Valentin and me alone with Amalie. Unless Valentin had a secret family we did not know about. That would have been mentioned in his file though. All our families were. Did his family die too? That would have been mentioned as well…

I shook my head.

Enough about Valentin. I thought angrily. *We have a mission to conduct. Now is not the time to get all moony.*

It was a good thing he wasn't in the same room with me investigating. If my mind was wandering this bad without him here, I did not want to think about how distracted I would be if he were with me.

A flush blossomed over my cheeks and neck, burning my skin. No, it certainly was *not* the time to be mooning.

"Watcha thinking about?" Jax asked and I could hear the smile in his voice.

"Nothing," I replied much too quickly. "How is your brother doing?"

"Oh!" Jax said, a pleased smile crossing his features, though a wry twinkle shimmered in his eye at my change of subject. "He's doing great, thanks for asking. He, our other brother, and my dad have been doing some family counseling and it's really helping their relationship."

A genuine feeling of happiness washed over me for a moment. I knew Jax worried about his father and brother after everything they had been through with his mother's death. It was good that Mr. Aldridge and his sons were working on healing.

My happy feeling soured when I realized that *I* could be doing the same thing. I shook my head.

"That's wonderful." I injected as much sincerity into my

voice as I possibly could.

"Yeah," Jax agreed excitedly. "Zav, my youngest brother, is looking into getting off his blockers. I was hoping to see them soon, but with everything that's been going on…"

"Yeah…"

With our arrest and twenty-four-seven surveillance, it was difficult to do anything but stay in the flat, train, or go to doctor's appointments.

"So, anyway," Jax said switching subjects abruptly. "Valentin looks good."

"Yes, he does," I responded without thinking, then cringed.

I waited for the ribbing Jax was sure to dish out any moment, but it never came. I looked behind me and he was inspecting something closely, as though he had forgotten about teasing me completely. A very difficult thing for Jax to do.

"What is it?" I asked, sidling up next to him.

"What does this look like to you?" Jax asked, holding up a vial of clear liquid that he had found in the dust.

I knew immediately what it was. It had been forced on me all my childhood and most recently during – and after – my captivity. It was a blocker.

"Why would my father have blockers with him if he was not planning on taking me with him?" I mused, taking the vial from Jax's outstretched hand. "The Coalition soldiers would not be taking those on assignment – if they even possess magic at all – and the soldiers who do have magic would not be taking blockers at all, they are suicide soldiers…"

"Daux…" Jax started as I began to pace.

"It doesn't make any sense!" I muttered, kicking up dust. "Why wouldn't the agents who searched here before us not have noticed this?"

"Daux," Jax repeated, a little sharper this time but I was

lost in thought.

"Seriously, it was just covered in a little dust. How hard is that to miss? It's like they dropped it there on purpose!"

"Daux!"

I stopped in my tracks, turning sharply toward where Jax was standing. A sympathetic look was etched into his expression, but for the life of me, I couldn't figure out why. My brows furrowed and I looked down at the vial in my hand, then back up at Jax's expression. A sinking feeling began to form low in my gut.

My father… My father…

"No," I whispered, shaking my head. "No, I do not believe it."

"Daux, I'm sorry, but you know I'm right," Jax said, approaching me with cautious steps.

"No," I repeated holding up my hand as if warding him off.

He repeated my name once more, but I shook my head. My whole body was trembling and I was seeing red. There was no way. It had to be something else, anything else.

There was no way.

There was no way.

There was no way!

"Daux!" Valentin shouted from behind me.

I realized flame was licking down my arm, heading for the evidence I held in my hand. Quickly, I threw the vial to Jax and whirled to face Valentin. Due to the fire or stress, I was not sure which, sweat was pouring down my brow and my chest was heaving beneath my armor.

"Breathe," Valentin commanded, moving towards me.

"I am!" I snapped, taking a step back.

He continued to advance on me, and I could see Félix and Himawari's concerned faces from behind him. I could feel the flames advancing across my chest and down my other arm now, licking up my neck. It would not burn me. No, the fire was a part of me. But it would burn my teammates, though and I wanted so badly to prevent that.

"Daux, don't focus on the fire," Félix called gently, approaching from behind Valentin.

"Don't come any closer!" I shouted, holding my palm up in warning but that only sent a shower of sparks from my fingers.

My heart was pounding in my ears and the minimal light from the small, high windows was beginning to seem much too bright. A tingling sensation began running up and down my arms, then the shaking set in. The flame spilled from my fingertips, down my back, and my legs, engulfing me in my inferno.

Air refused to stay in my lungs, the fire snatching it away before I could suck in another gulp. The room was tilting as if on an axis, spinning uncontrollably. Sweat was not drenching my skin anymore, instead evaporating as soon as it left my pores. I could no longer hear my teammates calling to me over the ringing in my ears. With the roiling, volcanic conflagration inside me, I knew it was only a matter of minutes before I erupted in a blast of flame.

Then, a cold shock ran up my left arm, causing my head to jerk up. Ice-blue eyes met mine through the flame, and the cold sensation began to spread. I looked down to see Valentin's cold fingers gripping mine, extinguishing the flame there. The tingling numbness began to recede, turning into the biting sensation of sticking my hands in a snowdrift.

Condensation dripped from our connected hands into the dust below, turning the ground there muddy and slick. Then, as the cold began to spread up my arm, the air around us became hazy and thick, like a fog had settled over us. A mist began washing itself over my face and I noticed that the flames there had ebbed.

"Breathe," Valentin begged, squeezing my fingers as another cold shock shot up my arm and settled just over my chest. "Breathe with me."

And despite the ice and flame battling for control over

my body, a tingling warmth ran up my spine. The image of my hands settling over Valentin's during our breathing exercise in my mind's eye was the likely culprit. As the flame waned over my torso, Valentin placed my left hand over my heart, then my hand right over my stomach. The action immediately sent a shock to my nervous system, along with the blast of ice he sent washing over my skin.

I inhaled one delicious breath after the other, inviting all the sensations – good and bad – to pass through. Droplets of rain scattered all around us, extinguishing the rest of the flame on my body – the atmosphere around us reacting to our opposing magics. Again, I was reminded of another time we had clashed, that day in the rain when Valentin poured his heart out to me with no hopes of forgiveness.

"Breathe," Himawari pleaded, appearing at my elbow and carefully avoiding touching me. "C'mon, Daux, breathe."

"You can do it," Félix encouraged, now at my side.

"Breathe with us, Daux," Jax said, his large hands settling on my drenched shoulders.

I sucked a huge sip of air into my diaphragm, my eyes never leaving the icy blue ones in front of me. The rain was pelting us now, but would soon taper off. There was no longer any heat source to encourage the phenomenon. The numbness began to fade and my heart began to slow. The only sounds I could hear were my teammates' breathing, their murmurs of encouragement, and the steadily decreasing pitter-patter of the magically caused rain.

Once the flame made no show of reappearing, my teammates pulled me into their arms, crushing me against them. All of us were soaked by the rain, our boots coated in the dust and muck. But I let them hold me. I needed them to hold me. Because my world had become untethered and I had no idea how I was going to deal with it without them.

Hopefully, the others would have found something useful in their search, because other than the vial, Jax and I found a whole lot of nothing on our first day back in Portnith. What is more, I had wasted too much magical energy panicking to continue to be much use to the others in our search. The blockers I had been on for so long had weakened me. My eyesight had begun to blur and I had needed to resort to the round-framed glasses I so loathed.

The others refused to continue the search without me even though I ordered them too. Valentin – given his experience on the task force sent to find my father – would have been able to lead them satisfactorily without me, and I could have gone back to the field office barracks and rested. Seethed, more like it. Maybe go outside and break some things. But no, they decided we were all going to go back together.

There went my plans to rage at nothing for my misfortune.

I could see the concerned looks they all shared when they thought I was not paying attention. The pity. It almost made me angrier. It wasn't fair for them to feel sorry for me. I should not be an object of pity. If anything, they should feel the same rage as me. They should feel the same intense, boiling fury that I felt.

Valentin especially should feel that way, after what happened to him, and what I assumed happened to him. You know what they say about assuming – don't do it. I would do well to remember that. It never bade well to entertain assumptions.

"What did you all find on your side of the building?" Jax asked as we were all lying on our bunks, still in armor.

Each Province in the NAF was supposed to provide its city with a field office and barracks for any Spec Ops agents who weren't stationed there. Since many agents were constantly on the move all over the NAF territories, even closer to home, these barracks saw a lot of use. The ones we were staying in now were no exception.

It was a long, squat building, as plain on the outside as the inside, and its drab grey exterior paint was slightly worn-looking. Inside though, was impeccably clean. Not a speck of dust to be seen, though, I was unable to use foresight to check to see if that was the case. The west side of the building housed the offices, and the east held the barracks. Each grey room was lined with three to four plain metal bunks and a corresponding number of plain metal armoires for storing weapons and anything else an agent may have brought with them.

There was no decoration and little tech at all. These rooms were for sleeping and not much else. Any operative staying here would be trying to get their mission over with as soon as possible and get back to their comfortable beds in their flats. Like me, except I botched our first day.

I shook my head, adjusting myself on the hard bunk to look at my teammates. They were all sitting on their bunks either looking at their holonavs or speaking to one another. We had chosen one of the rooms with four bunks, considering we had a larger team than most, and not all of us wanted a top bunk.

"We found the room we were held captive in," Félix supplied, dangling his feet off the side of his bunk – he had taken the top above Jax's.

"There was not much of anything in it," Himawari sighed, eyes glued to the screen of her holonav.

"So, you found nothing," I said, trying to keep the venom from my voice.

It wasn't like they had time to after I broke down. I shouldn't blame them for anything, not when they continued to help me when I didn't deserve it. Seeing as I was the one who got them arrested and almost labeled traitors to the

NAF.

"I didn't say that," Himawari snapped back, glaring at me. "We didn't have much of a chance to investigate before Jax pinged us to come back to the hangar."

I smirked a bit at her lack of hesitation. I wasn't offended; if anything, I deserved her ire for being tetchy. It was just funny to see her lose her cool after being patient with me and my poor attitude for so long.

"Sorry," I said, leaving it at that.

She continued to stare at me, but with little of the anger from before. It was almost like she was trying to look beneath my skin and see the mangled wreck inside. As though she wanted to see the writhing black mass that found its home inside the hole in my chest. Or every ugly little thing that traipsed through my mind.

I looked away from her in shame.

"There were some things we wanted you to look at in that room, Daux," Valentin said.

I could hear the disapproval in his voice. The weight of his gaze on me was almost heavier than my guilt. There was nothing I wanted more than a reset button at that moment. I might not have chosen to change the past entirely, but I would have taken back snapping at Himawari.

"We can do that first thing then," I said, forcing myself to meet his gaze.

The look in his eyes was indiscernible, but I held it anyway. I could do that. I could take responsibility and not hide in shame. I needed to stop feeling sorry for myself. It was pathetic.

"We will," he replied, continuing to hold my gaze.

I swallowed.

"Anyway," Himawari interrupted. "There was a lot to go over and we only scratched the surface, not to mention that the scene has been contaminated."

"Hardly," I scoffed and gestured for Jax to produce the blocker vial. "My father has magic. He's been taking blockers this whole time, the hypocrite."

The others sat up in interest at my declaration.

"Where did you find that?" Valentin asked, moving across the room to examine the vial.

I tried not to let my father's lie hurt me but it did. He had *magic.* This whole time – eighteen whole years – and I never once knew he had magic. Charles Deveraux, Governor of Arcadia, had magic and no one knew it. Not even his daughter. And he passed it on to me. No wonder he hated me so much. I was everything he never wanted to be, and he made me that way.

"In the makeshift hangar," I replied in a dead voice, allowing my body to fall back against the uncomfortable bunk. "It was buried in the dust."

"This is a new one too…" Valentin murmured, running his fingers over the expiration date. "He must have had a supply with him and this one fell out. The Coalition would not want him unleashing his magic by accident in their territories, and he is too valuable to turn away as a defector."

"The Coalition has their blockers too," Jax said, brows furrowing. "Why would they need a supply for him?"

"Their blockers are more potent than ours and take getting used to," Valentin replied. "They aim to eliminate magic rather than just block it. Charles would need time to adjust to them so they wouldn't make him sick or kill him, even if he has been using our blockers for an extensive period of time."

"How do we know that this wasn't dropped by one of the groups investigating after the escape? Or even planted?" Himawari asked.

All eyes turned to me and I realized that I had emitted the noise of anguish I was trying to hold back. Instead of burying my face in the uncomfortable pillow as I wished, I sat up and looked each of my teammates in the face.

"His…" I faltered, took a breath, and started again. "His signature was all over it. I saw the traces of it before I…

before I blew up."

"Daux," Himawari began, starting to get up from her bunk.

I waved her off, curling in on myself. I didn't want sympathy. I wanted my father behind bars or dead.

Or dead.

I wanted my father dead.

I wanted *my father dead.*

A laugh escaped under my breath, only catching the attention of Valentin who pursed his lips but said nothing. I couldn't believe I had fallen so far as to want another human being dead, but here I was, with a bleeding hole in my chest waiting to be filled by the death of the man who gave me life.

Oh, how the righteous have fallen.

"What magic do you think he has?" Félix asked gently.

"Probably something similar to my mother," I answered much more calmly than I felt. "Fire is my strongest element and the other three I can use rather weakly. And foresight comes from my mother's side, there is a record of it."

That there was no record of the Deveraux family's magic was strange. Magic was always registered, it was how the Academies knew how to educate magical children, how Placement exams were set up, and how society was able to operate. There was not a single record showing that my father or his parents had magic. He always blamed it on my mother… But it was him too.

His family had lied about their abilities for decades. How was I going to explain this to the Overseer? Or anyone else for that matter?

"Does this mean Amalie has magic too?" Jax asked.

I froze in place.

Amalie could not have magic. If she did, she would have been off blockers for months now and could be explosive in her magical presentation. And I had left her all alone with my friends, who knew nothing of the potential danger I had inflicted upon them.

"Rhiannan!" I gasped, pulling up her holochat on my holonav. "Answer, please answer!"

I waited for what felt like years – but was likely only a few seconds – for Rhiannan to answer and her smiling face to pop up on the screen.

"Hey, girly, what's up?" she asked over the sounds of my sister's voice singing loudly along with Hawthorn's in the background.

We were not supposed to contact other Spec Ops agents – or anyone really – while out on a mission. It was protocol, preventing compromising the mission. But I didn't care. I had to warn her.

"I need to talk to you privately," I hissed quietly so Amalie and Hawthorn would not hear.

I waited for her nod – the background of our holochat changing rapidly – and the sound of a door closing behind her before speaking. Rhiannan was now in a surprisingly yellow room, sunflowers decorating nearly every surface. This had to be her bedroom – it matched her personality perfectly.

"Amalie potentially has magic," I whispered, still afraid my sister might somehow hear me.

Rhiannan blinked for a second, processing what I had said, then nodded. "I'll get some temporary blockers ASAP. She didn't tell you she was on them?"

I shook my head. I hadn't any idea she was on blockers. My parents had let me think she did not have magic, and she never presented any signs. I never thought to ask her myself either.

My heart began to pound in my chest, making the hole in my soul ache with guilt. I failed my sister yet again, in more ways than one. This was going to be difficult.

"What if she fights me when I give it to her?" Rhiannan asked, tapping on her holonav screen – presumably to order blockers on my behalf. "Oral blockers taste terrible, it's not like I can slip them in her food."

"No, don't do that," I agreed. "She won't trust you."

I paused for a moment to breathe, to gather my thoughts.

"Just… Just ask her if she ever had to take medicine with my parents," I requested finally.

"And if she says yes?" Rhiannan asked.

"Then ask her if they were shots or oral, and whatever she says, tell her it's important that she start taking them again immediately. Do not scare her of course, make sure she realizes that she is not in trouble, but make sure she understands that it is important."

Rhiannan nodded; a firm set to her mouth before we disconnected with the promise of her updating me later. I was forever indebted to her and Hawthorn. There was no way I could repay them for putting them in danger like this. Whatever Amalie's potential abilities, they could explosively present themselves due to the suppression for so long. Or, they could be completely obsolete. Either way, it was safer to make sure she was not going to accidentally destroy their flat.

"Well," I huffed, slumping back against my bunk. "That's taken care of."

I flung an arm over my eyes, hoping to block anything and everything out, but only succeeded in knocking my glasses to the floor. They were quickly picked up and placed at my side by Valentin, who settled himself on my bunk. I was hyperaware of his presence still, and I didn't need him sitting that close to me. Not right now.

"You did the right thing," Félix said.

I agreed with him and said so, but it felt strange – wrong even – to put my baby sister on blockers when I had just gotten off of them myself. It was unavoidable though, and a ping on my holonav from Rhiannan a few moments later confirmed it.

Amalie was given an injection every few months since she was five. My parents had told her it was for allergies and she just went along with it. She *believed* them. Had she not felt the crushing feeling of the magic in her veins being dampened by the blockers?

After my mother was arrested and Spec Ops quite literally dumped Amalie on our doorstep, she had forgotten about it and when it was time for her next injection, she did not know how to tell anyone so she could get a new one. By the time I had been released from custody, she had figured whatever she was allergic to she had grown tolerant to and moved on.

She didn't even know she had magic.

My little sister had gone this long and no one ever told her she had magic.

Rhiannan said she took the news well and was fine with having an injection straight away once presented with the potential dangers, but that she had become subdued and was asking for me.

It was late. She was tired. Of course, she would ask for me. I was her big sister after all, even if she was angry with me. I wished I could be there for her, that I could call her but with the fact that I had already called Rhiannan while on a mission I could not risk another and getting reprimanded. I could not afford any infractions or anything that could potentially have Amalie taken away from me.

Chapter Eighteen

Rhiannan sent me a chat the next morning updating me on Amalie. She had gone to sleep fine but had crawled into Hawthorn's bed about three-thirty in the morning crying from a nightmare. It had taken another hour and a half to get her calm and back to sleep. The blocker also seemed to make her lose her appetite this morning.

I could not respond since it was against Spec Ops protocol, but Rhiannan would see that I had read her messages. How I longed to be back with Amalie, but I still had a few more days here in Portnith at the least. More, if all our investigations ended up as yesterday's did. I could not let that happen. I needed to keep my emotions in check – both about my father *and* Valentin. Something would need to be done about the latter, but thinking about that released a volley of butterflies in my stomach that I just did not need.

We were back in the building my father held us captive in, except we did not split up this time. I wanted to so we could cover more ground, but the others mutinied against me saying that if my magic was as uncontrollable as yesterday after being on blockers so long, they didn't feel comfortable splitting up. They wanted to make sure I was safe.

As much as I wanted to yell – to scream – at them, I did not. They were right to be concerned. They were right to be wary of me. I felt as though I was a ticking time bomb and it was only a matter of seconds before I went off and destroyed everything and everyone I loved. Never one to go off on a power trip, I let them overrule my decision. They deserved my trust in them. They deserved so much more than that.

"Are there any more blockers lying about?" Himawari asked, kneeling in the dust and running her fingers through the dust and grime there.

"Possibly," Valentin answered, joining her. "If the container was jostled enough to drop one, it could have dropped even more. It can't hurt to look."

Instead of investigating the rooms we had been held captive in, Valentin suggested we try and find more of my father's supply of blockers. He explained that we needed to find these blockers – if there were any more – so that we could trace them back to the manufacturer and get the purchase records. Just the one would do, but if we had more, it would be easier to track.

A private citizen buying blockers like that without a prescription would have drawn suspicion. My father would have had to use a front for that ruse, like a business where magic users with unstable abilities would work; though, long-term blockers wouldn't have been used in that scenario – which is what I suspected these were.

I shook my head and got down on my knees to search. The front my father used did not matter right now, we could figure that out later. What mattered was finding more of these blockers and turning them over to the evidence-collecting department the Overseer had set up for this very investigation. They would cut through all the red tape so we didn't have to waste our time doing it.

That would have been helpful when I was investigating my father the first go around, but there was no use in complaining about that now. Complaining – especially to myself – was something I was doing too much of these days.

After a few minutes of searching, the faint silver glimmer of my father's signature drew me to a far corner of the hangar. To my relief, Valentin had been right. There were several small blocker vials scattered around like they had been thrown from a crate when said crate had been roughly picked up to be stowed away in a hurry. But why was my father's signature on them? Wouldn't he have had his goons do the heavy lifting?

Maybe he inspected the crates? If he hadn't personally ordered them so he could distance himself from his escape plan, then it would only make sense for him to want to make sure he got what he needed – what he asked for.

Carefully, I scooped the blockers up and called for my team. "I found more in the corner over here!"

"We should take them to the evidence department," Valentin said, looking at the vials.

"The expiration dates match the other one and so do the batch numbers," I stated, handing them over for him to inspect closer.

"Then that would prove our theory that he purchased them through a third party," Valentin said, taking the vials. "Now we just have to figure out who did it on his behalf."

"And why," I continued for him.

"I'll bring these to evidence," he repeated and headed out of the building.

I watched him leave for a moment, then returned to searching the building. Since we had found the other blockers, it was best that we move to another section to try and find more indication of my father's plans. Valentin would catch up soon.

The rooms we had been held captive in were not easy to find. They were dark and windowless, obviously a space for either freezing or storing light-sensitive materials. My father had used them for prisoners. They had been overlooked in the sweep after my arrest, the doors obscured by debris and a Coalition-manufactured glamour that the military would not have been equipped to detect. My father had certainly covered his tracks.

But his rapidly weakening signature was not there. That was not surprising. We had been taken to him, not the other way around. Father expected others to be subservient to him, even the act of going to observe his prisoners would have been abhorrent to him.

No, he needed us paraded in front of him to inflate his ego. Nothing else would do. Even if one of those prisoners was his daughter. Scratch that, *especially* if one of those prisoners was his daughter.

Now that the lights were on in the room that I had been held captive in, I could see that it was filled with Coalition tech and supplies. Magic blocking cuffs, small boxes of sedatives, and a gun case filled with Coalition-issued firearms. Other handheld weapons such as cattle prods, cudgels, and Billy clubs. There was even a sword left behind in the mix, an old rapier. Its gilded hilt was reminiscent of the one that sat on my hip. Much more ornate than Valentin's simple blade, and even more decorative than my own. What was the Coalition doing with such a weapon? Or my father for that matter?

And why had they left it behind?

In the room where Talia and the others had been imprisoned, there were piles of firearms left behind in the struggle instigated by their escape. There had been a few Coalition soldiers captured in all the chaos, and none of them were talking. Two had even used special cyanide pills hidden in their teeth to kill themselves before their torture could begin. The other one had been sedated and had the false tooth extracted before he could end his own life, but he was only following orders from higher up, and according to the interrogation notes, he and the others had been barred from seeing who the alleged higher up was, further muddying the waters.

Did my father have high-ranking Coalition officials working with him? His status as one of thirteen Governors – some of the highest-ranking members of the NAF government – would certainly facilitate such a need for the Coalition to handle him with the utmost care. But how would my father have gotten in touch with such prolific officials in the first place? Governors' communications were monitored with the highest scrutiny, even their personal communications through their holonav comm-apps were monitored. Unless…

Had my father, or someone working for him figured out how to hack into the holonav mainframe and unlock hidden features? Surely if Félix, an 'amateur' but skilled hacker, could hack *my* holonav then my father could find someone with the same capabilities. And there was direct communication and handwritten letters to consider.

It would be much more difficult to ascertain what was in a handwritten letter unless the group monitoring my father's communications had a person who could see text through solid objects. And the last person I had heard of with that particular ability was retired and extremely ill. It would be much easier for my father to get coded messages out in physical form than digital. Though, my father hacking his holonav was something my team and I could not rule out.

After we left that room, we headed back into the large hangar to see if Valentin had returned. By the time we reached the room, he had found us, giving me a curt nod reminiscent of the old him to let me know he had handed over the vials. I almost smiled at the thought of him regressing into that angry stage.

I was glad he had not become the bitter young man I had known him to be in the past, even if I did wish he and the others were as angry as me at times. There was a nagging part of me that reminded me that I did not have to be angry either, but I ignored it. I *did* need to be angry – I *did* need my anger. I could not function otherwise.

That feeling had kept the ember burning when it threatened to extinguish. It had kept me alive with my sanity mostly intact. I was not going to let it go that easily.

As if on autopilot, I followed my father's signature back to the room he had us brought to face him. The one where he nearly broke Félix's jaw, where he tormented me by threatening to kill my friends and blocking my magic with my own magic-blocking cuffs.

His signature was all over this room, though this one was completely bare as compared to the last two. According to my memory of the place, there wasn't anything in there either except my father and a few of the Coalition soldiers he had used to capture us. Which… where did those soldiers even go? A few had been captured, we knew that, but none of the ones who had dragged me and my team to grovel before my father.

I spoke that question aloud to my teammates, puzzled.

"You're right," Félix agreed, looking just as perplexed as I felt. "There couldn't have been enough room on the helicopter for all of them."

"And I know for a fact that we didn't kill anyone here," Himawari said.

"There is no way they captured all of them in the chaos that was happening…" Jax stated, knowing that we only had a few Coalition soldiers in custody.

There were also the explosions to account for. Even with his Berserker magic, there was no way Félix could have caused that amount of destruction by himself.

I made eye contact with Valentin and he spoke my thoughts as easily as if he had read my mind.

"The incapacitated soldiers in the last room were taken into custody," he explained, gesturing to the room. "But any that escaped that didn't go with Daux's father likely went to designated points in town to detonate explosions in an attempt to show that Félix, and thereby any magic users in the vicinity, was dangerous and could not be trusted to save anyone who does not possess magic themselves."

"He wanted to show that we would cause anyone with weaker magic than us, or no magic at all, harm in our pursuit of justice," I said, trembling with indiscernible emotions.

Horror was rapidly overtaking them all.

It was entirely believable that my father would try to frame me – and my teammates – as the bad guys in this scenario. It surprised me that it had worked to some extent. The local soldiers regarded me with thinly disguised disdain at best and outright hostility at worst. His attack and escape had poisoned my image in the minds of my allies but in opposite directions. And it had spread to my teammates and friends in the same manner. He had sewn discord among all rungs of society, the relations between Spec Ops and the rest of the government had never been more strained.

I had to admit it was a rather ingenious plan on his part.

I would applaud him if I didn't want to rip his throat out.

"This place is a bust," I said finally, placing my hands on my hips. "We are not going to find anything else here. I propose we alert the evidence team of our theory, and the two rooms they missed, so they can search for any non-magical detonation devices. The Coalition would not be so stupid as to send volatile slave soldiers to start the explosions, and they would not use magic-bearing devices either."

"That's a good idea, Himawari, Jax, and I will head back there straightaway," Valentin agreed but paused before turning away. "Just wait here until I get back. The locals aren't too happy with you and Félix right now, and it's possible some would recognize you. Especially since the soldiers here are being so hostile. I'll bring back someone from evidence to guide us around to the explosion sites and help keep people away from the group."

I ground my teeth together, bristling at his suggestion, but nodded. He was right. We couldn't go wandering around upsetting the locals when the peacekeepers were more likely to allow us to be attacked than prevent it. Valentin's suggestion of a guide would be helpful. The signatures were fading faster every day that passed, and it would be helpful to have someone show us the places we needed to go in case they disappeared altogether.

We still needed to inspect the site of my father's escape.

For a moment, I stared at the empty hangar, wondering why they hid the helicopter so far away from where they escaped from. Then it hit me.

The realization slammed into me so hard that I nearly toppled to the ground.

My father had *known* we were going to be close to Portnith. He had *known* we were going to attack the base there and gather info. He had *known* my plans and that we were watching him. My father had to have known.

There was no other explanation.

How could he have figured it out though? We were so careful. We even used tech glamours so any anti-glamour magic technology wouldn't reveal our identities on the cameras in his office when Valentin, Himawari, and I visited. However, if my father were to have a secret disruptor in his office… That would have allowed him to see through our disguises.

That couldn't be the case! I would have noticed if Valentin and Himawari's glamours had been disrupted. And they would have noticed if mine had.

So, how could he have known? And how could we have been compromised?

As Valentin returned to the hangar with a young, blonde woman from the evidence department it dawned on me. This young woman looked nothing like the tall, willowy Hayley who had shown us around and answered our questions. She was petite and voluptuous, but her hair was the exact same shade as Hayley's.

Could she have been wearing some sort of tech that showed through our glamours? Maybe she recognized my voice? And how had they figured out our plans? Somehow, in some way, I knew my father's secretary had to be involved in my father's escape and my subsequent arrest.

And I was going to figure out how.

Later, as the woman from the evidence department – Brigitte, she introduced herself as– guided us towards the identified explosion sites I felt the tension surrounding my team rising to strenuous levels. Brigitte was fine, a little aloof, and she seemed to be giving me and Félix funny looks, but she was not outright hostile at least.

It was difficult enough seeing the destruction wrought on this city, reliving it as though it happened only yesterday. I was glad for her silence, even if her judgment came along with it.

The first explosion site proved my theory almost instantly. My foresight found evidence of an incinerated Coalition soldier in the wreckage. Bits of dark coalition uniform, of a leather boot, hair, skin, and bone so minuscule the untrained unmagical eye could not even hope to see it were littered among the rubble. Even with digital enhancements.

Nausea flared in my stomach, traveling up my esophagus until I thought I would truly be sick.

Breathe. I reminded myself and felt as my lungs and diaphragm expanded.

I couldn't tear my eyes away from the destruction before me. It was mitigated somewhat by the townspeople cleaning up the area – and construction crews removing debris after the initial investigations were completed – but that didn't change the harrowing thing that this soldier had endured. Innocent or not, it was a horrific way to die.

Heat warmed through my gauntlet and I looked down to see that Félix had slipped his hand into mine. He refused to look at me and squeezed my hand, swallowing hard. A sheen of sweat had broken out across his forehead and his eyes darted around the square like a prey animal looking for any chance to escape.

I quickly returned his gesture of comfort and began breathing deeply. In and out through my nose. In and out. In and out. In and out. In. Out. In. Out. In. Out.

The air felt like a lifeline, filling my lungs and diaphragm and soothing me. With each inhale and exhale I squeezed Félix's hand, reminding him to breathe with me, and after a while, I saw his shoulders moving shakily with each full breath.

"I know why there were no other Coalition soldiers captured," I said shakily once I was calm enough.

"Why is that?" Brigitte asked, pulling up her holonav to make notes.

"Because they were incinerated when the explosives went off. They were likely told they would have time to escape, but as soon as they activated the detonators, they were engulfed," I explained, feeling more than a little sick at my father's cruelty.

"And how can you be sure of this?" she asked sharply, but there was no malice in her voice.

"Test the soil and rubble if you don't believe me," I snapped, uncaring if she was being impartial or not. "You will find human remains that do not belong to NAF citizens at each detonation site most likely, as well as fibers and particles from Coalition-issued uniforms and footwear. Perhaps even burned Coalition weapons."

"There were burned weapons recovered from the sites," Brigitte said looking up from her holonav in horror. "We assumed the soldiers had abandoned them so they could assimilate into the chaos, not that they were... they were..."

"Instantaneously reduced to ashes?" Félix supplied tetchily.

Brigitte swallowed loudly. Behind her glasses, I could see a gathering wetness in her eyes. I felt little compassion for her.

"It's also possible that the soldiers were willing to die to avoid being captured," Himawari interjected softly, calling to mind the soldiers who had committed suicide while in captivity.

"It is something we will likely never know," I said, sweeping my eyes over the wreckage for one last look.

My eyes were beginning to strain. I would need to switch back to my glasses soon. I could feel my power taking a toll on my body, much as my desire for movement had when I was using the wheelchair. The periphery of my vision was beginning to blur. I could not take much more of this.

Valentin must have sensed my fatigue because he hurried to my side, nearly shoving Félix out of the way in the process, and placed his hand on the small of my back.

"It is time for our team leader to return to the bunker," he announced with authority. "She is still recovering from the incident and needs rest."

"O-Of course," Brigitte agreed, finishing up her notes on her holonav. "When should I meet you next?"

Valentin looked down at me and I gave him a shake of my head that would have been imperceptible to nearly anyone else. I could feel my body failing me. My magic was draining far too much energy. I could not go back out today. Looking for those remains had taken too much out of me, not to mention the stress of returning to this Gods-forsaken town.

"Tomorrow morning," Valentin said, thankfully understanding. "The rest of the team will be available to you should you need us, but our team leader needs to recharge."

Brigitte pursed her lips but nodded in agreement.

There was no way I could give this investigation more than I already had today. My limbs were beginning to feel weak and shaky. Immediately, I deactivated my foresight watching as the world around me dulled and my vision began to dim. I pulled my glasses from their pouch on my hip with trembling hands and slipped them onto my face, uncaring of who saw me. Still, as we made our way back to the bunker, I was hyperaware of Valentin's hand on my back, the heat radiating through my armor as though my magic was still searching for him.

The next morning, I awoke feeling as though I had been hit by a truck. I had fallen into my bunk the day before still in my armor, unable to do much of anything but stare at the pictures of Amalie that Rhiannan had continued to send me until Jax brought our team some food. After that, I showered and went back to my bunk listening to the sound of my friends' voices lull me into a fitful sleep.

But when Brigitte showed up at the bunker bright and early the next morning, I was ready; stiff and sore as I was.

She informed us that while I was recovering, her investigative team had found the incinerated unidentified remains I had predicted would be at every explosion site. Her tone and expression had been pained and apologetic, but I ignored her. I was in no mood to entertain apologies from people who could not be bothered to say them aloud.

However, there was something else lurking there. Something in her expression did not sit right with me.

"What is it?" I asked, attempting to sound polite. "There is something you're not telling us."

"I just…" she faltered, looking around at my team with concern. "I didn't know how to say it. But there is evidence to suggest that some of the fires and explosions, not all of them of course, but many were caused by magic. And not Berserker magic. Not to mention the fact that it appears as if the rooms you discovered yesterday have ties to a Coalition base that was raided a few months ago, and that the ones we had already cataloged show signs of being wiped of any evidence at all. I know you are aware of the last fact, but it is troubling all the same."

My brows furrowed, and the expressions of my teammates mirrored my confusion. Magic? Had my father brought in magic slaves? He could have done so since he snuck in a whole unit of Coalition Soldiers, but the amount of description in Portnith was far too great for a handful of slaves with shackled magic.

Slaves were volatile and unpredictable, but without their master's direction, they would not be able to wreak this much havoc unless there was a small army of them.

"The Coalition would never allow that many slaves back into NAF territory without their masters," Valentin said, voicing my thoughts.

"No," Himawari agreed, shaking her head. "A master cannot have too many slaves, it weakens their hold on them, so the possibility of Charles Deveraux controlling the amount he would need to cause this destruction is practically impossible *outside* of the enormous gamble the Coalition would be taking to allow that many slaves into Portnith for a terror attack."

"So, someone – sorry – several someones," Félix corrected himself, "would have had to possess unshackled magic to destroy the town this way. More than one person possessing fire or explosive magic…"

His voice trailed off, looking at me with wide eyes. Those blockers… My father must have used his "curse" to help aid in his terror attack – to further the narrative that magic was evil and no one without it was safe from people like me. I looked around at my friends surrounding me, people that I knew to be gentle and kind, and rage simmered beneath my skin.

Somehow the Coalition had recruited soldiers who possessed magic for the sole purpose of ruining the idea of it in NAF territories. The only places in the whole world we were allowed to be ourselves, the only places we were ever truly safe. My fists clenched so hard I knew my knuckles were whitening beneath the crimson of my armor and I wished I could feel the pain of my nails biting into my skin.

My father had tried to ruin magic for me, for everyone

and he must have used his own to do so. Something I never thought him capable of. So much for his anti-magic posturing bullshit. He could not even stick to his own morals. And if he would do that… Just what else was he capable of doing to further his agenda – whatever that may be?

The thought made me feel ill.

"Do you know what base the evidence in those rooms is connected to?" Himawari asked Brigitte, but from the horrified look she gave me, it appeared that she already knew.

"Captain Gladwin's intel base," I said before Brigitte could speak.

My skin crawled at the thought of wearing Gladwin's skin as a glamor. We had not been told the location of the base, as all the information the Overseer relayed to me for the mission was on a need-to-know basis. We were not navigating there, so we did not need to know. And if we were to be captured and interrogated by Gladwin's colleagues, then we would have been able to claim ignorance.

"The base I am referring to has connections to that name, yes," Brigitte said, but would not divulge further.

It did not matter. We already knew.

"Let's get going," I snapped, pushing my way out into the bright sunlight.

The others followed and soon enough, we were on our way to the town square where my father had escaped in his ancient helicopter. As we walked, seeing the square come into view much more quickly than I had expected, I realized Félix and I had taken the long way that day. He and I looked at each other with chagrin but refused to acknowledge that fact otherwise.

No one harassed us as we made our way into the square – thankfully – and the crater Félix created was still there, just a little off-center. The shop window I had crashed into was still broken, awaiting repairs, but the blood had been washed away either by the temperamental coastal weather or by the shop's owners themselves.

Absentmindedly, I ran my fingers over the shrinking scars on the back of my head and neck, feeling weak-kneed as nausea churned in my gut.

Flashbacks of what Félix had endured at my father's hand flooded to the forefront of my mind, unhindered by any attempt I made to dissuade them. My breath began to come in quick bursts, even as I tried to calm it, and once again, Félix slipped his hand into mine. His grip was much harder than it had been yesterday, nearly cutting off my circulation through my gauntlet.

I squeezed his hand back, struggling with my grip on reality at the same time. There was no time to panic though, we had to get through this. We had to fight it, or I was bound to lose my sister, my teammates, my freedom, and who knew what else as punishment. Once I saw that Félix was at least attempting to focus – attempting to breathe along with me – I activated my foresight.

Our signatures were still faintly wavering around the space, my father's hovering above them all, then disappearing over the skyline. There was no use in tracking it further, as it was disappearing before my eyes along with my own and Félix's. I had known it would not last long, and it would disappear fully by the time we set out to track it in any capacity.

I was surprised I had even seen it the first time considering I had thought my father didn't have any magic, seeing as he had been on blockers for who knows how long – effectively hiding that fact from me and the entire NAF. The only thing I could think of to explain it was that we shared DNA. Nothing else short of a miracle made sense.

I did not believe in miracles. Not anymore.

I only believed in what I could see. And what I saw at that moment, what made me let go of Félix's hand and rush forward against the warning of Valentin was… a child. A small child with deep brown skin and coiled hair wrapped in two braided buns on top of her head leaning over the crater where Félix had blown himself up trying to capture my father.

She was laughing.

I stopped in my tracks.

Moments later another child popped out of the crater, looking so identical to the girl I knew he had to be her brother. He stared at me for a second, drawing his sister's attention to me, and they both waved.

I blinked in surprise for a moment, then returned the gesture, forcing a smile on my face.

"They are healing," Brigitte said, moving to stand beside me. "While it is deep, the crater is not dangerous. Children play in it all the time now, pretending to be magic users."

"They may not hate us," I whispered with a hoarseness to my voice that I had not expected. "But their parents, their teachers, their law enforcement will warn them of the dangers of magic, of people who use it. They will grow to hate us, and themselves. My father made sure of that."

"You were here that day?" Brigitte asked.

I nodded my reply, not trusting my voice. Had she not realized that this was my fault?

"Then you will understand the apprehension," she continued, looking wistfully out at the growing group of children clambering out of the crater. "There are those that are frightened now, listening to people who are using their powerful voices to strike at the fear in our hearts, but the children see only the good that people like us do."

"Like us?" I rasped, looking down at her.

She smiled and waved a hand. A sparkling rainbow appeared in the bright sunshine; water droplets rained gently down on the earth where we stood. "Us," she repeated. "Humanity is resilient. They will come around again. They will have to, once their children start showing signs of magic. Or their neighbor's children."

That was an almost naively optimistic outlook, but if

society were to prevail at all – if tensions were ever to be repaired – then people would have to begin to accept one another. Magic was something that could not be changed easily, or at all. And if the NAF's citizens could not accept that, then everything would be broken beyond repair.

My team and I waited until the children left the crater, some hurrying home to their mothers and fathers, or school if it was still open. Others stayed behind and watched with inquisitive eyes and excitement escaping from their small frames with each movement. It made me homesick for my sister.

My father's escape from the square was hushed up, as much as something like this could be, but it did not stop onlookers of all ages from coming to peer at our investigation. Brigette and her team kept people from approaching, but they could hardly keep the townsfolk from having a little look in on what was occurring in their city.

The explosions had put many out of work and even more out of their homes. The death toll was something I did not even want to think about. How could I not though, as I trampled over the ruins of this city alive and well while these people had lost everything? Of course, the NAF government would be providing aid to these people, but my father – the governor of Heliorious and its provinces – had left everything in a muddle. His replacement, Interim-Governor Farris, was still wading through the mess he had made.

Many of these people would be living in shelters until the day came when Interim-Governor Faris was able to give them the aid they so rightly deserved.

Just another reason I needed to fix what my father had done, and quickly.

The citizens of Portnith deserved that much, even if they did hate people like me after all this. I could hardly blame them. I would probably hate people with magic too – if I had none of my own – after a tragedy like this.

We stood there as a team for a while, observing the

townsfolk and the military intelligence officers as they hurried about town seemingly oblivious to our presence there. Why had my father lured me and Félix to *this* spot to humiliate us and pain magic as evil as he believed it to be? Why this port town? It was not far from Eidolon, he could have just crossed the border there, why all the theatrics?

Yes, my father was dramatic. Yes, he loved a good show, but it would have been so much easier had he defected through Eidolon. Surely, he had a good reason for his theatrics. There was no way he knew about our plan to blow up the Coalition warehouse just outside of the town's limits. Perhaps me being here was just a bonus for him. So, why?

That question troubled me for longer than I cared to admit.

Chapter Nineteen

We stayed there, among the crumbling buildings of the once cheery town square for quite a while before we determined that there was nothing else to be gleaned from the location. Brigette led the way back to the temporary headquarters for the investigation teams and we followed in silence. She seemed slightly disappointed I could provide no more than the general direction my father's helicopter had flown off in. What had she expected? A definitive location as well as a concrete motive?

More importantly, what had I expected?

I certainly had not expected that my father or anyone else affiliated with the Coalition that day had possessed magic. I had not expected to find the blockers, the weapons, or the connection to Gladwin's intelligence base I had infiltrated. And I certainly had no idea what to make of it all, or how to piece it all together in a way that made any sense. My thoughts were swirling around in my head at such a speed I was making myself dizzy.

"Daux," Jax whispered from beside me in a hard plastic seat identical to the one I was sitting in. "You're making your lip bleed."

I straightened in the seat, unlatching my teeth from my dry, cracked lip, and shot him a weary smile. He returned it with a sunshine-bright one of his own, patting my shoulder as he stood to grab a few bottles of water for our team.

We were sitting around a large, round collapsible table

in conference with Brigitte and the three heads of the other teams investigating the scenes, and cataloging any evidence found. The Spec Ops barracks were not large enough to accommodate the large number of people the military had brought in, commandeering some from Spec Ops HQ to assist, so they had set up their meeting spaces in one of the local hotels that gratefully accepted the business.

Jax returned to his seat next to me, twisted off the lid of a bottle, and handed it to me. I accepted gratefully and took a sip, watching as he did the same for every member of our team, passing the water down until each of us had one. How had someone who had known such sorrow such shame become so kind? Why could I not be more like him?

Because you are not weak. An unkind voice said.

I now knew it was mine, though it sounded so much like my mother.

Jax's kindness was *not* a weakness. It was his strength. I was the way I had become because *I* was weak. I had no place to be passing judgment when I had chosen the opposite of Jax's strength to get me through my torment.

"Do any of you have ideas as to why Governor Deveraux may have chosen Portnith as a defection spot? Or why he chose to do so in such a public and dangerous way?" one of the team leads asked.

Darya Mehran was a short woman, barely brushing my shoulder with the top of her head at her full height, but that did not detract from her intimidating aura. Her golden-brown skin glowed under the soft lighting in the conference room and her inky black hair was scraped back into a tight bun on the top of her head. She wore the same drab white coat all the other intelligence leads donned along with black pants and boots that barely added to her height.

"I suspect that the governor decided he needed to make an example of magic users," Valentin answered her, leaning back casually in his chair.

I tried not to stare at the lean muscle his black tactical

shirt did little to hide, and refused to acknowledge Jax's smirk when he caught me looking away hastily.

"But how did he know there would be magic users with the authority to apprehend him in the area?" Mi Sang-Chul, another of the team leads asked.

He was older, greying at the temples and crow's feet behind his black acrylic frames. His was a stern, mistrusting face. I did not like him.

I looked between the four leaders and then shrugged. I had an idea, one concerning his secretary, but was unsure if I should say anything at present. I was not sure I could trust these people with that information. I needed to tell my team my suspicions immediately after this meeting, especially Valentin and Himawari since they accompanied me to my father's offices that day.

"Ms. Deveraux," Sang-Chul pressed, voice hardening.

"Sorry," I said, sitting up straighter and resisting the urge to roll my eyes. "We do not have any information indicating my father had any ideas that I would be in the area with my teammates and coworkers."

Sang-Chul frowned, clearly unhappy with my response. It was evident to the whole team that he did not trust us, especially me. I did not care because the feeling was mutual.

The third team leader, William Holden, cleared his throat, placing a thin pale hand on Sang-Chul's shoulder. The other man did not relax, but his eyes did soften a touch around the edges.

"This is your last day here and you have brought us some interesting discoveries in the days past," Willaim said gratefully, directing his words to the entire team, though his tone lacked sincerity. "It is beyond me how our teams could have been as incompetent as to miss the blockers or the hidden room in the warehouse. We are indebted to you for all the information you helped us to uncover."

"My father's... signature was leading me to most of the evidence," I explained hoping they would not see it as me knowing what to look for because I had inside knowledge.

"We are aware of your abilities," Darya said with a polite smile that gave nothing away. "Brigitte informed us of your connection to Charles Deveraux as well. It seems the Overseer believes that you alone are capable of apprehending your father."

Ah. That was what they thought. And with the way Sang-Chul's expression hardened again, they didn't much care for my boss, nor her interference in their investigation.

"I believe we need to all work together to apprehend my father and anyone working with him, as well as to hold back Coalition interference from *all* NAF territories," I said diplomatically. "My team and I – as representatives of the espionage department: Spec Ops – are willing to cooperate with the military, judicial, governing, and intelligence departments so that we may protect our nations and our freedoms."

"A pretty sentiment," Darya said but her smile still did not reach her eyes.

"It is not a 'sentiment'," Félix said hotly, crossing his arms over his chest.

"We are here, are we not?" Himawari asked, turning her dark, depthless eyes on the four team leaders. Brigitte squirmed beneath her gaze. "We are working with you, are we not? Our team leader has been cleared of any wrongdoing, and we are offering our services and knowledge. What more do you want?"

"Your Overseer has cleared Agent Deveraux, but who is to say the Overseer herself did not cover something up?" Sang-Chul asked, a mean-spirited smile curling the edges of his lips.

"Do you wish to see the transcripts of my interrogation?" I asked, raising a brow. "I'm sure, you as the intelligence liaison, would be interested to know Spec Ops interrogation methods as they only let the *very* best of your department participate."

Jax stifled a snicker next to me and the barely veiled slight, and I kicked him lightly beneath the table. Sang-Chul's jaw tightened but he said nothing.

"That will not be necessary, Agent Deveraux." Brigitte fluttered her hands nervously, shooting daggers at Sang-Chul.

"No," William added hurriedly. "We don't require that information."

But you also don't trust me or the Overseer. I thought angrily.

Nor did I, but that was beside the point.

Was this why the Overseer had not told them who I was? I had made a mistake in sharing who I was with Brigitte, but what was done was done. I could not waste time dwelling on such a small mistake. The investigation was over and there was no reason to beat myself up over it during this stupid briefing meeting.

"We were just curious as to why witnesses are stating Spec Ops agents were causing the destruction in Portnith?" Darya said, that horrid polite smile still on her face.

"You found the remains of the dead Coalition soldiers. They must have disguised themselves as Spec Ops agents in order to cause conflict among the government and the people," I snapped back as though it were obvious.

At least it was obvious to me.

Talia, Rhiannan, and their teams – as well as Jax and Himawari – attempted to help evacuate the town. They saved lives, there is no way they would have contributed to the destruction. Besides, the magic they possessed would not have caused flames and explosions of this magnitude.

But these people were refusing to see reason. They shut their eyes and minds to it in favor of the narrative they preferred to see pushed. They were power-hungry bureaucrats who had little care for the truth over solutions. It was obvious in the way they spoke to us, and in the way they looked at *me*. I was not angry, not at them. They were not worth it.

However, that did not mean I had to take their suspicions or censure.

"Whatever happened here," I started, rising from my seat, the water bottle Jax had gotten for me crushing in my fist. "Was the fault of Charles Deveraux and the Coalition. No one else. Not me, not my teammates, and not my fellow Spec Ops agents."

My teammates stood, following my lead, and Brigette shot us guilty looks. Our exchange earlier had clearly not meant enough to help defend me to her co-leaders. My heart hardened once again and I gave them one last sweeping glare before turning with military precision and storming from the table. The others followed, ignoring the protests from the team leaders we left behind.

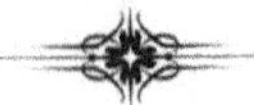

Back at the barracks we hurriedly packed our meager belongings, rushing to get away from Portnith as soon as we feasibly could. After the debacle of a meeting, we stormed out of there, deciding it was best to leave a few hours early.

"I need to speak with you all before we head to the hangar and are overheard," I said in a hushed voice.

It was still loud enough to catch their attention and they all moved to huddle in closer to hear what I had to say.

"Valentin, Himawari," I began, looking between the two of them. "Remember when we went to inspect my father's office?" I paused, waiting for their confirming nod before continuing. "I think his secretary, Hayley, must have recognized us somehow and informed my father. She may have even been able to track us in some way, or planted listening devices on our persons so they could hear what we were saying."

"Because?" Jax prompted.

"Because Darya had a point," I persisted vehemently, my

anger rising with each word that slipped from my lips. "There were Coalition soldiers – with *magic,* I might add – disguised as Spec Ops agents in Portnith. *My father* was in Portnith, only a handful of miles from where we blew up the Coalition warehouse. Both of those facts indicate that they had *some* knowledge of our plan, however insignificant."

"And you think Hayley is to blame?" Himawari asked, her expression grave.

"I can see no other possibility," I said.

Valentin nodded along silently, crossing his arms over his chest the way he always did when he was thinking deeply.

"Daux has a point," he said finally. "We should inform the Overseer of her suspicions when we make our report."

"And drag Hayley kicking and screaming by her hair from the Interim Governor's office," I suggested – a hint of malice in my voice.

The others stared at me, wide-eyed and shocked as if they could not believe I had said such a thing. I immediately regretted my choice of words, knowing that if my team thought I was unfit for duty, it could ruin me. It would ruin my chances of righting what had been done to me.

Rolling my eyes, I brushed my short hair from my eyes and turned my back on the group.

"Let's get going," I snapped without turning to look at them. "I am *sick* of this place."

Only one pair of footsteps followed me out of the bunk room. A cool hand encircled my wrist, halting me midstride.

"Daux," Valentin protested, turning me to face him, his eyebrows drawn and mouth set. "I am worried about you. I *need* you to talk to me."

And I needed to be rescued, I needed to be saved, I needed you. I thought angrily, but I did not voice those thoughts.

They would bring me no pleasure; they would not help the situation. If I spoke the words boiling in my throat, I would only be wounding Valentin. He did not deserve my ire, not anymore.

Despite that reasoning, I did not know what to say to him. I did not know how to respond in a way that would make him any less concerned for my well-being, mental or physical. When I did not respond immediately his grip on my shoulders tightened and the ground beneath me crunched as he dragged me forward.

My heart picked up in my chest, reminding me of the vow I had made earlier, not to let him get too close. I would rather hurt him with rejection than when I finally exploded. At least then he would be angry with me and the sting of my demise – whether it ended in my arrest or death – would not hurt him so much. At least there was that.

Before he could pull me into his embrace, I slapped his hands off my shoulders and planted my feet on the ground, envisioning roots burrowing deep into the dirt. I was physically and emotionally immovable. I would not be swayed by petition or passion. I could not let him get hurt. Not by me.

Shouldn't Angelov get to make that decision? Came the question in my mother's voice.

This was *not* my mother, nor was it an auditory hallucination. I knew what those sounded like from imprisonment. No, this was just… me. It sounded like my mother, yes but it was me filling in that role my mother vacated before she even allowed herself to love me.

What I could not figure out was why I was thinking more than self-deprecation and self-sabotage like I normally did in this tone. If I was trying to be like my mother, where was the bite of her words, the harshness of her judgments?

And I was the team leader, I knew what was best for *my* team. Valentin did not need me; he should not love me. I would destroy him as I knew I was destroying myself, and I could not let that happen.

"Daux," he protested once more, confusion replacing the

worry in his expression. "What's wrong? Have I done something to upset you? Please, just talk to me. I need you to talk to me."

The emotion in his voice nearly broke my resolve. I was too soft-hearted, too in lov—

No.

No, I could not think that. Thinking it would make it true.

I wanted it so badly to be true. I wanted to take Valentin by the hand and pull him close. To tell him every little feeling I hid deep inside my fractured heart and pray he would return them. My lips began to tremble, but I forced my hands to be stiff at my sides so I would not reach for him. I could not bare my soul to him. I could not handle the rejection.

"*I* need *you* to stop distracting me," I tried to say sternly, but the words came out shaky and sad.

I saw a flash of hurt cross his face for a flicker of a second before he registered the traitorous shake in my voice. I silently cursed myself for that as his hand reached up to cup my face, his thumb caressing my cheekbone with such tenderness I could have wept.

Why? Why was he so readily expressing affection toward me when I had shown him nothing but contempt? Even before he left and I was tortured I had not treated him kindly. We had worked on things… but why was he now so comfortable with me?

I knew the answer. It was one I could not allow myself to think.

Because thinking would make it true.

"I am here, Daux," he promised, eyes flashing with such earnestness I could not help but believe him. "I am here and I will never, *ever* leave you again. You can tell me to stop 'distracting' you all you want, but I am not giving up on you or abandoning you."

"You should," I argued, reaching up to place my hand atop his. "You should not care so much for me; we've fought like animals since we met."

"I am *not* leaving," he repeated. "I am not giving up on you."

He ignored the way my lips pursed and my posture stiffened. Ignored the flash in my eyes at his words. There was no getting through to him when he set his mind to something, I had learned that the hard way.

But. I thought as I stared up into those icy blue eyes I adored so much. *One way or another, I will drive him away. It is only a matter of time.*

"We are in this together, no matter what," he said.

I did not believe him.

I wanted to. Oh, I so desperately wanted to believe him. I wanted that so badly my chest hurt and my lungs ached. But I could not. It was not that Valentin was untrustworthy. Nor was it that I viewed any of his actions as a betrayal. There were just too many variables. Blind faith got people like us killed, or worse.

I had already endured the worst.

"You don't have to believe me," he whispered as though he had read my mind, gazing deeply into my eyes. "I don't expect you to believe me. But I believe in you, and in myself. Whatever may come, we *will* get through it. Together."

"You always were arrogant," I sighed, allowing him to pull me into his embrace.

"You wouldn't love me if I wasn't," he retorted.

I did not deign to answer him. Only laughed at his absurdity and wrapped my arms around his waist. Answering him would have been a death sentence. Either he meant what he said, and it would change everything, or he did not mean it the way I interpreted and I would face rejection. I could not handle either outcome at this moment, so, I let him hold me and prayed naively to unfeeling Gods that his embrace would never end.

Brigitte was the only one of the leaders to see us off to the jet, her expression apologetic.

"Thank you for your insight, Agent Deveraux," she said before I entered the hangar.

"I hope it helps both our investigations," I replied, leaving her behind.

As the door to the jet shut behind me with a click, the finality of the situation fell heavily upon my shoulders. My father had known about our plan. He knew enough to form *his* plan of defection in a way that would break the trust between the public and the governing bodies. I truly *had* been a partner in his escape, unwittingly or not.

My heart settled uncomfortably in my chest as I strapped myself in next to Himawari and Jax. We had a long while for my teammates to sit and analyze me, and my behavior, and I had nowhere to escape to. Valentin's eyes caught mine from across the jet as we took off, and my stomach lurched at the blue fire I saw there. He saw me. He knew. He was in my place at one point in his life; I could not hide what I was becoming from him. The thought terrified me more than my rage.

Chapter Twenty

The trip back home was not long but it was arduous. Each minute that ticked by was another that dragged on my nerves. All I wanted was to submit our report to the Overseer along with our suspicions about Hayley and get home to Amalie. I had gone through the holofile of pictures Rhiannan had sent me of their makeover session, karaoke night, and ice cream bar dinner over and over until I knew every detail of the pictures.

Every detail of my little sister's expressions.

I had not seen her so happy since before my Placement. My heart squeezed painfully inside of my chest, though seeing her smile did ease some of the guilt I harbored at having to leave her. There was nothing I could have done, and it seemed as though I had made an excellent decision on who should watch her.

Once we had boots on the ground back in Heliorious I made a beeline for the Overseer's office. Valentin insisted on coming with me, but the rest of the team was ready to get settled back into the flat. There was food to clear out of the refrigerator and shopping needed to be done to replace it.

When we reached the top floor of Spec Ops HQ, I breathed a sigh of relief. The Overseer's door was open and she was not in her office, which meant I was able to leave the mission report with one of her assistants. That meant I didn't have to be interrogated about my performance for now, and for that I was grateful.

Having Valentin there with me would have been an enormous relief should the Overseer have been in. But now that she wasn't, and we were all alone, my brain began to short-circuit. I had Amalie to get back to, I couldn't be thinking about Valentin and me. I could not think about whatever it was between us. If there was anything between us.

His comment kept floating back to me. That I loved him. And I had refused him an answer. How did one respond to a statement like that without revealing their innermost selves? How did one entertain the idea of intimacy without also contemplating the terrifying thought of being known and perceived by someone? To have my innermost thoughts and fears stripped down in front of Valentin and hope he wouldn't reject me was something I could not envision.

Everyone had their breaking point.

I was afraid to be his.

After uploading the mission report to the assistant's holonav and watching her upload it to the Spec Ops database, I dashed from the room without waiting for Valentin to follow. I was halfway through the lobby when a strong hand wrapped around my wrist, halting me in my tracks.

I turned to face whoever had grabbed me – to give them a piece of my mind – and found myself face-to-face with the very man I had been trying to avoid.

"Slow down, would you?" he groused, holding my wrist tightly.

"I have to get back to Amalie," I said, attempting to tug away from him.

He held fast, and I was once again taken aback at his strength.

"Amalie will still be there when we get back," he soothed, a soft smile playing around the edges of his lips. "We still have a whole shuttle ride back to the flat, and it's a few minutes until it gets here. You know they're never on schedule."

I hated it when he was right.

"Or are you trying to avoid me?" he asked leaning down to whisper it close to my ear.

I hated it even more when he read my mind.

"We are in Spec Ops HQ's lobby," I hissed, tugging at him once again. "People are staring!"

"Let them," he murmured.

However, I was not sure I heard him properly because I pulled my wrist away from him and began marching my way outside. My face was scarlet, and I wished I had taken my helmet with me to disguise the blush on my cheeks. Unfortunately, I had left it behind with the luggage, which the rest of our team would have brought back to the flat with them.

He lazily made his way outside to wait with me. And wait we did. Silently. It took another few minutes for the shuttle to pull up and unload the people getting off at this stop. Once it was nearly emptied, we boarded.

"Told you," he gloated, grinning at me.

"Hush," I snapped and let myself fall into a seat near the front of the shuttle.

To my misfortune he shoved my shoulder, pushing me toward the window, and sat down – ignoring my protests. He could have sat anywhere else and he had to sit here. Next to me. Right after that weird stunt that he pulled in the lobby.

What had gotten into him?

There was a time when he could not wait to get as far from me as possible. We had gotten passed that, sure, but it didn't change the fact that it *was* strange that he was insisting on sitting so closely to me now on a nearly empty shuttle.

What was he trying to do?

"You need to stop staring at me like that," he drawled, resting his head against the hard plastic of the shuttle seat.

I flushed again. "Like what?"

"Like you're going to flay me alive."

Oh.

Oops.

I had not meant to project so much anger or any at all. Valentin was not the target of it anyway.

"Sorry," I said, catching my head in my hands. "I'm just exhausted and I want to make sure my sister is okay."

"I know, and she will be. Rhiannan would have made sure you knew if something wasn't," he reassured me, patting my leg.

I peeked at his hand through my fingers when he didn't immediately remove his hand, then felt a flash of longing when he finally did. He was… I didn't know what Valentin was. I didn't know what these feelings were. There was one thing I did know, and it was that I was not sure I liked the way I was feeling.

About Valentin, or anything.

"Daux!" Amalie screeched when she caught sight of me in Rhiannan's entryway.

I could not speak, the lump in my throat preventing me from forming any sort of sound. She ran at me and I scooped her up into my arms, swinging her around as though we were the only ones in the room. I could feel the tears falling, so I buried my face in her hair to disguise them.

Oh, I missed her.

"I was scared you weren't going to come back," she whispered when I set her down.

"I promised you I would come home safe," I reminded her after swallowing down the lump in my throat. "I try to keep my promises the best I can."

"I know," she said, grabbing my hand.

Amalie's eyes were wet and red-rimmed. It was clear my absence had been taxing on her, even if she had refused to speak to me for weeks now. I would have to do something special to make it up to her.

"I missed you," she admitted.

"And I missed you," I replied.

"Even though I've been mean?"

"Even though you *had* been mean."

The tightness in my chest at her words made it hard to breathe. She had been agonizing over her behavior, afraid that if I had not made it back then she would have no way of apologizing. Or at the very least, making it up to me.

Just then, I became very aware of Valentin, Hawthorn, and Rhiannan watching us. Blood rushed into my face, coloring me red from the roots of my hair to my neck and ears. What was it about showing emotion that was so embarrassing? I loved my sister and there was no reason to be ashamed of displaying that love.

Clearing my throat, I stood to my full height and pulled Amalie close.

"Thank you so much for watching her while we were on our mission," I said to Rhiannan and Hawthorn earnestly.

"Don't mention it," Hawthorn replied, flushing a bit herself.

"Yes," Rhiannan concurred with a wide grin. "We were happy to have her. We all had a ton of fun."

I looked down to Amalie who nodded vigorously in agreement. I would have to keep them in mind when I needed someone to watch her in the future. However, I would have to set up childcare services for her too. Amalie needed structure, not to be shoved off on whichever of my friends were available at the moment.

"You've helped me more than I can express," I began, but Rhiannan held up a hand to stop me.

"I was happy to do it, and even if Hawthorn can speak for herself, she was too," Rhiannan said.

Hawthorn smiled. "It was a pleasure."

"Don't even think of trying to pay us," Rhiannan continued, eyes twinkling.

I rolled my eyes good-naturedly and squeezed Amalie tight.

"I wouldn't dream of it," I joked, earning a bright laugh from my friends. "Do you have all your stuff gathered up?" I asked Amalie.

She nodded and pulled away from me to grab her backpack from the entryway. She eyed Valentin warily, but he smiled and waved at her despite her surly behavior. It seemed he was determined to win more than one Deveraux girl over.

"I see things are looking up between you and Zima," Rhiannan commented wryly.

"What?" I asked, flushing again. "No, well, yes, I mean…"

"I'm only teasing," she laughed. "I'm glad you were able to work things out."

As Rhiannan continued to chatter, I looked over at Valentin, watching him speak with Amalie in such a serious manner that I nearly busted into giggles myself. It was so genuine and sweet; he seemed invested in what she was telling him.

When he caught me staring, he looked over and winked. I turned away in embarrassment. I could hardly focus on what Rhiannan was prattling on about because of the feeling of his eyes on me. By the time we said our goodbyes I was ready to collapse from the weight of his gaze alone.

As soon as we set foot back in the flat Amalie raced to my room to put away her things. From the silence in the place, I could safely assume that our teammates were now at the grocery store and would be returning soon.

A message from Félix confirmed that with a request for takeaway orders.

"Fé and the others want to know what we want from the takeaway place," I said to Valentin as I followed him down the hall to our rooms.

"Oh, the usual," he said pulling the plates of his leather

armor off, not looking up as I stood in his doorway.

"Okay," I squeaked out and turned away before he could remove anything else.

Hurrying to my room and closing my door behind me, I pressed my hand to my face. I needed to get a grip. Control myself. Valentin was making things much harder than they needed to be with his stupid loyalty and perfect face.

"What's wrong with you?" Amalie asked with her brows furrowed.

She was placing a book back on my shelf that she had borrowed while she stayed with Hawthorn and Rhiannan but had paused to stare at my dramatic entrance.

"Nothing," I said dismissively, waving off the question. "What do you want from the takeaway place? Everyone is too tired to cook."

"The one down the street?" she asked.

I nodded and she pulled the menu up on her holonav. She stared at the menu for a bit then closed her holonav screen with a swipe.

"Can I have the number four with rice? And make it spicy?" she requested, almost as though I would deny her.

"Of course, you can; it's whatever you want," I said, already typing our orders into the chat.

I barely even noticed that her chin had begun to wobble, but when I looked up her cheeks were only flushed and her eyes were glistening.

"Amalie?" I said, moving to press my hand to her forehead. "What's wrong, do you feel sick?"

"No," she whispered and wrapped her arms around my middle, burying her face in my stomach.

That couldn't have been comfortable, as I was still wearing my armor. I detangled myself from her momentarily to detach it, leaving only my plain black battlesuit, then pulled her back into my arms.

"What's wrong?" I asked her, brushing the hair from her face.

"I just missed you," she mumbled, hiding her face from me. "I thought you weren't coming back and I was scared. Now you're home and… I don't know how to describe how I'm feeling. It's happy, but also mad, and sad."

I held her tightly for a moment, glad she was expressing herself to me. Elated was a better word for it. I had been so concerned that she hated me for what happened with our parents and my arrest. For what happened to her because of it. For telling her off in front of my friends. It was clear she had complicated feelings about her current situation, but I was so happy she did not hate me.

"It's normal to have conflicting feelings," I reassured her. "It's good that you're trying to identify them. Thinking deeply instead of lashing out is a very mature thing to do."

Dr. Castillo, despite her infuriating loyalty to the NAF and Spec Ops, had some very good strategies for improving my relationship with Amalie. One was to wait until she was ready to speak to me, then to acknowledge her emotional autonomy, and praise her when she tried to relate to me or others. It sounded like it came straight from a childrearing manual… which it had.

She had given me a copy after one session where I had complained about Amalie's attitude not improving towards me or the others, even after starting therapy herself. It was cheesy, even patronizing at times, but it helped me understand that Amalie was going through something similar to me. And that I needed to help her before she became what I had changed into.

Bitter and angry.

"Daux," Amalie said, drawing my attention back to her. "Do you like Valentin?"

"What?" I sputtered, flushing at the sudden change in conversation.

"You know, like a crush?" she explained as though I needed it clarified in simple terms. "There is a boy in my online class with a crush on me, he says he likes me and wants to talk outside of class. So, do you have a crush on Valentin? Do you like him? You seem to want to talk to him an awful lot."

I blinked down at her upturned face and considered fleeing the room, but *he* – the topic of our discussion – was probably out there. I could not face running into him, not after what Amalie had just said. It would be too embarrassing.

"I… I am not sure," I said as honestly as I could.

"I think you're not being introspective," Amalie sniffed and squeezed my middle.

"That's a big word."

"I *am* almost twelve."

The look Amalie gave me looked so much like… well *me,* that I had to laugh. I was almost glad for this distraction so I did not have to ruminate over my guilt at being unable to disclose the full truth of our father's betrayal. I hardly wanted to tell her anything about it at all, much less all the horrible things he had done. Amalie kept giving me that look for a while before I sighed and replied to her statement.

"I *do* like Valentin," I said, ignoring the blush on my cheeks and her stare. "I more than like him. I don't know how to explain it; he and I have been through a lot together. We have grown a lot together. He cares about me… and about you too."

"You love him then," she stated matter-of-factly.

The truth Amalie spoke hit me like a tidal wave. It washed over me like a dam bursting from a neglected fissure. I had been ignoring my feelings for so long, knowing they were there but refusing to acknowledge them.

How could I when I had so much that I still needed to do? So many things to atone for? To burden Valentin with these feelings would be unfair to him. Now that Amalie had broken through that barrier that I had set up for myself, there was no ignoring my feelings any longer.

"I do," I choked out, tears blurring my vision and my

throat began closing in on itself. "I love him. I love Valentin more than I can comprehend."

"Not more than me though?" Amalie teased, satisfied that she had wheedled the truth out of me.

"No," I assured her. "Not more than you. Differently, I suppose, but not more."

"Good," she said and squirmed out of my arms. "I want to go watch a vid."

With that, almost as if our discussion had never happened, Amalie left the room. I barely even registered that she had said a boy from class *liked* her. I was left standing there, rubbing the tears from my eyes, unable to grasp the revelations Amalie had brought forth. I had thought it. I had *said* it.

That made it all true.

Every bit of it.

"Are you okay," Valentin asked.

I turned to see him standing in the doorway to my bedroom, his shoulder pressed into the doorframe. The way he leaned there, so casually as though he wasn't causing my heart to pound a mile a minute in my chest, made my brain malfunction.

My mouth opened and closed, gaping like a fish, but no words came out.

"Daux!" Amalie called from the common room. "Hurry, I want to pick together!"

"Amalie wants to watch a vid," I said hoarsely and pushed my way past him, trying to ignore the electric feeling that zapped through my battlesuit where we touched.

When I reached the common room, Amalie was seated on the couch remote in hand. She was searching excitedly through the digital archive of vids we had downloaded on our entertainment system.

"I want to watch something romantic," she said loudly, eyeing me with the knowing – and annoying – expression only siblings know how to make.

"Well, make sure it's age-appropriate," I snapped, flinging myself down onto the couch next to her.

"Isn't that *your* job?"

"I thought you were almost twelve? Surely you know how to regulate your media appropriately."

She just rolled her eyes at me but snuggled into my side. Eventually, we settled on an old vid, one about a woman who was promised to one man but was in love with another. A tale as old as time – one I would have lived had I not taken my life into my own hands. One Amalie might have had to endure had my father not defected and my mother not subsequently been arrested.

Once the beginning credits began to roll, Valentin ambled in, moving to sit in an armchair next to the couch. Amalie nearly screeched in protest, demanding he sit on the couch with us. Right. Next. To me.

I could have died right then. The ground could have opened up and swallowed me whole and I would not have cared. I would have been delighted even. Then I would not have had to endure an hour and fifty-eight minutes of torment orchestrated by my younger sister.

But such a fate was not meant to be, and I could feel that intoxicating electric spark through the layers of battlesuit and skin heading straight to my chest. It ignited the ember there, lighting a flame that blazed from the top of my head to the tips of my toes, turning my insides molten.

"I hope you don't mind if I join you," Valentin leaned over and whispered.

His breath brushed the shell of my ear and I forced back a shiver.

"Of course not," I whispered back.

Amalie shushed us from the other side of me and Valentin and I exchanged guilty, but simultaneously amused glances and settled back to watch the movie. Settled was *not* the right word though, because I couldn't settle down for the life of me.

Every little shift Valentin made beside me sent another spark straight to my heart. I felt like dying for the sensation of it. My body was as tense as a live wire and it felt as though every single one of his breaths was going to drive me over the edge into insanity.

I was not sure what I wanted more at that moment: to kiss him or to kill him.

The characters on the screen barely distracted me from my feelings. The only thing that kept me grounded was Amalie with her arms tight around my middle. Every gasp at the cheesy declarations of love, each jump when the characters did something exciting or disagreeable jolted me back into the present and reminded me to breathe.

At one point during the movie, I turned to find Valentin looking at me instead of the screen. His expression was pained, his blond hair messy, and his eyes slightly red. Longing flashed across his face and for a moment I was lost in the icy depths of his eyes. My breath hitched in my throat when I realized he was leaning toward me, closing the already short distance between us.

Slam!

The front door burst open, startling the two of us apart. Félix swaggered in, holding soft drinks and our takeaway orders aloft above his head with a long, loud cheer as he made his way to the dining area. Behind him strode Jax and Himawari, arms filled with groceries to last us until we could all make the trip together. Relief and irritation flooded through me, extinguishing the blazing heat that had been growing.

Amalie let out a disgruntled sigh and she stood from the couch, pausing the vid.

"What?" I asked her, my voice shaky and rough around the edges.

"Nothing," she said nonchalantly, stretching her hands above her head. "I'm hungry, we should go eat. Thanks for watching with us, Valentin."

"No problem," he responded, standing to his feet.

He sounded nonplussed as though nothing had happened between us at all.

They left the common area together, leaving me all alone. I blinked in surprise but stayed seated. How could Valentin act so normal? And why did Amalie sound so annoyed? Was she… had she been *watching* us?

Face flaming with embarrassment, I headed into the kitchen to help Jax and Himawari put away the groceries. I didn't think I could face Valentin or Amalie just yet, and if my friends noticed anything odd, they made no mention of it.

Once we all sat down to our meal, my face was schooled into an expression of calm. Or at least I thought it was because nobody asked me if anything was wrong or why I was making a face. Thankfully, dinner went off without incident. Amalie made no mention of Félix's eating habits, Valentin – other than sending me glances from across the table – behaved himself, and I didn't burn the flat to the ground.

In all, it went well.

We all finished the vid together, Amalie and Félix both in tears by the end with Jax consoling them both. Valentin still sat next to me but with *far* more distance between us than when we had started. Despite that, the electric feeling returned, running through us – through my veins – until I found myself as stiff as a statue by the time the film ended.

It burned through me and I could think of little else. It felt as though the air was being sucked from my lungs, from my bloodstream. Even the smallest of glances between us sent a jolt through me so powerful I was certain I would combust.

When the vid *finally* did end, Valentin stood abruptly and headed to the bathroom he shared with the boys. Soon, the sound of the shower could be heard and the others also began to disperse. Once we were all settled in our beds, I allowed myself to relax.

I had acknowledged my feelings for Valentin.

I had done that when I swore to myself that I would not.

There was no turning back from them now, though. The buzzing in my stomach and the tightness in my chest had been named, and that could not be taken away. What had I done? This was going to ruin everything. I couldn't let myself pursue this. Valentin, even if he did want me, deserved so much more than what I could offer him. No, I would push these feelings back and continue on as though nothing happened. I had my father to find, and I could not let anything stand in the way of that.

Chapter Twenty-One

A summons from the Overseer came the very next morning. Amalie had counseling all morning and her classes did not start until her session was over, so I did not need anyone to watch her unless we were sent out on another mission. Hopefully, that was not the case.

"Team Deveraux," the Overseer greeted when we entered her office. "Do sit down."

The Overseer's office was always neat, like her person, but today small holofiles were littered all over her desk, and older paper files in boxes sat scattered around waiting to be scanned into the system.

"Excuse the mess," she said unapologetically, waving a well-manicured hand at the boxes. "Some of these old files have become corrupted with age and system updates. My team and I are working to fix the issue. It just happens to be taking longer than we expected."

"Don't apologize," I said, injecting kindness into my voice. "You're incredibly busy. We understand."

"Yes," she mused, swiping through another file on her holonav. "I am. I have only called you in here today because of your current investigation. The information you have gathered has given us some important names and locations we need to be checked immediately."

"And by immediately you mean?" I prompted.

"You are scheduled to leave within the next few hours."

I almost shot from my seat. The Overseer knew – *she*

knew – that I had Amalie in my care. She *knew* I had been unable to set up childcare for her because as soon as I was cleared for assignments, I had been shipped off to Portnith.

As though he could sense my thoughts – my feelings – Valentin gave my hand a quick reassuring squeeze. I saw him shake his head imperceptibly from my periphery. My magic was strong, even if I was still recovering my full potential, but I knew I was no match for the Overseer in my current state. It would be more than foolish to act on my anger now and attack her. Valentin believed I was going to lash out verbally, which would also be a mistake.

No, the noxious feelings inside me burned too hot for verbal attacks. I wanted to sink my teeth into her, to burn her flesh until it was blackened and peeling.

I could see the look she was giving me. I had failed to respond in the mere seconds she had given me to do so since finishing her sentence.

My hands balled into fists, nearly crushing Valentin's fingers. I felt rather than saw him wince.

"With all due respect, ma'am," I began, injecting as much politeness into my voice as possible. "I have not had the opportunity to enroll my sister, Amalie, in any childcare services. I was not given a clear timeframe in which I was to be cleared for duty and have been unable to fill out the forms since I *was* cleared as I have been on assignment."

The Overseer raised a brow at me, then began tapping on her holonav without responding to me. The tension in the room could have been cut with the rapier I had strapped to my hip. Even without my foresight activated because I was still on temporary blockers while off assignment, I knew Jax would be sweating through his armor. Félix would be fidgeting with his stress ball, squeezing it so hard his rapidly strengthening fists would threaten the weak barrier of synthetic rubber with each clench. Himawari would look poised and composed, I knew from experience, but inside she would be screaming for someone, anyone, to say something and break the terrible silence.

"There," the Overseer said finally, lowering her arm and holonav. "I have expedited your childcare request. You have four days starting from the moment you step out of this office to choose an agency and a team of caretakers. I understand wanting to properly vet the caretakers, so send your choices to my assistants and they will run the necessary checks. Once they have been cleared, I will push the paperwork through personally. If you finish early, report back here and you will start your mission."

I nearly slumped over in relief, shocked at this kind of accommodation coming from the Overseer because of her apparent dislike of me since my father's escape.

"Thank you, ma'am," I said through teeth I was straining to unclench.

"I am not doing this for you, Deveraux," she shot back, smoothing back her numerous braids. "I may have my problems with you and your team, but your sister is innocent in all of this. I would hate for her to be mistreated due to the rushed nature of our line of work, and because I did not give you an adequate time to prepare."

"Thank you," I repeated, the tightness in my body refusing to release.

"While I take issue with your failure, and how you conduct your missions on occasion, I see no need to put your sister under any undue stress. It would be unfair."

What is unfair is mistreating me and holding me personally responsible for my father's actions. I thought.

I had wanted to say it aloud, but I was in the Overseer's bad books already and I *was* grateful that I had some time to procure care for Amalie, *and* had help in doing so.

I nodded my thanks to the Overseer and, without waiting to be dismissed, I stood. My teammates followed suit, though I wasn't surprised they did so. All four of them were fed up with being treated like traitors within the Spec Ops ranks. Such treatment from the highest of higher-ups made the feeling that much worse.

"Since you are likely in a hurry to set up all the necessary matters for your sister, Deveraux, I will be sending the debrief to all of your holonavs personally," the Overseer said as though we had not just disrespected her authority in her own office. "I do not want any outside help brought in on this mission, please. Your team only. I suggest Angelov look over and help plan while you are looking over agencies and workers."

"Of course, ma'am," I said stiffly.

Then I turned on my heel and stormed from the office. The others were not far behind. I could hear Jax whispering with Félix and Himawari at my flank. Valentin strode confidently beside me, his blond hair gleaming in the hard lights of the Spec Ops HQ hallways. It should have felt nice to have them validate my ire in this way, leaving the Overseer's offices before we had been formally dismissed, but I was too distracted by what I needed to do for Amalie.

I hated leaving her so soon when I had just gotten home. When she had just admitted that she was afraid I would never come back for her. The Overseer's assistants would know what red flags to look for in the potential candidates I chose; I knew I could trust them, but it felt like I was failing my sister by not doing it myself.

She deserved to interview potential workers with me. I did not want just anyone coming into our home to watch her. Or, if she were to go to an overnight facility, I would want to scope the place out personally so she could feel safe. However, due to my failure, that luxury was no longer available to me. Once again, I had failed Amalie.

A scream had been building in the back of my throat for the past hour and a half, and it was threatening to unleash itself on the whole flat. Amalie, as if sensing my bad mood, hurried off to find Valentin instead of helping me choose a childcare agency like she was supposed to. Probably to force him to play a game with her or watch another vid.

She had taken a real shine to him since she had forced me to admit my feelings for him, which only made those feelings that much stronger, seeing her clinging to his hand and leading him around the flat.

However, it wasn't that cute now when I was trying to set this up for *her* and she was off goofing around.

Breathe. I reminded myself.

Directing the air down low into my belly, I felt my diaphragm strain against my muscles and skin. Then I exhaled. In and out, in and out, in and out. In. And out. In. And out. In. Out. In. Out. In. Out.

Amalie was a child and I was her guardian. She did not have to be a part of this if she did not want to be. I could not force it on her, no matter how important it was for me that she had an opinion on her care. It was my responsibility. Not hers.

"Need some help?" Himawari asked.

I looked up to see her standing in my doorway, a soft look on her pretty face. The dark colors she wore were her signature as a shadowmancer – all greys, blacks, and violets – but they only enhanced her near-ethereal beauty. They never took away from the kind smile she gave our teammates and me.

"Yes," I sighed, shifting on my settee so she could sit down next to me.

"What's bothering you?" she asked once she joined me, peeking over at my holonav.

So much. I thought, but could not bring myself to say it aloud.

I sighed again.

Himawari waited patiently, silent and open, until I was ready to speak. She was always like that, a gentle presence when the need arose. On the job she was fierce – a force to be reckoned with – and bullheaded to a fault. But at home…

At home, she was as gentle as an elder sister trying to coax a younger sibling to dry their tears. Himawari was a protector and a comforter and I had never been more grateful to know her.

I took a deep breath, noticing that she mirrored the action. Then I spoke.

"Amalie isn't interested in helping me choose a childcare service for her," I complained, letting my head fall into my hands, obscuring Himawari's view of my holonav.

"She *is* eleven," Himawari reminded me wryly. "Most eleven-year-olds I know would not be interested in choosing their babysitters, much less want to entertain the idea of being babysat."

"That…" I paused my argument, reflecting on what Himawari had just said.

Amalie had wanted to play a game with me and Valentin. *I* could not play a game as I had a limited amount of time to vet a very long list of candidates who would potentially be caring for my sister. So, I told them they could play together when Amalie showed decreasing interest in helping me.

I could not give her whatever she wanted, as much as I wanted to, as much as it might ease my guilt. Amalie was old enough to understand that I was doing something for her benefit, but that did not mean she was at a place where she was ready to be an active participant in her upbringing. She deserved gentleness and she needed time to play. I could not hold it against her that she was more interested in playing with me and my teammates than helping me care for herself.

"You *are* right," I said finally through a tight throat. "I'm just overwhelmed and I didn't want her to think I didn't care about her opinion on this."

"Even if she does think that," Himawari began reassuringly as she slipped an arm around my shoulders, "she will come to understand that is not the case. Why don't we go through some together and have Amalie weed through a handful of our top picks with you after supper?"

I could have cried with relief. Not only did I have less than two days to go through all these agencies, I had to go through individuals working there for in-home care if Amalie wanted to stay in the flat. Himawari had just offered me a lifeline.

A screech and a crash coming from the direction of the common area jolted the two of us from our embrace and we rushed into the hallway to see what had caused the commotion.

Amalie stood in the center of the common room atop the coffee table with a toy firearm in her small hands. Jax was lying face down on the rug, seemingly playing dead, all of the couch cushions scattered about the floor. Félix was tied up to a floor lamp with a sock gag in his mouth, begging us to save him with his eyes. Valentin had another toy firearm – the twin to Amalie's – in his hands, his aim was trained on Amalie from behind mine and Himawari's bathroom door.

All of them looked up at us when we rushed into the room.

Then Amalie's firearm misfired a foam bullet into the back of Jax's head, lodging itself into the coils of his wet washday hair.

Himawari and I exchanged a look, both of us attempting to stifle our laughter – I bit my lip and she covered her mouth with her hand.

Then Valentin fired at Amalie while she was distracted, and nearly as soon as the foam projectile hit her side, she launched herself off the coffee table and into a small pile of couch cushions, hollering in mock agony. Her cries did not lessen until moments later when they transformed into an alarmingly accurate death rattle. Then she fell silent.

Félix began screaming through his gag to be rescued and Valentin started toward him to remove his bonds but stopped, staring down at Amalie for a moment before raising his toy firearm and putting a foam bullet between her eyes.

Her tiny body gave a jerk, then fell still, her hands falling open and her firearm clattering from her hand.

Himawari and I watched, enraptured by the little drama unfolding before us. Then Valentin did the unthinkable.

Félix thrashed and screamed as his supposed rescuer aimed the firearm at him and fired. Félix slumped over instantly, but when he did Amalie sat up whispering furiously at Valentin.

I caught snippets like, "No! *I'm* supposed to be the bad guy!" and "I was going to come back from the dead once you rescued him and kill you both!"

I am sure I would have overheard more, but Himawari was already dragging me away, back to my room. Once inside with the door shut the two of us collapsed into fits of giggles. I could not speak even if I had wanted to. Any air I sucked down immediately was exhaled in laughter and my ribs ached for want of trying to inhale normally.

We could still hear their bickering from behind my closed door, which did not help with the uncontrollable laughter. Anytime we got remotely calmed down a noise would come from down the hall, or Himawari and I would just look at each other and it would set us off again.

Eventually, Himawari grasped my hand and squeezed as tightly as she could while holding her breath. Her face began to purple and I stopped laughing long enough to try and stop her, panic rising in my chest.

"Himawari!" I exclaimed breathlessly.

"I'm fine! I'm okay!" she gasped finally, clutching our entwined hands to her chest. "I just—I needed to stop laughing. I couldn't breathe."

"And asphyxiating yourself is the only way to fix that?"

"It wasn't asphyxiation, I was holding my breath. It's nearly impossible to asphyxiate yourself that way."

I just rolled my eyes, then bit my lip in an attempt to stave off laughter again.

"Don't you start!" Himawari admonished, grabbing my

wrist to activate my holonav. "We have childcare agencies and workers to vet and we can't waste any more time."

That sobered me up and I entered my passcode, unlocking my holonav to reveal the page I had left off on. "Right, so… I can share some of these with you. But it will take a while since I have barely made it through a fourth of them."

"Did you filter any out?" Himawari asked, unlocking her holonav.

I had already thought to filter out any agencies that wouldn't line up with the care I wanted, or needed, for Amalie. However, that still left far too many to go through without help. Once again, I felt a rush of affection for Himawari and her kindness.

"What?" she asked when she caught me looking at her.

"I love you," I said, even though the words burned my throat when they came out.

A pretty pink blush tinted Himawari's cheeks at my declaration, and she busied herself with the incoming agency files on her holonav to distract herself from her embarrassment.

After a beat, she looked up at me, her jaw working. "I love you too," she said, then looked back down at her holonav, signaling that was the end of our exchange.

I didn't blame her for her embarrassment. She was the kind of person who did things for others without expecting anything in return. An expression of gratitude or affection would turn her into a blushing mess and she would deny any thanks.

We as a team needed to do better at making sure she accepted praise and make sure she knew that all of us appreciated her. She deserved it.

We worked in silence for the remainder of the afternoon, our quietness punctuated by cries and screams of agony as my sister terrorized our other teammates with her games of action and intrigue. By supper, we had whittled down the list into something more manageable for me to go over with Amalie, or with help from the rest of my team.

Once again, I was struck with the notion that I would be unable to do much of anything without my team. I relied on them far too much. But was that really a bad thing?

As Himawari and I finished up and made our way to the dining room, I felt a conflicted air settle in the space in my chest. How could I keep pushing them away when I needed them so desperately? I knew the answer to that question already. I could not.

Chapter Twenty-Two

Finally, I was getting somewhere. With Himawari's help, I had made it through half of the agencies and had selected a handful to look over with Amalie should she want to, like we had the night prior. Hopefully, she would work with me on choosing her favorites and then I would go through the remaining agencies and we would repeat the process until we came to a decision.

It was unlikely we would be going with a boarding agency, considering Amalie was still under surveillance and Spec Ops would want to keep her here at the flat. Himawari had thought of that while we were going through the agencies that morning, which once we filtered those agencies out, made our load a lot lighter. Soon I would be finished with all of this and I could rest easy that Amalie would be cared for whenever I was away.

My sister and I sat on the couch together after breakfast that morning, music from Amalie's favorite band playing softly from the entertainment system. She was sprawled out on the large sofa, her feet digging into my thigh as she looked over the agencies I had picked this morning. There were three added to last night's two, for a total of five agencies with specific caretakers for her to choose from so far. I was looking over her counselor's guardian notes, the things I was allowed to see from her sessions, along with her report card from this quarter of the semester.

The notes were nothing starting, they documented

Amalie's frustration with life – especially with me. I had expected as much. I went from being a big sister she looked up to, to a parent and someone who took away the only way of life she had known. At least, that was how she saw it; though, it was our parents who took that from her.

The counselor understood that, and encouraged me in her notes to be patient with Amalie. Regression would be normal after a bout of progress, and allowing my anger or frustration to take hold would only reinforce certain core beliefs Amalie had about herself, and the world.

The counselor's note also informed me that Amalie was showing renewed interest in interacting with her peers, as I had witnessed last night with her dramatic mock gunfight with my male teammates. I knew Félix had loads of cousins and a few younger siblings. Maybe I could set up something with him so she could interact with kids her own age once this situation with my father settled down. And there were also kids from her online class to think about. Kids who would not have been there for the humiliating moment Spec Ops had pulled her out of class after my mother's arrest.

The amount of relief the counselor's notes gave me was insurmountable, even if Amalie was still experiencing these negative feelings toward me. I was just glad she was beginning to understand that I was not trying to make life miserable for her; that I was trying to help her.

The small spark of happiness that flowed through me at the thought of her interacting with other kids face to face was a welcome reprieve from the constant heaviness and strain of the emotions I had been carrying. For a moment, I felt like my old self again.

I had always intended to try to convince my parents to allow Amalie to live with me once I had gotten established as a Spec Ops agent. They most likely would not have allowed it, considering Amalie had magic and they did not want me to find out about it. But I would have tried.

I was not prepared for the responsibility another human

being was, or the toll it took on a body. She was worth it though, trying to figure all this out. Amalie was worth everything.

"Daux," she said from behind the translucent screen of her holonav.

"Hmm?" I hummed, looking over the notes on her report card from her teacher.

"I still like the ones from yesterday better." Amalie's voice was soft, hesitant.

As though I might be angry with her for interrupting, or making an autonomous choice. Or both. The gentle warmth that had been building inside me as I looked over the positive notes from her counselor and teacher was extinguished instantaneously. Once again, she was afraid because of something my parents had instilled in her.

Inhaling deeply, making sure it was calm and even so as not to spook her, I turned and smiled as genuinely as I could. The fear in Amalie's expression waned before my eyes even before I opened my mouth. A good sign.

"That's okay," I reassured her. "Those are all very good agencies, and I liked the ones from last night better too. I just wanted you to have options. It is ultimately you who will be spending time with the caretakers, so you deserve a voice."

Her lips began to wobble slightly and it was a few moments before she spoke again, her little throat bobbing in desperate attempts to swallow her emotions. I waited patiently for her to get her words out, knowing if I moved to hug her or force her to speak, she would clam up.

"Thank you," she whispered, not trusting her voice to go an octave louder.

"Of course. I love you," I said and patted her knee before turning back to her report card.

A moment later she whispered back, "I love you too."

Hours later, my hands balled into fists at my sides, I stood outside my grandparents' senior care facility. I stared up at the old building marveling at its old-world beauty on one hand, and on the other, I was seething with anger and resentment. I could barely force myself to climb the hand-carved limestone steps – each step feeling as though I was being weighed down by lead weights.

It truly was a pretty building – large and stately with brownstone exterior and navy-blue shutters on each of its many, many windows. Columns rose in the front, more for decoration than support, giving the building even more of a distinguished aura. Had I been younger, maybe I would have been happier that my grandparents were staying here. Perhaps I would have been excited to visit them.

Right now, however, it felt as though I were marching to my execution. Or into a sentencing. I knew in my very bones that this visit was not going to be pleasant for any of us. I just had to keep my cool.

Keep your head on and everything will be fine. I thought, placing my hand on the shiny brass doorknob with trepidation. *Don't start a fight in the old folks' home.*

Valentin had promised to meet me at the Home after running some last-minute errands of his own, but he was late. It was well past eleven-thirty now, and I had no more time to waste. The Overseer had given me four days to get care settled for Amalie, and that time was nearly up. I had to work out everything now. Unfortunately, my grandparents needed to be a part of those plans if something were to happen to me.

It hurt to think that the grandparents I loved so much gave up as easily as they did when it was so obvious my parents were abusing me, abusing Amalie. Even if they couldn't have saved us from them, my grandparents *could* have done something. They could have slandered my father and outed him as a bigot. They knew first-hand how evil he was. They prided themselves as people who were descendants of those praised freedom fighters in the war.

Why had my grandparents not done anything?

Why had they not saved me?

Pain lanced up my arm and I looked down to see the brass doorknob glowing in my hand. I dropped it immediately and summoned a small gust of wind to, hopefully, cool down the metal before someone else burned themselves on it.

Soon, the knob stopped glowing and I looked down to see my hand was bright red. There was no blistering or burned skin – probably due to my affinity for the element of fire – which was a relief. I could not afford to get into trouble for harming someone accidentally. Not when I was supposed to be taking blockers. I could not explain what was happening with the blockers and why my magic was fighting against them… It was unsettling.

I looked around me, spotting several security cameras lining the porch with one situated directly above the front door.

A sigh escaped me and I shook my head. I was surely caught now. Hopefully, the people manning the security desk would not review the footage and I would not have Spec Ops agents on my tail as soon as I left, waiting to arrest me for breaching the 'deal' I had made with them.

Without another moment's hesitation, I yanked the door open and stepped inside. The home was just as nice inside as it was outside. Wall-to-wall carpet in a deep navy to prevent slipping, with the beadboard walls stained a deep brown and gleaming like they had been freshly polished. Eclectic lamps and light fixtures lit the entrance, giving the effect that I was entering a grand party.

It was *very* old world in its design. I knew my grandfather would have picked it because of my grandmother's love of pretty things. The fact that I knew that hurt.

Steeling my spine, I marched up to the reception desk. It

was a solid rosewood and polished with a mirror-like shine so that I could see my reflection in it. Behind it sat a young man with brown skin and curly black hair wearing a navy suit jacket. When he saw me, he offered me a genial smile and began gathering what I assumed to be a sign-in book and a pen.

"Hello, and welcome to Heliorious Senior Living Home," he said in a musical, but soft voice. "Please sign and date your name here and who you will be visiting."

I offered a tight smile and signed my name, then my grandparents' names on the indicated line. The book was heavy, bound in rich leather, and filled with thick cream paper which was embossed with elegant script and lines to indicate what should be signed where. The pen, too, was heavy in my hand as I slowly wrote each letter of my name with painstaking care.

I did not want to risk burning the book or crushing the pen in my hand while I wrote.

"Daux Deveraux to see Alma and William Winchester on Godsday, the thirteenth of Trenquillity, eleven-fifty-five a.m."

"Oh, you're here to see the Winchesters," he commented, his smile growing as he looked at my signature. "That's wonderful! They hardly ever get outside visitors. You must be one of their granddaughters."

"Yes, I am," I said, trying to sound cordial. "Where and when can I see them?"

"Well, according to their schedule they will be resting in their private rooms," the man explained, looking briefly at his holonav. "But we can bring them down to the common area if they are up for it."

"No, I would rather see them privately. If they are resting, I would hate to drag them down here when I am perfectly capable of going to see them."

With a pang, I realized that not too long ago, I would have been unable to walk up a flight of stairs, much less down a hallway to see my grandparents in the home's common room. I wondered if some of the people here felt as trapped as I had. The familiar wash of guilt found me once again.

I was angry at my grandparents, but maybe they could not have done anything to save me and Amalie. Maybe they saw their decline and knew they would have been unable to do much of anything. But their lack of trying? I was only able to escape my parents by going to the Academy, and Amalie with Father's defection and Mother's arrest.

Anger and guilt swirled and boiled in my stomach as some fresh-faced carer with choppy brown hair and a pretty smile led me to my grandparents' rooms. She wore scrubs, indicating she dealt with more of the demanding tasks of the Home. They were navy, as was what seemed to be the uniform color around here, and pristine. It gave the impression that even if this was a care home, it was a high-class establishment – if the décor was not enough of an indication.

"Here we are," the carer said, knocking on the door lightly before keying in and opening it. "Mr. and Mrs. Winchester, you have a visitor!"

Notes of tuberose, orange blossom, and amber wafted through the open doorway. A hint of coffee and pipe smoke filtered through the bright smell of my grandmother's signature perfume. Heart pounding, I hesitated in the doorway, peering into the sun-filled suite.

It was as if my grandparents had been frozen in time. Other than a few extra lines on their faces, and more white shooting through their hair than grey, they looked very much the same. There was nothing to indicate any reason they would be unwell enough that they could not respond to my note.

They sat at a small dining table; remnants of their finished breakfast strewn about the red checked tablecloth. A newspaper – *"The Rising Sun"* one of the only physical printings left in Heliorious, often exclusively delivered to facilities such as this – dangled from my grandfather's strong, but liver-spotted hands.

My grandmother was dressed in a bottle green dress and her hair was done up in an elegant chignon. Her makeup was even done. It was as though she was expecting company. Expecting me.

In her hand was a book, an old romantic story about star-crossed lovers during the Wartime era. A popular novel even today, but one she had read to me often when I was young. It had a place in my heart and on my bookshelf.

I knew the first line like the back of my hand.

"My little Deer," Grandmother whispered when she caught sight of me, bringing a delicate hand to her lips.

And I stared, like my nickname, fear flooding every molecule of my being. What should I say? What should I do? Since I had last seen my grandparents, I had become so many things. I had been Placed, become a Spec Ops team leader, brave, loved. Then I became a failure and a killer. All in the name of a system that hated me. What would they think of me now? The thought alone paralyzed me.

Chapter Twenty-Three

I straightened my spine as far as I could and stepped into the room, very aware of the one-person audience we had with the carer cleaning up after my grandparents' breakfast. Once I was halfway through their living room, making my way toward the kitchen and dining area, I paused once again in fear.

This was a mistake.

My grandfather stood from his chair, the newspaper falling from his lap. His blue eyes were watery, but not from age. Tears welled in the corners of his eyes and fell gently over his wrinkled cheeks.

I flinched instinctively, taking a few steps back before knocking into something hard. The smell of magic and mint enveloped me.

"Valentin," I said without turning around.

"I told you I would be here," he whispered, brushing his cool fingers over my shoulders.

"You are *late*," I bit out with a smile.

He only chuckled in response. I could have punched him.

Valentin promised to do this with me, promised to stop me if I got too angry or tried to run away. I was almost disappointed he showed up. I *wanted* to run away. I wanted to scream and cry, to throw a tantrum like a child. But he was here now, and I no longer had any of those options.

How ironic it was that Valentin Angelov was now my conscience.

"Daux, is that truly you?" Grandfather asked in a voice that was slightly shakier than I remembered. "Your eyes… They look so different."

"Yes," I replied stiffly. "It's me. And I am wearing glasses, that might be why."

My grandparents exchanged glances with each other, then turned back to face me. I could not discern what passed between them at that moment, but panic spiked in my heart. They had perfected the decades-long art of speaking without words, and even with my foresight had not been able to decipher such a language.

"Will you introduce us to your friend?" Grandmother asked, leaving the subject of my eyes alone, and stood from her seat with the same elegance I remembered from my childhood.

I wanted to dig my heels in, to resist the politeness of this interaction. But my *conscience* would not let me, even if I decided to do so.

"This is Valentin Angelov; we are in Spec Ops together and he is my teammate," I said, stepping to the side so I was no longer blocking Valentin from view. "Valentin, these are my grandparents, Alma and William Winchester."

I was fully aware of how wooden and formal I sounded, cringing internally at the sound of the words leaving my mouth.

"Pleasure to meet you," Valentin said amicably, striding across the room to shake my grandfather's hand.

"And you," Grandfather said, shaking Valentin's hand warmly.

"Thank you for coming to see us," Grandmother said, moving to shake Valentin's hand as well. "Both of you."

Words failed me, causing an awkward silence to fall over the four of us. The carer hurried from the room after finishing her cleanup and closed the door softly behind her. The sound made me jump, deafening in the silence.

"Daux," Grandmother said soothingly. "Why don't we

sit down and talk about why you're here?"

I stared for a moment, then nodded. I allowed my grandmother to lead me to the pink velvet couch, settling myself stiffly next to her. Valentin sat next to me and my grandfather took his place in the brown leather armchair next to the couch.

After a moment, and a nudge from Valentin, I spoke, "Amalie has magic and she didn't know a thing about it."

My grandparents shared another glance, then turned back to me.

"We hoped this wouldn't happen," Grandmother said with a sigh.

I schooled my expression and my tone into neutrality. "So, you anticipated it potentially happening?" I asked.

"Yes," Grandfather said, guilt and regret dripping from his words.

I almost hated him for it.

I wanted to hate him for feeling anything akin to guilt when he did *nothing* to save me and Amalie. It would have been so easy, but all I felt was pity, and I hated myself for that instead of him.

"I want to wean her off blockers, but I am currently scheduled to leave the country for an indefinite period to try and track down my father, or anyone who may have been involved in his defection," I explained, my hands balling into fists on my lap.

"Daux is working on setting up a team of carers to watch over Amalie while we are gone," Valentin continued for me, squeezing my wrist. "While they may be equipped to care for Amalie if she is weaning off, we don't feel safe doing so not being present. And there is always a chance that any of us may not return."

My grandparents caught on quickly.

"Once we were placed in here by our daughter – your mother, Daux – we were deemed unfit to care for either you or Amalie should we request that," Grandmother started, her voice shaking.

I stopped her.

"What do you mean Mother put you in here?" I nearly shouted, standing from my place on the couch. "The records say you voluntarily entered the facility!"

"Daux," My grandfather coaxed, as though I were a wild animal that needed gentle treatment. "Please, sit down. Let us explain."

"How am I supposed to believe anything you say?" I seethed, feeling the ember in my chest sparking to life, igniting the fire in my veins.

"Daux," Valentin snapped.

My head jerked toward the sound of his voice, the ember exploding with a vengeance before dimming at the ice in his eyes. I took a deep breath and released it through my mouth, then sat down again, my movements ridged and jerky.

"You are right not to trust us Daux," Grandfather murmured, leaning forward in his chair. "But please, let us explain. You and your sister were not the only victims of your parents' lies and abuse."

I tensed at his words. Could it be true that my grandparents had not abandoned me?

It turns out that it could. That it was.

Shortly after my father had forbidden my grandparents from seeing Amalie and me, my mother had begun her cruel tricks – at my father's behest of course. That came as no surprise to me. What did surprise me was the extent of my mother's gaslighting.

It had gotten to the point that both my grandparents were convinced they were ailing and unable to live alone anymore, despite their physicians and healers finding nothing wrong with them. They, at my mother's encouragement, checked themselves into Heliorious Senior Living Home not long after.

Now they were considered infirm because of the "mental break" they had, witnessed by my mother, and were under constant observation and care. It was not until my mother's arrest had their freedoms started coming back to them. The staff was finally beginning to see that they were in their right minds and always had been.

"So, you… you were basically prisoners," I said, hot, angry tears gathering in my eyes.

"Yes," Grandmother replied, her wizened hands gripping mine tightly, unafraid of the magic that could spew forth and burn her.

How had I not seen it? How had I allowed myself to be manipulated by my parents yet again? They wanted animosity between my grandparents and me. They would be happy to know that I was at odds with them. My parents would be pleased to know they were winning.

"Our imprisonment was not nearly the same as yours, Daux, but we were prisoners all the same," Grandmother continued.

Her fingers squeezed mine so hard I could barely feel the blood flowing. My incarceration had been horrific, but surely theirs' had been terrible as well. They were stripped of decision-making rights, they could not contact me or Amalie for fear of retaliation by my parents, and they were at the mercy of the state. Only now, with my parents uncovered treason, were they beginning to regain some of those rights.

My anger towards them began to ebb. They could not have done anything to help me, not with what had been done to them. To be angry with them would be futile, and erroneous.

Valentin's hand found my wrist, his thumb stroking over my thundering pulse point. My heart stuttered in my chest, painfully aware of his presence here and what it meant to me. What it could mean that he was here at all?

I pulled air into my lungs and looked between my grandparents as I exhaled. I could forgive them. What happened was not their fault, not at all. However, now I knew what I needed to do. What I should have done ages ago. It was time to see my mother.

Valentin had insisted I wait until the following day, Mournsday, to see my mother. I had just had a horrible truth revealed to me and needed a clear head and a fresh start if I wanted anything to come of my visit with my mother. I hated it when he was right.

Besides, I had wanted to rush from the senior living home and storm the interrogation chambers where my mother was likely being held. That would not have boded well for me, as it would be seen as an act of aggression toward Spec Ops on my part; though my ire was only directed at one specific person in the building at the moment.

Valentin had been able to calm me enough for me to complete my original intention for the visit. Since my grandparents' condition was finally being investigated, they would be able to at least take charge of Amalie's care should something happen to me. Along with this, my grandparents requested that I bring Amalie around for a visit as soon as I returned from my upcoming mission, which I reluctantly agreed to. If I had believed my grandparents abandoned me, then Amalie was probably led to think the same, if not something worse.

Valentin and I were also able to have someone from the home contact Spec Ops to open a line of communication for the investigation into what happened to my grandparents. Although, that was pretty cut and dry. But these things needed to be on "paper" – more like in a database, as paper was hardly used anymore – for anything to happen.

It seemed as though my parents' treachery had gone further than even I had anticipated. The very thought prompted a deep feeling of unease to settle in my gut. Just how far did the web of their lies and deceit go?

I waited until Amalie was sitting in the dining room doing her online classes before slipping out. I sent a message in our team chat to remind everyone where I would be going and to make sure Amalie got her homework done in case I wasn't back in time.

My heart was racing in my chest long before I made it to Spec Ops HQ. Headquarters did not have a prison – not officially. Since it was not a traditional prison, it was not legally zoned or labeled as such, and therefore not known to the public.

My elevated heart rate did not just have to do with visiting my mother. It had more to do with the fact that just a few short weeks ago, I was imprisoned here. I had no desire to relive those memories. But I had to know why my mother chose a man who left her to this fate over her parents. Over her *children*.

Dev met me in the lobby, grim-faced and somber.

"Zima said to be expecting you," he said, holding his hand out for me to shake.

I raised a brow at it.

Was he serious? Did he expect me to shake his hand after he tortured me for weeks straight, all the while knowing I was innocent?

I guessed not, because he dropped the appendage as though I had burned him – which was impossible as I had taken a temporary blocker this morning – as I was required to do – just in case my emotions got the best of me today.

Having the grace to look shamefaced, Dev gestured for me to follow him and led the way through a maze of unfamiliar halls until we reached a lift. A lift I remembered very well. I was drugged up the last time I set foot in it, but I remembered it like it was yesterday.

I dug my fingernails into my hands to keep from dwelling on the memory. I was here of my own free will now. They were not going to put me back in that room. Not without a fight.

I did not deign to speak as the lift took us up to the correct floor of the prison. I was too focused on slowing my heart rate to be polite – not that I was very interested in being polite to Dev at the moment.

He made no motion to speak to me either. I was just fine with that.

Once the doors slid open, I followed Dev down the white hallway, soothed by the sounds of my boots thudding against the flooring. Sound was not permitted in this wing, but I was not an interrogator. So, I let my footfalls thud louder against the floors until we came to my mother's door.

"I want to warn you before you go in," Dev began, shooting me a concerned glance. "She's not in her right mind. She might not even recognize you."

I struggled to bite back a laugh. "I am not sure she ever was in her right mind."

Dev stared at me a moment, lips pressed tightly together before nodding and unlocking the door. I stepped inside the bright room, blinking a bit against the bright white that had seared itself into my mind's eye long ago.

"I'm going to have to lock you in," Dev said, closing the door slowly. "But I will be right outside. Just signal at the camera in the corner of the room. I will be watching the feed on my holonav and let you out."

"Thanks," I whispered.

He closed the door behind me fully and I heard the lock click into place. Strangely, I did not feel panicked. For some reason, I trusted that Dev was not going to keep me locked in here with my mother.

My mother…

It took me a moment to find her, but it was a spartan room. As soon as my eyes fell upon the lump on the cot in the corner, I knew it was her.

Stepping forward, the squeak of my boots against the floor caused her head to shoot up from the bed. When she caught sight of me, she whirled on the cot and sprang to her feet, only making it a few steps before restraints connected to the wall behind her jerked her backward.

"You!" Mother howled, her voice hot and wild as a beast.

"Me," I whispered.

My mother was a beautiful woman; age had not changed that. But whatever happened between now and the time I saw her last did. Her face was visibly lined and sallow, her hair lank and dirty, falling around her shoulders in matted clumps, looking browner than blonde it was so caked in oil. Her nails, which were usually long and painted red, were free of polish and bitten to the quicks. And her blue irises were now a muddy color that stood out starkly against her pale skin.

I had always thought my mother was one of the most beautiful women in the world, despite her ugly heart. Now she was wan and disturbed. The sight of her eyes so changed sent a wave of fear through me. What was happening? Why were my eyes changing? My mother's? My teammates'?

"What do *you* want?" she spat, spittle gathering in the corners of her cracked lips.

"Why did you have my grandparents stripped of their rights?" I asked, moving to stand just out of reach. "They were your parents! How could you do that to them?"

"I have only done what *you* have done to me and your father!" Mother screamed.

"*Father* defected. *You* helped him. My grandparents' only crime was loving me!" I raged back, looking down my nose at her.

Disgust could not even begin to describe how I felt. It was far deeper than that. How dare she compare her actions to my own? My parents committed *crimes* – moral and societal. I was innocent on all charges. Blameless, despite being blamed.

How dare she compare me to herself.

"You always were stupid," she hissed, reaching for me

with hands that formed claws. "Weak and stupid. Fascinated with that *curse.*"

"My *magic* is not a curse," I snapped, looming over her. "The only curse I have ever had the misfortune to endure was being born to a selfish *bitch* like you!"

She recoiled at my words, shocked that I would speak to her in such a way. I had not so much as argued with her since I was a small child and had not known that speaking out of turn would get me slapped.

Then she smiled. It was an ugly thing to behold.

"There is that nasty little mouth," she jeered, her lips bleeding slightly from the wide grin she displayed. "Only an unsightly little creature such as yourself would speak to her mother in such a way. You are scarred and pale, your skin is dry, and your *hair*! Oh, darling girl, only a vile little beast would speak to a loving mother in such a hateful way."

"Aren't you one to talk? Have you looked in a mirror lately? Do not make me laugh! You have never been a mother. A monster, yes, that suits you much better," I murmured, disgust leeching into my voice, my expression.

A monster…

I looked down my nose at the woman who had given birth to me, realizing I had surpassed her in height if not anything else. It was astonishing what this place had done to her, my once beautiful mother. I tried not to think about what I had looked like sealed away in here, but I could not help but wonder if this room had brought out the monstrousness in both of us. Mother's was just more visible at the moment. I had been bathed since my time locked away here.

"Yes," I sneered. "Monstrous. Simply monstrous, Mother. Your insides match your outsides now."

"How dare you!" she screamed, thrashing against her bonds. "How dare you, how dare you, how dare you! You little witch, you evil little beast! I wish your father would have brought you with him if only to hand you over to that Gladwin – oh, yes, he would love to have a 'chat' with you after what you did!"

My mother's tirade stopped just as quickly as it had started, her eyes bulging in their sockets, making her gaunt face appear even more skeletal. Her shackled hands slapped over her cracked lips as though she could take back the words that had spilled out. Like she wished to pull them back from the ether they had evaporated into. She had slipped up; she had said something she was not supposed to. It was not my intention to cause her to do so, but I could not stop the triumphant grin that spread across my face. Gladwin again? The facts were beginning to add up and I couldn't help the euphoric spark that danced in my chest.

"Thank you, Mother," I said, leaning forward to kiss her protruding cheekbone.

Then I signaled to the camera in the corner of the room, narrowly avoiding her clawed fingers as they slashed at me. I had heard enough. It was not what I had come to hear, but it was enough. The door opened, revealing Dev's familiar grim face and I exited into the hall, relishing in my mother's howl of agony as I made my way solemnly back to the lift.

Chapter Twenty-Four

I need to see the Overseer," I said, approaching the secretary's desk.

She looked up at me, pressing her glasses back up her nose. I could never remember her name. It was something like Rachel… Raquel? Rebecca? It did not matter now.

"She's busy," Rachel, Raquel, Rebecca said squinting down at her holonav.

"It's important," Dev said from behind me.

His deep, smooth voice startled the secretary from whatever schedule or file she was looking at.

"Oh… Oh, of course, right away, Dev," she fluttered, standing from her desk and rushing to the inner offices where the Overseer and her assistants worked.

"Are they ever going to take me seriously again?" I complained, running a hand through my short hair.

"It pays to have someone like me behind you," Dev chuckled.

His laughter died down when I shot him a look, but he was right. Dev could still decide that I was suspicious and worth that title, but he trusted me; though, I did not know why. In addition, he *did* apologize to me when he came to release me. And he helped me now, which I did not expect him to do after I purposely vomited on his shoes the last time I saw him.

I still can't trust him. I thought hatefully as we waited for the secretary – whose name I still could not remember – to bring us back to the Overseer's inner office.

It was only a moment later that she returned, red-faced and flustered.

"She wants to see you now, I apologize for earlier, she has a busy schedule," she explained, but I brushed passed her before she finished speaking.

I stormed past the assistants and their desks, ignoring their stares and the way they rose from their seats as if to apprehend me, and slammed the Overseer's door open.

To her credit, she remained seated, staring cooly up at me from her leather chair.

"Deveraux," she said cordially, as though I had stopped by for a casual visit.

"Did you know my father was affiliated with Captain Gladwin?" I demanded, striding up to the desk.

The Overseer blinked up at me, her mouth falling open a fraction of an inch. It was the most surprised I had seen her in a long time. The most emotion other than distaste I had seen from her in even longer.

"I will take that as a 'no'," I said.

"I need more context on this, Deveraux," the Overseer said slowly, rising to her full height. "I need verification. Where did you hear this information? Who is your source?"

I was not a short woman by any means, but the Overseer towered over me, her lithe frame shaking with what I could discern was fear and anticipation. She had no idea. Granted, neither had I, but I was shocked.

All it took was for me to insult my mother just a little bit for her to spill an important bit of treason that threatened the international security of the NAF. It seemed like it was more than the interrogators had been able to learn in the few short weeks since her arrest.

"I can't verify the truth of the claim," Dev called from the doorway. "But I can verify Daux's source. I was watching the camera feed from Annette Deveraux's cell as

Daux was speaking to her. Annette admitted in a fit of rage that Charles Deveraux was going to meet Captain Gladwin once he escaped – and that Gladwin had it out for Daux."

I turned, not expecting this show of support from Dev, and he smiled apologetically at me. I nodded, somewhat dazed, and turned back to the Overseer, whose face had become a mask of calm. She stepped around her desk, moving to stand directly in front of me, and placed her hand on my shoulder.

I resisted the urge to bare my teeth and shake her off. Resisted the urge to spit at her feet.

"You can check the security footage if you do not trust Dev's word. He will have it recorded on his holonav," I supplied, steeling my spine against the weight of her onyx-eyed gaze.

"Thank you," she whispered fiercely. "I know you know what this means, so I will not insult your intelligence by summarizing, but you have broken this case wide open for us. I am glad you convinced me to wait to send you away."

"Me too," I said, shrugging her hand off my shoulder. "I still need to pick a caretaker for my sister."

I made it halfway to the door where Dev stood waiting for me, before pausing and turning back. "I will be ready to go by the deadline, if things have changed, please let me and my team know so we can prepare accordingly."

The Overseer nodded grimly, and I left with Dev following on my heels. By the time I reached the lobby, emotion had begun to overtake me. Relief and rage burned through me, fighting for dominance.

Dev, who was still behind me, placed his hand on my shoulder and gave it a reassuring squeeze. I wanted to punch him but refrained. Instead, I reached within myself, pulling air into my lungs and then exhaling it in a gust. In and out. In and out. In and out. In. And out. In. And out. In. Out. In. Out.

"Are you sure you want to do this?" I asked Amalie as we stood in front of our grandparents' door in the senior living home.

A fierce expression danced across her face and once again I was struck by how much she looked like me. The set of her mouth and the blazing fire in her eyes, the resemblance was unmistakable. I had explained everything to her and her counselor before this decision to visit, but I was still apprehensive.

Without looking at me, she nodded, her small hands balling into fists at her sides.

So, I knocked on the door.

Our grandfather opened it wide, his eyes first falling to me, then to Amalie. Tears once again welled in the corners of his eyes and he stepped to the side to allow us entry. Amalie strode in ahead of me, her back straight and tall. Pride blossomed inside me and I followed her with a small smile.

"Oh my," my grandmother breathed from her place on the couch. "Amalie, you have grown so much."

Amalie seemed not to know how to respond to that, so only offered our grandmother a smile in return.

"Please," Grandfather said, gesturing to the couch and armchairs. "Do sit down, girls."

I sat down on the couch next to Grandmother, smiling encouragingly at Amalie and patting the space next to me. Grandfather waited for her to pick a place to sit, watching her with wary optimism. Carefully, Amalie padded her way over to me, snuggling into my side as I slipped an arm around her.

None of us could blame her apprehension. I had walked in here only a couple of days ago gearing for a fight, but now that I knew the truth, I was eager for Amalie to have a relationship with our grandparents. She had been banned from seeing them before she could even form core memories. It would take time for her to trust them.

I needed them to get on well though, just in case something happened to me while I was gone. I promised to come back, but that was a promise I could not always keep. Amalie needed family and people she could trust around her in case that ever were to happen.

My grandparents kept staring at us as though they could not believe we were there as they conversed with Amalie. The damage their daughter – my mother – had done went deep. They likely thought they would never see us again. My throat tightened a little at the thought.

I was once again grateful for Valentin joining me on my first visit. There was no way it would have gone as well as it had, and now I got to do the same for Amalie.

"I am scheduled to leave tomorrow," I announced when there was a lull in the conversation.

"That's why we're here," Amalie added with a look that begged for my approval.

I smiled down at her before continuing. "Amalie and I have chosen a caretaking service to oversee her while I am gone, and any other time I am called away. Whenever you like, you can contact them and they will bring her to see you if she is not in counseling or class."

"You can also ask for progress updates if you want," Amalie piped up. "Daux filed all the paperwork and everything."

The glimmering expressions our grandparents threw our way told me I had made the right decision in coming here with Amalie today. I knew she would be cared for properly if something were to happen to me.

"Are you okay with that, Amalie?" Grandmother asked.

Amalie looked from her to Grandfather, then me, before answering.

"Ye—es," she said nodding. "I know Daux wouldn't

allow something she thought would harm me. Everything she is doing now she is doing to protect me and give me a good future."

I nearly snorted at the obviously practice lines, but affection tamped my amusement down and my arm tightened around her middle.

"And what about your magic?" Grandfather asked gently. "Are you interested in seeing if it will manifest?"

Amalie's face fell.

I had informed my grandparents about her magic and that she did not know of it until recently. I had wanted to wait until we saw them for a serious talk about it.

"I don't know," she said, her voice small and fragile.

"That's okay," Grandmother reassured her. "You are still young, there is plenty of time to decide if you want to see if it manifests."

Amalie smiled, her expression taut around the edges, but genuine. "Thank you."

Her reaction was all I needed to know and I steered the conversation toward her most recent report card. Grandmother and Grandfather exclaimed with delight over Amalie's academic accomplishments in her online classes. Soon, she began to emerge from her shell, sharing little bits of information about herself and our grandparents hung on every word. It felt as though the wounds in my chest were closing over the longer I sat there.

A pang of anger flashed in my chest, sweat slickening my palms as they clenched into fists.

If only we could stay this way forever, I might be able to heal. But I had a job to do if I wanted to keep my sister with me – if I wanted to keep her safe. "If onlys" would only distract me. I had to live in the now. For Amalie.

I felt an echo of Amalie's nervousness as I stood in front

of Talia's plain wooden front door once again, debating whether or not I should knock. Himawari, the ever-soothing presence she was, stood next to me – rolling her eyes at my inability to take action. We had decided to say a quick goodbye this evening and ask her to see us off tomorrow, to be there with Amalie so she did not feel so alone. Rhiannan was off on a mission of her own, and I trusted Talia to comfort Amalie as she had always comforted me.

But I could not bring myself to knock on the Gods' forsaken door.

Himawari, fed up with my inaction, lifted her fist and knocked gently three times. It swung open gently, revealing Gwyn Hier, Talia's teammate.

His dark glare from me to Himawari was telling, but he did not tell us to get lost. Instead, he called for Talia over his shoulder, not taking his eyes off Himawari and me. His voice was deep and gravelly, the kind of voice that reverberated in one's bones. His glare did not make his intimidating voice easier to withstand.

"Daux!" Talia exclaimed once she reached the front door. "And Himawari too! Long time no see!"

She wrapped us both in a bone-crushing hug, her short brown hair tickling my cheek. When she pulled away and released us, she turned back toward Gwyn and shooed him away. "Go brood somewhere else, why don't you? Let me talk to my friends."

With a final glare at me, Gwyn grunted his ascent then turned on his heel and left.

"So, what's up?" Talia asked, leaning a hip against the doorjamb.

I chanced a look at Himawari who nodded encouragingly at me.

I took a deep breath in and then out. Talia was my friend. My *best* friend. I could ask her a simple favor. But my guilt for her arrest still lingered and I could not bring myself to do it. Another breath in, another out. In and out. In and out.

Do it for Amalie. That voice that sounded so much like my mother but was actually me said.

Fine. I would do it for Amalie.

"Could you see us off tomorrow?" I blurted. "With Amalie I mean? She has been very clingy lately and I'm concerned how she will take me leaving. Especially with her new caretakers coming to stay with her tomorrow."

"Oh, duh," Talia said with a smile and a knowing look. "Of course I will. I'd do anything for you, you need only ask." She turned to face Himawari now, cocking her head toward me as she did so. "She should know this by now, but I guess she still needs some pushing, huh?"

Himawari laughed at the blush that crept up the back of my neck. "She sure does."

"Okay, okay," I said defensively, holding up my hands in a surrendering gesture. "I will come right out and ask next time, gracious."

"That's better," Talia said and reached out, chucking me on the chin with her fist affectionately.

I rolled my eyes and grabbed her retreating wrist to pull her into a hug.

"Thank you," I whispered.

She patted my back gently before pulling away, sending a wink to Himawari.

"What are friends for?"

Chapter Twenty-Five

Amalie's arms were wrapped around my middle, squeezing me as though she was afraid to let me go. Talia stood close by, her eyes red-rimmed and wet. It was difficult to say goodbye, difficult to let go. I may not come back from this mission – the chances of coming back from any mission varied, but there was always a chance – and this time I would be leaving my sister without a guardian. My grandparents were still sorting out their conservatorships and would be unable to care for Amalie should something happen in that case.

We were all terrified of that.

I knew my friends would do what they could to prevent Amalie from becoming a ward of the state, but there was only so much they could do as they were not her relatives. Not to mention that they were all Spec Ops agents themselves.

"Amalie," I said gently, growing increasingly anxious the longer she clung to me. "Talia has promised to stay with you while your caretaker is here to make you more comfortable. I need to go now; you have to let me go."

"You're not going to come back," she whispered into my armor-clad abdomen. "You're not coming back this time, I just know it."

"Thanks for the vote of confidence," Félix teased on his way out the door.

I shot a look at his back but said nothing.

Amalie had every right to worry, I did not want her to, but I would not begrudge her for doing so.

"I will come back," I promised her. "And I will be one step closer to bringing Father back to face justice."

"He can stay where he is," Amalie pouted.

"I would like that too, but he has to pay for his crimes, Amalie."

"Fine…"

I tilted her face up to look into mine. I saw myself reflected there in the lines of her cheekbones, and the shape of her eyes. The pointed nose that was dusted with a smattering of freckles from her time in the sun that our mother would have hated and bleached with lemon juice – or frowned upon magical concoctions.

"I love you," I told her.

Her green eyes welled with tears and she hugged me tightly once more before releasing me.

"I love you too," she whispered before moving on to hug Valentin almost as tightly as she had me.

Talia and I moved in unison toward one another, reaching for each other as easily as breathing. I ignored her sniffles as she ignored my trembling. She knew – just as I did – that Amalie's words held weight. I may not return.

"Thank you," I said, pulling back from her embrace.

It was for more than just being with my sister that I thanked Talia. I was thanking her for being my friend – something that had been rather difficult as of late. I was thanking her for caring about me, about my family, and for so many other things I could not express.

From the look she gave me, she understood very well what those two words meant.

"Don't mention it," she replied with a puckish grin, her brown eyes sparkling with more than unshed tears.

I hugged her one more time, then picked up my gear and headed for the door with Valentin at my side. I paused for a moment, looking over my shoulder into the flat I had called home with more affection than any other place I had lived. Talia had her arm around Amalie's shoulders and was leading her into the living area, wiping tears from both their faces.

My heart sank with the knowledge that my sister was right and I would be breaking my promise to her. I was not coming back from this mission. I was not going to die, I had too much to accomplish before that happened. However, the sister Amalie knew would be too far gone. I was going to find out exactly how Gladwin and my father committed their treasonous acts, and that was going to break me for good. I knew without a doubt that I would be returning to Heliorious a changed woman. A woman my sister would not recognize. A woman I would know all too well.

We were headed to the border between Eidolon and New Palogenia. The intel I had gleaned from my mother led to some interesting developments when another Spec Ops team returned from investigating strange instances with the border security there. Their investigation had uncovered guards accepting bribes from Coalition citizens with unsavory intentions, as well as NAF citizens who wished to defect with national secrets. Gladwin had potentially come through here multiple times disguised as any one of these people. He may have offered bribes or used a glamor, or traditional means of disguise to get across the border. It would be easy with security this lax.

The moment my boots touched the beautiful grassy knolls of New Palogenia's border with Eidolon, I knew something was off. The air – even without my foresight activated – felt off. Smelled off. I could not put my finger on what it was, but I knew.

From the look on my friends' faces, especially Valentin's, they knew too.

Our auto driver set the cloaking device as soon as my team exited the vehicle – ready to walk a distance to the immigration processing center – rendering it invisible to the naked eye – or even my foresight. The driver would deactivate the cloaking device once we returned, with or without our target.

Everyone here was hopeful for the former.

I could have cared less either way. Gladwin's head on a pike outside Spec Ops HQ would have satisfied me the most, but we needed him.

It was so odd that we had needed a man whose visage I had worn like my own skin once. A Coalition captain, a war criminal, an all-around vile and evil man who enslaved and abused people with magic – and the Gods knew what else he did to them. I felt that if I knew exactly what he did with the enslaved magic users under his command, it would only solidify the wavering desire to bring him back as a corpse.

There would be no coming back from that, though. I would most assuredly be arrested again and never see the light of day again.

A border patrol guard approached us from his post in front of the immigration processing center, offering to lead us to the main offices. They had been waiting for us.

I declined.

"I want to see the processing floor," I said, placing my hands on my hips and hoping to look authoritative.

I must have had the desired effect because I noticed the way his eyes flashed to the rapier on my hip. He swallowed, nodded, and then led us inside the large, squat building made of gray concrete. It was situated just inside the New Palogenia border so the Coalition could not attack it without directly declaring war.

Inside, there were only a handful of guards monitoring the immigration process. It was telling that there was no one attempting to immigrate *out* of New Palogenia. All the immigration was coming from Eidolon – or others who had been given leave to travel to Eidolon and then they defected from the Coalition there.

I had forgone my colorful armor in favor of the black tactical gear Valentin preferred, as did Jax. Himawari still wore her customary shadowmancer garb, and Félix a toned-down version of his berserker armor, but they hardly looked out of place with us all in dark clothes. We hurried to position ourselves at each of the exits: me at the front, Jax and Himawari off to each side where the office corridors were located, with Valentin and Félix located at the very back in case Gladwin attempted to flee. We each had undetectable listening devices in our ears that would allow us to talk to one another discreetly.

I surveyed the area watching for any suspicious behavior. It was a large space with a depressing air as somber-faced people filed in one at a time. The room was open except for the stalls running parallel against one another from the back of the room to the front. The immigrants were directed through the front of the room and then pointed toward which offices to go through after all their papers were checked at the stalls.

Half an hour passed, then another, and another. I was beginning to grow frustrated at the slow-moving line of immigrants held up by the bored guards checking their papers.

That was when I noticed him.

He was nothing like the man whose likeness I had stolen for our infiltration mission, and his hulking sidekick was nowhere to be seen, but it was Gladwin nonetheless. He had short white hair and tanned skin, and his height was considerably shorter. Whether he was hunched over in a disguise or glamor, I was not sure, but those black soulless eyes were unchanged. They seemed to eat the light around them, swallowing it into the nothingness of their depths.

"It's him," I whispered, not daring to move.

"Where?" Jax asked.

I could see him from the corner of my eye inconspicuously craning his neck to scan the crowd of people.

"Fifth row from Jax, about to get his papers checked," I said back, my gaze not leaving Gladwin's form.

"What do we do?" Himawari asked, tensing to converge on the stall.

"Nothing, we wait," I commanded, tensing up myself.

"What if he recognizes us?" Félix questioned.

I had already thought about that. If he recognized us, he would have turned around already, or he would have made sure his papers had faults in them that needed to be corrected before entering the country through the center. We looked too much like the guards in the center to draw much attention.

And when he made it through, I knew he had not seen us.

Jax and Himawari moved first, Valentin and Félix heading up behind Gladwin at the rear. I waited. Waited until he saw me and broke into a smile.

I returned it with one of my own and slowly made my way toward him, reaching him before Jax and Himawari as he closed the gap between us with his quick strides.

"You," he said, delight shining in those depthless eyes.

"Me," I snapped back, unsheathing my rapier.

He did nothing. Did not even flinch when I pointed the blade at his chest. With a flick of my wrist, I could have him slit open with his innards spilling onto the gray concrete flooring and he did not even *flinch*. I expected as much. He was known for being a little unhinged. Lucky for me, I was too.

"Captain Gladwin of the Coalition," I said, my voice ringing out for the whole room to hear. "You are under arrest."

"I don't think I am," he taunted, tapping the edge of my rapier away with the back of his hand. "I have a woman to meet."

"Who?" I demanded, pointing the blade toward one of those horrible eyes.

"Wouldn't you like to know?"

With that, he sidestepped me and grabbed the hilt of my rapier, pulling me toward him. I had anticipated this sort of maneuver and let him pull me with too much momentum, sending us both sprawling to the ground. What I had not anticipated was my rapier skittering across the concrete away from me.

Quickly, I grabbed Gladwin by the hair and slammed his head into the ground once. Twice. Dazing him. Still, he fought back, arching his spine off the ground in an attempt to throw me off. He threw a calculated punch that caught me on the ear, making my head spin and ears ring.

Enraged, flame engulfed my raised fist, the light dancing across the now pale face of Captain Gladwin. With my other hand, I wrapped my fingers around his neck and slammed his head against the concrete again. His dark eyes glimmered with firelight and hatred as he gazed up at me from where I had him pinned on the ground. Almost as if he were daring me to hit him, to burn that perfect pale skin of his. To maim him, scar him, kill him.

I grinned.

"Daux, don't!" Félix warned.

I did not heed him.

Bloodlust swam across my vision, honing in on the man below me. A breath in, a breath out. And I swung my fist downward.

A cry of pain filled my ears when my fist connected, but not the one I was expecting.

"Félix," I gasped.

My hand, my magic, had seared part of the way through the armor at his shoulder. The heat of my rage had burned through something so durable as a berserker's armor.

Bile rose in the back of my throat, threatening to spew

from my mouth and nose. I could smell the burning of his armor and his skin all over again. My fault. *My fault.* Always my fault. Just as it had been last time. I was too much of a coward to kill my father, too weak.

And now, as I was trying to right that mistake, I had hurt Félix again.

"Félix," I whispered again, afraid to touch him.

"I'm okay," he ground out, pushing himself to his feet and dragging Gladwin with him.

I allowed him to, sliding off our prisoner's body onto the cold, unforgiving concrete.

Relief and rage rushed through me in tandem, colliding with one another in a nauseating hurricane of emotion. I wanted to take him into my arms. I wanted to punch a hole through his stomach. I wanted to apologize. I wanted to scream obscenities at him.

I settled for silent inaction.

"You," Gladwin said again, smiling down at me.

"Me," I repeated with a snap, shoving Félix out of the way and hauling Gladwin away from him. "You're lucky my teammate stepped in."

Valentin and Himawari rushed to help Félix to his feet, checking his injury without so much as a glance at me or Gladwin.

"Oh, I am *sure,*" Gladwin retorted, a smug expression crossing his beautifully cruel features.

"You *are* lucky," Jax interrupted, grabbing him by the elbow and snapping magic-blocking cuffs on his wrists. "Agent Deveraux was going to kill you, and none of us were close enough to stop her except for Agent Gurrero."

Gladwin turned his dark gaze to meet mine, raising a sculpted brow at me in an appraising gesture. I suppressed a shudder at the glimmer in his dark eyes.

"You're Charles' girl?" he asked, looking me up and down. "Older than I thought."

My skin crawled at the way he said that. I didn't bother

to hide the way my lip curled in disgust at his words.

"I am," I said, crossing my arms over my chest. "And *you* are under arrest."

"Agent Deveraux," Gladwin grinned, showing all his teeth reminiscent of a wild animal.

"What?" I snapped.

"Nothing, it's just... Isn't it your custom to say something like, 'Anything you say can and will be held against you in a court of law'?"

"And you said my name?"

He winked and before I lost my temper again, I shoved away in disgust.

"Get him away from me, Jax, before I really do kill him."

"I might kill him myself," Jax said, leading the vile man out of the building and toward the checkpoint.

"Oh, but don't you need me alive?" I head Gladwin say as Jax herded him away.

Gladwin's cry of pain indicated that Jax's pacifism was morphing into my current mindset rather than his own. I would have smiled if it were not for Himawari and Valentin leading Félix my way. My heart sank into my toes, my stomach following with it.

"Félix, I—"

Valentin held up a hand to cut me off.

"Don't," he snapped, eyes frozen and cold as ever.

My mouth snapped shut with an audible click and I could feel the muscles in my jaw feathering as my eyes burned against the tears that threatened to gather there.

Fine.

I would not care then. They were the ones who wanted me to open myself up to them, how dare they condemn me when I try and do what they wanted? But even as I thought such things, I knew they were not true. That's what made everything that much harder.

"*Don't* get in my way next time," I snapped instead, allowing the anger to take over.

Félix paled and seemed to shrink in on himself at my words and I hated the disgusting glimmer of pride that wormed its way into the hole in my chest. Hurting my friend was nothing to be proud of, and yet a part of me took pleasure in seeing the hurt in his dark eyes. He was so much older looking now than when I first met him, but a harsh sentence from me made him look like the solemn little kid I met at our Placement Ceremony.

"Daux," Valentin warned, face hard and cold.

But the damage had already been done. I turned away from them toward the awaiting auto. There was nothing left to say, for I had already broken everything beyond repair when I allowed Félix and Valentin to get hurt the first time. They just had not seen it yet.

Chapter Twenty-Six

The trip back to Heliorious was filled with silence punctuated by long stretches of staring in my direction when the others believed I would not notice. Himawari and Valentin had Félix all bandaged up so well that when he saw a healer it would not take more than a few minutes to undo what I had done to him. At least, that was what I heard them whispering to each other.

I sat with Gladwin under the guise of making sure he made no attempts to escape his cuffs, but really it was to absolve myself of my prior actions; though, I knew nothing could truly fix what I had done. So, I acted as though I did not care about what I did or anything else, ignoring Gladwin's attempts to rile me or start a conversation, only speaking to remind him that anything he said was being recorded and would be turned over as evidence. That shut him up for good, thankfully.

Soon, we were back at headquarters and I could dump Gladwin off on the awaiting interrogation team. But not before I made sure they knew to do absolutely everything in their power to break him. I wanted him to feel like I had felt. I wanted him weak. I wanted him powerless. I wanted him begging for the death I would have so willingly given him only hours before.

And I wanted to watch.

We were greeted by several teams and a small troop of military personnel to escort us inside HQ from the hangar. I recognized a few of the team members, but none of them acknowledged me or my team other than to state why they were there and to follow them.

We did so without question, marching in tandem with our escort. Pride and shame swirled within me, mixing in a horrible whirlpool deep in the pit of my stomach. I wanted to throw up. I wanted to cheer in victory – however small this one was.

My team was silent as Gladwin was herded off – with a wink in my direction – towards the interrogation wing. They were also silent as we made our way up the lift toward the Overseer's office. A gnawing in my chest warned me that my friends may rat out my attack on our newly acquired prisoner, but they would be justified in doing so. I would not stop them.

But when Rachel, Raquel, Rebecca – I still could not remember her name – ushered us into the Overseer's inner office, none of them made a sound. Not Valentin with the cold fire in his eyes that burned me to the bone. Not Himawari whose shadowy judgment I could feel as if she had manifested it into the room. Not even Félix who I had injured.

"Good job, team Deveraux," the Overseer stood to her impressive height and moved around her desk to shake each of our hands.

She shook mine last, lingering a bit.

"I was wrong about you once again," she said smoothly. "And once again, I am sorry."

None of my teammates responded to her statement. Their silence was judgment enough.

"Thank you, Ma'am," I said stiffly.

"You all have accomplished something great today," the Overseer spoke to all of us now, pacing in a way that reminded me of a lioness in an enclosure. "The capture of the Coalition Captain Gladwin was something I never thought I would see, and yet here we stand. It is all thanks to the five of you."

We all murmured half-hearted platitudes of humility, but she held up a hand to stop us.

"Your treatment, while protocol, after the defection and escape of Charles Deveraux, was something Spec Ops is not proud of, and in no small connection to your success, you will be repaid for your suffering."

Rage burned through the shame in my gut at her words, reducing it to ash. I even tasted it in the back of my throat, like acrid smoke curling from a dragon's mouth. Like scorching brimstone.

How dare she and the NAF "repay" me for doing my job? How dare they frame me, my teammates, and my friends as criminals and then act like "repayment" was all that needed to be done to fix their mess? I wanted to rip the Overseer's throat out with my teeth.

It was as insulting as it was immaterial.

As it was, I had no cause to be insulted. At least not on behalf of my friends. I had betrayed them. They would not appreciate my ire.

"Thank you, Ma'am," Valentin said on my behalf when I found myself unable to respond.

The Overseer did not seem insulted by my silence. She didn't even seem to notice, heading back around her desk to sit down. For that, I was grateful. That way I would not be tempted to attack her.

"My assistants will be in contact to facilitate the matter," The Overseer said, steepling her fingers. "You are dismissed. And thank you for your service."

"You are welcome, Ma'am," I ground out when I found my voice and turned on my heel, storming from the room.

The others followed along behind me. I could feel their stares behind my back, and hear the ghosts of their whispers brushing against my ears. I could not care. I should not care. It was not fair that I should care. I should have become a heartless shell, but the guilt was eating me up from the inside out. Gnawing at the hole in my chest, ripping the flesh and crushing the bone.

We separated when I stopped at the interrogation floor, looking over my teammates' closed and exhausted expressions before keying in with my holonav. They would be taking Félix to be healed. I was surprised no one said anything to the overseer about my attempt on Gladwin's life – and Félix's injury as a result.

I do not deserve – or want – their protection, I told myself.

That was a lie.

"If you do not get him off balance as soon as possible, you will not get anything out of him," I nearly shouted at Dev in his rather impressive office.

It was a bright space with crème walls and warm brown leather furnishings, offset by the teak wood desk and bookshelves. He must have been promoted recently, as he certainly would not have been giving us a tour all those months ago if he were very high up in the interrogation squad. Not unless our team was going to be conducting much more intimate missions alongside the interrogators – or working as interrogators ourselves.

"Daux," Dev said soothingly, a tone I recognized from the white room.

I shuddered.

"My team is preparing a strategy right now," he continued in the same tone. "I am overseeing this interrogation personally."

"How did that turn out for you with my interrogation?" I asked waspishly, my hands resting on my hips.

A sheepishly amused expression crossed his warm features, and he leaned back in his comfortable-looking leather chair.

"Not well, I am afraid. You're too much of a fighter," he replied. "Not many people can withstand that many sessions with their minds intact."

That was where he was wrong though. My mind was not intact, but he did not need to know that. I was sane enough to refrain from attacking him. Besides, I liked Dev well enough before the interrogation. I did not blame him for carrying out his job the way he was ordered. I did. We all did, like clockwork – gears moving smoothly together in a well-oiled society. Until something, or someone, like my father removed himself and brought everything to a halt for a little while.

"Or the white room torture," I snapped back, throwing myself into one of the plush chairs in front of his desk.

"Or the… white room technique," he corrected carefully, eyeing me warily.

"Are you going to report me for insurrectionist language, Dev?" I laughed, something dark and dangerous leaking into my voice. "I have been bringing in such great results lately, surely the Overseer and the Governors would not want me arrested again just because I used one wrong word?"

I was toeing a dangerous line here, but I had already started down the path and there was no turning back now. I was loath to admit that I was relishing in the thrill of it.

Strangely enough, Dev laughed. Long and loud, as though I had just told the joke of the century. Even more strange, it was a genuine laugh. He genuinely thought my blatant disregard for the rules that had been imposed upon me was funny.

"No, I will not be reporting that you used the 'wrong word'," he said once he had calmed, mirth still evident in his voice and expression.

"Thank the Gods," I said sarcastically, though I did partially mean it. "I am serious though, the longer you sit on this one the more time he will have to think about how to mess with you. He has a talent for getting under people's skin."

"Do you think it's a talent, or do you think it's something else?" Dev asked, a sudden gravity coming over him.

"What do you mean? Are you asking me if I think Gladwin had magic?" I asked incredulously.

The idea was almost ludicrous. A captain in the Coalition military able to use magic? The Coalition hated magic except when they could exploit it. Their core belief was that magic was a curse, that it was wicked. Why would someone as high-ranking as Gladwin be able to wield it with impunity?

"We used the magic blocking cuff on him to restrain him during his arrest, as is protocol," I said after a beat. "So, I have no idea if he is able to use any of the elemental styles of magic or any abilities he might have been born with. I think he is just naturally annoying."

"I am going to tell you something in the strictest confidence, Daux," Dev said, voice lowering to a near whisper.

I leaned forward toward him, my heart leaping into my throat. Surely this was not a trap to get me into more trouble? I waved the thought away. Whatever Dev had done to me, he had always been honest with me. I could at least hear him out.

"There is overwhelming evidence that the Coalition leaders and their high-ranking officers may *all* possess magic," he whispered.

"What?" I asked, unsure if I had heard him correctly.

"We believe that, through interrogating your mother and captured members of the Coalition military, the Coalition leaders use magic as easily and often as you or me," he repeated.

"You must be joking," I said rising to my full height, hands balling into fists. "If you think I am going to believe that. My father and mother *hate* magic, they *tormented* me because of it. He would not have defected if he knew."

"He and your mother believed it to be true and he defected anyway," Dev said. "I'm sorry Daux, but it is true. Or at least, it is true according to your mother and our interrogation records. And our methods don't lie, you know that first-hand."

I slammed a hand down on the immaculate teak wood desk and ground my teeth together to keep from screaming. My father hated magic. He *hated* it. He would not use it. He would not. Why would he punish me, force blockers on me, if he did not truly hate it? Why would he have used blockers himself?

I asked Dev as much.

He looked at me with such pity in his dark eyes that I nearly gouged them out with my fingers. It would have been so simple, hook into the socket and pull. But I refrained.

"Those blockers you found are being analyzed, but we are fairly certain that they are not real blockers," Dev said carefully, watching my every move.

"What. Do. You. *Mean*?" I ground out between my teeth.

"I mean that the chemical composition of the vials is not like any blocker we have ever seen, nor is it manufactured in any of the NAF territories," he continued, appearing nonplussed. "They even appear to contain magic-*enhancing* chemicals, rather than ones that dull the ability that are normally found in blockers."

What in the ever-absent Gods' names did that mean? That my father was taking magic enhancing injections rather than blocking agents? Why would he do that? He hated magic. He hated it.

I tasted smoke in the back of my throat again.

"My father hates magic," I snapped, forcing the flame back into submission inside me. "He forced blockers on me, abused me, belittled me all because I had a '*curse*' as he put it. There is no way he would have magic-enhancing injections, much less use them. Unless he was stealing them for another purpose."

"What purpose would that be?" Dev asked, unconvinced.

"I'm not sure…" I paused, deflating. "Maybe he caught wind of a lab making magic-enhancing serums and decided to take some with him when he defected so the Coalition could test them. Perhaps to create something to counteract them?"

"It is plausible…" Dev relented, still seemingly unconvinced. "Of course, we should insinuate the former to throw off Gladwin in either case. He will either be so offended that we would assert such a thing, telling us that it's absolutely not true or he will play it off like it's nothing, which is likely a defense mechanism for the smarmy bastard."

"Which may tell us it *is* true?" I hedged.

"We would have to hook him up to the machine to know for sure, but yes. It would be a good head start."

I nodded slowly, still trying to process the fact that what we found were *not* blockers. My father could have been taking enhancers, not blockers. All this time, he could have lied to me. Lied to everyone.

Why would he defect then?

And how did I move on from this?

One step at a time, I told myself. *One step at a time.*

Gladwin sat across from one of Dev's interrogators in one of those horrible white rooms at one of those bolted-down metal tables, smirking infuriatingly. The captain was young, mid-thirties maybe – at the most – and even in the white scrubs of his prisoner's garb he was irritatingly beautiful. Almost like one of the mythical fae from the Eidolon Highlander myths with his delicate facial structure, long black hair, and his unsettlingly black eyes.

I wondered how it was possible that I could hate someone *more* than I hated my father.

Then I took another look at Gladwin's face through the screen – remembered what it was like to wear his likeness as if it were my own. Ah yes, it was quite easy to see.

I could almost feel the slick oiliness of the glamour I had once worn of his likeness. It was a sickening feeling, almost as sickening as watching him in real-time through the cameras.

Dev and I sat in the observation room, its grey walls lined with screens that were connected to the security cameras in each of the white cells. Lighted buttons and dials lit up the control panels, too many for me to ascertain what they all did. A microphone was mounted to the center console of the control panel where we were situated.

It was not a large room, but it could comfortably fit a small group of observers if needed. As it was, Dev and I were seated facing the south side of the room, watching one screen, in particular. This screen showed us Captain Gladwin and his interrogator. I was glad my mother's cell was not pictured on this wall. I would have gotten too distracted. The image of her suffering the way I had would have been too enticing for me to resist.

"Where is that little blonde girl?" Gladwin asked the interrogator as we watched. "I hoped she would be the one to interrogate me, she is my arresting officer, after all."

We both wore earbuds connected to the sound system of Gladwin's cell cameras, allowing us to hear the conversation easily without interference from any other camera feeds.

"That is not how things work around here," the interrogator – a tall woman with warm brown skin, black hair, and strong features – answered him.

"Pity," Gladwin sighed, pretending to deflate a bit.

It was as if his whole personality was an act. A charade. A silly, flirtatious man with nothing important to hide. I knew better. We all did. I wondered if those soldiers I had encountered while wearing Gladwin's likeness had been dealt with justly, or if they were mutilated and murdered for the transgression of being tricked by my glamour.

The thought made me sick.

"What is your connection with Charles Deveraux and his wife, Annette?" the interrogator asked in a bland tone that I vaguely recognized. "Are you affiliated with any of the neo-traditionalist groups in Heliorious?"

Gladwin only offered a smirk in response. We knew he was affiliated with these groups, and he knew we knew it. How else could he sneak into the country and extract Coalition sympathizers, or put plans in place for them to defect by themselves? There was no way he *did not* have at least a foothold in neo-traditionalist movements all over the continent.

"How about dear little Valentin Angelov?" Gladwin asked, observing the interrogator's reaction carefully.

The woman – Suna, Dev had whispered her name to me as we watched – gave nothing away. I recognized her as the woman I almost choked to death during my imprisonment. My eyelid twitched, but I said nothing.

Nobody but my team called Valentin by his first name, and only a handful of people outside of us actually knew it. It would have been common knowledge had people bothered to look at his file, but most just went along with using his nickname – Zima. A nomenclature that no longer fit his personality. Something had come along and melted that cold heart of his.

Someone.

Someone he could no longer trust.

Someone he *should* no longer trust.

I swallowed back a sob that threatened to escape my throat. I could not have Dev knowing that the missions he and the Overseer were tasking me with affected me this much. He would have me removed from the room. I needed to be here. I needed to watch them break Gladwin. I needed to see him as broken and shattered as my mother had been. As *I* had been.

"What about Angelov?" Suna answered his question with a question.

"Why not have him interrogate me?" Gladwin suggested, smiling winningly at her. "It would give us a chance to catch up, and reminisce on the old days."

"What is he talking about?" I snapped to Dev.

"I believe he is referring to the incident when Zima's team was killed," Dev whispered back, almost as if he were afraid Gladwin would have heard him even though the comm system was clearly off – indicated by the glowing red button on the control panel lettered with "OFF" in bold white over top of the hard plastic.

"What would he know about *that?*" I hissed, hands clenching into fists.

"I'm not clear on the details," Dev said, watching as Suna expertly tried to wheedle more information out of Gladwin, while he expertly evaded each attempt. "But I know Gladwin was involved in their deaths."

His words sent my innards dropping to the floor, as though we were going through a turbulent patch in a jet.

Gladwin had been involved in the deaths of Valentin's previous teammates? *And* knew his name? Just who was this man, and why was he so interested in my… my teammate? How did he know so much about him?

"How involved?" I asked once the words came to me.

"There are conflicting reports," Dev said, eyeing me warily. "Some say he was there personally, and others say he was orchestrating the whole attack they got caught up in."

"If he was orchestrating it, or if he was there, why did Gladwin not make sure Valentin was dead?" I questioned, frustration overtaking me as I watched Gladwin smirk and simper during his verbal interrogation. "Why not wait to make sure he was dead too? I know he happened upon his team as they were dying. Surely Gladwin would have factored that in if he's as great a strategist as we're believing."

Dev watched the screen for a moment longer, before pressing the comm button to "ON" and speaking.

His voice chilled me.

"If you do not cooperate, we will resort to more drastic measures," he said in the very same dead voice I had heard during my first interrogation.

I stared at him in disbelief. *Dev* was the one who presided over that? I almost felt betrayed, but then realized he had been watching over us since the beginning. He had been involved in my case since my arrest, so it made sense that he would have been involved before that too.

"Go ahead, I look forward to it," Gladwin goaded, searching the barren room for a camera, or anything to indicate someone watching him.

Dev turned to me; brow raised.

Was he asking my permission?

I looked to the screen – looked at the man who had caused me and Valentin so much suffering. I smiled.

"Break him," I said, waiting in gleeful anticipation for his torment to begin.

I hoped he would not break too easily. I wanted to savor this.

When I returned home that evening, Amalie ran for me from the dinner table, wrapping her arms so tightly around my middle that I feared she would cut herself on my armor. I hugged her back in relief. I knew my earlier prediction had come true – that I would return wholly changed – but I was able to keep my promise to her. I was alive and I came home.

"You came back," she whispered.

"I promised you I would," I said lightly, running my fingers through her hair.

"I almost didn't believe it though…"

I forced a laugh, knowing the others were in the dining

room, just down the hall – knowing they were listening to us. Judging me for hurting Félix. Adjudicating me for nearly killing Gladwin.

I deserved every ounce of censure.

Amalie dragged me into the kitchen and began filling a plate of food for me, but did not force me into the dining room. Instead, she rushed in by herself, grabbed her plate, and returned to my side by the counter.

"I know everyone is mad at you," she said matter-of-factly, then shoveled a forkful of food into her mouth. "So, I'll eat in here with you so you aren't alone."

My heart, which was warmed by her actions, sank in my chest. The others made no effort to hide their displeasure to my sister, which meant they were *incredibly* angry. I could not bring myself to face them.

I had become cowardly as well as despicable.

A monster – beastly, as my mother had so aptly put it when I visited her in her torture chamber.

The food, which would otherwise have been delicious, tasted like ash in my mouth. But there was no helping it. I shoveled forkful after forkful into my mouth, barely chewing whatever dish it was before swallowing.

"So," Amalie hedged as we ate. "What did you do to make everyone so mad at you?"

If I had not practically inhaled my food, I would have choked on it.

"I know it's your fault Félix is hurt," she continued, ignoring my reaction. "But I don't know why. No one would answer me when I asked. Himawari said they didn't want to put bad thoughts about you in my head. Jax said you just had a disagreement with all of them. Valentin said it was better I didn't know."

A sigh escaped me, and I placed my plate in the sink. How could I talk to her about what happened? How did one discuss these things with a child? I was surprised by my friends' restraint, considering how angry they must be with me – I might not have been so generous – though I did appreciate that they had kept silent.

I did not need Amalie to know everything that had happened. Not because of my shame – which was great – but because I was unsure about what I actually wanted her to know. Much of what I did for Spec Ops was not something a child needed to know.

I stifled a bitter, sulfur-tinged laugh. I had been a child not much older than Amalie when I had enrolled in the Academy, and I had learned in great detail what I would be doing if I was Placed in Spec Ops.

But Amalie was not me. She did not need to know what I knew. She did not need to imagine what I saw on my missions.

"We can talk about that in my bedroom," I said, unwilling to be overheard by the others, lest they think I was whitewashing the truth for my own benefit – and in their well-placed anger – overshared on the gory details.

She looked at me with lips pursed for a moment, then placed her own dish in the sink and nodded to me. "Okay, let's go then."

That reminded me of myself – myself before I became who I was now, cowardly and spiteful.

Once we were in my room with the door closed securely behind us and Amalie was settled on the chaise lounge with her knees pulled to her chest, I finally began to speak.

"I hurt Félix," I said, forcing myself to hold her gaze. "And I hurt him because I was trying to kill a man and he stopped me."

"Did you do it on purpose?" she asked, her face giving nothing away.

"Did I do what on purpose? Hurt Félix? Or try to kill someone?" I asked in response.

"Hurt Félix," she clarified, face still impassive.

"No, I would never hurt him on purpose."

"I didn't think so. But I wanted to be sure… You have

been very angry lately."

My chest clenched at her words, her observations. She was too young to be worrying about my anger. Much like I had been too young to worry about our father's.

"Amalie... I... I'm sorry," I whispered.

"You don't have to apologize for *being* angry," she said, shrugging her slender shoulder. "Only when you *act* angry is when you need to apologize. Jax told me that."

"Jax is right," I said, feeling my throat close in on itself.

Another reason I was grateful for my friends – friends I had no right to hold as dear as I did. I doubted Amalie would have any good influences in her life if it were not for them. I would have been unable to provide that for her if it was just the two of us.

"And were you trying to kill the person Félix was protecting on purpose?" she asked after a few heartbeats, allowing me to regain my composure.

"Yes," I answered honestly, holding my chin high, awaiting her judgment. "It was a lapse in judgment. He is better for us alive rather than dead. Félix was right to stop me."

"Why were you trying to kill him?" she continued.

I could hear the curiosity in her voice. I would have been that curious too, at her age, but that did not stop my skin from crawling at her question. I needed to be honest with her; however, honesty was becoming difficult. My shame was growing, as well as my fury. I should not have to have this conversation at all, much less with my kid sister. She was just a child for the Gods' sake!

"He—he is a very bad man," I began, thinking of Gladwin's bottomless black eyes. "He has ki—hurt very many people, and done much worse. I allowed myself to get too angry and I lost control. I wanted revenge, and I thought that killing him would be the best way to get it."

Death was too good for Gladwin. As much as I was frustrated with my friends and ashamed of my actions towards them, I was grateful they had stopped me. Gladwin enduring the same torture I had undergone was a better revenge than me killing him quickly. And now the NAF would get valuable Coalition information. It was a win-win.

"Why are you smiling?" Amalie was looking at me curiously, a hint of fear and concern glinting in her blue eyes.

Panic surged in me as I scrambled for an answer. "I-I am, I was just thinking about how grateful I was for my friends. They stopped me from making a bad decision, a dangerous decision."

It was not a lie, not completely. I could not bring myself to lie outright to her. Not when she was treating me with such maturity, such fairness.

I decided against telling her what I had said afterward. She did not need to know about that side of me. Instead, I changed the subject entirely, asking how she was doing with her caretakers. The excited way in which she prattled on nearly drowned out the sound of footfalls from the hallway leading away from my door. I tried to ignore the chilled feeling that clambered down my spine, but it stayed with me for a long while after – spreading through my veins and twining around my lungs.

Which of my teammates had been outside my door? Were they listening to me tell my sister half-truths? Judging me?

What did he, or she, want?

Chapter Twenty-Seven

I awoke the next morning from a restless slumber, Amalie in a tangle of blankets next to me. She had stolen most of them sometime in the night, contributing to my lack of rest but most of it was due to my mind being flooded with memories of the day before. Gladwin's capture and the beginning of his torture at my and Dev's hands. Félix's injury, and my reaction. The person outside my bedroom door, listening to my conversation with Amalie.

I had a sinking suspicion that it was Valentin based on the sound and length of the footsteps. How would I confront him? How should I?

Was that even the best idea?

Probably not, but I did not like being spied on in my own home. For all I knew, he could be reporting back to the Overseer on me again like he had last Katalyst, the first month we had been teammates. And why would he not? According to him, I was untrustworthy if he felt he had to spy on my private conversations with my sister.

Ultimately, I decided against confrontation. I was still a team leader and picking a fight was beneath my station. I had enough to deal with.

Soon Amalie would begin to stir under her mound of blankets and I would have to drop her off at the care center before I met Dev at Spec Ops HQ to observe Gladwin's interrogation again. I would be bringing Valentin based on what Gladwin had inferred yesterday. Dev had insisted. That was before I suspected Valentin of spying on me, however. This revelation was going to make observing the interrogation more than a little uncomfortable – grating even, knowing his eyes would be on me part of the time. Watching my every move, every expression.

Shaking my head against the thoughts, I pulled myself from the bed, my tired bones groaning. I needed to prepare Amalie her breakfast before taking her to the care facility but to do that, I would need to venture out into the kitchen.

I sighed and pulled on a robe over my nightgown and slid on my glasses.

Hopefully, none of the others would be awake yet.

Padding out into the hallway, I activated my foresight just a tinge to listen for any sounds of breathing coming from Jax's and Valentin's rooms. Soft, steady breathing sounded from behind both doors. Carefully, I hedged my way out toward the common area, listening for stirrings from Himawari or Félix's rooms. Nothing.

With a breath of relief, I made my way into the kitchen to make breakfast. Moments later – while I was starting the coffee pot and tea kettle – I heard the sound of footsteps behind me. Not the ones outside my door last night, thankfully, but small ones accompanied by a tiny yawn.

"Good morning, blanket thief," I said without turning around.

"Good morning," Amalie replied, coming up behind me and wrapping her arms around my middle. "What's for breakfast?"

"What do you want?" I asked, patting her hands as I pulled her arms off me. "We have to leave soon."

Amalie thought for a moment, then began pulling leftover waffles from the freezer. "Can we have these together?"

She sounded so earnest that I did not have the heart to refuse her, even though my gut was roiling with anxiety. There would be enough left for the others if we had some of the waffles, it was what they were made for, but I could hardly bring myself to stomach them once they were prepared and we sat down to eat our meal.

The sweet, fluffy smell of the waffles made my digestive tract flip. But I soldiered on, to make my sister happy. However, I all but could not eat another bite when Valentin and Jax walked into the dining room.

The food instantly turned to real ash in my mouth and I had to chase it down with water, hoping no one would notice any black on my teeth. The flavor of smoke stayed behind in my mouth, making each further bite taste bitter and unpleasant.

"Good morning!" Amalie greeted them with sleepy cheerfulness.

"Morning," Jax said in reply, his sunshiny grin lighting up his handsome face.

Valentin only smiled his response, stoic as ever.

My heart was racing, my thoughts jumbled and fueled with anxiety.

Were they going to tell her the whole truth? She was too young, too innocent, to know all of what I had done. I did not want her to be afraid of the world, or of me. I was terrified of her hating me again. She had *just* started to open up.

Amalie did not need to know.

Looking up at Jax and Valentin, I could see that they were both staring at me with trepidation. Their eyes darted between me and my sister; tension identical in the lines of their bodies.

Smiling, I placed a hand atop Amalie's free one, curling my fingers around it so she could not be easily pulled away from me. I could tell they wanted my sister far away from where I could do her harm. How silly. I would never hurt Amalie.

I once would have thought that about Félix as well.

I wondered if my father thought *he* would never do

another person harm before he did, then liked it too much to stop. I wondered when I would turn into him. I wondered if I already had.

Instead of wondering further, I spoke.

"Jax, Valentin," I said, my voice dripping with sugar to hide the venom. "I wanted to apologize for how I acted yesterday. It was out of line and completely inappropriate. I am sorry."

Jax blinked at me, a hesitant smile crossing his features. Bemusement. Good. That was the desired effect.

Valentin, on the other hand, narrowed his eyes. I was taken back to our clash on one of our very first days of training together. The others had requested we duel. The exhilaration that flowed through me as we displayed our magic with equal parts recklessness and calculation was indescribable. I felt something similar now, staring Valentin down at the breakfast table, daring him to call my bluff.

"Minimal harm done," Jax joked, trying to ease the tension. "I don't speak for anyone but myself, Daux, but I forgive you."

I looked down at the table, a sheepish smile in place. "Thank you, Jax. That means a lot."

I could tell by the set of Valentin's jaw from beneath my lashes that he did not believe me. I did not blame him. My false apology was as ridiculous as the sweet act I was putting on. Jax only believed it because he wanted to. He wanted his friend back; he wanted me healthy and whole.

I hated to lie to him.

But I was not sorry.

Okay, maybe I was a little sorry for hurting Félix. I could not have them taking Amalie away from me, or keeping me from her, over something as simple as that misunderstanding.

I almost scoffed at my own thoughts.

Misunderstanding?

No. It was just rage.

A rage that had allowed me to hurt not one, but all of the people I cared about on that mission. Surprise flooded my chest at how easy it was to shove down how much I cared. Deep down, I was surprised I was still telling myself that I did not.

"Daux," Amalie whispered, breaking me from my thoughts. "You're squeezing my hand too tight."

I let go at once, jumping back a smidge.

"I am so sorry!" I fluttered, checking over her hand for any tender spots.

She pushed me away and grabbed her plate with a laugh.

"Don't be silly," she said, mirth lacing her tone. "I'm all right. We need to go get ready."

I nodded, standing to my feet. Jax had returned to the kitchen to help Amalie clean up, and Valentin stood in front of me, preventing me from retreating to the kitchen myself to get away from him.

"What is going on with you?" he asked, voice low and careful.

It sent shivers down my spine – the danger in his tone.

"Nothing," I insisted, injecting syrup into my voice.

He did not buy it, a hand coming up to grab at my bicep when I attempted to brush past him.

I could feel his anger, it sang to meet mine in the form of his magic. Hot and cold flooded through me, colliding inside the hole in my chest. The feeling was euphoric and almost knocked me to my knees – or into Valentin's arms.

"Daux," Valentin said lowly into my ear – when had he gotten so close?

"I don't know what you're pulling," he continued, breath fanning the shell of my ear. "But it needs to end, now. We need you at your best. *I* need you at your best."

I pulled back to look him in the eye, despite the weakness in my knees. He was so beautiful.

"And you shall have me," I whispered, then blushed when I realized what I had said.

Two spots of color brightened Valentin's icy complexion, which was now considerably more colorless due to his bleached hair.

"At my best, I mean," I amended, pulling away from him to hide my mortification.

As I hurried away, I heard him cough slightly in embarrassment over the sounds of Jax and Amalie in the kitchen.

I had flustered him too.

Gods help me.

Amalie was dropped off at the care center without incident. Thankfully, she had listened to me and hurried when I rushed her so I could leave ahead of Valentin. Dread had filled me at the thought of being alone with him after dropping her off, not only because of what I had said accidentally this morning, but because of what had happened the last few times we were alone together.

He made it too hard to stick to my resolve. I was unraveling at the seams and I did not want him there to pick up the pieces of me when I came undone. He deserved more than that. He deserved more than me.

But, after the way he held me and told me he would never let me go, I could not get the image of a dark-haired child that resembled an equally dark-haired husband – both of whom belonged to me in my placement exam simulation – out of my head. I was not sure I even wanted to have children, Amalie might be more than enough for me, but the idea of being settled down enough with someone to even think about it… was attractive.

Especially if that someone was Valentin.

However, he deserved so much more than anything I could give him.

Isn't that his choice to make? That same soft, sweet

voice resembling my mother's asked. *Is it not Valentin's choice to decide whether he wants you and anything you have to give?*

A deep flush heated and colored my skin, the reddened flesh visible from the neckline of my black tactical shirt and jacket all the way to my hairline. Thankfully, my hair was now well past my ears, having grown since it was shaved in Katalyst and we were now well into Victoris. And since I was off blockers for missions, I was able to use a few magic growth serums to aid in the lengthening process. At least no one would be able to see the blush staining my ears red.

It was bad enough that the color on my face was visible behind the large gold frames of my glasses. Thankfully, the abhorrent blush was gone by the time I reached Spec Ops HQ. Even more wonderfully, Valentin was not on time.

I met Dev in the plain, high-tech lobby and entered the lift with him.

"Zima knows where the viewing room is," Dev explained when I asked if we should wait. "He can meet us there when he arrives, I'll send him a message letting him know."

I frowned but nodded, grateful I did not have to spend any time alone with Valentin in the lift. Or walking down the long hallways in the interrogation wing. Not after what I accidentally said this morning.

I could feel my earlier flush creeping up the back of my neck and I ground my teeth in an attempt to push it back.

By the time the lift opened and we were down the hall at the viewing room door, Dev had finished his message to Valentin. I wondered fleetingly what he had included in that message that took him so long to compose it, but I refused to let my paranoia get the better of me. There was no reason for Dev to betray me. There was nothing *for* him to betray.

The moment Dev opened the door, I could see on one of the many screens that Suna was back in Gladwin's room. Despite the interrogation having lasted long past the time I left yesterday evening, Suna – and Dev – looked no worse for wear. Looking closer at her, she was a pretty woman, her long black hair was wound into a bun at the top of her head, and her golden-hued complexion had a healthy warmth to it. A clear nodule was in her left nostril indicating a piercing, but it was clearly unsafe to wear during her work. And only added to the colorlessness.

I had nearly killed an interrogator with my bedsheets before they took them away. I would not want to see what Gladwin or another prisoner would do if they ripped a metal ring or post from Suna's nose. It certainly would not kill, but it would not be pretty.

I suppressed a shudder at the memory of my vision streaking, then flooding, with red during my time in one of those rooms. So much blood. My own blood.

I had scratched deep gouges in my face and it had taken a strong healer to combat the blockers in my system to close the flesh without leaving scars. No one bothered to inform me of any medical procedures that had been done to me while I was drugged and driven out of my mind. Reading my personal Spec Ops file came with consequences it seemed.

A soft creak from the door behind me caused me to jump and whirl around. Valentin stood there, peering at the screen over my shoulder. I stood to the side so he could see better, quashing a tremble at his nearness as he moved to stand next to me.

"Hello, Zima," Dev said with a mild smile.

"Dev," Valentin replied, crossing his arms.

Then he softened a bit, offering the other man a small smile. Dev did not appear offended by Valentin's standoffish behavior. He was probably used to it if he had Valentin's contact info to send him private messages.

"So, he mentioned my former team?" Valentin asked after a beat, watching as Suna questioned Gladwin.

The captain looked a bit worse for wear, his long black hair was mussed and his dark eyes had purple smudges beneath them, as though someone had taken a palette of Himawari's eyeshadow and smeared her favorite colors beneath his eyes. It pleased me more than words can describe to see him in such a state and I had to fight the grin that threatened to overtake my features. Since Dev and Valentin were both present, I struggled to keep my face as neutral as I possibly could.

"You specifically," Dev said, answering Valentin's question.

"He wanted to know why you were not one of the ones interrogating him," I said, my eyes not leaving the screen.

Valentin scoffed his answer. I understood completely.

I had felt the same way when Gladwin had asked for me yesterday as well.

Dev handed Valentin and me pairs of earbuds and we all slipped one into our ears, allowing them to connect to the camera feed so we could hear the conversation in Gladwin's cell but still converse amongst ourselves should we need to. Just as Dev and I had done the previous day.

"What is your connection to Valentin Angelov?" Suna asked with clinical sharpness, almost as if on cue.

Gladwin smiled as though he had not spent the night fending off interrogators and nightmares. I remembered the images the drugged food and water had shown me and shuddered. There was a time when I would not have wished such treatment on my worst enemy… but now I could not wait for him to reduce to the same broken state I was in when I left this place.

"I killed his teammates," Gladwin said conspiratorially, leaning forward toward Suna as though he was telling her a secret between friends at a sleepover.

Suna cocked an eyebrow at him, writing something down with her holonav. "You killed them personally?"

Gladwin's smile broadened and he shook his head.

"No, no," he said. "I *did* have them killed though, so I may as well have done the job myself."

"But you were there? In the NAF territory where Angelov's team was attacked?" Suna pressed, hoping to get as much information out of Gladwin voluntarily as she could. "Were local neo-traditionalist movements involved?"

"Perhaps." Gladwin's smile turned secretive. "May I speak with them? Valentin, and Charles' daughter?"

Suna's eyes flickered toward one of the cameras for a fraction of a second, grimacing. Gladwin looked into one of the corners, likely unable to see the cameras there as they were hidden well in the walls of the cells but his gaze met mine all the same. Those hollow, dark eyes of his sent a shudder down my spine. It felt as though he was looking into my very soul.

Then, his smile stretched into a grin.

It was like he was looking into the deepest parts of me and saw something… a kinship.

The sudden urge to rip my skin off arose unbidden and strong. I wanted desperately to throw up that silk black oily substance in my chest and rid myself of anything Gladwin may see mirrored in his own soul, but I could not.

Instead, I dug my fingernails so deeply into my palms that I broke skin, taking comfort in the pain I was able to inflict upon myself.

"They're watching us, aren't they?" Gladwin asked, lounging back in the hard metal chair he sat in. "I bet Miss Deveraux can't *wait* to hear what I have to say about *'dear Daddy* and *Mommy'*."

The last words he spat like a sneer, but his demeanor bounced back to his regular gods-may-care attitude he normally adopted in a few seconds. It was as though he had never been angry in the first place.

"I am unaware if anyone is observing this interrogation or not," Suna lied smoothly.

She would not have told him if we were there or not, whether she was privy to the information at all. It was against interrogation policy to give the interrogated more information than necessary. They were not allowed to have any power in the relationship. It made them harder to break.

It was why they had allowed me to think Félix's injuries had never been healed, why they had allowed me to believe all my friends were still jailed in the same way I was after they had long been released. That they were still being tortured in the same way I was.

I took a deep breath, then another. I would be calm. I would not jeopardize this. I would not show weakness. Not in front of Valentin and certainly not in front of Dev.

Gladwin clicked his tongue against the roof of this mouth, his dark eyes glittering with amusement. "There is no point in lying to me, my dear," he crooned, leaning toward her conspiratorially. "There is no way Deveraux and Angelov would want to miss my torment, not after what I put them through."

I grimaced at his words. Gladwin had hurt Valentin, not me, and I hated him for it. My initial dislike of the captain was based on principle, and that he somehow helped my father commit treason. The revelation of Gladwin's involvement in Valentin's teammates' deaths only fueled my hatred for the man.

But he had never harmed me, not personally.

Unless he had.

"What does he mean?" I asked, my nails digging further into the flesh of my palms.

"I don't know," Dev said back, puzzlement crossing his features.

"He's just trying to get under your skin, Daux," Valentin soothed, placing a strong cool hand on my shoulder.

I could feel the coldness of his palm sinking through my jacket and shirt, eliciting a shiver.

"I want to know what he means," I insisted, relaxing a little under Valentin's touch. "Was he there that day in Leumièr when my father escaped from Portnith, or did he have neo-traditionalists there in his place?"

"It's not impossible," Dev said slowly, staring hard at the screen.

Valentin's lips tightened into a thin line as the realization of what I was saying, what I was implying, what Dev had all but confirmed dawned on him. The Coalition had roots in the NAF that went much deeper than we could have anticipated. Just how far had they grown?

I smiled. Gladwin – though he knew I was listening – did not believe me capable enough to understand his implication. He surely believed the version of me my father had spun him. Of course, I should not assume, but I *knew* without a doubt he believed me ignorant of his direct involvement that day.

He never expected me to put the pieces together.

Maybe choosing him as a glamour was beneficial in a way. I had needed to get into his cruel mindset, to understand him, so I could play him convincingly to any soldiers I happened upon. Simply put, I knew him – at least a little.

"How is he getting into the country? And how did he orchestrate Valentin's team's demise without anyone knowing of his involvement until now?" I demanded.

"I always thought it was strange that such a small group of soldiers could get the drop on your team, Zima," Dev said, awestruck.

Valentin was silent, jaw clenched so tightly I worried he would crack a tooth.

But before we could continue that conversation, I could see Suna secretly gesturing the predetermined sign of distress toward one of the cameras. Gladwin was speaking to her, his face distorting with a fervent expression that reminded me of my father. And my father had *magic*. Who was to say Gladwin did not as well?

"We need to get someone in there with Suna," I said, rising from my seat in a panic. "She could be in serious danger!"

"We have him on blockers," Dev protested, attempting

to stop me.

"She's asking for assistance!" I yelled.

Valentin stood in his way and I ran from the observation room. If I was right, then blockers would not stop what Gladwin could do. What he was *about* to do.

My boots echoed loudly against the white tile flooring as I ran towards Gladwin's cell, my heart hammering in my chest. Suna may, or may not, have helped Dev interrogate me, but she was just doing her job. I did not fault her for acting upon her orders, just as I could not fault Dev. I did not wish to see her harmed.

I readied my holonav to connect the input key to the door, flinging it open when I heard the click of the lock. It banged against the wall with a crash that startled Suna from her chair and I charged, flinging her behind me.

Then the room exploded.

Or… It felt as though it had, but when I opened my eyes – my body curled around Suna's, shielding her from the supposed blast – nothing had happened. We were safe, alive, unharmed.

That could not be! I had *felt* the wind rushing around me, the heat of an explosion, rubble, and debris hitting my back as I sheltered Suna from the worst of the blast with my own body. I had *felt it.* Pain *still* rippled down my spine where the worst of the explosion had hit, but there was no injury. My tactical gear was pristine.

So, what had happened?

Because this horrid white room was just as horrid and white as ever.

Roughly, I shoved Suna from the room and slammed the door shut behind me. I could hear her shouts and fists banging on the door behind me, but I ignored them. Turning, I made eye contact with one of the cameras in the room, giving the imperceptible signal for "follow me" at Valentin and Dev should they still be in the observation room. Then I stalked forward to Gladwin, my rage mounting at the sight of his smirking face.

"I *knew* you would be watching, Daux," he crowed, looking quite pleased with himself.

Cursing, I reached across the table, grabbed him by the collar of his shirt, and hauled him forward. I was going to gouge his eyes out. I was going to light him on fire. I was going to—

The door slammed open again and I paused. Valentin strode over to me, Dev following determinedly behind him. He did not remove my fist from Gladwin's shirt as I expected, instead, he stood next to me and crossed his arms – an icy expression marring his handsome face.

"And the gang's all here," Gladwin sang with delight.

"What did you do?" I snapped, shaking him a little.

"Now, now," he said, smirking. "That would be telling."

With a snarl, I lifted him by the neck of his shirt and slammed him down onto the table. The sound of his body's impact reverberated in my ears, in my bones. A pleased thrill ran through me and I moved to throw him again, my magic flaring up inside me and giving me the strength to lift Gladwin, who was nearly twice my size.

Before I could do so, Valentin grabbed my wrist. Hard. His fingers clenched around the joint so tightly I feared he would break it. I let go of the captain, snatching my hand back from Valentin with a hiss of pain.

"What did you do?" Valentin asked, much softer than me but his voice was devoid of any geniality.

"Hello, Valentin," Gladwin said as though they were old friends, ignoring my teammate's question.

"What. Did. You. Do?" Valentin repeated with more force, ice crystals forming on the ends of his hair.

"Oh?" Gladwin's smirk turned into a grin. "This?"

One second, we were standing in the dreadfully white cell, and then the next we were in a lush tropical forest. Much like the one we hauled Dr. Moreau through on the Floral Islands. I shuddered at the memory. The sound of the

Coalition soldier's screams as they were being torn apart by the non-mutated animals still haunted my nightmares.

"What are you doing?" I snarled, stepping forward only to be blocked by the table between us.

But there was no table. At least, not one that I could see. All I could see between us was a dirt path – foliage and fallen leaves from the tropical trees above us lining the trail.

Luckily, I had not been required to take a blocker this morning as my presence was requested for the interrogation and I activated my foresight, pulling my glasses from my face as my senses began to heighten. The ground and the foliage began to blur, a myriad of colors and shapes, until it became a wash of misty grey before my eyes. Then, the screams faded until they were nothing more than a faint ring in my ears.

It was a glamour.

Or… something similar. Glamours were impossible to cast in the cells – electronically or otherwise. The security tech and magic warding cast on the rooms prevented them, and other kinds of illusionary magic or tech.

"How?" I snarled, grabbing the collar of Gladwin's uniform and shaking him slightly.

He grinned, placing a hand atop mine. A shudder of disgust ran up my spine, but I could not pull away from him. The illusion flared to life again, pushing past my senses until all I could see, hear, and feel was the rainforest.

What was I doing here? What was Gladwin doing here? I knew I should capture him, or kill him, whichever would work just fine for me. But as I held the collar of his black Coalition uniform in my fist, I could not bring myself to act.

His eyes were so black and devoid of light, like one of the antimatter holes left in the farthest corners of the universe by the Gods' immeasurable power. I felt like I was being swallowed whole, atom by atom sucked into the depths of nothingness.

"You want to let me go, don't you, Daux?" Gladwin

asked smoothly. "You want to let me walk out of this chamber safely and unharmed. You can even come with me if you would like. I can take you to your father."

My father? I was angry with him. He had hurt me and my friends, had he not? But I so desperately wanted to see him. I wanted to help him on his mission, whatever that was. I wanted to be a good daughter. I wanted my father's love. I wanted that more than *anything*.

"Ah, such fun we shall have, don't you think?" Gladwin asked me, cupping his hand to my cheek.

Yes. I wanted to whisper, but the words would not form in my mouth. I was frozen in place, unable to twitch an eyelash much less move my lips.

"Daux," came a harsh voice to my right, icy and cold.

The darkness was cut by a prickle of light for a fraction of a second before it was back with full vengeance. I could hardly breathe. The sound of my blood rushing in my ears was the only thing other than Gladwin's voice I could hear.

"Daux!" the frozen voice shouted close to my ear.

A low moan of pain slipped through my lips as I pushed at the hands grasping me. There were too many. I could not breathe.

Then I saw it.

White.

The ceiling was white.

What ceiling? I was on the Floral Islands with Captain Gladwin. He was taking me to my father. I was not in Spec Ops custody anymore. I was safe. Gladwin had saved me.

But the ceiling was white and I was not on the Floral Islands. Valentin had a sword made of ice magic at Gladwin's throat, a crimson ripple of blood dripping down his pale skin where the magic weapon had pierced his skin.

Gladwin's expression was fierce and manic, his black eyes glowing with an unknown power. His teeth bared at Valentin like a cornered animal. Valentin stood above him, sword pointed directly above Gladwin's jugular, face impassive. His bleached blond hair was disheveled, his pale skin was slightly flushed, and his chest was heaving with exertion. He had launched the table across the room, and it now lay in a mangled heap beneath a large dent in the white wall.

If I had any artistic talent in my battle-worn hands I would have painted this scene, but I settled for immortalizing it in my mind before looking around the white cell.

Dev was nowhere to be seen. He had entered the room right after Valentin and me, had he not? No, I was sure he had. Where did he go?

"How did you do that?" I asked Gladwin, scrambling to my feet.

There was no way. *There was no way.*

Gladwin did not have magic. He could not. The Coalition hated magic. There was no way Gladwin would be using it, much less showing it to me and anyone else at Spec Ops HQ who could be watching. But here I was, having fallen victim to some sort of glamour that ensnared me *through* my foresight, and through the anti-magic tech in the cells.

Gladwin's manic grin widened, showing far too many teeth and I flinched at the sight. It was like the skin of his face had nearly split in two, like a wolf's. I shook my head and rubbed my eyes, hoping it was part of the illusion, but when my gaze fell on the fallen captain again, I could still see too many of his teeth.

From the sneer on Valentin's face, he could see them too.

Bile rose in the back of my throat and I could barely swallow it back down. I gagged, the muscles in my throat spasming involuntarily as I tried my hardest not to expel the waffles I had eaten that morning. Was it more of a glamour? Or was his face really…

I could not bring myself to finish the thought.

"It's the enhancers, isn't it?" I asked once I was sure the contents of my stomach were not going to expel themselves all over the pristine white floor. "That's how you're doing this. That's why your face is…"

"My face is what?" Gladwin asked, his voice a low rumble. His lips remained pulled back in that frenzied smile, showing *all* of his teeth, splitting his face completely in two. His eyes somehow darkened even more than they already were, the iris completely swallowing the white. "Like this?"

His jaw – impossibly – unhinged, his teeth lengthening into needle-sharp points. Gladwin's body began to grow, his extremities lengthening as he stood to tower over Valentin who gazed up at him with a horror that I had never witnessed on my teammate's face once since I had met him. Not even when he had been injured. Not even when he saw the destruction my father had wrought in Portnith.

"Gods above and below," I swore, using the archaic expression, and pressed my hand to my mouth.

"If the Gods will not return to us, we shall become them," Gladwin said in that horrible deep, slithering voice. "Remember, Rage, I am *Fear*."

It wormed itself into my ears, into my brain, trying to find purchase in my neurons and cells. This time I *was* sick, my breakfast spraying through my fingers and onto the clean white floor. Gladwin's laugh shattered through the sound of my retching, the same horrid slithering sound accompanied by a cacophony of thunder and crashing boulders.

It set my equilibrium off balance and I found I could not rise to fight or escape even if I had wanted to. I was trapped, imprisoned in this horrible white room with a monster I no longer knew how to identify. Gladwin was no longer human – if he ever had been.

He was becoming something different. Something more.

He was becoming a God.

A shout from behind me jerked my attention away from the man-God before me, and I turned to see Dev rushing back into the room with a hastily assembled army of agents and interrogators. In his hands were several syringes filled with a clear liquid. Blockers.

"Valentin!" Dev yelled above the sound of Gladwin's laughter, tossing him a syringe. "Use it! Use it fast!"

Dev was going to fight this *monster* with *blockers*? I pushed myself to my feet, my mind spinning and shouting incredulous half-formed sentences at me as I rushed toward Gladwin, flame blazing in my hands.

I had to help. I had to protect them.

"No," Gladwin boomed, stopping me in my tracks.

The flame in my palms sputtered, nearly dying like the ember in my chest. Why was I stopping? Why was I not fighting?

Obey me. Gladwin's oily booming voice reverberated in my mind, but he had not spoken. *Obey your Fear.*

The flames in my hands sputtered again, but they did not die. Gladwin's command shook me to my core. I had no idea what he was doing to me, why my foresight could not dispel it, and how he was even doing so. The Coalition *hated* magic. They *despised* it. Their entire international organization was founded on its rejection of anything and everything magical.

The enhancers.

The memories of the mutated plants and animals I had seen in my classes at the academy – in pictures and in real life – flew to the forefront of my mind. Bears with balding, scaled patches shining through their coarse fur. Their jaws unhinged like a snake to devour its prey with rows and rows of teeth like a shark. Insects with far too many legs to be classified as such and in such vibrant colors that they would surely be eaten by any animals who caught sight of them if it were not for the noxious poisons that they secreted that scientists were still trying to understand.

Brightly colored ferns, poisonous black roses, foxgloves that could kill with one sniff of their pollen. Trees that rotted from the inside out before they reached their desired height and bleed corrosive sap when cut into. One of the worst was the child-eating plants, which thankfully had been culled long ago.

These mutants often did not make it past their maturation, dying soon after a reproductive cycle, which made it easy for non-mutated animals and plants to encroach back into their territories and kill the young mutations. Mature mutated flora and fauna were forces to be reckoned with, but the non-mutated animals had adapted to combat them well enough.

Gladwin reminded me of these monstrosities.

Had the Coalition experimented on the natural flora and fauna of our world to create these enhancing serums? Had the mutations been an effect of those experiments? Had they intentionally tried to destroy everything just to bring the Gods back? Or, in their hubris, done such a thing to fashion themselves into new Gods?

If the Gods will not return to us, we shall become them. Gladwin's earlier words echoed back to me.

In an instant, I leaped into the fray unencumbered by my earlier nausea. Valentin needed me. They all needed me. One more person was all it took to change the tide of a battle in some cases. One well-placed slash with a sword. One well-aimed shot with a firearm. One good strategy. A scrap of intel. It was what we had been taught at the Academy.

Valentin was defending himself furiously with his sword, all pale and icy cold. Like a prince in a fairy story. His eyes flashed haughtily as he spun away from a quickly timed swipe from Gladwin's claws. The others behind us sent their magical attacks his way and someone even had a firearm, carefully aiming their shots at Gladwin when there was an opening.

I could hear Gladwin's commands in my mind telling me to stop, to blast Valentin with white hot flame enough to render him into ash on the spot, but they were merely whispers now. I don't know what had changed, but it did not matter.

That ember in my chest roared against Gladwin's

commands, burning into my very soul. Burning up through my bloodstream, my throat. Flame erupted from my palms, up my throat, and past my lips leaving the smell of sulfur and smoke in my nostrils as the heat boiled in my stomach.

Gladwin's screams of agony and rage pierced my ears. The sound was unnatural. Unholy. But I did not let up the force of my magic, watching as the shallow cuts and bullet holes cauterized as my flames burned his flesh. Skin bubbled and oozed with blood and oil, flesh melted, hair singed.

I had wanted to do this for ages, and now I had gotten my wish.

Satisfaction roared through me, fueling my magic, burning the flame hotter. I would have a sore throat later because of the smoke, but I did not care. Fire could not consume the dragon that created it. I was no different.

I only let up my magical attack when Gladwin's horrific body fell; though, still not dead from the burns I had inflicted.

"Now!" I screamed, feeling the rawness of my throat already.

Valentin understood at once and jammed his blocker syringe into Gladwin's neck. Dev followed suit, as did many others who were also now carrying blockers. Healers rushed into the room just as Gladwin's form began to shrink back to its normal size. Healing light, warm and soothing glowed over him as they reknit his skin and muscle, saving him from my burns. Every so often, another blocker would be administered to stave off the effects of the enhancer.

We did not know how long it would stay in his system. We did not know if the effects were permanent or not. Once his body was in a healed enough condition to move, someone – one of the healers no doubt – hooked him up to an IV drip. The bag was filled with magic-blocking serum.

Valentin and I stood next to each other – I did not know when he moved to stand beside me, nor when he had grabbed my too-hot hand in his ice-cold one – and watched.

Gladwin's eyes began to flutter as the healers worked over him, a new healer moving in to take another's place when their magical and physical energies were depleted. Then, his eyes opened and I gasped.

Looking up at Valentin in disbelief, I saw that his face was set, tight and grim. Rage shone behind his lovely blue eyes. I looked back down at Gladwin to make sure I had seen what I thought I had, squeezing Valentin's hand tightly despite our sweating palms.

Gladwin's eyes met mine, a wicked smile plastered over his ruined, but healing, lips when he saw the horror written on my face. His eyes, those horrible blacker-than-black eyes, were no longer dark. They were no longer the same familiar, nauseating shade that threatened to swallow me whole only minutes before. They were now a terribly, frighteningly familiar shade of ice blue.

Chapter Twenty-Eight

I could not remember how I came to be sitting in the Overseer's office, much less how I got there in the first place. All I remember was looking into Gladwin's eyes and nothing else. There was no way it was another illusion, not with the large amount of blockers pumped into his system.

I unsuccessfully attempted to suppress a shudder.

His eyes were the exact same shade of blue as Valentin's. The shade I had grown so fond of. It was now tainted by Gladwin's monstrosity. How was he able to control me the way he did? Why did foresight not dispel the illusion?

"Why did Gladwin want you in that room so badly?" The Overseer voiced my next question aloud as if she had read my mind.

I swallowed uneasily before answering. I did not want her to know more than she needed to. "I am not sure, Ma'am. All I know is that he specifically wanted Valentin and me in the interrogation room with Suna. He mentioned both of us by name."

The Overseer pursed her lips, tapping her fingers together thoughtfully. Valentin shifted in his seat next to me, and I started. Again, I had not realized he was next to me. Numbness ran through my limbs, my brain, feeling heavy and thick. Whatever Gladwin had done to me, it had left its mark.

"Dev tells me you believe that Gladwin was

experimenting with these 'enhancers'? That he called himself 'Fear'?" The Overseer spoke again, this time directed toward Valentin.

"Yes," he answered simply, his own movements slow like mine. "He said something in the interrogation chamber..." Valentin paused, looking at me, seemingly asking me for something with his eyes.

I swallowed again, my throat burning from the smoke I had exhaled earlier.

"He said 'If the Gods will not return to us, we shall become them'," I said, forcing back the urge to be sick again at the memory of his horrible voice.

If it were possible, the Overseer's expression grew even more grim, her steepled fingers forming into a fist she rested stiffly atop her desk. I did not like that look. I did not like what it meant, and what it could mean. I did not like the fear that rose unbidden in my chest, drowning out that disgusting numbness Gladwin had left me with.

My father wished to become a God.

All of the Coalition leaders must wish to become Gods. They must all be using magic. My father had magic. He took blockers to hide it... or did he?

"My father..." I gasped, shooting upright to stand from my chair, stumbling on weak legs.

"Was using the enhancers," Valentin finished for me, rising to guide me back to my seat. "It's likely your mother was too."

"But why? They are not Coalition leaders," I protested, head spinning. "Why would they be allowed to use an enhancing serum?"

"Because of what they can give the Coalition," the Overseer answered through gritted teeth. "He was a *Governor*. That comes with an immense knowledge of our government, our borders, our people, and our history. All of that would be of the utmost importance to the Coalition, more so than any other person who should wish to defect from the NAF."

"I need to find him, I need to stop him," I said struggling to rise from my chair again.

Valentin grabbed my hand, pulling me back down. "And we will. Gladwin has been hooked up to the machine again. He'll give us that information and more in a few days, whether he wants to or not."

From the grave set of his face, I knew he was thinking about his teammates and how Gladwin claimed he had been involved. Now, maybe, Valentin would have some closure. That day in the rain when he had confessed his grief to me – when I still hated him – flashed in my mind. He had been as angry as me once. I wondered what had changed. Had I done that? Surely not; to think so would be incredibly arrogant.

I could not help but think about how he had changed after that day. It was like a weight had been lifted off his shoulders. He was still a hard-ass and more stoic than the most seasoned soldier, but there was a softness about him now. Especially with me – and with Amalie and the rest of the team. His edges were not so sharp, his eyes not so guarded, his voice not so cold.

A fluttering stirred in my heart when I realized he was still holding my hand. The memory of what I had accidentally said to him this morning burned in my ears. Had it only been this morning? It felt like a lifetime ago now.

"Okay," I said, struggling to speak around my thoughts. "But we need more information on these enhancers. There is no way they have just emerged from thin air."

"I'm inclined to agree," Valentin said, smiling softly now that I was calmed somewhat.

I resisted the urge to stare at his mouth, instead looking straight ahead at the Overseer who frowned slightly at me.

"Are you all right, Deveraux?" she asked, concern lacing her tone and immaculate brows furrowing. "You look positively ill."

A nervous laugh escaped me and I struggled to school

my face into a neutral expression.

"Yes, of course," I assured her, ignoring a warning look from Valentin. "I am just feeling a bit rattled from Gladwin's revelation."

She nodded with understanding, dropping the matter of my strange behavior. "I am troubled about that as well," she admitted after a beat. "Still, there have been no findings of any enhancing serums – experimental or otherwise – being made in any of the NAF territories. At least, not that we can find, and if *we* cannot find evidence of it, then it is certainly well hidden indeed."

"Gladwin's... transformation reminded me of something," I said slowly, looking between Valentin and the Overseer. "The mutations. Our world's plants and animals began changing shortly before the war... and they changed in ways that were incredibly similar to Gladwin."

"But all the mutations have incredibly short lifespans," Valentin interjected.

"They do, but what if that was a flaw in the experiments the Coalition was trying to eradicate?" I insisted, sitting up straighter in my seat. "If Gladwin were using them, they must have worked out that little kink in the experiment. They must have perfected the serum if someone as vain as him were to inject it into his body. And what if the enhancers don't just enhance *magic* but the most powerful thing about a living thing? What if it enhances the very *essence* of something? Gladwin is a psychopath, a murderer, and Gods know what else, so he developed monstrous traits as well as enhanced abilities."

"Gods above and below," the Overseer swore, hand to her heart and forehead as though she could not determine whether she was going to faint or be sick.

Valentin called for one of the Overseer's assistants to bring her some water, and she accepted it gratefully, gulping it down so readily that some sloshed over the side and onto the lap of her leather trousers.

"Dr. Moreau may have some insight into this matter," she said when she finished the glass and could breathe, brushing the water from her lap.

There was a sickly pallor to her dark skin, but she waved off another glass of water, instead pressing the empty glass to her cheek to let the cold soothe her.

"Dr. Moreau?" Valentin asked.

"The doctor we rescued from the Floral Islands?" I tilted my head in confusion.

"He studies the world's flora and fauna, mutated and non-mutated," The Overseer explained in a shaking voice. "It is an odd task for a Spec Ops agent, but it has led to new ways of combating both groups when necessary. He may have data on the mutated plants and animals that could help us understand Gladwin's transformation and the enhancers. I will have him gather his data and send anything pertinent to Dev and the both of you."

Pulling my hand from Valentin's, we both stood and nodded, understanding the Overseer's words as a dismissal. As we turned to leave, the room was flooded with the Overseer's many assistants. Her orders, harried and terse, followed us out into the hall. The sound only served to punctuate the growing silence between us, one that I was scared to breech. It felt as though Valentin were millions of miles away from me, and if I were to reach out to touch him, I would find his hand just out of reach.

My hand hovered over the blocker I had sat on the bathroom counter, the crème-colored marble stark against the glass and surgical steel of the syringe. I was not on active duty, but I also was not inactive either. I had not been given directions to take blockers until called – nor had I been told to hold off. I swallowed, my throat still raw from the smoke and flame.

I had not spewed flame from my mouth before and I was scared that – because of whatever was happening to me when I took these blockers – I might accidentally burn down the flat with everyone inside it.

I would need to practice more; I would need to control whatever this was. Using all that energy to attack Gladwin nearly drained me dry. It was all I could do to trudge to the bathroom to shower after Valentin and I had returned home from headquarters. Feeling this weak shamed me. I hated that my muscles still ached after training. I hated that using my magic took so much more out of me than it used to. I felt so *useless*.

Before I realized what I was doing, my fist had closed around the syringe and crushed it. I hissed in pain, dropping the instrument, but not before large glass shards had imbedded themselves into the skin of my palm and fingers.

"Dammit!" I cursed, flinging the remnants into the trash.

Just then, a knock sounded from the other side of the door.

"Hang on a second!" I called, cursing under my breath as I wrapped a pristine white hand towel around my bleeding appendage.

When I opened the door, Valentin stood there, expression cool and guarded. Then he saw my hand and the crimson liquid seeping through my makeshift bandage. My hand throbbed and I pulled it close to my chest as if it would ward off the pain.

"What happened?" he demanded, shoving his way into the bathroom, closing, then locking the door behind him.

"I cut my hand," I replied dumbly.

"How?"

My eyes darted toward the bathroom trash receptacle before I could help myself and he brushed past me to look inside it. There, on the bottom of the empty receptacle, lay a bloody and broken syringe. Valentin turned toward me once again, face grim.

"How?" he repeated, a touch of anguish in his voice.

"I crushed it," I admitted, jutting my chin in the air. "Accidentally."

"Why?"

Was there a point in arguing with him? No, I supposed there was not. I sighed.

"I was angry."

"So, you crushed a blocker?"

I nodded, unwilling to say anything more.

Wordlessly, Valentin began pulling a first aid kit from beneath the sink and setting out supplies to clean and bandage my wound. I watched as he prepped his own hands and sanitized the counter before holding his hand out to me, waiting.

I hesitated for a moment, afraid to cross that thousand-mile gap between us, but when I laid my hand in his I found the distance to be much greater than I had imagined. His hand was gentle as he unwrapped the bloodied towel to inspect my wound, but there was a tension to it that I remembered from our first days as teammates. My chest tightened painfully, tugging at the jagged edges of my heart.

He was silent as he picked the shard of glass from my hand with tweezers. He held it so close to his face I could feel his cool breath on my skin and I had to fight to hold back the shivers. I did not want to embed the glass any further into my skin or risk him stabbing my wounds with the tweezers. It hurt enough already.

The steady clink, clink, clink of the glass as each bloodied shard landed in the sink reverberated in my ears. He was so, so quiet I could hear him blinking. Nausea churned in my gut, but not because of the blood and my torn flesh, but because I love—I loved… I loved him. And I was too far gone to have him.

"Daux," Valentin said as he disinfected and bandaged my hand.

I hummed in response, unable to form words for fear of

blurting out my feelings for him.

"I am… concerned about you," he admitted.

I looked away, unable to meet his eyes.

Of course, he was concerned about me. All my teammates and friends were. Even my grandparents seemed concerned when I last visited them. I had been changed; I had *chosen* to change. I was resigned to it now.

"You needn't be," I murmured, pulling away from him and heading for the door.

He made no move to stop me, much to my relief. I did not need the extra pain. Once I captured my father, this would all be over. I had no illusions of things returning to normal, returning to the way they were before, but I would not need to be so vigilant about fending off my teammates' concerns for me.

"Thank you for bandaging my hand," I whispered, leaving him alone.

Information regarding my father's location came in the middle of the night. Luckily Amalie's care team had someone on call for this very scenario and was at the flat within the hour. My sister did not even stir when I and the team left for the Overseer's office. Not even when I leaned down to whisper goodbye and kiss her forehead.

When we entered the office, Dev was there waiting for us, looking as well put together as he always did. I was unnerved by his unruffled appearance, knowing the dark circles under my eyes resembled bruises and my braid was uneven. My team was not faring much better than me, Jax was fighting back yawn after yawn; Félix and Himawari had barely managed to tame their hair nests; even Valentin looked as though he could barely keep his eyes open.

The Overseer was implacable as always, not a hair out of place. A jolt of envy ran through me at her perfect box braids and bright-eyed appearance. I had to remind myself she had a lot more practice at being up at all hours than I did. She was standing against her desk, her eyes locked onto the screen of her holonav when we entered her office, wreathed in her usual black ensemble.

Dev cleared his throat, catching her attention and her head snapped up.

"Oh, good, you're here," she said by way of a greeting. "Please be seated, I know you are all tired."

We obeyed gratefully, Félix, Jax, and Himawari taking a spot on one of the brown leather couches that were pushed up against the wall. Valentin and I sat in each of the chairs sitting in front of the Overseer's desk. Dev remained standing, unconcerned about tired legs.

Sometimes I wondered if he was a robot.

"Dev's interrogation team has uncovered that your father's last known location was in Athor," the Overseer informed us once we were seated. "Gladwin confirmed your suspicion about the secretary, she has been arrested and has told us everything she knows."

Athor? Why would my father go to Athor? I was pleased that my suspicions about Hayley were right, but how in the world were we going to get into Athor unnoticed?

"And how are we supposed to get into Athor?" Félix asked, voicing my thoughts.

Athor was a country on an arid continent southwest of Eidolon. A place of constant contention between the NAF and the Coalition with both Governments taking over the territory and driving the other out many times during the NAFs early days. It was now a no-man's land, rich in oil and self-governed. The Athor Government was allied with the NAF but pockets of Coalition loyalists continued to cause trouble since the last conflict over the country.

"We will have to get you as close to the country as possible without alerting any Coalition bases in the area," the Overseer said, frowning at her holonav momentarily. "Jet most of the way at least. You will have to leave immediately if you want to catch up with your father. I will send you the coordinates before your journey over so they are not intercepted by untrustworthy parties."

"Someone needs to inform my grandparents," I snapped, allowing myself a small slip from the mask I wore in front of the Overseer – the one I tried to keep in place in front of everyone else. "If I die retrieving my father, they are to take over my sister's care. They need to know I am leaving, not what for or for how long, just that it is happening."

A look of displeasure marred the Overseer's elegant features, but she acquiesced with a wave of her hand. One of her many assistants rushed into the room, holonav at the ready.

"Write a missive to the Winchesters, Agent Deveraux's grandparents, and inform them that their granddaughter Amalie is currently being watched over by her care team as their other granddaughter is on a mission with an indefinite return date," the Overseer commanded.

The assistant nodded, already typing furiously on her device as she hurried from the room. Then the Overseer turned back to us, eyes narrowed and shrewd.

"Be prepared to leave at a moment's notice," she said, rising from her desk to see us out. "We are still gathering more information from Gladwin by the second, but we cannot overtax him or we will kill him, as I am sure you are aware."

I grimaced but held my tongue. It would not do to pick a fight now.

The Overseer continued, explaining that Gladwin's information was disjointed and incomplete. They had my father's location, but not enough specifics. They did not want to send us in blind in case there was more danger than anticipated. It was highly possible that another team would be dispatched alongside us, which would make stealth a lot more difficult to maintain.

I quickly suggested Talia and her team, considering the heavy hitters with the Demos twins and the ranged stealth attacks Gwyn and Talia could carry out. The Overseer twitched a brow at me, no doubt contemplating Talia's "involvement" in my father's escape, but nodded. It was not a confirmation of my request, but a promise to consider it.

That was all I could ask for, I supposed.

The five of us returned home, heavy-limbed and dead-eyed. Amalie's carer's breezy goodbye barely registered in my ears as she brushed past me and out the door while I pulled off my boots. I blinked, dropping them to the floor, and shuffled down the hall to check on Amalie. She was fast asleep still and I dropped a kiss to her soft hair before leaving, then closed the door quietly behind me.

I knew I would be unable to sleep if I tried, so I headed to the kitchen to make myself some tea. The others were sitting around the dining room table, eyes glazed and posture slumped.

"Herbal or caffeine?" I asked from the doorway between the rooms.

A collective grumble of words I could not discern emanated from the group. I pursed my lips and sighed.

"Herbal it is," I said, turning on my heel to make the tea.

Once it was finished seeping, I gathered five mugs and placed them on the table with cream and sugar. Then I retrieved the teapot and poured tea into each of the mugs, pushing them toward my friends as each was filled.

I took no cream in mine, only sugar, and watched blearily as Félix nearly caused an overflow in his mug with cream. He stopped right before it spilled over the rim, eyes on his holonav.

Jax heaped spoonful after spoonful of sugar into his, then grimaced when he took a sip. Himawari switched hers with him after lightly sweetening it. Jax barely seemed to notice, blinking groggily at the new mug of tea before him. Valentin was the only one of us who took it black, watching the rest of us with weary amusement as we blundered through preparing our drinks.

None of us spoke for a long time, all lost in thought. Of all the heinous, disgusting things I expected the Coalition to be behind, creating new Gods was not one of them. I thought of all the blockers my father had forced on me, on Amalie, and shuddered. Just how many of those were blockers that we had been dosed with? What if he had injected us with enhancers as well? Would that explain the shadows in my teammates' eyes? Would that explain the darkness in my own?

But they would just cancel each other out, wouldn't they?

Even after years of blocker usage, my magic had not dimmed. That was not how blockers worked. They only blocked the ability to use magic; it did not destroy the ability itself. There were ways to take the ability from people, which were typically used on criminals, but regular blockers could not do such a thing. I would be powerless otherwise.

The ember in my chest flared in protest at the memory of my magic being dampened and my hand clenched around my mug of tea.

"So," Himawari began after a while. "What are we going to do?"

I swallowed a large gulp of tea before answering her. It burned my already raw throat on its way down. I savored in the pain.

"We are going to go to Athor and arrest my father," I said simply.

"But it's *Athor!*" Himawari exclaimed incredulously.

"I know."

She shook her head disbelievingly at me, but I held up a hand in surrender.

"I have a plan," I said, toying with my mug. "It won't be easy, but it's the only thing I can think of."

"Okay, let's hear it," Valentin said, looking at each of

our team members and then finally to me.

I let my gaze lock with his, my heart swelling and breaking at the same time. Then I spoke.

Chapter Twenty-Nine

Y ou cannot be serious," Valentin all but shouted when I had finished relaying my proposal.

"I am perfectly serious," I said and took a sip of my tea.

"Tell that you lot don't agree with this madness?" Valentin begged the others, running his hand through his hair.

Himawari shot Valentin an apologetic look. "I'm sorry, but Daux has a point."

"She does," Félix agreed.

Jax was the only one who looked torn about my idea.

"I can see how it would work," he spoke slowly, weighing his words. "But I can also see the danger it would pose you, not to mention all the things that could go wrong."

I sighed, resting my forehead in my hand. "Listen, my father is crazy if he thinks he can become a God. But if what I suspect is true," I swallowed hard, looking down at my thighs – the place he used to give me my injections. "Then he will want to finish what he started."

Valentin gave a strangled cry and slammed his fist down on the table.

We all jumped at his display of emotion, staring at him wide-eyed.

"You cannot be serious, after what we saw those enhancers do to Gladwin!" he yelled, uncaring of the late hour or his volume. "Your father will destroy you as he has always hoped to do, Daux. You *know* that."

"I do," I snapped, rising from my seat. "I know better than anyone what my father is capable of doing, and what he has done to *me*. I am willing to take the risk of letting him believe I want to join his cause – the risk of letting him get close enough to try to inject me – if it means bringing him down for good."

No one commented on my choice of words, no doubt believing them exactly as I had intended them to do; however, a glimmer of recognition shone in Valentin's eye. Had he caught the double meaning in my words? I hoped not, because he was the only one who could stop me from killing my father the moment that I allowed him close enough to inject me with those foul enhancers.

Athor was as dry and hot as I had heard it described. It felt as though it was leeching the moisture from my skin. The trip in had been long, days. With the tumultuous nature of the country's history, we needed to travel by boat. A civilian leisure ship that felt as though it moved as slow as a crawl.

Our weapons were easy enough to stow, especially when we informed the captain who we were and that our mission was important to the international security of the NAF. Travel back would be organized with Athor's governing body upon my father's capture, which would be much quicker. I wondered how we would be returning home when the Overseer found out what I was planning to do.

My lips were dry and cracking, not because I had been chewing on them. Nervousness bubbled inside me, shaking my arms and tensing my shoulders even as I attempted to breathe, breathe, *breathe* as my grandmother had taught me.

It was no use.

As I crossed the hot sand, the sun glaring off the grains in a way that nearly blinded me, I felt as though I was going to pass out from sheer anxiety. My teammates had been a steady presence at my side, but they would not be for much longer. If I was going to get close to my father, I needed to be alone, which meant my friends would have to stay out of sight. They knew and agreed to the plan.

We would get my father to take us to his hideout, and I would incapacitate and arrest him. At least, that was the plan on paper. The Overseer had denied my request for Talia's team – or any other team – to join us. We were on our own.

My fears had started before we even set foot on the jet. Valentin had indeed noticed the double meaning in my words and stared at me relentlessly while preparing for our mission. I had tried to ignore him. Attempted to send him innocent smiles and lighthearted jokes his way. He was not having any of it. Joking and smiling had not been a part of my personality for a while now, and using them as a distraction only seemed to heighten his distrust of me.

He had literally cornered me in front of the closed front door before we left the flat while Amalie was in the corridor with the others saying goodbye.

"I know what you're planning," he had said, staring down at me with a weary expression, his blue eyes shadowed and sad.

"Do you now?" I asked, injecting a hint of saccharine sweetness into my tone.

"Daux," Valentin warned, voice low and harsh.

I liked that.

I liked the electric feeling that had been building between us since he had returned home. I liked the way the rasp of his voice slid over my skin like the satin of the red dress from the gala I had hanging in the back of my armoire.

Brazenly, I placed my hand on his shoulder and stood on my toes to stand at eye level with him. If I was going to die or lose myself on this mission, I might as well enjoy my final moments in Heliorious.

"Valentin," I breathed, my breath fanning over his

shock-parted lips.

I watched as his tongue darted between them for the briefest of moments and wondered how it would taste. If it would feel cool like his hands, or hot and blazing like the fire I had expelled from deep in my lungs. I wanted to find out – if only to distract him and myself from what I was going to do when I got to Athor.

"Daux," he said again, voice pleading and velvety.

He smelled so intoxicating – ozone and mint; the cold, magical smell of him soothing the burning in my throat. Just as I was about to close the hairsbreadth gap that I had left between us, he shoved me backward into the door so hard the back of my head thudded dully against it. A thrill ran up my spine when his hands found my hips. I could feel the coolness of his fingers through my armor and my body began to hum with magical energy in response to his touch.

"Don't do this," he breathed against the shell of my ear.

I trembled at the feeling. "Do what?" I asked coyly, a smirk curling at my lips. I had him right where I wanted him, now if only he would *cooperate!*

"Trick me," he whispered. "Distract me, whatever you're trying to do."

"And is that *really* what you think I am trying to do?" I asked in a voice like silk as I twined my fingers into his hair, pulling him closer. "Distract you?"

His breath hitched. There was hardly any space between us and no space left between me and the door. If someone had still been in the flat and happened upon us, it would seem as though I had been trapped, but really, it was I who had trapped Valentin like a fly in a spider's web. The thought soured my stomach a little, but I ignored it.

"Stop," he groaned against the skin of my neck. "Please, not like this."

I frowned. Like what? Valentin had flirted with me, surely, I could do the same. He might not love me as I did him, but that did not mean I could not initiate a kiss. So, what if I was the only one with feelings? People who didn't love each other kissed all the time.

Why couldn't we?

"I don't care if you don't want to talk about what we both know you intend to do in Athor," Valentin said, attempting to pull away from me. "But I won't do this. I won't let you do this to me, to us."

That familiar feeling of rage burned within me and I could taste sulfur at the back of my throat, burning the tender membrane. His rejection stung as though I had been slapped, and only steeled my resolve. My father would die. I didn't care what usefulness he had to the NAF. He was a dead man, and I didn't care what it cost me. Not even if I lost Valentin.

"If you don't want me, then let go of me," I hissed, yanking my hands from his hair.

And he did, the coolness of his hands quickly replaced by the burning heat of my anger. I had barely noticed Amalie's tearful goodbye when we joined everyone in the corridor. I attempted to pay attention, to wipe away her tears like a big sister should, but all I could think of was Valentin and his hands dropping from my hips, effectively letting me know how he felt. About any possibility of *us*. I should have known. I was too damaged for him, for anyone.

I regretted that now – how I had acted, and thinking he would be interested anyway – and on the jet as we flew over the Cassacania Ocean to get as close to our destination as possible. He refused to look at me, or I had refused to look at him so I would not know if he had attempted to do so himself. And on our trek to Athor, neither of us had spoken a word to each other.

Now, in the heart of the bustling city, our armor and battle gear shrouded in light-colored robes and scarves to protect our heads from the scorching Athor sun, Valentin still ignored me. Instead of his usual place beside me, he stood to my six, keeping a watchful eye out on the crowds around us. Jax stood beside him, behind Himawari who was to my left, and Félix to my right. To anyone else in the crowd, we would have looked much like a group of friends out on the town. Perhaps going to lunch at one of the street stalls, or shopping in the popular market district.

But to a practiced eye, one would have caught the subtleties of our movements. They would have seen our eyes sliding over the crowd with more than the curious or excited eye of a group of young people out for a day of pleasure. They would have seen the subtle outline of our weapons beneath our robes – or understood that Himawari's staff was not a fashionable walking support as she pretended it was now.

I was counting on that.

I was counting on my father and his people seeing us – seeing me – and trying to finish what he started in Portnith. Anticipation thrummed through me, over my skin, in my brain. I could not wait for the moment I saw the flash of betrayal in my father's eyes the moment he realized I wasn't going to go along with his stupid plan. I would *never* allow him to become a twisted version of a God, nor would I allow him to make me into one either.

Once we were in a good vantage point I dropped the protective scarf around my shoulders, allowing my short golden hair to show. The others browsed casually around the massive amounts of street vendors, sampling their wares on occasion as I sat down in the middle of the square on the lip of an old, but beautifully kept fountain depicting one of the many forgotten Gods. This one appeared to be a Goddess of wealth or commerce with the beautiful robes which were carved onto her stone body and a jug of coins she was tipping into the fountain. Her belly was swollen with child and her exquisitely carved lips were turned up in a smile indicating the comfort and happiness one could achieve with financial stability.

It was a beautiful town square, full of color and music that distracted from the blistering heat of the sun reflecting off the sand and stone. For a moment, I allowed myself to feel glad that Athor and the other nations around them had been able to remain mostly independent from the Coalition, for the controlling government surely would have destroyed the beauty of this place for its brutalist ideals and architecture. I was also glad they had favored their won independence from the NAF. It was interesting to me that they could have peace without the same governmental structures we had.

I allowed myself to think on these things for a while longer, observing my surroundings from my place at the fountain. Too soon enough, however, I saw a group of men in robes similar to mine standing on a rooftop observing the square just as Himawari spoke into my earpiece.

"We're surrounded," she whispered, attempting not to sound nervous.

Everything was going according to plan.

I smiled. "That's what I was hoping for."

In a flash, several disguised Coalition soldiers converged on us and began herding my unresisting teammates toward the fountain. I stood with my hands slightly raised so they would not get antsy. The whole thing was inconspicuous; not a single local noticed. From the outside looking in, it would have seemed like we had met up with another group of acquaintances.

I grinned up at the soldiers watching from the roof and turned to the ones surrounding me and my teammates.

"State your business," one said in a hushed, almost conversational tone.

He was tall, and intimidating, with dark skin and eyes. His head was shaved and his limbs were long and thick like tree trunks. He looked as though he could snap me in half with his bare hands.

I never thought I would see someone bigger than Jax. I shot him a surprised look and he shrugged.

"My father wants to know why I'm here?" I asked

innocently, tilting my head. "I would have thought that was obvious. I wish to join him. The NAF betrayed me, betrayed my friends. I want to help my father finish what he started."

"I was hoping you would say that," said a smooth voice that ran chills through my blood.

I turned to my right and looked up into a familiar pair of green eyes, plastering a smile onto my face to hide my wrath.

"Hello, Father," I said, opening my arms to him.

My father enveloped me in his own long, slender limbs, resting his long-fingered hand on the back of my head as he pulled me into his chest. I had longed for him to hold me this way once but now I merely felt a painful tug at my chest. This felt off, wrong. I could feel my teammates' eyes on my back. The tension was rolling off them so thick I could cut it with my rapier.

"Hello, my little deer," Father whispered joyfully.

We had been herded away from the hustle and bustle of the square and into an awaiting auto without a fuss. We were so complacent that my father's men had not even searched us for weapons or insisted on magic-blocking cuffs. They truly believed we were defecting after my father's plan to have us arrested had turned us against the NAF. I was a little surprised at how thoughtless they were, but pleased at our good fortune; though, there was a nagging thought in the back of my mind that warned of impending danger. As much as I wanted to ignore it, I could not.

My father had wanted to talk somewhere secluded; somewhere no one would find us. I thought rather wryly that it would be a good way to get rid of us should the need arise, but I complied readily to show him I was on his side. My teammates were much more reluctant – Valentin especially – but I paid them no mind. *Everything* was finally going *my* way. I was not about to ruin it.

Soon, we were nearing a small home well on the outskirts of town. It was one story and made of the same soft brown stone that most of the buildings were in this country. The home was situated near the edge of a steep butte, far enough away to prevent any danger, but close enough that many people would stay far away. We had not passed another house or settlement for many kilometers and could not see any of them in the distance. Still, I did not worry despite the warnings in my head. I had everything under control.

When the auto stopped and we all exited the vehicle, my team and I made to follow my father into the house but the soldiers with him stopped us.

"Only you beyond this point, Daux," my father said warmly, but there was a threatening note beneath that cordiality.

I nodded my obedience with a complacent smile, waving back my friends to stay with the soldiers outside. None of them appeared happy with the decision, but I hardly cared. I was so close to achieving everything I had worked so hard for – killing my father and screwing over the government that had first betrayed me.

Inside opened straight into the kitchen with a plank floor, swept neatly, and the interior walls were made of the same materials as the outside. The only furniture in the room was a wooden table with enough chairs for my father and his men. An earthen oven and stove were affixed to the far-left wall with plain cabinets and an outdated refrigerator spanned the back.

My father gestured for me to sit, and I did so immediately. He sat across from me, studying my person with the same intensity as he had always done when I was a child, scrutinizing my every move.

"I assume your mother is not coming to meet me?" he asked, crossing one leg over the other leisurely. "Gladwin was supposed to retrieve her; he is good at smuggling defectors out of NAF territories. He had done one such retrieval several years ago, I believe your Angelov would be familiar with the endeavor."

If my father was trying to get a rise out of me with that jab at Valentin, he wouldn't. Not today.

"Valentin is aware of the circumstances of his teammates' deaths," I began, allowing some anger to show, but shaped it so that it would appear as though it was aligned with his own. "And no, Mother has been arrested and will be unable to join us for some time. I could not get her out of custody but you did a good job ruining my reputation with Spec Ops. I see why now."

"You were always too good for what the NAF intended for you," my father sighed, giving me a pitying look. "Shame about your mother. I assume Hayley told you where I would be? Or at least gave you a hint?"

"Oh yes," I nodded enthusiastically. "And I am sure Gladwin will be able to get Mother out of custody. He is known to be very persuasive. I am sure they will take Amalie as well, yes?"

"That was the plan."

Had my father really intended this from the beginning? Had he truly wanted to take us all with him? I did not believe that even for a second, not even as my heart twisted painfully in my chest, crying out for a father I knew would never *ever* choose me not even if I had been exactly what he wanted. As for my mother and Amalie? They were just pawns in his game, as I had been.

"Father," I hedged, injecting as much deference into my tone – my expression – as I possibly could. "I know you had me on blockers when I was a child… but some of those clues you left me in Portnith…" I paused, looking up at him respectfully. "They were not blockers. I knew you were trying to tell me something, but I did not know what. The Spec Ops intelligence sector took them to the labs and they could not understand the chemical composition of them."

"But now you know what they are?" he asked, a twisted sort of pride gleaming in his eyes as he shifted forward in his seat.

"I…" I swallowed thickly. "I remembered that sometimes the blockers burned when you injected me. Blockers feel cold to me, not warm. The heat made my insides burn… My eyes would grow dark, and my *magic*—"

"Your magic is the same as my own," my father finished for me, a wry grin on his handsome face.

He went on to explain that the Deveraux family had always had an affinity for flame out of all the four elemental magics, but never registered their magic. Most of the family line believed in the Coalition's message that magic was evil, that it was a curse – and that they took blockers to counteract it. It was not until the Coalition began seeing success with their enhancer experiments that a few members of the family with ties to the opposing government began to enhance their magic secretly. They believed, like many others, that if the Gods left and cursed them then they would replace the missing deities.

He had used these enhancers on *me*.

And somehow, some way, he had been able to get them to me and my friends. Those shadows in their eyes, the darkness in my own.

"Did you intend…?" I began but was cut off.

"For you to become a God as well?" Father asked mirthfully. "Of course I did. There was once a whole pantheon, so many seats to fill, and who better than my own flesh and blood to fill it with me?"

"Amalie too?"

He nodded his answer, teeming with pride that I had figured it out.

Rage boiled in my blood, and if I was not careful, my magic would get the better of me. He had *experimented* on me. On *Amalie*. I wanted to lunge for him, to wrap my hands around his throat and burn him alive as I squeezed the air from his lungs.

I did not do that, however.

Instead, I asked, "Will you do it again?"

The fanatical gleam in my father's eye blazed brightly and he stood, crossing the kitchen to grab a box from the counter. Nestled inside was a syringe just waiting to be used. Just waiting to foul someone's blood and magic with its disgusting contents.

I tried not to let my disgust show, but was unsuccessful because my father tutted me.

"You always did hate needles," he said with a strange sort of affection in his voice.

I gulped, forcing a nervous smile onto my face. I just needed him to get close enough to me so I could kill him. Just close enough to ram my blade through his black heart. To punch a flaming fist through my father's chest – just as Félix had done to Fear in my hallucination – leaving him with a real hole to match my figurative one.

Blood thundered in my ears as he made his way closer to me. Each step was agony. My hand itched to grab my rapier, to summon a ball of flame and hurl it at his face – the face that had contributed to my own.

Just as he reached me and was about to lean down to press the needle into my neck – just as I was about to run him through to the hilt of my blade – a shout sounded outside. A commotion followed, punctuated by gunfire and the familiar crackling sound of ice, lightning, and Félix's explosions. Then it seemed as though the world was going black.

"No!" I shouted, looking toward a window to see a shadow streaming past. "NO!"

"What is going on?" My father demanded, pulling me around to face him.

His pale face was red with rage, eyes bloodshot and manic.

"I don't know!" I cried, struggling to break his grip.

"They said they were with me!"

They had said that. They had agreed to let me handle this my way – unaware that I had planned to kill my father – and had agreed to take a back seat. They promised that they would not interfere. And they had lied.

My father rolled his eyes and shoved past me, rushing from the house, and leaving me to follow behind.

Outside was a disaster. My teammates were outnumbered, and these soldiers were not as inept as the ones we had killed in the Coalition warehouse. Two of the men had Himawari cornered at the edge of the cliff, guns raised. Her shadows writhed around her like a mythical beast – blacker than I had ever seen them – and she held a hand to her neck, as though she had been wounded. Jax, Félix, and Valentin battled the small hoard of the soldiers that remained, using their combined magics to ward off the bullets that hailed down on them.

But Valentin's ice magic was melting faster than he could conjure it, and the arid conditions made the crystals harder to form. He was unsteady on his feet, his swordplay sloppy and erratic.

Jax called a lightning bolt, taking careful aim at one of my father's men, but when he released it, the bolt fragmented into anyone who stood too close. Félix saw what was happening, and before he was electrocuted, he tackled Valentin – who was still moving sluggishly – and used an explosive blast to launch them both away. They landed in a heap, much too far away for the small blast Félix had emitted.

I expected to see Jax's face twisting in anguish when he saw what he had done, but only a somber, resigned look crossed his face when the bodies fell and the dust settled. And that was when I saw that his eyes were as black as my own had been the first time I reacted to my blockers… no, the first time I involuntarily took an enhancer.

I activated my foresight, searching Félix's irises, then

Himawari's. They were both black as an empty night sky. A glinting in the sand caught my eye and I saw a syringe glinting in the sand. It was half buried, as though it had been dropped.

I stepped past my father, shocked and enraged. How dare he use enhancers on my friends again? I had agreed to it to get close to him, but I never intended for him to use them on my teammates. He must be so desperate to recreate the pantheon that he had his men attack my friends and force the enhancers on them.

I would *kill* him.

I felt the burning pull of magic and rage in my chest and whirled toward my father, unsheathing my blade and making to point it to his throat. I had to finish this quickly if I was going to ever have to opportunity to do it at all.

Except my father was no longer standing behind me where I had left him. Spinning around once again in search of him, I was knocked to the ground. My breath burst from my lungs, leaving me gasping as my chest *burned*. I tried to scramble away, to lift myself upright so I could breathe, but I found myself pinned to the sandy earth with my rapier just out of reach.

Looking up, I saw the face of my father looming above me, wrath in his eyes.

"I knew you would betray me," he said, his voice deadly calm. "I always knew you were no good."

I spat up at him, the glob landing on his cheek, and when he reared back to slap me as I knew he would I arched my back, flinging him off me, and scrambled to gain the dominant position. My hand found the hilt of my rapier, and I swung it upward to aim it directly at my father's skull.

Something sharp pierced my neck as I did so, and I looked down at my father's grinning face. I had been here before, in my simulation. My father was below me and I was about to deliver the killing shot. Then he pulled out his own gun and shot me. But now it was different. Now, he held a syringe full of dangerous chemicals to my neck with his thumb against the plunger and there was nothing I could do to stop him from pressing it.

Chapter Thirty

I felt the prick of the needle sliding under my skin, into my vein. Power like I never experienced burned through my blood, and a cry of pain ripped itself free from my clenched teeth. I screamed against the burn, the complete opposite of the cold, icy feeling of the blockers. It was so much worse than the small amounts I had been unknowingly injecting into myself.

My father had used enhancers on me with the blockers so I did not transform into a monster like Gladwin, at least not until he wanted me to. That was why my eyes were so dark in my memory. That was why he had never wanted me to go to the Academy. I remembered it all now.

It was why he pretended to hate my magic. He *experimented* on me. His own daughter.

He wanted to turn me into a God along with him and Mother. Even poor Amalie. I couldn't even bring myself to dwell on that thought.

With an enraged cry, I brought my rapier up again, angling the sharp point of the blade directly at my father's eye. He needed to pay for what he had done.

"Damn you!" I screamed, yanking the syringe out of my neck with my free hand and keeping my blade point aimed at him so he would not move. "Damn you, and damn everything you ever did to me!"

I drove the syringe into his hand so hard it stuck into the hard-packed, sunbaked earth, pinning him there. I ignored his cries of pain. All I wanted was to see him bleed. All I wanted was to make him pay.

Who would care if I brought him back as a corpse?

"Daux, no!" Valentin cried, causing me to pause.

Still, I held my rapier aloft, the tip – dangerously sharp just for this purpose – hovering inches from my father's eye. It glinted dangerously in the blinding rays of the sun, hypnotizing me momentarily. In my mind's eye, I saw a flash of red coating the blade as I retracted it from my father's eye socket but the moment never materialized in reality.

"Daux!" Jax shouted from somewhere to the right of me. "We need him *alive!*"

The soldiers my teammates had been battling were either dead or dying, their bodies littered across the sand, some with Himawari's strange shadows still writhing around them. I felt hollow. There was no grief for the men who had helped my father, the men who had tried to kill or poison my friends. I wondered when I had grown so callous.

The wind whipped my short hair around my face, strands sticking to my dry, cracked lips as I stared down at the man who gave me life. I so readily wanted to take *his* life with my own hands. How dare they? How dare my teammates judge me? They all had loving families who encouraged their abilities, not cursed their existences. Their parents didn't look down on them as the scum of the earth, as though they could not bear to be in the same room as them let alone share DNA. Their families did not use them as experimental chattel in their quest for unrestrained power.

Not a single one of their family members plotted their downfall, and arrest, all while knowing they could kill themselves. Not a single one. So, how could they judge me? My heart, which had been scarred and shattered since before I was released from that white pit, squeezed painfully inside the gaping hole in my chest as I gazed upon the fear on my father's face.

I tried to smile, but a sneer crossed my face instead.

He did not deserve one.

I knew *exactly* what he deserved, and I had made my decision.

"Are you afraid, Father?" I asked though I knew he was.

I could see him trembling. I relished in it as much as I had enjoyed the memory of torturing him in my Placement Exam simulation. I wanted, no, I *needed* to hear him say it. I needed to see he was as afraid of me as I had been of him once upon a time.

"Go ahead, little deer," my father snapped, his graying blond hair falling into his face. "Give in to your base desires like the mutated animal you are!"

"I plan on it," I whispered and reared my sword arm back.

My anger boiled inside of me as I saw a triumphant smile flash across my father's face. He thought of me as a mutated animal? Fine. Then I would show him my teeth and claws. I would tear his beating heart out of his chest and crush it in front of his face as the light faded from his eyes. He is the one who made me that way after all.

"Daux, *no!*" Valentin screamed causing me to falter before my rapier could pierce my father's eye.

I spun to face Valentin, stamping my boot down on my father's broken leg so he would be in too much agony to pull his hand free and try and crawl away. His screams barely registered in my ears as a white-hot rage overtook the anger boiling inside.

"He is *my* father," I cried as Valentin approached with his hands raised. *"I* get to decide what is done with him, not you, not anyone else!"

"But, Daux," he started, reaching out his hand as if begging me to take it. "He is a valuable asset. If you kill him now, we will have lost an opportunity to stop the Coalition's plans for the enhancers."

From behind him, Himawari and Félix approached, their

eyes flashing that same horrid blackness I knew would be echoed in mine. They too, held their hands up, weapons discarded in the sand – placating me. Himawari's mouth was parted to beg me to calm down, to think critically.

A snarl ripped from my throat like a beast, my boot grinding down harder on my father's leg, his cries finally reaching me. And they were terrible, ugly sounds that turned my stomach and made my skin go cold and clammy. But I did not relent; he never did once for me.

"Daux," Valentin begged pleading with his light eyes. "Daux, *please!*"

And my rage struck like lightning. As it reached its crescendo, my vision fractured and I saw myself. Saw me as I am and I was now. Two sides of the whole me separate, apart, but together. One with fire in her eyes and flowing golden hair. The other was broken and trembling, a gaping hole in her chest that oozed with the same oily black color of her eyes.

They stared at one another across a divide, and, as one, they lunged for each other, falling into a dance of such passion and rage I never thought myself capable. They struck, slashed, grappled, and ripped at each other. Blood dripped from their noses into split lips.

My naked form, my short hair, my bruises, and my bloody nose all snapped me into place in this strange world my brain conjured up as these two facsimiles of myself battled each other as if to the death.

"Stop!" I shouted.

I felt every blow that they landed as though they were attacking me and not each other. At first, it seemed as though the version of myself with fiery eyes was going to win this battle, but with every strike from my black-eyed form she began to falter, her blows growing erratic and slow.

I took a faltering step forward, demanding they stop once again, but they paid me no heed. Then, the black-eyed one dealt a finishing blow, and the fire-eyed girl's head snapped back before she collapsed in a heap to the ground. Pale hooked fingers closed around her throat, her face quickly growing blotchy and purple.

Like Suna's had when I strangled her in my cell.

"Stop!" I demanded more forcefully, feeling as though my throat was the one that was being crushed. "Stop it, you are killing her!"

"That is the *point,* you coward!" the black-eyed one finally spoke.

Coward. The word echoed through the canyon in the strange space we occupied. It resonated through my brain.

I had called myself that word many times, but now I recognized the voice that used it.

"You," I breathed, accusatorially.

"Me!" she shrieked back.

"Who are you? You're not my mother, you're not me, so *who?*"

Her hands slackened on the neck of the fire-eyed girl below her and she grinned, showing all of her very sharp teeth. They were blackened with the very same substance that oozed from her chest. I recoiled at the sight, remembering Fear and his monstrous smile.

"Oh, Daux," she purred. "My little coward. I am you."

"No." I shook my head.

That was impossible. I was not this creature. I was not this *monster.*

A laugh cackled its way up her throat, throwing her head back with the force of it. The black hole in her chest shook, pouring the sludge down her stomach and spewing it onto the face of the girl she choked.

"You are though," she insisted once her laughter had subsided. "You are me and I am you. We are one."

"Who are you?" The words tore from my throat, leaving it stinging and burning the way it had when I spewed fire at Fear.

My hands were balled into fists at my side and I

desperately wanted to use them. To knock her off the girl she was tormenting; to shove her into the canyon; to remove her from my life forever.

She was the reason for all of my troubles, I just knew it.

"I am Rage" she answered as though it was obvious.

Perhaps it should have been. I was *angry* all of the time, even before I went into that white cell. I had always carried it with me like I carried the ember of my magic.

"Like Gladwin was Fear," I whispered, finally reaching the conclusion Rage was waiting for me to make.

"I am Hate, I am Fury, I am Destruction," she replied, flashing her razor-sharp teeth. "I am many things, just as you are. But I am you, and you are me. And this little weakling too."

Her words shattered my mind and I nearly fell to my knees with the weight of them.

I *was* her – I was Rage – my hands around my own throat, squeezing the life from the other copy of my body with all that wrath and pain. Choking that beautiful, perfect version of myself until the black sludge in my chest spread out into my veins, from my fingers and leeching into the perfect skin I was so intent on destroying.

No one was here to save me this time. No one could save me from *myself*. There was only death and destruction in my heart and it was bleeding into my *soul*. There was no one here to reverse this. No one but me.

I – with my blood-slick hands around my own throat – couldn't stop myself from squeezing. She flickered, like the ember in my chest. Sputtering, dying. The glow illuminating her body, the fire in her eyes, flickered in tandem with the ember in my chest. My magic… my *soul*.

"Breathe," I whispered to her – to my soul. "Please, please breathe."

"I can't," she said.

It was like she had spoken inside my head because her lips had not moved.

I supposed that was where we were, inside my head

"Please," I begged her. "Please, you have to. You can't give up!"

Why was I so determined to save her? I was already ruined beyond repair. There was no way I was going to be able to be that girl again. Even if I could be happy after all this, I would never be whole. Not that I ever was to begin with.

Just then, I realized that Rage was holding my gaze. All my fury was pouring out of those black eyes, like twin oceans roiling in a storm. Twisting and capsizing anything that dared cross their waters. The oily sludge that spread from her fingers and the hole in her chest poured from those eyes like inky tears, tracking down her parchment-pale face and neck.

And those thoughts, all those negative things floating through my mind, were hers. Rage was projecting all those maddening things onto me now, and my soul. She was trying to ruin and drown me in her misery.

"You're coming for me next, aren't you?" I asked her.

Rage's lips parted in a wicked mockery of a grin, showing teeth blackened by that terrible substance she hoarded inside of her. I knew now, that once my soul stopped struggling in her arms, I would be next. And my death would not be pretty.

Lightning struck once again – fracturing my vision in two. I saw Jax calling down bolt upon bolt of lightning, striking out with fearsome power as the remaining Coalition soldiers swarmed him.

My vision cleared and I was back, Rage's black-slick body filling my line of slight. I then made my decision. It was easy, like deciding to kill my father.

I swallowed and allowed a breath to pass in and out of my lungs. Then another. Finally, I took a step forward, crossing the divide between the three of us as though it was not a thousand-foot drop of open air. Rage hissed, clenching her fingers around my soul's throat. Both their eyes bulged in their sockets, one from anger, the other from strain.

When I reached them with my hand stretched to them like Valentin had reached his out to me, begging me not to kill my father. Only now I was trying not to destroy myself. My soul grasped my hand tightly, pulling at me, pleading with me to save her – to save myself. My other hand lifted toward Rage, and I implored her to take it.

Her grin had now fully turned into a snarl and her teeth grazed dangerously close to my soul's cheek.

But she was me, they both were. That meant *I* had the power here and I was not about to let myself die by my own hands. Wanting my father dead wasn't the issue, and it never was. He deserved death and any other punishment that came his way. But my rage, which I had allowed to fester, was killing me from the inside out. There was no other way around it; I had to make peace with myself.

I gripped Rage's wrists and pulled them away from my soul's throat, ignoring her furious scream as I did so. Once my soul was free, she fell to her hands and knees and began to cough up the black sludge, spewing it on the ground in stinking puddles. After I was sure Rage would not lunge for my soul again, I released her and began to implore her with upturned palms.

"Please," I said, taking a tentative step forward, then another. "Let us be free."

"You just want *her* to be free," Rage spat, with all the venom built up inside of her. "You want to *become her again.* You don't want me? You would *abandon me?* After all I have done for you? I. *Saved.* You."

I now stood in front of her emaciated, trembling form and I reached for her, pulling her struggling body into my arms. I kissed her short hair as she struggled against me.

"You did save me. I am so grateful for that. But you are killing me now, and you need to let me go," I said, feeling her tremble violently against me.

"You're going to leave me all alone," she shrieked, sobbing into my chest. Her fists beat against my back, my chest, and my shoulders. Her bare feet kicked against my greaves, stamping the ground and my boots in her wrath.

"No," I placated, holding her tightly. "I still need you to protect me. I can't do that on my own. I need you, but you need to let go of control. We need balance, you and I."

She shrieked against my chest at those words. How dare I do this to her after all she did to protect me? How dare I betray her? Didn't I understand that she had her hooks so deep into my heart that there was no undoing them?

I only soothed her and let her rage. That was all she knew. I would not punish her for being what she was created to be. I would not be my parents. I would not inflict that upon myself any longer. I did not deserve to be treated that way when I was a child, and I did not deserve to be treated that way now. Especially not by my own hands. Rage was a part of me now, whether I wanted her or not, and I needed to accept all ugly parts of myself.

My soul, finished with her expulsion of Rage's black sludge, stared up at the two of us with a determined but serene expression on her face. She nodded to me, entreating me to continue. To take control of Rage so that we could become one again.

"I need you to let me go," I repeated to Rage, softly but with authority.

This was *my* mind. *My* body. I was not going to allow my rage to control either any longer. I was grateful that she had helped me to live through hell, but now she was ruining everything I thought I stood for.

My father… He could die for all I cared, but the NAF did need him. And his punishment would be far slower and more torturous than anything I could provide him with. It would be over far too quickly if I killed him myself. It was best to just let him rot in a white-walled cell like I had.

Abruptly, Rage stopped her shrieking sobs and pulled

away.

"Fine," she rasped. "I'll let you go, but don't forget, I will *always* be a part of you."

"I'm counting on that," I replied then smiled then turned to grasp my soul's hand, pulling her to her feet.

As this world began to fade around me, I could have sworn I saw a sinister grin cross Rage's face. It was the same one that was mirrored on my own when I came back to myself, facing my father once again.

Chapter Thirty-One

"Father," I said, kneeling over him so my face hovered above his own. "Do you fear death?"

"All men fear death," he spat.

My grin still in place, I straightened to my full height and took a deep breath, feeling that anger dance beneath the surface of my skin. I pointed my rapier at him once again, while the gasps of my teammates rang out across the cliff.

"Unluckily for you," I crooned with the softness of a loving parent – something he never was. "I will not be sending you to meet your beloved Gods."

"You-you're not going to kill me? You stupid child, you could never follow through with anything," he rasped, struggling beneath me.

"Now, now," I tutted. "That's just not true. Now on your feet… foot. I have places to be, you see."

"I'll see you dead!" he threatened.

"Promises, promises," I laughed, jerking the syringe from his hand and ignoring the spray of blood that coated my fingers as I did so. "I will be counting down the days, Father. Stand. Now."

Grabbing him by the collar of his shirt, I yanked him to his feet and passed him off to Valentin who was standing in shock next to me. Of course, he would be surprised. He had not seen what I had seen. He had not been there to witness what my mind had tried to do to itself – what Rage had done to me. He could not hear her voice in my head – *my* voice –

crowing with pleasure at the torment my father was sure to receive once we brought him back to Heliorious.

We could hardly wait.

Jax, Félix, and Himawari hurried over to me, expressions of concern on each one of their faces. I opened my mouth to reassure them that I was okay and that I had everything under control, but Himawari pulled me into her arms before I could get a word out. Jax and Félix followed suit shortly after.

I could see now that I had worried them beyond forgiveness. They had seen my struggles and tried their best to help me, and I shut them out. They were there for me at my lowest point and kept pulling at me when I refused to stop digging further. I could not have asked for better friends than them.

"If you do something like that again," Himawari said, pulling back from me slightly so I could see the shadows dancing in her eyes. "I *will* kill you myself."

A laugh escaped me before I could stop it, earning a glare from her.

"I'm sorry, next time I will…" I paused.

"Let us help you when you decide to commit patricide?" Jax offered.

"Yes," I agreed, pulling the three of them in tightly once again. "Exactly that."

"You're forgiven then," Félix said, pinching my cheek.

I bit his finger lightly before he could pull away, earning a squeak and a flick to my forehead. It seemed, just like that, all was forgiven. No atoning, no begging for clemency. With all that I had put them through, they absolved me without pomp or ceremony.

"I don't deserve any of you," I told them with all the sincerity I could muster. "I truly don't deserve you."

"Friendship isn't about who deserves what, Daux," Valentin said from behind us.

We whirled around to see that Valentin had bound my father in cuffs and gagged him with his own tie. A nice touch, I thought. Rage would always be pleased about that sort of thing, perhaps. But I was not about to let her ruin this moment.

"I know," I replied, wishing with all my heart that he could forgive me too. "But after what I put you all through today… and what I have been putting you through for these past few months, I truly do not deserve your loyalty or your friendship. And I am forever grateful that you have chosen to be my friend, and chosen to stay with this team."

"There is nothing to forgive, Daux," Valentin said roughly. "You lost yourself momentarily, and now you're back. We're all glad for it; please don't forget that."

I swallowed around a lump in my throat. I would never forget. My father might have tried to turn me into a monster, but *I* got to control my destiny. Not him. Not Rage. Me. Standing here with my friends, I knew that I was not alone.

"I won't," I whispered, feeling the tears gathering in my eyes as the first one landed. "I won't ever forget."

Himawari let go of me to hide her sniffles, finding herself wrapped in Jax's embrace. Félix, unsure of what to do with himself, took hold of my father and began leading him toward the house. Most likely to inspect it for any more enhancers, or anything we could use to further our investigation into the Coalition's plans to bring back the Gods.

However, I was staring too intently into Valentin's face to notice much of anything else.

There was once a time when I would have been ashamed to have him see me cry. Now though… now was different. I was different, for all that rage I had bottled up for so long, I now felt as small and weak as a kitten.

I would have killed my father today if my teammates had not been there. I still might, given the moment he was no longer valuable to the NAF. My friends had prevented me from treason, and murder; though, I was less concerned about the latter. Father deserved every sort of punishment coming to him.

Despite all that anger though, my friends were all able to get through to me and show me that there was no coming back from the path I was on. Rage was consuming me, and they refused to let her take me alive.

My heart, as broken as it was, swelled large enough to fill that hole in my chest and stuck there, sealing the entire space up. I could never do enough to repay them for their love and trust, but I would spend the rest of my life trying to make up for it.

Valentin's eyes blazed as the crowd of Spec Ops agents and officers hurried around us, pushing us closer to each other. When he put his hands to my cheeks, I realized that my tears had spilled over. I was not ashamed. I was not angry.

I was consumed with a far more powerful feeling. A multitude of them.

Gratitude.

Serenity.

Love.

And when Valentin pulled me in close so that our lips were only inches from each other – his breath ghosting over my skin – leaving me shivering, *I* let go of that lingering glimmer of anger. It would always be there with me, but I no longer needed to cling to it the way I had been. I realized now, as Valentin's lips lifted and pressed ever so softly to my forehead, that I had other things to live for. And live for them, I would.

Chapter Thirty-Two

Not long after we had boots on the ground in Heliorious the, Overseer summoned me to her office. Me personally. None of my other teammates had gotten her summons. That was not exactly strange, I had been bidden to her office alone multiple times since I had joined Spec Ops. What struck me as strange was that, in her message, she noted that my father was in the same cell as I had been during my interrogation.

Why would she say that? What was her motivation for doing so?

I suspected she was trying to manipulate me in some way, which was unnecessary because if it had to do with nailing my father to the wall, I would do almost anything she asked. I wanted him to pay for his abuse and his crimes. I wanted him to pay dearly.

"Ma'am," I greeted the Overseer when I entered her office, my hands clasped respectfully behind my back.

"Deveraux," she responded, returning my greeting. "Do have a seat."

I sat in one of the stiff leather chairs in front of her desk and waited expectantly. Her dark eyes watched my every move like a cat waiting to strike its prey. Everyone was a means to an end to her, I knew that now. I was nothing special to her, just a tool for Spec Ops and the NAF to use accordingly. I did not blame her for those views, she regarded herself as practical. Pragmatic even. I did, however, dislike her for them.

"You were prompt in responding to my message," she said, watching me carefully.

"My father is in custody, I assumed I would be useful in some capacity," I replied honestly.

The Overseer nodded. "You will be. The interrogation squad would like you to speak with him. We need to hear it from him how long he was poisoning you as a child."

A shiver of dread ran up my spine. I had not told her about his more recent plans to poison me and my teammates. I had not even had the chance to speak with them about it. My father had just been incarcerated less than a few hours ago.

"Is the white room torture not working?" I asked, tilting my head to the side in a show of mock innocence.

I could not help myself.

The only indication that the Overseer noticed was a nearly imperceptible flinch. Hardly a twitch of her hand, but I had well-trained eyes.

"It will take some time for that line of…" she paused as though the next word tasted vile on her tongue. "Torture, as you put it, to take effect. We need results now, and the quicker he bends to our will, the better."

"You want me to torture my father?" I asked.

I had no qualms with doing so, but I did not particularly want to use the same sort of mind games the interrogators typically employed. Dev included.

"No, no!" The Overseer waved a hand. "Nothing like that. I was hoping you would *talk* to him, as is Dev. I thought if he were to break his composure around you, the child who caused his downfall, he might…"

"Break easier," I finished for her.

The Overseer nodded grimly, as though she hated to acknowledge such a statement.

"Fine," I said, standing to my feet.

"Fine?" she repeated incredulously.

I nodded and turned toward the door, then paused.

"He may be my father, but he tried to extinguish the only life I have ever known that allowed me to be myself so he could become something he shouldn't. He tried to make me into a monster," I told her, allowing air to slip in and out of my lungs easily, soothing my racing heart. "I did not accept because *you* asked, I accepted because he deserves any punishment that comes his way."

I held the Overseer's gaze for a long moment before she nodded at me. As imperceptibly as the flinch, but I saw it all the same. I was dismissed. Facing forward, I pushed open the door and headed toward the Spec Ops interrogation floor where I spent so many agonizing days as a captive and an ally.

A shiver ran up my spine as I walked through that white, empty hall to cell four-fourteen. It was almost poetic that my father had been placed in the same cell I had because of his machinations. Almost as if it were divine intervention. I wondered if it still smelled like vomit, or if the multiple rounds of cleaning products that had been used since then had removed the scent.

I hoped not, but it was unlikely my father would be tormented by the smell of my bile. It was common practice for the interrogation teams to remove anything that would titillate the senses, no matter how foul.

Still, a girl could dream.

I paused for a moment outside his door, waiting. Breathing. This visit wasn't my idea. I had to remind myself of that so I didn't turn around and run back the way I had come. The Overseer thought it would rattle my father if I went to visit him – if I were to try and interrogate him – and cause him to slip up. I had accepted this "request" of hers and I could not refuse now, not when I was already here.

The interrogation teams were doing exactly as they had with me the second time, talking and asking questions until words were no longer enough. They didn't care what you had to say, not when they could just probe around in your brain and take what they wanted. This was just a scare tactic, something to throw Father off and make him lose control. A broken, unbalanced mind was much easier to play around with. And when it came to interpreting those results, something pliable and soft was much easier than a mind with walls and chains surrounding it.

I did not enjoy being a pawn in the Overseer's scheming, but the thought of tormenting my father was too much to pass up, even if I was apprehensive about my boss' motives. Valentin had given me a hard stare when I called him on my holonav minutes before to tell him about her orders. I wanted the team to know I was potentially going to be out late and not to worry.

I had responded to the Overseer far more enthusiastically than I probably should have. I might have given her reason to distrust me further.

Shaking my head to clear my thoughts, I began my mantra. One breath in, one breath out. In and out. In and out. In. Out.

Then I pushed open the door.

My father was sitting there at the table, head in his hands. His normally close-shaven facial hair had grown in stubbly patches. He had never been able to grow facial hair well, but he refused to take any of the magical tonics that would encourage hair growth stating that he didn't want that "evil" inside his body. This statement was now comical to me, considering he possessed the ability to use magic himself, and had this whole time. Even more so that he had used enhancers on himself to try and fashion himself into a God. It was just another lie.

His skin had taken on an unhealthy pallor, almost sickly gray, and his blond hair – almost the same shade as mine –

was lank and dull. My father was a handsome man at one time, but now he looked unhealthy and pathetic. The inside now reflecting outwardly. Once again, I took a sick sort of satisfaction in his misfortune.

He did not look up as I sat down across from him at the table. I waited patiently, smiling at his dejected form until his now dull blue eyes looked up from beneath his hands to meet mine.

"Hello, Father," I said softly but without compassion.

He had put me here almost singlehandedly once; he deserved no sympathy from me.

"Here to gloat, daughter?" he asked in a raspy voice I hardly recognized.

I tilted my head to the side, feigning ignorance. "Why would I do a thing like that?"

Almost in spite of himself, my father threw back his head and laughed.

"You are certainly nothing like your mother," he said once he had quieted.

"I'll take that as a compliment," I said, keeping my tone neutral.

"No," he continued as though I had not spoken. "No, Daux, you are so much more like me than she or I ever realized."

I grinned, ignoring the flash of Rage that shuddered through me, urging me to grab him by the throat and smash his head into the table over, and over, and over again until blood coated the horrid whiteness of these walls and brain matter and skull fragments littered the table.

His revelation was nothing new to me, I had always known I had favored him in his quiet, analytical temperament over my mother's loud and shallow personality. He was trying to get under my skin but did not get to dictate my emotions. He did not get to upset me any longer, as I knew he was trying to do right now.

"If you're trying to hurt me, you will have to do better

than that, Father," I said calmly, relaxing into the hard metal seat beneath me as much as I could.

This room, this man, neither of them scared me any longer. I had survived them both. Yes, I had been hurt here, and yes, my father had tormented me for years, but I had beat them. I was stronger than the things that tried to break me. They could not hurt me unless I allowed them to, and I would not permit that. Not again.

"You were always such an irritating child," he spat vehemently.

"Because I was so much like you?" I countered with a pleasant smile.

I was referencing his magic – the magic I inherited from him. The ability he pretended to loathe. The gift I once thought he tried to extinguish in me.

The look he fixed me with would have had me cowering in the corner when I was younger, and I was shocked with the poise and grace with which I held myself steady. He could not lift a finger to hurt me, but I could use words to destroy him and body language to render him obsolete.

I was in control here.

The mere thought nearly brought tears to my eyes, but now was not the time for that.

"How did you meet Captain Gladwin, Father?" I asked. "Was it when I was a child? When you started using the blockers on me? Or was it before even that, when you became involved with the neo-traditionalist movement?"

Even if he was a prisoner, I knew he would not respond well to me beating around the bush. My presence alone would be enough to shake him; there was no need to be clever.

"Is that what you're after?" he sneered. "The other interrogators have already asked me those mundane routine questions."

"I am not an interrogator," I responded, folding my hands on the table in front of me. "I am your daughter and I am asking you a question."

"You are no daughter of mine."

I laughed at that. I could not help myself.

"Will you answer or not?" I asked, cool disdain leaking into my voice.

"No."

I knew this would not be easy; he was not going to just spill all his secrets the moment I walked through that door. I was prepared for that – for his intimidation tactics. I had all day, and he had nowhere but here to be. How long I stayed depended on how much he was willing to give me and I wasn't leaving until I had what I wanted.

"Did you know they are interrogating Mother?" I asked nonchalantly.

A smile nearly broke out on my face when he took the bait. He would have known what they were doing to my mother, but my father was a selfish creature. He did not like it when other people played with his belongings.

"What are they doing to her?" he asked.

My father's entire body was trembling with rage. The possessive light in his eye nearly took me back to my childhood. The childhood I was forced to relive in this very room.

"You know *exactly* what they are doing to her," I whispered for fear of the sound of my enjoyment leaking into my voice. "They are doing what they do to everyone who winds up here; they are doing to her exactly what they did to me."

I leaned in close, fixing my father's gaze with my own. Green met green and a flash of lightning would have sparked between us had I not kept my magic in check.

"And guess what?" I said, my lips curling back over my teeth in a gruesome display of a smile.

"What?" he snapped.

"They are enjoying every second of her torment, and it is all thanks to you."

Despite his abuse and his infidelity, my father loved my mother. In a sick and twisted way, of course. But he did love her the only way he knew how. Though, could that truly be called love? Was possessing something enough to claim to be love? I would have said yes once, but after I met Valentin, I was no longer sure.

It was so satisfying to see the flash of rage crossing my father's face as I spoke those words. To see him tremble under the weight of the knowledge that my mother was being tormented by someone other than him. I wondered for a moment if he had thought that way about me too.

Which was silly, because his orchestrating my arrest was a form of personal torture.

"Amalie is enjoying spending time with the grandparents you banned her from seeing, by the way," I threw at him, leaning back in the hard metal chair.

"Yes," I continued, seeing his eyes darken with the very same rage I possessed within my own soul. "She is doing very well now that she is out from under your thumb. Her magic will flourish without enhancers, her education is all mapped out. She will be attending the Academy as I did."

"Stop," he hissed through gritted teeth.

"Her favorite subject is the theory of magic," I went on as if he had not spoken. "It is helping her see she is not the abomination you brought us up to believe all magic users were. It is so beautiful to see her coming out of her shell with the other children. She is making so many friends—"

"Stop!" he roared, the chair he sat in screeching backward as he stood to his feet.

I tilted my head to the side, observing him. My reaction seemed to anger him more; he wanted my fear, my deference. He was incensed that he no longer had it. How pathetic that this man needed the fear of his child to feel whole. The submissiveness of his wife. The uneasy admiration of the province.

"Or what?" I asked, examining my fingernails. "You will

get angry? You'll punish me? I am *trembling, Father.*"

A familiar flame blazed in his eyes and I knew he was right where I wanted him, like a fly trapped in a spider's web, struggling to free itself before the corrosive venom of the mutated arachnid burned its fragile body to mush.

"You are *my* child! You *will* listen to *me!*" he yelled, looming over the table in a way that would have been menacing if I still feared him.

"I thought you said I was no daughter of yours? Which is it?" I blinked, feigning innocence. "Do I obey you unquestioningly or do I view your existence as an insect under my boot? I think I prefer the latter."

In a flash my father launched himself across the table, his large pale hand reaching toward my throat. I expected such a reaction, but the force of his fingers wrapping around my windpipe knocked the glasses from my face, sending them clattering to the white tile floor.

I was not scared, nor was I worried. There would be agents in the room within a matter of minutes if I did not restrain him myself. My father might have been bigger than me, but I was stronger – I had intact magic. He had lost his. The Overseer had personally started his injections of the chemical that would eventually terminate his ability to use magic as soon as his arrest was processed.

"Are you sure you want to do that?" I croaked out, flame dancing across the fingertips I held mere inches from his wrist.

"You would not burn me," he said, but there was fear in his voice – in his eyes.

"I would, and I would do so with pleasure." My Placement Exam simulation showed me that much.

I would be more than happy to see that pale skin of his blister under my hand.

For a moment, his hand flexed around my throat and I could feel the muscles constricting against my trachea. Then, as if defeated, my father slumped away and returned to his chair. I leaned down, my eyes fixed on him the whole time, to retrieve my glasses. Once they were back in place on my face, I allowed a large sip of air into my lungs, expelling it with relish.

"You were always so insolent," he sighed, eyes on the floor. "Never listened, never obeyed, always wanted to play with that gift of yours. You did not want to take the blockers and enhancers even though I told you they would make you stronger. Why couldn't you just be a good child? Why did you make me do these things?"

"I am not here to have that discussion with you," I said, allowing a molecule of sorrow to leak into my voice. "I am here to talk about your involvement with Captain Gladwin and the Coalition – your use of the enhancers – as your *child.*"

He said nothing but I was not leaving until I got what I came for, and I meant that. I would stay however long I needed to for him to break down and tell me even one little thing. I wanted this torment even more than I had wanted him dead. I didn't care what he admitted, I just wanted to break him, and once he broke, the interrogators would take over. I would take however long I needed, even though I knew Dev would be chomping at the bit to hook my father up and learn his secrets.

I could not help but think at how sad my father looked, slumped over in his chair across from me. Pathetic even. It was with no effort on his part, I knew he would never stoop so low as to try and garner my sympathy. I was not so important to him, and he now knew I was no longer easily manipulated.

He barely touched the meal that had been brought to him – white, bland rice, one of the same meals I had been served. I refused any food they would have left for me; I could not stand bland food anymore, not that I liked it all that much before.

"Why are you still here?" he asked, his voice filled with

regret and anguish.

"I am waiting for you to answer my questions," I said, ignoring his pain. Uncaring of it.

The curse he threw my way did not bear repeating, but I continued to ignore him, waiting for him to break. Waiting for that one little slip-up that would allow me to leave and all of this would be over.

When his hand reached for the bowl of rice I flinched inwardly, thinking he would throw it at me, but he only lifted his spoon with the grace he always possessed and took a bite. I watched him eat, remembering all the meals we shared in silence – me too afraid to utter a sound out of fear of his wrath. Now he sat before me, weak, unable to use his status and power to get what he wanted.

"Why did you and Mother not tell Amalie she had magic? Or me?" I blurted, unable to help myself.

"Because," my father answered, pushing his rice around in his bowl. "She would have turned out exactly like you, and then I would have two difficult children to deal with. You refused any effort I made to strengthen you; she would have followed your example."

"*You* are 'difficult' yourself, though," I pointed out. "You had magic. You *used it.* You liked using it."

My father's shoulders tensed at that and I waited with bated breath for him to lash out at me. He was trying to be careful, that much was obvious, but my words had rankled him. If I kept pressing along that vein, maybe he would finally blunder.

"Is that why you turned traitor? Because you wanted the Coalition's scientists and doctors to eradicate everyone else's magic, but allow you to keep yours? So, you could rule over everyone else as Gods, all-powerful, while we were all weak and subservient to you?" I prodded.

"Why else would I give up all my power here?" Father said sullenly before he could stop himself. "You forget, I *tried* to give you the same abilities as well. Gladwin was only the beginning. He was the first successful experiment. I wanted us to be *Gods,* Daux!"

His eyes shot to me, widening in horror when he saw the catlike grin that was creeping its way across my face. I had my admission of guilt, his lack of remorse. I could leave satisfied now.

I stood to my feet and saluted the camera I now knew was affixed in the corner of the room, invisible to the naked eye, and turned on my heel to leave. I refused to even glance back at the man I once called father. A traitor, an abuser… a pathetic excuse for a human being. I barely registered his cries of rage as the door swung shut behind me, locking him in that prison of colorlessness.

Chapter Thirty-Three

Coming home after that interrogation was like the sweet first sip of cool water after a long, arduous training session. The flat smelled of Jax's cologne, the heavily spiced smell of whatever had been cooked for supper, and… well, just like home. The smell of one's home is unique and personal. It is comforting in a way that not much else is. It can soothe the most frayed of nerves, ease the most harried of minds after a long day, and bring the utmost comfort when that comfort is most needed.

I felt as though I could bask in that comfort for hours, just standing there in the doorway, but I noticed a small movement out of the corner of my eye from the darkened living room. When I turned my head toward the movement, I saw Amalie lying on the couch, her white-blonde hair fanned across the cushion. Her chest rose and fell with steady, even breaths and I knew she was asleep.

My heart began to crack, the chasm of my chest threatening to shatter open once more, even though it was slowly beginning to heal.

Amalie must have been waiting up for me when she fell asleep.

The hairpin fractures my friends had forcibly sutured together along the shell of my heart groaned against the threads cementing them in place. Why did love have to hurt so much? I waited a beat for my chest to burst open and my heart to spill out and shatter once again to the ground, but it held fast.

I pressed my hand to my sternum and rubbed the phantom ache there. It was dull, echoing. Dropping my hand, I made my way to the couch and brushed my fingertips over my sister's forehead, pushing her bangs out of her face. She was soft, delicate. But made of sterner stuff than my father had thought. Much like me.

He may have broken us, but we were capable of being repaired. We were strong.

After a moment, I scooped Amalie up into my arms and carried her into our bedroom. She mumbled a bit of nonsense as I carried her and held fast to me when I tried to place her underneath the covers. It was a gentle feeling that fell over me. Motherly. It should not have belonged to me, but it did, and I owned it gladly.

I carefully detangled her fingers from my black tactical shirt, pulling the thick covers up over her slight frame. She mumbled a bit more, making those innocent sleeping noises, and I pressed my lips lightly to her forehead for a fraction of a second. Then I left so as not to disturb her.

It was such a strong feeling that came over me that I had to lean against the closed door for a moment to catch my breath before making my way back down the hall and into the kitchen. I had not eaten since before the Overseers summoned me and I was ravenous. The aromatic scent of tonight's leftovers wafted through the air still; though, they would long be put away by now.

It was a delicious scent that tantalized my empty stomach and I could hardly pile my plate high enough or reheat it fast enough. I didn't even take the plate to the dining room table, just stood there shoveling my face full of roasted meat and rice, relishing in the flavor. Savoring the sensation of fullness rapidly flooding my empty belly.

I enjoyed every bite.

Once I was finished, I turned and deposited my plate in the dishwasher. When I twisted back around, I jumped at the sight of a dark figure that now leaned against the countertop. My hand flew to my throat, I knew that the only other people who could be in this flat were my sister and my teammates, but I was still startled nonetheless.

"Valentin," I breathed, a relieved smile tugging at the corners of my lips.

"Daux," he said, face stoic and stiff compared to the languid grace with which he leaned against the counter.

My heart began to race, and I feared it would pound out of my chest. His eyes blazed with icy sharpness that burned my insides. He was the same Valentin I had seen many times over, but the way his gaze made my heart race…

When had he changed? Why did he now seem so altered to me?

After all that we had been through together, I was still too afraid to think what I was feeling. I truly was a coward.

Valentin did not appear any different than the last time I had seen him in person. It had not been long since then; however, my reaction to him surprised me. My heart was beating much too fast during what should have been a normal meeting between friends. My face was too flushed. My limbs were too shaky.

Perhaps it was because I could only see the wild, fervent gleam in his eyes. Perhaps it was the memory of his lips brushing against mine like the brush of a butterfly's wing.

I hadn't even heard him enter the kitchen, but from his tactical attire, he had just returned from the outdoor training facility – probably getting in a late-night training session. From the sleepy stillness that settled over the flat, it seemed the others had declined to join him. Now he was leaning against the countertop, a glass of water halfway to his lips.

Those very same lips that I nearly kissed a few days ago. His bleached hair – black roots finally showing and normally carefully styled – was tousled and wet in a way that slightly obscured his eyes. But that piercing shade of blue still shone through.

Piercing me right through the throat as I stared back at him, frozen in place. Could it be that he was experiencing the same confusing feelings as I was?

"Hello," I greeted him shakily, breaking the frozen atmosphere.

Valentin stared at me a moment longer then downed his glass of water, placing it in the sink before actually acknowledging me.

"Hello Daux," he said in an even voice.

At the time I was too keyed up to hear the tense undertone in his voice; however, when I retired for the evening, I recalled how tight his voice really sounded.

"How are you?" I asked, slowly wringing my hands for something to do.

Valentin shrugged and turned to clean his glass, finally taking his unnerving, pale eyes off me then placed his dirtied hand bindings in the recycling disposal basket. He then returned to the sink and washed his hands. The awkwardness in the room was palpable.

"Tired," he rasped, finally answering my question. "You?"

"I am fine," I replied, watching as he dried his hands on a towel.

Neither of us spoke after that and the silence was quite awkward. We stood in the kitchen, neither of us speaking, neither looking in the other's direction. For the life of me, I did not know how to break the tension. But I didn't have to.

Valentin's hand grasped my upper arm with more force than he had ever used on me – outside of sparring – and spun me to face him. His eyes flamed with such an intense blue fire I thought I would burn to ashes beneath them.

"Valentin…" I whispered, unsure of my voice. "I'm sorry. For everything. I never should have tried to kiss you like that. I should have trusted all of you. And I never should have jeopardized your lives the way I did."

He didn't speak, did not even acknowledge my apology,

but the fire in his eyes only intensified and I could feel my skin flaming. What was going on? Why was he affecting me so? And why did I think his eyes looked so beautiful?

Before I could answer any of my own questions, Valentin closed the minimal space between us. I watched – heart hammering – as he placed his hand on the back of my neck. The coolness of his fingers stung my heated flesh in a deliriously wonderful way and he leaned his forehead to mine, closing his eyes with a weary – but somehow pleased – sigh.

My mind blanked and my body began running on autopilot. The only action I could focus on was remembering how to breathe. Valentin hardly ever touched me in this way; though, there were instances where I was positive that he was going to kiss me but did not. Times where he held me while I was sad, or angry, or frustrated. When I needed bandaging… Other than those few times, the closest we had ever been was sparring or patching one another up. I had no idea how to force myself to respond so I just let him stay there, breathing deeply. In and out. In and out.

"Daux," He whispered, finally opening his eyes to meet mine.

"Y-yes?" I replied shakily.

"I missed you."

Shock traveled down my spine like a bolt of electricity. Though I knew Valentin didn't dislike me anymore – and hadn't for a while – I was still surprised to hear he would miss me. With the way I had acted, I was sure he would have written me off completely. I was sure all my teammates would have.

"What?" I asked, hoping to prompt him to repeat himself.

"I missed you," Valentin said, more forcefully this time, cold fingers pressing into the back of my neck.

"I'm confused," I whispered, beginning to pull away from his embrace. But he stopped me, wrapping his arm around my waist and drawing me in closer. Blood began to roar in my ears, and I was sure he could hear my heart thundering in my chest.

"Why?" Valentin murmured against my ear.

Why was I confused? Valentin wasn't a very affectionate person, at least not until recently. Nor was he effusive. I had just been trying to ignore the tension-filled dance we had been doing for some time. I had only figured out what that meant now.

I thought there may have still been some animosity between us because of how I had treated him, but perhaps it was more. I long ago realized that I admired Valentin far more than I had let myself believe. I loved him. Maybe we both felt the same… Was that even possible?

I remembered how Valentin's eyes blazed when I turned my father over to Spec Ops instead of killing him. I remembered how weak my knees felt. I remembered that I made myself forget, letting myself believe that Valentin was merely my teammate and nothing more.

However, I realized that Valentin showed his care for his team and me in subtle ways, avoiding overt emotional interactions. But with me… he became almost tender. When he would help me bandage myself, cautiously averting his eyes from seeing unnecessary nakedness. Talking with me when my burdens became too much for me to bear.

Was it more than the friendship and admiration we shared with each other?

I knew it was on my part, but he was still so hard to read.

"Why Daux?" Valentin whispered again, his lips grazing my ear this time.

I trembled. My already shaking limbs began to betray me. He felt it. I knew he felt it because I felt him smile against my skin. It appeared he had figured out his feelings before I had.

"I don't know…" I breathed. "I just…"

Valentin seemed to be tired of waiting for me to respond

as he slowly dragged his hand from my neck and down my bare back, tracing small patterns on my sensitive flesh.

"Just what…?" He murmured. "Is it truly hard for you to believe that I missed you?" he asked.

"N-no," I gulped as another tremor rocked through me. "W-we are friends."

Valentin's fingers paused on my spine and I felt his body stiffen slightly against mine.

"Friends?" He asked.

"We are… Aren't we?" I replied hesitantly.

"I thought someone as perceptive as you would have noticed by now…" Valentin said, his voice slightly harsher and raspy.

And then, all at once, I understood what Valentin was trying to get me to realize. His strange behavior these past few months. The tense air in the room when I realized he was there with me.

Valentin had been falling in love with me. This entire time, Valentin had been falling in love with me, and I refused to see it.

"Oh," I whispered.

"Oh," he repeated.

Valentin held me a few moments more before releasing me and brushing the hair from his eyes.

"Goodnight Daux," he whispered.

Then he left and I was alone.

It felt like hours before I could bring myself to move from my spot in the darkened kitchen. Once I did, I found myself holding my breath and using every ounce of my stealth training to sneak from the kitchen, nearly bumping into a solid wall of muscle as I did so.

"Oof!" I exclaimed when two strong hands grasped my forearms to keep me from falling backward.

"You all right?" Jax asked.

"Fine," I said, shaking my dazed head to clear it a bit. "What are you doing out here?"

Jax could not hide his sheepish expression from me, not even in the dark and I saw Himawari's door quickly shut from across the living area. My eyes flashed back up to his face and he would not meet my gaze. I was heartened to see that there were no shadows in his warm brown eyes. I would have to discuss everything with them soon, but now did not seem like the right time.

"Oh, well… have a good night then." I grinned up at him before extracting myself from his hands and made my way down the hallway.

Before I entered my bedroom, my hand on the doorknob, I paused and turned back toward Jax.

"You both deserve to be happy," I called in a soft voice so as not to wake Amalie. "Don't let fear or embarrassment stop you."

"Thanks, Daux," Jax said, rubbing the back of his neck in mortification.

"Don't mention it," I laughed and turned back to enter my room.

"Daux," Jax called.

I paused again, looking down the hall at his shadowy form.

"You should take your own advice sometimes," he said, then turned back toward Himawari's room and disappeared into the dark.

I blinked at where he had stood for a minute before drawing up the courage to turn to the room across the hall from mine. Then I took a deep breath. Then another. In and out. In and out. In. Out. In. Out.

And I knocked.

Chapter Thirty-Four

The next day was excruciating. Valentin, whether embarrassed or put off by my reaction, was pretending as if nothing happened between us. He had ignored my knock on his door, and I – too embarrassed to knock again – had retreated into my room. Any time I laid eyes on him the next morning I would flush a horrific shade of red. I could still feel his breath on my skin and his fingers on my back and neck.

I had no idea how to bring up what had happened in the kitchen just last night. There were rarely any opportunities for us to be alone and I sure as hell wasn't going to discuss it in front of our teammates. And to add to the problem Valentin was most definitely avoiding me, running away and not talking to me about what he had admitted in so many words.

That pissed me off.

Valentin decided to embrace me that evening – not me – and we *were* going to talk about it. Whether he liked it or not.

And that was exactly what I set out to do. After an excruciatingly awkward dinner, Valentin had disappeared into his room to "meditate" as his excuse for avoiding me. So, instead of moping like I wanted to, I helped my other three teammates and Amalie clean up, then returned to my room.

Sitting in front of my vanity mirror, I contemplated how

I should even approach Valentin, much less the topic of that evening. When the idea came to me, I acted quickly so as not to give myself time to chicken out. I brushed my hair until it was soft and smooth, pinched my cheeks to add some color, and worried my lips so they were pink and full. Then I yanked open my bedroom door and stepped out.

At the same time, Himawari froze in the middle of the hallway. Shocked to see each other so suddenly we both froze. The sound of Félix and Amalie's laughter coming from the common room punctuated the tense silence.

"I'm just going to Jax's room… to talk," Himawari said nervously like she had been caught sneaking out by a strict parent.

I nearly laughed, biting my lip to stifle the sound. We were apparently on similar missions.

"Have a nice night then, Himawari," I smiled and gave her a small wave before pushing her, slightly stunned, toward Jax's door.

Apparently, he had not told her about our conversation last night.

My heart began to pound violently in my chest after she quietly slipped into Jax's room and I approached Valentin's. I pretended not to hear the whispers coming from beneath Jax's closed door and raised my knuckles to knock.

"Breathe Daux," I told myself. *"You have killed a man, many men, before; you can have a* conversation *about your feelings with Valentin."*

Then I knocked.

Valentin's door swung open almost immediately and I tried to swallow my anxiety. But that did not prepare me for what I saw. Water droplets fell from Valentin's wet hair and onto his bare torso. His skin was tinted pink from what I could only assume was a hot shower. I resisted the urge to run my fingers over his flesh.

Only when Valentin cleared his throat did I realize I was staring. I startled and forced myself to look into Valentin's eyes.

"I thought you were Jax," he said.

"No," I replied dumbly.

"He asked to see me about something important."

Valentin was beginning to sound exasperated and *I* was starting to lose my nerve. The whispers coming from Jax's room had turned into laughter, indicating that Jax had no intention of coming to talk to Valentin tonight.

"Well, he's busy right now," I said, swallowing hard.

Valentin cocked an eyebrow at me. I did not even need to pinch my cheeks earlier with the rush of blood that was staining them now.

"Can I come in?" I asked, not allowing either of us to escape the situation.

Valentin sighed but moved to the side to allow me to enter. I stepped in and flinched at the sound of the door closing behind me. Valentin's room looked the same as it had the last time I had been in here, dark and cozy.

I felt anything but comfortable with the uneasy energy I had coursing through my veins. I had to say something now or I would lose my nerve.

I whirled to face Valentin but faltered at the sight of his bare chest and arms before me. He was always so covered up, so put together, and now he was shirtless – the sunburst scar on his side that he had gotten when we destroyed the Coalition warehouse on full display.

Hesitantly, I reached my hand out to touch it, my eyes locked with Valentin's. Just waiting for him to tell me to stop. My heart was in my throat as his jaw clenched, but he said nothing. Made no move to dissuade me.

When my fingers grazed over the raised skin the muscles beneath jumped, tensing and contracting as though my featherlight touch was electrocuting him. Then I remembered that electric current that had been running between us since we returned from Portnith the second time.

I wondered if he was feeling it now.

"Does it hurt?" I asked, unsure if I was asking about the electricity between us or his scar.

Valentin shook his head stiffly, making no move to stop me as I traced my fingers over the sunburst shape of the scar tissue. The raised flesh dipped and grooved where it had knit together under Hawthorn's inexperienced hands. I remembered my anger that day, bitter and tangy in the back of my mouth.

I had wanted to scream at her, to stop her from healing him though I knew it was the best course of action. I would have lost him had she not used what meager healing ability she possessed. The thought punched right through the scabbed-over hole in my chest.

I nearly doubled over with the pain of it.

Valentin had almost been taken from me, and I, in my selfishness, had almost let it happen. I had been so blind and had allowed Rage to rule me for far too long. I did not want that anymore; I did not to live that way any longer.

I wanted to be soft, wanted to be loved, and to give love in return.

Before I could lose my courage, I placed the hand I had been tracing Valentin's scar with on his waist and the other to his cheek, then I lifted myself onto my toes. When I was only inches away from his face, I paused, searching his expression for any hint of displeasure or warning to stop.

"Can I?" I whispered, my voice slightly hoarse, scratching its way from my throat.

"Yes," Valentin breathed, cool air ghosting over my face.

The shaky inhale he took when my lips first pressed to his burned my insides. It felt like I was being electrocuted and my skin was lighting on fire, except I had felt both of those things and neither of them came close to this sensation.

Then he grabbed me, his hands bunching in the fabric of my robe as he pulled me as close as he possibly could. Our bodies were completely flush with one another, not a hairsbreadth but our clothes between us. The Coalition could have bombed Heliorious at that exact moment and I would have felt nothing but Valentin's searing kiss and his hands on my hips. Would have heard nothing but the sound of his breath in my ears and his whispered, "I love you; I love you; I love you" over, and over, and over again until it was in time with the beating of my heart.

When he pulled away for air I could have wept.

"Valentin," I whispered, clinging to him as though I would die if I let him go. "Valentin, Valentin, Valentin."

"Yes?" he laughed breathlessly.

I could not say much of anything, other than his name. Over and over again like it was a prayer to those far away, silent Gods. To Rage who hiding somewhere inside my heart. It was so wonderful how easy it was to hold him. How well we fit in each other's arms.

"I love you," I murmured against his chest, marveling at how warm he was. "I love you, and you saved me."

"You saved yourself, Daux," he argued, tilting my face to look up at his. "But I love you too. I have for a while now."

"I'm sorry I was too distracted to see it," my voice trembled as I spoke, but I had never felt braver.

I had already kissed him, already admitted my feelings, and he had accepted them. There was nothing left to fear. Nothing could compare to the joy I felt at that moment. Not revenge, not killing my father. This… this was bliss.

"What you went through was a lot, more than a lot," he said lamely, searching for the right words. "Most people don't go into those interrogations and come out whole, and even less find themselves again. You are so strong. I'm sorry I couldn't have been more help, that I wasn't more help."

"But you were," I insisted, touching his cheek. "You helped me more than you could ever know. I would not be here right now if it weren't for you."

"No, you wouldn't," he agreed cheekily, kissing my nose.

The ember in my chest exploded into a roaring flame, clearing out the ashes of my heart. Was I fully healed? No, not remotely. Though, I was on my way there. Now, I would allow my friends – and whatever Valentin was to me, lover, partner, whatever he wanted – to help me. I should have done so from the beginning, but I was so blinded by my rage.

"I'm here now," Valentin whispered against my hair and I realized I had spoken all of those thoughts aloud.

I smiled up at him and stood up on my tiptoes to press my lips to his once again. I was not healed yet, not even close. But with the love of my friends and family, I knew nothing would keep me from becoming stronger than I had ever hoped to be.

Chapter Thirty-Five

The next morning resulted in gagging noises around the breakfast table. Apparently, Amalie had awoken and decided to snoop the night before, listening to my conversation and subsequent kisses with Valentin before sneaking back to bed when I returned flushed and out of sorts. Then she decided to tell everyone else what she had discovered.

"Well," I said, looking down my nose at Himawari and Jax. "You two have a lot of nerve teasing me when neither of you slept in your own rooms for the past two nights."

With a triumphant smirk, I stood from the table, ignoring their indignant sputtering as I brought my dishes to the dishwasher.

"We have a meeting with the Overseer in a couple of hours," I called over the renewed gagging and teasing noises from the dining room. "Hurry up!"

The spring in my step died rather quickly when I remembered I would have to discuss the enhancers with my team. With Amalie. Nausea hit me like a wave and for a moment, I thought I was going to heave up my breakfast.

"Daux?" Valentin said from behind me, his hand resting on the small of my back.

I jumped, turned to face him, and found myself pinned between him and the sink. That alone would have sent my heart pounding and blood rushing to my face, except for the fact that I was very terrified of losing control of myself right in front of him. I still needed to work on vulnerability it seemed.

"You okay?" he asked, brushing a cool hand along my cheek.

Gods above, he was so beautiful. The blond in his hair was beginning to grow out, showing the inky black roots of his natural hair color, his eyes were bright, and there was a bit of a light pink dusting his high cheekbones.

"I…" I started, biting my lip.

His thumb ghosted over my mouth, pulling my lip from my teeth. I would have trembled, instead pulling away from him slightly, and grabbed his hand in mine.

"I need to talk to everyone before we meet with the Overseer."

"Sounds serious."

I brought his hand to my lips and kissed his knuckles, ignoring the way his breath hitched when I did so. "It is."

"Then we," he coughed lightly and pulled his hand away. "We better get back in there."

I nodded and he led the way. Everyone was still joking and laughing with one another, but stopped when they saw the expression on my face.

"What's wrong?" Jax asked looking between me and Valentin.

Himawari sighed, rubbing a hand over her face. "I think I know."

"What do you mean 'you know'?" Jax asked, brows furrowing.

She did not answer, only turned the dark depth of her eyes on me. Thankfully, they were her normal blacker than night shade and not the flat black they had turned in Athor. Félix watched me carefully too, his pink stress ball holding on for its life in his hand. Jax stared hard at me, then Himawari before his expression smoothed out and he nodded.

"I see," was all he said.

"Well, *I* don't." Amalie crossed her arms over her chest. "What's going on."

"You all felt what happened in Athor," I said. It was not a question.

They all nodded, with the exclusion of Amalie who pouted, feeling left out. Even Valentin, who had not been forced to take blockers because of his punishment mission, knew what I was referring to now.

"When everyone's eyes turned black," he said, his voice barely above a whisper.

"When our magic began to change," Himawari added.

Jax swallowed, his throat bobbing. His body language told me that he would rather be anywhere else than the dining room. I knew why. He had killed, and he had felt next to nothing.

"I heard a voice," he whispered, blinking rapidly.

"What did it say?" Himawari asked before I could.

Jax took a deep breath. Then another. And another. Himawari laid a hand on his arm, massaging the muscle there, her jaw working lightly. I looked away from them, feeling as though I was invading an intimate moment I was not supposed to see. Instead, I allowed my gaze to fall on Valentin, who was staring at me too.

"It said Justice had been served," Jax said eventually. "That the Coalition soldiers had deserved what they had gotten. It was their punishment for their cruelty."

"I was afraid of that," I said aloud.

My father had tampered with too many of our prescriptions, having the blockers replaced with enhancers. He knew – like he had the night he captured us in Portnith – that to hurt me he needed to hurt my friends. And to hurt my friends, he needed to destroy the very thing that made them who they were – their magic.

"What does this mean?" Félix asked, his stress ball squeezed as flat as a pancake.

I turned to him, my heart in my throat and Rage in my

eyes.

"It means that my father was trying to turn us all into Gods."

Soon after our harrowing conversation, everyone was ready to leave. We had decided that it was best to keep this revelation to ourselves for now. The Overseer did not need any more ammunition against our team, and I was not keen on being arrested a second time. I warned Amalie – who had sat in silence as we recounted the many times seeing shadows in each other's eyes, the hallucinations, the strange instances of losing control of our magic when we were on blockers – that she could not repeat anything we said to anyone else.

She accepted this without a word, her face pale and eyes watery. She was still quiet as I was opening the door for one of her caretakers – Crystal. The small woman with bright blue eyes, curly brown hair, and golden-brown skin bustled into the flat, already chirping about Amalie's schedule for the day. I saw my sister make a face but did not have time to press her on the matter. So, I leaned down and kissed her cheek with the promise to bring her back ice cream and headed out the door.

"Hello, everyone," the Overseer greeted us, standing in front of her desk as we entered.

We all said our greetings, remaining on our feet as she was still standing in front of her desk. A show of respect. Valentin grabbed my hand and gave it a reassuring squeeze. I took a deep breath. In and out.

She did not know. She did not need to know. We would

be okay.

"I have a lot to apologize for," the Overseer said, beginning to pace in front of her desk. "But mostly to you, Deveraux."

"There is no need—" I began.

But the Overseer held up a hand to cut me off.

"Let me tell you how sorry I am for my part in all your suffering," she begged, dark eyes earnest. "I mistrusted you, erroneously. And that caused a lot more strife than trust, which we needed the latter. We always need the latter in this occupation. I am sorry."

I was struck by the sincerity in her voice. So much so that I could not find it within myself to be remotely angry with her. Maybe I would later, but not now. Especially when we were keeping such a secret from her. One that could very well shatter Eturnus to its core.

"I forgive you," I said, striding over to the tall woman with my hand outstretched.

She took it in hers with a grateful smile and gave it a businesslike shake before releasing me and hurrying around the other side of her desk.

"Do sit down, please," she asked, gesturing for us to do just that. "We have a lot to discuss."

So, we did. My father's capture, along with the information still being gleaned from my mother, Hayley, and Gladwin broke open the Coalition's true intentions for magic and the people who used it. It was time we struck back, and struck them hard. The NAF would no longer be taking a defensive stance and allow the Coalition to blaspheme the gift that had been bestowed upon us when the Gods left.

My father would no longer be controlling my life from the shadows. When we returned home, my teammates and I agreed that we would discreetly look into the enhancers and their effects. Dev still wanted the team's input on the information gleaned from his interrogations, so we would be able to use Gladwin's accounts to at least understand something of what was happening to us.

I knew, that for better or for worse, we needed to understand how to control the effects of the enhancers. I needed to understand Rage. For now, she was complacent, but what if she decided to rear her ugly head again? And Jax… whatever had happened to him, he needed to be able to control. Someone as gentle as he was, did not deserve a vengeful God controlling his magic. We had to become stronger. We needed to.

Somehow, that thought was not daunting. I would rely on them more now, and that made it all more bearable. It felt as though I had risen from the ashes from my own destruction. Like I had been reborn. I knew without a doubt, from embers and ashes – like the flame that had always resided in my chest – we could become stronger than ever.

Acknowledgments

First and foremost, dear reader, I would like to thank you for reading. I would like to thank you for believing in Daux, in all of her friends, and in me. We all appreciate your support more than you could ever know. Félix would love to take you all out for mangonadas, even if he drained his bank account doing so.

To the team at Winged Publications, thank you for your patience and commitment. Without you, I would not be able to share this story to the best of my ability. To my editor Katheryn Eckert, thank you for combing through this manuscript and pointing out all the errors and inconsistencies. To my publisher Cynthia Hickey, your endless patience and enthusiasm for the craft is inspiring. Thank you.

To my friends Kat, Stou, Jooj, Holly, Morgan (Rose), Rachel, Jasmine, Janine, and Autumn: I could not have done this without you. Your love and support throughout life and writing this sequel (and the series as a whole) means everything to me.

My wonderful Bookcord friends and lovely beta readers Kai, Cheesy (Daria), Guinvere, Elsye, Jennifer, Nikki, Cole, and Rhianna thank you for your passion, your friendship, your support, and your help with this project. May the memes and the book recs never end. Kai, your tiktoks and reviews mean the world. Keep your flames burning.

As for my parents, I couldn't be more grateful to have two sets who love me and show so much love and excitement for my stories and characters. I would not be who I am (or where I am) without you. I am forever thankful for all of you Mama, Shane (Dad), Dad, and Sarahbeth (Mom 2.0). Thank you for making me laugh and encouraging me in everything I chose to do. I love you. And to Dad and Sarabeth, thank you for flinging my book at library patrons whenever you can. It means the world.

Siblings, I bite my thumb in your general directions. Jokes aside, thank you for putting up with the people who live in my head and demand I write stories about them. They thank you for only thinking I am a *little* bit crazy. I thank you for being the banes of my existence (I wouldn't want anyone else as my siblings so I love you, dorkfishes).

Pat and Tammy for supporting me and always lending an eager ear for hints about the series. And for your wonderful company. I couldn't have done this without you.

Usagi and Squeekers, I love and adore you with all of my being. Thank you for all your snuggles and kissies, and demands for food when you have already been fed. I would fall to pieces without the two of you.

My final acknowledgment and thanks (as always) will be to my husband, Zach. You are my backbone, my rock, and my universe. I love you with all of my heart and soul. Thank you for always encouraging me to try, try, and try again. You never let me give up or give in to negative self-doubt. I would be lost without you. This series is always dedicated to you, because without you I never would have gathered the courage to write it, much less try to publish it. I know, without a doubt, that with you by my side I can do anything.

And I thank you for that. I could write Shakespearean sonnets about you, but you don't care for Willy Shakes so I shall refrain. They would fall flat anyway because I love you *so* much more than words can express.

Did you miss book one *I Am Become*? Get it here

Katelynn R. Butler grew up in East Tennessee and has been reading and dreaming up her own stories since she was a child. She procured her first library card at eight and has continued to ransack her local libraries since, reading anything she could get her hands on. She spends most of her days writing fantastical tales like the ones she adored growing up. Otherwise, she can be found baking, crocheting, researching vintage and historical dress, or spoiling her two rescue cats. I am Become is Katelynn's first novel.

www.ingramcontent.com/pod-product-compliance
Lightning Source LLC
Chambersburg PA
CBHW070408310726

48977CB00003B/603